Lycan Legacy

A Soulmark Series

Rebecca Main

www.RebeccaMain.com

www.ViaGraphia.com

Table of Contents

I

Magic wasn't a science. Merida believed it was a *feeling*. A sixth sense. An indescribable knowledge set deep in your bones. One that couldn't be disputed or swayed. One that held you until death did you part.

Merida, the local witch doctor—emphasis on the *witch*—perceived magic as a precious gift.

Her gift was particularly powerful, but she knew precisely how to wield it—re-emphasis on the *doctor*.

Merida liked to keep to herself. She lived on the outskirts of her village in a comfortable little cabin that certain villagers liked to call a shack. She didn't mind an awful lot what they said, for she understood their nature well, and they, hers.

It was an anomaly, her little village, for she wasn't the only supernaturally inclined inhabitant.

Amongst the mundane, who carried on about their lives in willful ignorance, was a pack of wolves—or rather, a pack of lycans. They lived together in a strange sort of harmony, politely ignoring each other's vast differences in favor of focusing on surviving.

The pack brought security to the community, for no outsider dared to test their strength.

Merida brought safety and reassurance. Her remedies and tonics were regarded as acts of miracles in the eyes of those brave enough to try them.

As for the humans, they reminded the supernaturally inclined of their place in the world: beneath them. For one singular outcry from them meant the gruesome end of the others.

Everyone had their place and role to play in the village. It was understood by all that so long as no two factions intertwined irrevocably so, the tentative peace would remain. Merida believed heartily in this fact. She also thought, if no one was any the wiser, she may intertwine as she pleased. And so she did with Luc Blanc.

Luc was the second son of the alpha.

He was beautiful and passionate and utterly wild. Merida had been smitten at first sight, along with the rest of the general populace. Their entanglement spanned years. With each event that brought them together, the need to know more about the other grew stronger. Until that need turned into an ache.

An ache that no spell or potion could rid. An ache that could only be subdued by their union.

Again, and again, and again.

"You look so stern whenever you work," Luc pronounced, lounging comfortably on the many furs strewn over Merida's bed.

The lines creasing Merida's forehead did not lessen, though a few more appeared with the raising of her eyebrows. Her look of unimpressed amusement was met with a satisfied smile from her lupine lover.

"Hush," Merida said. "I'm working."

The wolf reclined with an exaggerated huff until his lithe body was stretched artfully atop the bed. "When you asked for a short break, I assumed it would involve *sleep* not work."

"And you were wrong," she replied smartly.

Her hands took up the task at hand with uncanny ease, while Merida chanted a spell under her breath. Eyes half closed, her hands chose pinches and spoonfuls of this and that across the large wooden table that sat in the far corner of her home. Luc watched, mesmerized as always by her confidence and magical ability.

Most of Merida's home was littered with supplies. Pots and bowls were lined flush against the walls. Jars and boxes found themselves stacked upon rickety handmade shelves that remained aloft purely by magic. Even Merida's bed was framed and cocooned with enchanted elements. Dreamcatchers of various sizes and lengths hung at either end of her bed. A set of candles bordered the piece of furniture. They never dulled or diminished, no matter how long the wick remained aflame. Last was an arrangement of mirror fragments that formed the shape of a diamond if one turned their head an inch to the left.

It was rare for Merida's patients or customers to see the inside of her humble home. She kept her business dealings to the small domed dwelling only a short walk away.

"What are you making?" Luc asked once Merida finished her chant with a small sigh. Her pale blue eyes flickered to Luc. His face held the pinched look of curiosity one got when they attempted and failed to portray indifference.

"A tonic to reverse the effects of the murwood and mugroot draft I gave to Margery Travers last week," Merida replied.

"It looks complicated."

"It isn't," she replied with a breathy laugh. "There may be many ingredients, but I've found the strongest spells need very few. What matters far more is the intent behind them. I crafted the draft with weak intent, and so my concentration in fixing its remedy need not be all-consuming."

Luc snorted with amusement and rose to rest on an elbow. Merida stopped her idle stirring of the tonic to grace the second son with a generous once-over. She enjoyed the coarse hair across his chest and the way it trailed far below the blanket covering his most noteworthy body part.

"Tell me, is the draft you made for Ms. Travers the reason why the youngest Travers brat lost his voice?" he asked.

Merida smirked and set aside the tonic. She glided over to the bed, wide hips swinging back and forth as she stripped from her long robe.

"Perhaps," she purred with a wicked, all-knowing smile. "She's yet to ask for any sort of remedy, but it's only a matter of time."

Luc sprung forward with a burst of laughter, looped a muscular arm around Merida's waist, and dragged her forward. They tumbled around on the bed until the wolf's might pinned down the witch.

"You are brilliant," he proclaimed somewhat reverently and brushed a wayward swath of deep brown curls from Merida's face. The witch blushed and averted her gaze in an attempt to conceal her pleasure.

"It's not difficult," she admitted. "Not really. Everything has a purpose. A beginning and end. Magic follows this course to a fault. There is no spell, potion, or hex made that cannot be undone."

Luc took on a thoughtful reprieve, studying his lover's rosy cheeks and small, pert nose. Merida allowed him his moment, tracing her fingers over his square jaw and cleft chin.

"And what remedy is there to this?"

Merida's questing hand was stolen by Luc's roughened one and placed over the patch of skin treading below his rib cage. There a dark mark adorned his fair skin in the form of two arrowheads nestled into one another. Merida eyed the mark with a pang of discomfort.

"You know as well as I this is a *gift*. Somewhere out there is your perfect match. The other half of your soul," she said with tired longing. "Finding them is the remedy you speak of, Luc. Find them, and you will know happiness to your heart's content. Do not think cruelly of this blessing you only see as a curse."

Luc remained silent for a time until Merida began to squirm beneath his weight. His gaze grew dark with unabashed heat at the action, and he pressed his growing shaft against her with firm insistence. Merida locked eyes with Luc and drew in a sharp breath at his expression.

"My heart is content with you," he said. His brown eyes began to speckle with gold. "You are my happiness."

"And you, mine," she atoned, meeting his hungry kiss with equal enthusiasm.

Farewell

- Chapter 1 -

I tend to avoid wearing white. The color against my skin only accentuates my fair pallor. But here I stand, drenched in white lace from neck to toe, marveling at the sheer beauty of the brilliant white draping me. A sigh tumbles past my parted lips as the wonder and awe fade.

"Are you wearing your hair up or down?"

I glance to my left. Juniper, or June as close family and friends call her, sits with her legs tucked beneath her at the end of the nearby stiff-backed couch. She observes with wide-eyed admiration as I grant her a soft smile.

"Mother hasn't decided yet," I respond.

June hums. "You'll look stunning either way. I wish I were as pretty as you, Winter."

I give a good-natured shake of my head as my first reply. "You're very sweet to say so," I say as all of my mother's ingrained teachings of niceties and pleasantries kick in.

Remember, Winter, when given compliments, always accept them graciously. No one likes a woman who fishes for praise.

I cast my eyes back to the full-length mirror a few feet in front of me. Staring back is a lovely woman, but I wonder if anyone else catches the sadness that always seems to linger in my slate gray eyes.

"Did you know the white wedding dress was made popular by Queen Victoria in the 19th century?" June continues with careless enthusiasm. Her honey-blonde hair, dressed in wavy curls, swings in front of her face as she leans forward. "Isn't that so interesting?"

"I did know that, as it happens," I reply and give my younger cousin a warm smile. *But do you know white is a common color of mourning in several Asian cultures?*

"Oh," she murmurs a bit dejectedly. Her sky-blue eyes dart to the floor then back to me, their vigor and excitement returning only as a teenager can conjure. "You must be so excited to be with your soulmark, Winter! How long is it since you last saw him?"

I flush unwittingly and look away from the mischievous grin now present on June's face.

"Twenty years, give or take."

June makes a noise that is a cross between a sigh and whine. "I think the betrothal is rather romantic!" A startled laugh crosses my lips before I can help it, but June charges on. "Truly! You actually found your soulmark, *and* you get to marry him. You're so lucky, Winter. I wish I could be with mine... wherever he is."

At the sudden sound of dejection in her voice, I step from my small pedestal and walk to her side. Kneeling down—much to June's distress—I grasp her hands.

"June, you know as well as I, I'm not lucky at all," I say with gentle finesse. She sets her sights upon our clasped hands and swallows.

"Because of the curse...."

I swallow as well and nod. "Yes."

"But the soulmark curse only prevents you from having children," she goes on with sheepish hope. "You can always adopt."

The words sting, even when delivered with such earnest. The curse upon my family—my pack—is as old as the lycan curse. It prevents us from carrying children to term with our soulmarks, and it mercilessly stunted the growth of our pack. *It's done more than that. The curse has taken apart the pack piece by piece.* And I am the last of the Blanc family line.

Centuries ago the Blancs flourished and were incontestably the strongest pack in Northern America, not to mention the oldest. Without the added boost of bound soulmarks integrated into our pack, we were forced to adapt to stay strong.

Our males become more aggressive and territorial. Our she-wolves, which we possessed in unusual abundance, created a strict hierarchy among themselves to rival the men. Mine is not a pack that is easy to live in, but I am lucky enough to bare our pack's namesake and enjoy the rank of fifth in the pack.

"We'll see. Regardless, I'm sure it will be more than enough to know I'm with my soulmark."

June stays quiet. Her eyes lift slowly to mine as she takes her bottom lip between her teeth to worry at the pink flesh.

"What is it?" I ask.

"Are you going to tell him about the curse?"

I blink back in response, and then give a quick shake of my head. "You know I can't do that, June. We're—"

"Not allowed," she finishes. June urges me to stand then makes a fuss of dusting off the bottom of my dress. The task is pointless, for the room we occupy is kept in pristine condition at all times. Any speck of dirt that dare enter the house would be banished immediately upon sight. Most visitors applaud the neatness of my home, but I cannot shake its sterile hold no matter how hard I stare into its gleaming surfaces.

When June persists in her chore, I drag her up by her arm. "Stop that," I scold without any bite. "And please don't feel any sorrow for me, okay? I'm going to be just fine and happy as can be," I assure her. *Even without children.*

June shoots me a small smile. "I just want you to be happy. You always try to make sure that I am."

"That's what cousins do," I tease. June's smile grows, but a touch of forlorn still lingers in it. "I wish I could go to your wedding."

A soft "aw" makes its way from my mouth before I envelop the seventeen-year-old into a hug. "Me too," I mumble against her head then plant a kiss there.

Truth be told, June is far more a sister to me than a cousin. During our shared childhood, she was a constant source of comfort to me. Her brightness eclipsed the dark life I lived at home.

Where my parents tore me down, June brought me up.

Where my parents questioned my merits, June never even thought to ask.

Where my parents disciplined and groomed my wolf and me for the prestigious life as their daughter, with June, I could be free—to an extent, at least.

"Your fitting went well before I came?"

June's question snaps me out of my reverie, and as she pulls back to retreat to the couch, a more subdued smile arises onto my face. Catching June's eyes, I nod to her question.

The dress will be taken in one last time, due to my mother's insistence. The local seamstress, a low-ranking she-wolf in her mid-fifties, made no protest even as I had. In the end, I can't fault the seamstress for her submission. No one says no to the alpha she-wolf.

Apparently, not even me.

"It went well," I say. "Would you mind unbuttoning the back for me?"

June is back on her feet in a second and behind me. Her slender fingers work the parade of pearl buttons from their loops, and my chest expands with great relief.

"Thank you," I breathe.

"Tell me again how everything is supposed to look?" June asks once she's finished. A small chuckle bursts from me.

"Haven't I told you this a hundred times?"

I walk behind the privacy screen at the other end of the room and change from my wedding dress into my daily wear—a cozy, thick wool sweater paired with slick black leather leggings. I tear away my treacherously high wedding shoes in favor of the fuzzy slippers I like to wear around my home.

"Let's make it an even one hundred and one," she quips. Another laugh is elicited from June's playful demeanor.

"White and red roses and lots and lots of greenery." I flop down on the couch. The cushions begrudge but an inch of leniency, and I give an exaggerated grimace as my snowy hair tumbles in front of my eyes. I brush the curly strands away with the back of my hand. "You know it will look picture perfect since my mother is at the helm."

June nods along with an eagerness that befits her age. "Aunt Adele throws the grandest parties."

"What else?" I cock my head to the side, a mischievous smile crawling into place as I pretend to think. I cup my chin in hand and smile wider. "A four-course dinner with the seasons *finest* game and vegetables, and a cake topped with powdered sugar and a winter berry compote." My mouth waters at the mere thought of the tasty dessert.

June grins back. "Isn't that your dream cake?"

I nod. It had been one of the only elements of the wedding I had taken a stand on. The "naked cake" trend appeals to me greatly, and it fits my style far more than the traditional frosted cake. My mother hadn't been pleased with my insistence, but she caved eventually so long as it "stopped my perpetual whining."

"It is!"

"Good! It's your day. You should get whatever you want."

I take June's hand and squeeze. She is effortlessly affectionate and supportive, as always. I wonder if she realizes I look up to her just as much as she looks up to me.

"And when you get married, what will it look like?"

"I want something rustic and dreamy. With wildflowers everywhere."

My smile widens. Rustic chic is what I want too. Although my sentiments on the matter are relayed to my mother, I get a distinct inkling it will be far more winter chic than a classy rustic affair.

"Wildflowers suit you," I say. "They're resilient and beautiful. They grow where they please, sometimes in the most unlikely of places. In cracks and crevices. In the heart of the darkest wood."

June blushes. "I can't believe how much you know about flowers and plants—especially since you never went to college!"

I keep the warmth to my smile even though inside I cringe. Not going to college had been... *difficult.* Yet, bound to the will of my alphas, I couldn't disobey their orders to remain and put my efforts into what they deemed to be of the utmost importance—the pack.

"The library and internet are a powerful combination," I say at last. *They most certainly had been.* I force down the resentment that ignited in my belly at the reminder. The library became my refuge. My childhood fascination with plants turned into a more studious pastime to fill the void of the higher education I was denied.

I clear my throat, the sound a gentle rumble, and pin June with a playful squinting of my eyes. "But back to your dream wedding... a certain Toby Jensen wouldn't happen to be the one you picture waiting for you at the end of the aisle, would it?"

June lets out a high-pitched squeal and grabs the nearest pillow to throw at me. I delight in the rush of color that floods her cheeks. "Winter Blanc!" she shouts as if the scandalized tone will bring me to heel. I laugh merrily instead.

"Don't tell me he's not. I thought you two were madly and deeply in love."

June's rosy cheeks deepen to crimson. "Toby and I aren't like you and Atticus, Winter. We're not soulmarks."

"No, you're not. But you and Toby aren't like the rest of the couples in the pack. You're genuinely in love. So many of our pack mates are together through arranged circumstances. You're lucky your parents and his approve of your relationship."

Her shoulders drop from their stilted position, but her blush only recedes a quarter. A sense of hope pervades me as I think of my cousin's relationship with her boyfriend. They make being in love look easy. And although they are young, ages seventeen and nineteen, their relationship is far more mature than several others in the pack.

It lightens my heart to know she will be in Toby's safe care once I leave for Montana.

Thoughts of the American state raise my heartbeat, or rather, ideas of Atticus do. Our matching marks, three intertwined rings, were discovered when we were children at a great meeting of the North

American packs. As fate would have it, Atticus accidentally touched the soulmark still forming on my lower back as he valiantly helped me pilfer a box of cookies.

The box of cookies my small, five-year-old hands strove for had been far out of reach. Heedless of the difficult task, I stretched to the very tips of my toes. As a by-product of my determination, my shirt had ridden up in my efforts. A gentleman, even at age eight, Atticus had attempted to assist my cookie heist and inadvertently touched my soulmark while giving me a much-needed boost.

The moment was electric. Literally.

He dropped me in shock, wide-eyed and shaking. I succumbed to tears of confusion and a small bit of pain from my landing.

It was a match made in heaven.

I duck my head to hide my smile. My interaction henceforth with my soulmark was conducted via letters and heavily monitored by my family. In rare occurrences did we speak over the phone. We certainly never *saw* each other. Secret social media stalking was my only means to garner a glimpse into Atticus Hayes's life. That, and the short secret messages we embed in our letters to each other.

They are trivial phrases snuck into boring paragraphs that express our excitement to be with one another and clue the other in to the more meaningful details of our life. Our secret code took years to get right, but the painstaking effort was worth it. I can't speak of Atticus's experience throughout our exchange, but our letters have always been subject to my parents' disapproving eyes. Having the means to express myself without the threat of my parents' censorship was *everything*.

If our discovery had taken place anywhere else, my parents would have whisked me away to some tower and kept me hidden—along with their secrets—for the rest of my life. I shudder at the thought.

At the time, I could not comprehend the soulmark curse upon my family. Why was it bad? Why did they look so ill whenever I expressed my joy and excitement? Five-year-old Winter did not understand their disdain and anger. Nor could six-year-old Winter, but at age seven, my parents made sure I did.

The soulmark is a weakness to the Blanc pack, for it does not bolster us as it did the other packs spread out across the world. It is a curse, they had explained, for the purpose of marriage is to procreate, and we cannot with our soulmarks—souls bound or otherwise. If those outside the pack knew of our weakness, they would surely take advantage, and the Blanc pack would come under attack.

They told me those who *truly* understood the importance of the pack's survival proudly did as our ancestors and removed the cursed mark from their skin in solidarity with the pack. That I, the daughter of the alphas, would forsake this privilege to prove my commitment to the pack was a grave disappointment.

As those who do forsake the pack in such a way are met with sometimes *fatal* unkindness.

To show my solidarity with the Blanc pack's plight, I am not to bind my soul with Atticus... regardless of our impending union. *This* is to be my concession to alleviate their disappointment.

The thought makes me ill.

Tomorrow I leave for Montana with a dozen or so of my pack. And the following day I will be Mrs. Winter Hayes. My heart gives a nervous flutter.

"Our parents are okay with it *now*, Winter, but they aren't the ones who need to approve it. You and I both know that," she ends with a small, rebuking voice.

I hold back a grimace. "Haven't you heard?" I ask playfully. "I have an in with the alphas. If Toby is the one you want, I'll put in all the requisite good words needed to make it happen."

June tries for a smile. "I trust in your capabilities of persuasion when it comes to Uncle Malcolm, but Aunt Adele is another matter."

"My mother is a staunch supporter of having the best... so just make sure Toby can prove he treats you the best, and you'll be golden, kid." June frowns as I lean forward and punch her in the arm.

"I'm not a kid. I'm seventeen."

"Well, I'm twenty-five, so to me, you'll always be a kid."

June rolls her eyes but then softens.

"You'll really put in a good word for Toby with your parents? I mean, we don't plan on getting married tomorrow or anything"—June laughs a touch hysterically —"but knowing he's got their approval will go a long way for us."

"Have I ever let you down before?"

I'm tackled into the hard couch cushions, June's squeal of excitement nearly bursting my eardrum. "Thank you! Thank you! Thank you!" Hauling her off is a more difficult task than I anticipated, but somehow, I manage through a storm of thunderous laughter passed between us. "Oh, Winter, I wish you weren't going. I'm going to miss you."

A lump forms in my throat. "We can talk as frequently as you want. I'm only a text or call away, okay?"

June bops her head up and down happily.

"You know who might end up missing you more than me?"

My eyes widen as I take in a steadying breath. "Don't say—"

"Knox!"

I release a groan. Knox Bernard does not approve of my marriage or soulmark with Atticus. He's been one of its most vocal opponents throughout the past few years. Worse are his demands that I go through the same soulmark removal process as the rest of the pack, even though a betrothal contract was signed a long time ago with the Hayeses.

"He'll get over it," I tell her dryly. There are few things I envision missing about home, and Knox doesn't make the list.

Silence overtakes the small space between us, and my thoughts drift to the new pack I'll be joining, the Adolphus pack. How different will they be from mine? And what exactly does it mean to be a "new age" pack and leave tradition behind? I smooth my features into something serene as a pit of doubt begins to well in my stomach.

Mother and father have nothing nice to say about the Adolphus pack, and our chance meeting with Irina Adolphus at the Celestial Court did little to change that opinion. They insist her pack is no good. Impulsive. Dangerous. Feral. Mother frets over my survival among them, for I possess none of those qualities. My upbringing ensured me to be a groomed, well-behaved woman, docile yet amiable enough to sway decisions.

"There you are!" My mother's voice rings throughout the guest powder room with shrill exasperation. "It's almost six o'clock, Winter," she reprimands me as she marches into the room, her heels clicking like stakes against the floor. I stand with grace endowed to me through years of training, and June follows suit with far fewer airs of polite society about her.

"Hello, Aunt Adele."

My mother dons a patronizing smile as she stares down her niece. "Shouldn't you be home doing homework?"

"It's winter break!" June announces. "And—"

My mother's hand is in the air, palm thrust forward before June can prattle on. "Go home,

Juniper. Don't keep your mother and father worrying about your whereabouts."

June doesn't lose her smile as she envelops me with a brief hug. "I love you," she blurts out. "Your wedding will be beautiful! I can't wait to see all the pictures and go over every detail, Winter. Bye! Bye, Aunt Adele."

A cheery wave is delivered before she exits the powder room, but I am the only one to return it.

"Sit, Winter." I do so and prepare myself for one of her lectures as she remains standing. "It's important we discuss a few... *private* matters regarding your marriage."

The implication of her words drives a flush of red to my cheeks, and I deftly avoid her steely gaze.

"That's really not necessary, Mother."

"Oh, Winter!" Her voice echoes her mild embarrassment, and immediately I realize I have misinterpreted her words—a scenario I attempt to avoid at all costs. "You're twenty-five for heaven's sake. I'm well aware of certain... *private activities* you participated in. Though, while on the topic, you should do well to avoid those scenarios with your soon-to-be husband. Interested parties might take offense later should your marriage to that man become null and void."

A prickle of doubt crawls across my skin. "Interested parties" referred to Knox Bernard. To my parents, he is the perfect suitor for me.

"Forgive me," I say with a demure air. "I misunderstood."

"That much is clear, Winter." She barely contains a scoff. "The matter I wish to speak to you about is one we have discussed before. But one who marries outside the pack can never be reminded too often, lest they end up like the Maces, Parishs, or Steinbecks."

A cold thrill runs down my back at the mention of the families who have chosen to leave the Blanc pack over the last decade. Since they had nothing nice to say about our pack upon their departure, their ability to speak further had been removed.

"I assure you I'm aware of the consequences of such actions." The words are spoken quietly as I look past June to the bay window at the end of the room. Snow falls peacefully outside. The soft, white crystals drift down at their own leisure and blanket our property. "I won't say anything about the soulmark curse."

"And...." The slight chill about the room is nothing compared to the arctic tenor of her voice. The hope I attempt to keep safe in my heart for better tomorrows trembles.

"And I won't let him complete the soulmark," I answer.

My mother makes what she considers a pleased noise. It is the cross between a purr and a growl and does little in the way of reassurance.

"Excellent. You must realize, Winter, the Adolphus pack is destined for doom. These 'new-age' packs are too erratic. They have nothing to keep them balanced and structured, and that's what we more traditional packs have in spades." She tsks and stands in one fluid act, then strides to the window. "If the Adolphus pack loses their squabble with the Wselfwulf pack, I don't want my daughter tied down to a wolf who cannot appreciate our set of values. Your father and I only want what is best for you, Winter."

Knox surfaces again in my thoughts. His hawk-like eyes and sharp jaw conjure in my mind. Even there their intensity is unnerving. Knox doesn't so much want me, as he does the prestige that comes with marrying the last member of the Blanc line. It doesn't hurt that his courting efforts are accompanied by a sizeable inheritance in tow—an inheritance he garnered through suspicious means.

How can my parents want me to be with a wolf whose loyalties lay first and foremost with his own self-interest? They might doubt my ability to survive among the Adolphus pack, but I *know* I cannot endure a life alongside Knox Bernard.

"Are you even listening to me?"

I gulp, and I'm unable to hide my startled expression fast enough for my mother's eyes. "Of course," I reply, turning my expression into one of shocked disbelief. "You were reminding me of the importance of keeping our other pack secret. About the true origins of the lycan curse." Mother's chin thrusts high into the air. "I won't speak of the lycan curse to the Adolphus pack, Mother. If brought up, I'm well versed in directing the conversation in another direction. I would never confirm the curse's origin to our pack."

For a moment, I wonder if I have guessed incorrectly, and a knot of worry winds itself around my stomach. Could I be wrong? Mother always follows her reminder of the soulmark curse with that of the lycan curse.

"You do have an affinity for stretching the truth," she concedes. Her chin lowers, and her eyes become hooded as she studies my reaction. I know better than to react to her words, but the small slight still stings.

"I'm loyal to the pack, Mother. Above all else."

A hint of approval dashes across her face in the small twitch near the corner of her mouth. But this is not the type of approval that leaves me reassured. Instead, the knot in my stomach tightens like a snake ready to devour its prey.

"And here I had my doubts these last few months. I'm so pleased you say this, Winter. Your father and I have spoken at length about this arrangement of yours and have agreed upon a way to use it to our advantage."

My cool facade finally breaks, a frown creasing the skin between my brows. "The advantage is being able to call the Adolphus pack our allies through this marriage. They'll help in whatever future qualms we may have—"

"Don't be so naive, Winter," my mother interrupts. "The association of our pack with theirs is a sully to our name. To request any type of aid from them is unthinkable."

I stay silent a moment, collecting myself as best I can. "Then what advantage do you speak of?"

"This war of theirs is not beneficial to the lycan community. It's causing too many waves and needs to be settled with haste." Mother turns her back to me, staring out into the night. Her reflection is stony in the glass windowpane. I attempt to garner her true emotions through the pack bonds, but they are unreadable to me, as per usual.

"What will you have me do? Mediate the situation?"

My innocent question draws an uncouth bark of laughter from my mother. I shrink back into the couch in response.

"Mediate the situation?" Her laughter slowly dies down, and she faces me. The stony expression is swept away in favor of one of pure condescension. "Oh, Winter, don't be ridiculous. Anyone with eyes can see a resolution between the two packs by mediation is out of the question. The only way their feud will end is with blood, and whoever claims the most will be the winner."

"What do you want me to do?" I ask, my words turning colder. My mother's expression remains the same.

"This need for bloodshed needs to come to a head. Sooner rather than later."

"And you want me to instigate the fight?"

My mother rolls her eyes. "Nothing so dramatic as that, Winter. Honestly, girl. We only wish for you to keep us updated on the goings on of the Adolphus pack. What their thoughts and plans are for their confrontation with the Wselfwulf pack."

"You want me to spy on them?" I ask. My question is delivered with quiet restraint.

"I want you to do as your father and I command, as a good daughter should, not ask meaningless questions," she responds. The alpha in her voice makes my wolf bend in submission, and without thought, I stretch my neck to the side in a silent offering. "You must understand, Winter, that you are in a unique position. Without completing the necessary elements of the soulmark binding, you will never entirely leave the Blanc pack, not under my careful watch.

"And though your union to that man will tie you a certain degree to the Adolphus pack, you will likewise never be completely part of their pack. I don't want you to think of this business as spying. Think of it as proving your loyalty to the Blanc pack. Perhaps we should not have shielded you as we did from the *rougher* aspects of pack life. I wonder how you will survive among those savages. Even for this brief period of time," she says.

Shielded? What utter nonsense. My loyalty to the pack was ensured through persuasive hands and fits along with verbal lashings until I learned my place as their daughter: to be sometimes seen and never heard.

I suck in a harsh breath that my mother ignores. Really, I shouldn't be surprised at the request, and yet I am. Mother has always enjoyed testing our pack mates' loyalties, why not her daughter's as well? I dare not think of what consequences might occur should I fail, for I learned long ago the pain it could wreak went beyond the physical.

"Don't think too hard on it, Winter, dearest. You'll get wrinkles, and we can't have you spoiling that lovely face of yours," she chides before striding out of the room. "And remember, there are more players in this game than you realize. Should you disappoint us, there will be others who face the consequences of your actions."

BY THE MOON

- Chapter 2 -

It's undoubtedly quieter without June's running commentary whispering in my ear as we fly to Montana. The journey is many things without a true friend or ally nearby.

Bittersweet.

Somber.

Stark.

How I manage without her shine is a remarkable feat. The pack mates who accompany me are not the liveliest of peoples. Worse still, my only bridesmaids are my cousins Lucy and Jessica. They're a vicious duo who are equally cruel apart.

My mother has three sisters, Cora, Jules, and Margaret—but only two if you were to ask her. Aunt Cora is mother to Lucy and Jessica and holds the rank of third she-wolf. Aunt Margaret is June's mother. Her rank fluctuates near the bottom of the top ten she-wolves. It is a fact that constantly makes my mother and Aunt Cora cringe. As for Aunt Jules, she left the pack without a word to be with her soulmark. Nobody discovered her departure until days after the fact.

An invisible clamp tightens around my throat.

Her desertion those years ago make my circumstances more disliked. That is the nicest way of putting it.

I stand alone in a canopy tent planted on a short wooden platform outfitted as a makeshift bridal suite. December's icy touch is impeded by two sets of mini heaters at their full strength in the cozy space, and lush cashmere blankets adorn most of the allotted furniture. A pair of chairs are left unoccupied at the back of the tent near its zipper door. My cousins refuse to wait inside the outdoor bridal suite in favor of the warmer indoors, even if the suite is right next to the ceremony venue.

If the bridal suite is anything to go by, our winter ceremony will be the epitome of rustic chic—heavy on the *chic.*

I smile softly. For all her bark and bite, my mother did an exquisite job in planning the wedding.

The wedding is held on Adolphus land as a gesture of goodwill, and as both a symbolic and literal gesture of me leaving the Blanc pack to join another. Yesterday, I spent the day sequestered to my hotel room as my mother set off with my cousins and aunts to oversee the last of the wedding preparations.

It wasn't until the rehearsal dinner that I got to spend time with Atticus before the ceremony. Even then, I had been kept away from him as much as possible by my pack mates. The experience would have been far lonelier if my soulmark had not taken the less-than-subtle snub in stride and snuck me winks and smiles throughout the night. When I returned to my room last night, I discovered a batch of warm apple cinnamon morsels delivered courtesy of Atticus from Baudelaire Patisserie and Café.

The sweet treat melts in my mouth, accompanied by an appreciative moan. A simple note had been left near the plate. It read:

Life is about to become immeasurably sweeter.
Counting the seconds until tomorrow.
-A

At this very moment, the note lay hidden among one of the many suitcases traveling with me to my new home. Hidden because, if any were to see the unauthorized communication, a scene would inevitably be made.

I force my gaze away from the analog clock perched atop a small pine dresser. The time to wed is inching closer and closer, but I won't be escorted out until the clock strikes eleven. I suppress a yawn. Lycan weddings are held at night, and ours will be no different. Our ceremony will take place at eleven, followed by a midnight feast. And feast, I will.

When my eyes wander over to the tall mirror propped up in the far corner of the tent, I give pause. My dress is like something out of a dream. Lace hugs my torso and arms, while a skirt of tulle pools out around me like I'm royalty. The dress reminds me of some fanciful ballgown with its rose appliqués and natural waistline. But my favorite element is the lace and how it overlays the simple bustier and hugs the caps of my shoulders all the way to the edges of my wrists.

The back is just as stunning, showing off the lace's floral pattern against my bare back before disappearing into the tulle skirt. I give a small spin and glimpse the pearl buttons that line the skirt's long train. Every piece fits perfectly together. I don't just look beautiful, I feel it too. I relish in the thought before it can be taken away from me by some cruel comment by my cousins later in the night.

My hair is half up and woven with ivy and greenery. The rest cascades down my back in billowy curls. The foliage is a necessary interjection of color, but it's not the only one. My bouquet is an elaborate display of red roses, which are far more cumbersome than they ought to be. The deep crimson is mirrored in my lipstick.

The last piece of color resides on my wrist. Staring down at it brings a spot of color to my face. A gift from my soulmark on our wedding day. It was delivered to me in the evening from my father as my winged eyeliner was being finished by the makeup artist.

A bracelet made of diamonds and emeralds. The sight of such a gift left me breathless. I missed the look of approval on my father's face at my look of awe, but my makeup artist assured me how sweet it had been to witness. I don't bother to inform her that our relationship is strained at best. He does not approve of my new rank in the Adolphus pack as a beta.

If I married within the Blanc pack, there is no doubt in my mind my parents meant to groom me to be the next female alpha.

"Vanity is unbecoming, Winter."

My mother's voice startles me from my deep reverie, and I turn sharply to see her entrance. A cold draft follows in behind her, but she secures the tent's flaps closed behind her quickly enough.

"Mother," I greet cautiously with a healthy dose of surprise tossed into my tone for good measure. I glance at the clock. There's still five minutes left until 11:00. "Where's Father?"

"He'll be here soon enough. I wanted to give you this." She holds out a square jewelry box.

I blink back, then take the offering from my mother before I can be scolded.

"Don't open it yet," she snaps as I go to do just that. I sigh and set the jewelry box near the clock. "Open it later. In *private*," she stresses. The alpha in her voice is undeniable, and her order rolls over my spine like a grindstone pressing into my bones.

"Of course, Mother," I agree and swallow past the discomfort of such an onerous order.

"Good," she says with a relieved sigh that is most unnatural coming from her. I look over my shoulder to see her expression. It is foreign to me. The gentle joining of her brows and the soft pout on her lips makes her look almost... nostalgic. Again, I swallow. "You look a vision, Winter."

"Thank you, Mother," I reply, my voice just above a whisper.

For a moment we linger in peace and silence, as daughter and mother alone. Then her sweet facade breaks, and her shoulders jerk back as she straightens her spine. "Your father is walking up now. Grab your bouquet, Winter. It's time."

+++

Unacquainted faces trump the familiar as I am marched down the aisle. A violin quartet serenades from somewhere in the massive glass building that hosts our ceremony, and, in unison, the crowd stands to greet my father and my entrance as we walk the silk-lined aisle.

I attempt to keep my eyes from wandering too far around the glamorous room or become too distracted by the scent of evergreen, mint, and the strong presence of the guests' perfume. After all, the man at the end of the aisle is looking at me. A shaky breath rattles out my lungs as I avert my gaze to the aisle runner halfway into our voyage. A warm hand smooths itself across my own, and I peek up at my father. He looks solemn and proud and ready to carry out this arrangement made so long ago. He doesn't spare a glance back in my direction, but I believe it for the better.

As I sweep my gaze back toward the ground, I am caught by heavenly blue eyes. I draw my shoulders back and stand taller at his intense regard. My lips draw to a part as I sweep my gray eyes over his frame.

Beautiful.

The closer we get, the more in awe I am of the man I'm meant to take as my husband. Even in my preposterously high heels, he stands an inch or two above me. He's muscular, but not overly so. The three-piece suit he wears is tailored expertly over his broad chest and thick arms, but the growing smile upon his face turns my cheeks to red.

Strong, clean-shaven jawline.

A not-too-wide nose.

Perfect lips.

Joyful eyes.

Counting down the seconds....

I duck my head in embarrassment steps before my father brings us to a halt in front of the grand altar. Pictures of Atticus I had sought out over the years through social media did the man no justice. He's too handsome for words.

"Who here gives this woman to this man to be wed?" the officiant asks, a man of small stature and hair as white as mine.

"I do," my father replies. His lips brush the warm apple of my cheek before delivering a brisk nod toward Atticus who takes a step forward. As my father retreats, Atticus advances, his hand outstretched for me to take. I lift my eyes to him in a flutter of lashes derived from the butterfly wings waving around in my stomach.

He smiles back at me, a dazed expression settling on his face as I slip my hand into his palm. We settle ourselves before the officiant, Atticus smiling like it's Christmas morning, and me, in turn, as red as the roses in my hand.

"Please, be seated. I am Jackson Walters, and I will be the officiant for today's ceremony. Welcome family and friends. We are gathered here today to witness and celebrate the marriage of Atticus and Winter. We are not here to mark the start of a relationship, however; we are here to recognize a bond that already exists. Atticus and Winter discovered their souls in one another at the start of their lives, ages eight and five, respectively.

"What shock must have run through these two fine wolves at the contact. They were both far too young to understand the gravity and precious gift they received that day. Now, twenty years later, and the two may finally begin their journey together on this night."

Jackson's steady cadence stands in stark contrast with his elderly form. Atticus, who still holds my hand in his, squeezes it lightly.

"Let us not forget, the soulmark is our kind's most precious gift. Tonight, we have been given the privilege to witness its beauty. Much like in the way we stop and stare in amazement at the beauty of nature, we find ourselves here, together, to revel in the emotions their union evokes. Let us be thankful we need not traverse valleys or climb mountains to experience something so indescribable.

"Tonight, let us celebrate love. Let us celebrate the joining of souls as they were always meant to be—as one. Lucille, Winter's cousin and maid of honor, will now read for us an untitled poem by R.M. Drake."

Lucy's heels tap sharp and succinct against the polished wood floor that spans the ceremony hall. She ascends the raised pulpit seated several feet behind the short line of my bridal party. My cousins wear long maroon dresses and hold a small bouquet of white roses. Lucy passes her bouquet off to her sister as she goes by to stand at the pulpit without her floral accessory. She looks the picture of perfection, and pride gleams in her eyes.

"You will be the clouds
and I will be the sky.
You will be the ocean

and I will be the shore.
You will be the trees
and I will be the wind.
Whatever we are, you and I
will always collide."

Whispered sighs and gentle sniffles trickle into my ears during Lucy's reading. I've heard it practiced a dozen times since my mother decided upon it over a month ago, but the words still fill me with longing. I center my focus on Atticus, only to catch him staring unabashedly at me in return.

His thumb swipes across the back of my palm, bringing the hair on my arms to stand on end. And then he mouths a single word. *Hi.* A short laugh threatens to burst from my lips at the genuine and friendly greeting. I bite at the inside of my cheek before coyly mouthing my own "*hello*" in return.

Anticipation curls in my stomach, stirring the butterflies there into a frenzy. I cannot pull my eyes away from the man before me. A tingling erupts along my lower back, my soulmark aching in reminiscence.

"—As long as you honor the promises that you will make to each other today, you will create a life of love and happiness." I suck in a sharp breath at the officiants ringing words. Atticus slips forward a step, re-earning my attention and wide eyes.

The officiant prattles on, but there is nothing but the sound of my own heartbeat. It drums on at a pace far faster than any other in the room.

Atticus turns my hand in his and presses his thumb into my palm. My fingers latch around it with greed, and I find comfort in the small act.

"Atticus, do you take Winter to be your lawfully wedded wife, to have and to hold, for better or for worse, for richer, for poorer, in sickness and in health, until death do you part?"

Atticus's chest puffs up. "By the moon, I swear it."

"Winter, do you take Atticus to be your lawfully wedded husband, to have and to hold, for better or for worse, for richer, for poorer, in sickness and in health, until death do you part?"

I hesitate, my lips parting but no words passing by them. Atticus waits patiently in return. No worry or doubt crossing his features as I summon my courage.

"By the moon," I say at last, "I swear it."

"It is now time for the exchanging of rings," Jackson announces, far more upbeat than before. I twist and pass my bouquet to Lucy who takes it without a word. When I straighten, Atticus is accepting a pair of rings from his best man, the Adolphus pack alpha.

"Wedding rings have long been a symbol of love," Jackson tells the crowd gayly. "They are a tangible symbol of the vows you have just made to each other. Atticus and Winter, let these rings be a sign that love has substance as well as a soul. And despite its occasional sorrows and hardships, love is a circle of happiness, wonder, and delight. It is my hope, and that of those who surround you today, that you and your family are always encircled by love.

"Atticus, repeat after me: with this ring, I thee wed."

"With this ring, I thee wed."

A glimmering emerald winks back at me in the abundance of candlelight and soft overhead lighting. The pear cut stands alone against a white-gold diamond band. Atticus slips the ring over my finger, and a well of emotion stirs in my heart. Instantly, my eyes become glossy at the sight of the beautiful ring, and a moment later, Atticus presses the band onto my finger.

"Winter, repeat after me: with this ring, I thee wed."

"With this ring, I thee wed."

There is no hesitation this time around, only the strongest urge to put myself in this man's arms as I slip his simple band over his finger.

"Atticus and Winter, you have come here today of your own free will and, in the presence of family and friends, have declared your commitment to each other. You have given and received a ring as a symbol of your vows. By the power vested in me, I now pronounce you husband and wife! You may now share your first kiss. Congratulations! Friends and family, I now present to you, Mr. and Mrs. Hayes."

Those in attendance burst into applause as Atticus winds his arm around the small of my back and ushers me forward into his strong embrace.

"May I?" he murmurs. I nod, a lump in my throat forming as he bends his head toward me. Our eyes remain open and focused on one another until we are mere inches apart. My eyes close, and the sweet press of his lips to mine comes a moment later. They are gentle in their insistence, dragging themselves over my lips, once and then again before capturing my full bottom lip.

A pleasurable sigh escapes me as Atticus pulls back, tilting his forehead to rest against mine.

"Hello, Mrs. Hayes," he whispers once more for only me to hear.

+++

What happens next is nothing but a blur of motion. We thank our guests as they leave the ceremony hall toward the parade of horse-drawn carriages meant to take them to the reception at a private and secure venue. Pictures with our families and the prominent wolves of our packs occur next. Then they too are ushered away to the reception for Atticus and me to have a short set of photos taken. Just the two of us.

As silly as it sounds, stars remain in my eyes even when the flash photography ends.

Our carriage ride over is passed in relative silence. A bashful shyness engulfs both of us as we hold hands in our carriage and sit close together to share warmth beneath our thick lap blanket.

"Did you enjoy your gift yesterday?" Atticus asks as we turn into a long winding drive off the main road. In the distance, a large, wooden building stands in the distance. Old-fashioned lampposts light the lane, bringing a magical ambiance to the midnight air.

"I did," I tell him, giving his hand a small squeeze. "It was *delicious* and had just the right amount of caramel."

Atticus squeezes my hand back and keeps his voice low as he answers. "Good. Zoelle will be happy to hear it. Unfortunately, I'm not much of a cook, but Zoelle is. I, on the other hand, am pretty good at being able to convince her to make something for me."

I laugh at his admission and peer at him through my lashes.

"Don't worry, I'm not the best cook either," I tell him. "I could eat sweets all day."

"I'll have to remember that," Atticus murmurs as we reach our destination.

Warm hands rest on my waist to escort me from the carriage's belly. But as my feet land safely on the snow-covered ground, they remain. A strange nervousness keeps my eyes trained on the pretty pearl tie pin he wears, instead of looking into his sapphire blue eyes.

"I know our relationship isn't what most consider normal, but I want you to know that I've been looking forward to this day for a long time. To be quite frank, I'm thrilled it's here. And although we are technically husband and wife... I think we should keep things pretty slow between us." Atticus clears his throat as his cheeks turn a little pinker. "Does that sound all right to you?"

I nod. It's all I can manage with the knowledge of how close his fingertips are to touching my soulmark. I release a slow and calming breath even as my thoughts whirl. His sentiments are appreciated, but I can't help but wonder how long we will be able to stand by this rule. It isn't just his innocent touch that makes my body stir. There is a hunger he tries and fails to keep out of his eyes, and our bodies continue to angle toward one another in each other's presence.

There is an unspoken suspense building between us, one we won't be able to ignore forever—*despite my parents' wishes.*

Atticus clears his throat, and I avert my gaze to the reception hall ahead of us.

"I guess we should head inside," he says and pulls away. Atticus takes my hand, and together we walk inside as husband and wife.

+++

The night's activities far surpass my expectations. The dinner is wonderful, the speeches are heartfelt, and the band plays all the right songs. Ryatt, Xander's younger brother, and Quinn, his soulmark, make sure my glass is never empty.

It may or may not be the real reason I am having such a marvelous time. The champagne softens all the raw edges of my nerves, and after a bit of time, being on Atticus's arm is the only place I want to be. *If June were here to hear my sentiments, she would squeal in delight.*

The only threat to my night of bliss is the surly faces of the Blanc Pack. In my champagne-induced haze, I came to realize that as long as I don't make eye contact with them, I will remain untouched by their disapproving glares. My no-eye-contact rule also helps me push away the feeling of disloyalty that comes with glancing their way.

"Are you having a good time?" Atticus asks, his warm breath and lips brushing the top of my ear. I shiver a little but give a happy nod and look his way to bestow a gracious smile.

"How can I not be?"

Atticus smiles broadly, his pearly straight-white teeth dazzling me. "Good. I'm glad."

"Congratulations, brother," an increasingly familiar voice states from behind. Atticus and I turn to greet the Adolphus alpha, Xander, and his fiancée, Zoelle.

"You know," Atticus says, his broad smile still in place as he swings his arm across the back of my shoulders, "you only have to congratulate us once. This is your fourth time."

Xander laughs and tugs his fiancée closer into his side. She's a beautiful woman with dark skin and the most lovely, dark curls acting like a halo around her face. "Ah, but this time we come bearing gifts."

"More cinnamon morsels?" I ask eagerly. The champagne buzzes through my veins as I recall the delectable treat, but then I'm coloring as the three laugh at my brazen enthusiasm.

"No, I'm sorry." Zoelle's cheeks retain a healthy glow from her laughter. "But I can make those for you any time. The gift I wanted to give you is from my coven, the Trinity Coven."

I freeze as she holds out a small purple bag to me, but it is Atticus who takes the gift on our behalf. With as much discretion as I can manage, I scan the faces of those who monitor us. Nobody seems to be watching our interaction closely—at least not that I can tell. *Good, it won't do well if my pack mates see me accepting a witch's gift, regardless if she is the alpha's soulmark.*

"Thank you," I finally manage to say, albeit a bit breathlessly as my heart thunders on at an unusually clipped place. Tonight, only pack is allowed. More specifically, those of the lycan variety. Zoelle's presence had been a quick concession on the Blanc pack's part, but behind closed doors, they fumed at the indignity.

Atticus sports a playful frown after dumping the contents into his palm. "Rocks?"

"Fertility stones," Zoelle corrects, the color growing brighter on her cheeks. Atticus lets out a boisterous laugh that draws the eye of a fair few, and I swiftly deliver an elbow to his side. He looks down at me in question, but I scoop up the stones and put them back into the bag with remarkable speed. I hold them back out to Zoelle.

"I don't have any pockets. Would you mind making sure these get set aside by the other gifts?"

Zoelle nods pleasantly in return. "I know the gift is a bit unorthodox, but Yule and Winter Solstice gifts like these are intoned with even more energy and power. You don't have to use them right away, but they've been known to do the trick."

"Thank you, Zoelle. How... thoughtful." And it is to an extent, but no amount of magic will give Atticus and me children.

"If you're curious, they're rose and smoky quartz, moonstone, and aventurine. They're commonly used for fertility," Zoelle adds and gives an impish shrug.

Years of practice are the only reason I am able to keep my emotions in check as the sorrow of the soulmark curse unfurls inside of me. I prepare to offer some excuse to leave the small group when a vision of chestnut curls and honey brown eyes make their way over to us. Lucy.

"Winny, why aren't you dancing with your handsome new husband?" In a gesture that is easily mistaken by the group as a friendly squeeze on

Atticus's bicep, I see the more malicious curl to her smile as she lets her hand linger. Lucy shares her sparkling smile with the group. "You'll have to forgive me, Winny, but I absolutely must insist on stealing at least one dance with your husband. You don't mind, do you?"

Numbly I move my head side to side, and I'm startled when Atticus's lips briefly graze my cheek before allowing himself to be whisked away by Lucy. I watch their departure in a slight daze, my fingers coming to brush over the area.

"Don't worry," Xander says to me with warm affection. "I don't think Atticus can stand to be parted from you for more than one dance."

I give a grateful smile, half produced from habit, the other from genuine relief. Even though I know better than to give into this sort of simple jealousy, my mother's words of this "sham union" ring dutifully in my head. The words grow like some kind of weed, sprouting taller and reaching farther as the seconds tick past.

I catch Atticus's blue eyes from the dance floor, which hosts only members of the Adolphus pack. He shoots me a wink and grin, then spins my cousin at a dizzying pace. Her chestnut curls fly haphazardly about her face, strands sticking to the sticky gloss painted on her lips.

"See," Zoelle teases with a charming air, and indeed, my sprouting jealousy washes away as I turn my attention back to the alpha couple as proper etiquette dictates.

My mouth opens to impart some passing nicety when I am affronted with a most alarming sight. "Oh my God," I say and release a whimper. I stare in abject horror at the couple entering through the back of the building like lurking shadows right toward us.

Both alphas turn to see what causes me such alarm and in tandem let out their own pleased gasps.

"Irina!" Zoelle cries with delight and rushes determinedly through the crowd, Xander hot on her heels.

"Wait—" But my plaintive cry is ignored.

They can't be here.

I swallow thickly and duck my head with more speed than necessary. *Be natural,* I scold myself. *Maybe nobody will notice.*

It's a foolish thought. Naive. I steal a glance their way. At least there isn't a scene being made... *yet.* Once my pack mates catch wind of this invasion, there will be hell to pay. Since our last encounter with Irina in the Dark Court, my parents have become disenchanted with the dominate she-wolf. For much of the wedding planning, Irina had been the main point of contact before mysteriously falling off the grid when final details needed to be organized. Of course, we connected the dots upon seeing her at the Dark Court as to why she was so unresponsive and another had taken over her role.

My father won't forget the slight. My mother cannot.

Though I hold no true misgivings for the woman, I still can't conjure warm feelings for her uninvited presence. And the night had been going so well.

A warm hand settles between my shoulders, and I jerk at the unexpected touch. Atticus wears a bemused expression at my reaction. Lucy isn't as kind.

"Did you enjoy your dance?" I ask, struck with a strange sort of breathlessness as I wait for his answer. I turn my back to the Adolphus alphas and the new guests. Thankfully, Atticus keeps his eyes on me. If our pack ties were stronger, he would be keener to my mild distress, but they haven't developed substantially—not yet, at least. The majority of my pack bonds still lie with the Blanc pack. Atticus also isn't privy yet to the subtleties of my body language... unlike Lucy.

Her honeyed gaze is piercing as she replies for the two of them. "Your husband is a lively dancer," she answers sweetly, a bell-like laugh chimes from her a moment later as she nudges Atticus with a playful smile. "I'm not sure if you can handle him, cousin."

"Nonsense. The soulmark makes certain of it," Atticus corrects her with a suave charm to his words.

He doesn't take his eyes off me once, and so I put on a smile I hope is convincing, place a hand on Atticus's flank, and attempt to steer him away from the reunion in the back.

"Let's grab a snack from the dessert table," I suggest. "We'll speak with you later, Lu—"

"Who are they?" Lucy asks. Her eyebrows pinch together as she studies the newcomers with Xander and Zoelle.

"Oh, just some close family friends I think who wanted to wish us a quick congratulations. They won't be staying long." I want to say more. I want to drag Atticus off and mollify Lucy's curiosity somehow, but Atticus isn't budging, and Lucy's shoulders become stiff. "I'd love a cupcake," I say in a last-ditch effort to steer their attention away.

"That's Irina." A note of shock lingers in Atticus's expression and voice when he looks their way. Then a wide smile splits across his face as he shakes his head in a good-natured fashion. "And she brought her soulmark with her. Hot damn."

He's striding off before I can stop him, but as I give chase to remind him how *not* good this is, a hand latches on to my arm and halts my progress. Lucy tugs me back, her brown eyes splintering with gold.

"What the hell are they doing here, Winter? Did you invite them?" I rip my arm from her grip, checking the delicate lace for any rips or tears.

"No," I reply back, my voice full of steel. "Of course not. They've come on their own accord, or by that of the Adolphus pack."

I'm not one to snap back or become aggressive, but Lucy brings out the wolf in me. The feat is rather remarkable really, for my parents made *sure* my wolf spirit was tamed to their hand and leashed to a point where I should rank far lower in the Blanc pack. I'm not sure how I managed the rank of fifth in the Blanc pack, perhaps by my parents bolstering alone. Regardless, my higher rank infuriates Lucy to no end.

As Lucy's eyes spark with more golden flecks, mine do the same. Our lips draw back into soundless snarls.

"Fix this," she says, her voice baring trace notes of command. I arch a brow. I might not be as physically strong as Lucy, but my will, when tested, can be just as strong as my parents.

"Go grab a drink and make yourself busy," I order back, throwing my weight into the command and seeing her flinch back. As the new beta of a different pack, my rank far outreaches Lucy's now.

Sneer still in place, she turns heel and strides toward the bar. I sigh in short-lived relief. Irina is on the receiving end of a larger-than-life embrace by Atticus. Her smile is unapologetically bright. When he sets her down, he delivers a hearty slap to the tall and slender man waiting beside Irina. He jostles from the force but wears a small, sincere smile.

I wind my way around tables and chairs, avoiding our guests with as much tact as I can summon while not tripping over my gown. Irina and her soulmark catch sight of my advance with the others following suit shortly after.

"Hello," I announce with an easy smile, my hands coming to clasp in front of me. "I didn't know we were expecting you, Irina."

Her copper eyes drill into me with mischief and knowing. "I do believe I said weeks ago I would do my best to make it."

"Of course," I reply, unable to tear my gaze away from her new eye color. *I swear they were green like ivy the last I saw her.* I shift closer to Atticus. "You've... changed a bit since I last saw you," I comment.

Irina smiles coolly back. "I died since you last saw me," she explains calmly.

My gaze shifts around the group's occupants with uncertainty. "Pardon?"

"Oh, everything turned out quite all right, I assure you. Here I am, better than ever." The gentleman at Irina's side splays a hand across her hip and looks down at me with a warning in his icy blue eyes.

"Wonderful," I respond.

The gentleman extends a pale hand in my direction. I take it and hide my balk at the cold touch. "It's a pleasure to make your acquaintance, Mrs. Hayes. My soulmark has only kind words to speak of you."

A trickle of apprehension draws up my spine, and I straighten. Alpha eyes are upon me, and they do not belong to the two beside me. "How sweet of you to say, Irina," I manage to get out. "Atticus, I think we need to keep making the rounds. It was wonderful being able to meet both of you."

I avoid looking Atticus directly in the eyes as I make our excuses and my apprehension grows. Xander's demeanor changes an instant later. His face draws blank, yet cordial as he stares over my shoulder.

"Adele," Xander greets with a small nod a moment later. "From my understanding, you met my sister once before. Allow me to introduce you more formally. Adele Blanc, my younger sister, Irina Adolphus, and her soulmark, Jakob Vrana. They traveled all the way from Austria to wish Winter and Atticus well on their wedding day."

My mother's rage calls the entire Blanc pack to attention through the pack bonds. I know without needing to turn around that all eyes of the Blanc pack rest upon our entourage.

"And here I thought you'd be too busy gallivanting around in that dismal tomb preoccupying yourself with who knows what," Adele offers with a cruel smirk. Her hand comes to rest on my shoulder and the fine point of her manicured nails strum my skin.

"As the newly installed Royal Household, our calendar is rather full, but we wouldn't dare think of missing the wedding of the year," Irina says.

A coil of tension winds around our group and seeps into the watching crowd. My hands clasp onto each other more tightly as I shift myself toward my mother. Her influence through our bonds is strong, and the need to stand by her outweighs the call to side with my new pack and husband.

"I was under the impression that only *pack* would be in attendance for the ceremony and reception, Aleksander."

Xander, unmoved by my mother's hostile tone, gives an innocent shrug. "Irina *is* part of the Adolphus pack. By their soulmark, Mr. Vrana is accepted as part of my pack as well."

His blasé delivery prompts my mother's nails to dig into the soft flesh of my shoulder and urges me back with intentions meant to be seen as "motherly" concern. Xander's eyes narrow at the gesture, and I feel Atticus's warm hand shackle itself around my wrist.

"I didn't realize we were attending a funeral tonight, Adele," a new voice enters. *Knox*. My eyes shutter closed a brief moment at the cold opening. "Then again, with the pack's most beautiful she-wolf leaving our ranks, I suppose it is. But are the vampyrés"—he spits out the word like it's dirt—"really necessary?"

Another hand upon me, this one Knox's, grips my hip and guides me forcibly back to stand behind my mother. The dark-haired wolf shifts forward in my place, breaking Atticus's hold. My husband releases a soft growl.

"And who are you?" Irina asks, her nose twisting up into the air as her copper eyes narrow. The raven-haired beauty wears her disdain like a crown. Then again... she is royalty among the Dark Court now. When I met Irina all those weeks ago, I had not seen this side of her. I saw a she-wolf doing her best to survive and be strong. Now she is as cold as marble as she stares down my familial pack.

Knox ignores Irina and stares down Xander instead. Zoelle scowls back at Knox in Xander's stead, for his eyes remain trained on my mother. A wise move.

"This is Knox Bernard," I pipe up, earning a feeling of ire through the Blanc pack bonds. "Oh my, it looks like everyone's glass is empty," I rush on. "Perhaps we could all benefit from a refill."

"Quiet, Winter. This conversation is strictly between Mr. Adolphus and me. Though, I'm sure your father will be interested in the topic. Fetch him."

The order she issues is beyond reproach and is delivered far more roughly than I expect. I walk away, my eyes staring blankly ahead as I obey. *She only issued the order so harshly as a power play*, I tell myself. The Adolphus pack is strong, and she needs to remain steadfast in their eyes. *Don't take it so personally.*

I do anyway, keeping my tears at bay through a series of controlled breathes. Quinn and Ryatt watch me pass by silently, their expressions matching in concern and intrigue. I appreciate their silence, for all around me whispers twirl about the sudden scandal.

I block them out. Years of training make the action effortless.

"Father," I say in my most placating voice. He turns and regards me. His tumbler is topped to the brim with an amber liquid and ice sloshing up the sides. "Mother asked for you."

His eyes flit to the scene at the other end of the room and then back at me. I hold myself tall, smiling at the few pack mates he surrounds himself with. They all wear matching expressions of impatience, though I cannot determine if it is from my disturbance or what courses through the Blanc pack bonds.

"Gentlemen, if you'll excuse me." We walk back over together, the members of our pack knowing better than to stop and make small talk with me. I feel their watchful gazes on my back but keep a placid smile on my lips as we pass back through the crowd.

Upon our arrival, it is clear harsh words have been spoken. Mr. Vrana, the blond vampyré, stands in front of Irina and glares daggers at Knox.

Xander shows his anger in the pinching of his lips and the narrowing of his eyes. My mother, however, is as red as can be. What can possibly have been said in under three minutes to ignite their anger in such a way?

"Malcolm, we're leaving," my mother says through a snarl once we are close. I stop in my tracks, my heartbeat thudding to a comical stop.

"What?" I ask. But nobody hears my soft-spoken question.

"What's going on here, Adele. And why is *she* here?"

I cringe at my father's harsh delivery and can only watch as he steps forward past my mother to enter into the thick of the argument. My mother allows him entrance and retreats back a few steps to be by my side as the scene unfolds.

"They are the *epitome* of uncouth, Winter. How you will deal with their vulgar and boorish ways, I do not know. But I do not envy the task," she says, not bothering to keep her voice down.

I catch Atticus's worried look, but before he can come to my aid, Knox makes a scathing comment in his direction.

"You didn't need to start a fight," I say.

"Me?" She scoffs and leans closer. "These dogs can't help but take the bait. They're wild, Winter. The sooner you can prove where your true loyalties lie, the sooner you may come home. And I do hope that day to be sooner rather than later."

This comment is whispered but lacks none of her previous severity. Before more can be said between us, my father spins on his heels to face us.

"Adele, let's go. Winter, farewell," he says stiffly and walks past us without another word. His face, I note, is as red as my mother's.

"Do remember to call, Winter," my mother says loud enough for everyone to hear. "Often, if you must."

RUNNING WILD

- Chapter 3 -

It's an awful end to a rather lovely wedding. The Blanc pack leaves upon my parents' abrupt departure. Only a handful of them wish me well and say goodbye. Lucy's self-righteous airs as she air kisses my cheeks before leaving is almost too much to bear.

The Adolphus pack do their best to reinstate the peace and reset the mood to a cheerier tone, but their efforts are a waste. The more drinks pressed into my hand to appease my obvious distress only proves to make me sadder.

Even the champagne has turned against me, I realize sullenly.

My head rests against the cold glass window of the limousine taking Atticus and me back to his home. Our bridal suite at the town's most beautiful boutique hotel is forgone once my stomach took a turn for the worse. Atticus assures me we have it for a few nights, and if we want, the following night we can spend our time there. But for tonight, he thought it best to bring me back somewhere undoubtedly safe: his house. Well, *our* house.

"We're here," Atticus murmurs, touching my arm with gentle care.

I step from the limousine onto wobbly legs. I'm immediately aware that the ground is too slippery for my drunken feet to find adequate purchase. But I don't have long to worry about my plight. A hot palm slides around my back to my middle, hooking me into Atticus's side and shepherds me forward.

"You have a pretty house," I mumble. And it is. The house is a Dutch colonial painted some darker shade of blue with white trimming around its windows and on the posts. It's darling, like a real-life dollhouse.

"*We* have a pretty house," he corrects, sweeping me up into his arms. The sky above is finally free from clouds, and the stars blink back down at us, as well as the luminous moon.

My wolf quivers with anticipation of the coming full moon, but it fades from my system almost as soon as it comes.

"Pretty," I mumble once more, sinking into Atticus's embrace. He unlocks the door on his second attempt and brings us inside. When the door closes behind us, he sets me down, and the world slants sideways. "I think I need some water," I say, mouth suddenly tacky and dry.

Before I know it, I'm seated on some couch in the next room and a glass of water is thrust into my hands. I take a grateful drink and then another.

"I think Ryatt and Quinn were a bit too enthusiastic about making sure you were 'well hydrated,'" Atticus says. He takes a seat on the floor in front of me, lounging back on his forearm and sipping at his own glass of water.

I pause with my glass halfway to my lips and study Atticus. He's abandoned his suit jacket and tie, or perhaps lost them. Either way, the view is a pleasant one. His shirt, no longer crisp and perfect, hugs the muscles of his arm. Just as his vest does to his chest. When I drag my eyes to his, I note the purple shadows beginning to form beneath them. A flutter stirs in my stomach as I see the warmth still present in them.

"It was nice for a while," I tell him around the lip of the glass, gaze drifting south once more to his chest.

"Do I have a stain somewhere?" Atticus asks.

"Huh?"

A goofy grin spreads across Atticus's face, and he runs a hand through his hair, ruining its stylish combed-back appearance. "You're, uh, sort of staring... at my chest."

The deep chuckle that follows my blush is one of pure masculine satisfaction, and I strive for some semblance of modicum in my drunken state. "I was just looking at your pocket watch. Well, the chain of what I assume is your pocket watch," I tell him matter-of-factly.

His goofy smile remains, but he obligingly ceases his laughter and takes out his watch. With a flick of his wrist, he tosses it to me. I fumble to catch it, spilling my water on the couch and my dress.

"Whoops."

I awkwardly set down my glass, and by the time I have righted myself, Atticus is offering me his handkerchief. I blink at it in confusion, taking it as well.

"For your dress," he explains. My mouth forms an O as I dab at the fabric of my dress and then the couch. Satisfied with my work, I take my time inspecting the brass and gold accessory. I'm well aware the entire time Atticus studies me.

"It's quite old," I finally manage to say, peering at him through lashes that are growing heavier and heavier by the minute. "Is it a manual wind watch?"

Atticus nods in surprise. "It was my great-grandfather's. I have it taken in every now and then to make sure it keeps running smoothly."

I make a short humming noise in the back of my throat as I lean over the couch's edge to deliver the heirloom back to Atticus, not expecting to lose my balance in doing so. He catches me as I windmill over, and a short shriek surges out of me as I tumble into his hard chest.

Half on and half off the couch is an uncomfortable place to be, and so I scoot my bottom half off as well. The process takes much less effort, but the landing is far less comfortable.

"Oof!"

"That's a lot of skirts," Atticus remarks, attempting to help me find a more comfortable seat on the floor between himself and the couch. The bottom half of my dress disagrees vehemently at the course of action, and soon, I quit my efforts.

"It's pointless," I tell Atticus, batting his hands away as he continues to try and right my skirts. "You don't have to do that." But my words don't reach him, and I sulk back against the couch, watching as he fusses with the long train. "I said, '*You don't have to do that*,' Atticus."

He passes me a wry smile and finishes rearranging my volumes of skirt into something far more manageable. "Of course, I do, wife."

His light teasing brings a pleased flutter to my stomach, and I fidget with my hands. "I don't think husbands are supposed to do that. Tidy and clean." With my admission, I direct my attention to my fidgeting hands.

Atticus goes back to his earlier position, sprawling out further this time on the wooden floor and propping his head upon his hand. I swallow, my eyes drifting over the mightier swell of his bicep in this position. When I meet his blue eyes, there is a different sort of warmth creeping into them.

"And what is a husband supposed to do for his wife?"

My heartbeat gives a hard thump at the retort, and I stall to think of an answer. My fidgeting hands go up to my hair and begin to pick out the bits of ivy and greenery. They also dislodge all the pesky bobby pins keeping everything in place until I'm free to start untangling all the knots.

"A husband is supposed to provide for his wife."

"And a wife?"

"A wife is supposed to take care of her husband."

"And these are mutually exclusive roles?" Atticus's voice is a mixture of confusion and teasing, and I find my sights drawn to him unconsciously.

"They're... they just are what they are," I say. My answer is wrong. I know the moment I say the words out loud, but I refuse to take them back. I straighten my spine, ready to defend my answer if necessary.

Right or wrong, drunk or not, my answer is what I grew up being taught, and nothing will change it.

Atticus leans in toward me, moving like some lithe feline as he treads into my personal space. "Anytime you want me to take care of you, Winter. Just say the word, and I'm yours."

He seeks something out in my eyes at his confession, but I'm not used to a confrontation like this. I don't know how to respond, or what the right answer to give is. Or if there is one. With a gentle exhalation, I pull away from his silent inquisition and search out my water. There isn't much left, but I down the rest of the contents anyway.

"How about I show you your bedroom?"

I blink in surprise but accept his request when he stands and holds out a hand to me. Somewhat speechless, I follow him upstairs. I'm thankful the room doesn't try and spin or tilt out of my reach as I climb unfamiliar steps into a dark hallway. Atticus leads me left, and at the first door, we stop.

"This is your room," Atticus tells me. "I sleep at the other end of the hallway in the master bedroom.

So, if you need anything, like water or... uh, or anything else, I'll be there, just knock."

Atticus's evolving bashfulness is intriguing. His cheeks turn pink, and his hand becomes warmer around mine. I blink, his previous statement completely slipping away from me as his warmth sinks into my body. I lick my lips, still parched.

"Can we talk about one more thing before you go to bed?"

Again I blink, pulling my thoughts forcibly away from the sheer amount of heat he projects. I understand we lycans run hotter than the average human, but Atticus is on another level. The flame of life burns brighter inside him than any I've met before.

"Winter?"

"Yes?" My response comes quicker than I mean it to, but Atticus quirks a grin and brushes some of my snowy white curls over my shoulder. I still at the action and acknowledge my cheeks to be the same color as his.

"Tomorrow is a full moon. Normally, the pack would run together in our wolf forms as one because it strengthens our pack bonds. Unfortunately, with the current climate between our pack and the Wselfwulfs, doing so is too dangerous. Instead, we run on a schedule to make sure each wolf gets the chance to run while making sure our borders are constantly watched."

"I can feel the moon's power rising already tonight," I say, my words slurring together in the middle. I scrunch my nose and try harder for the composure I can usually call at will. "During the carriage ride," I explain, "and after."

Atticus doesn't let go of my hand. For a moment, he just stares down at me. His eyes flit over every centimeter of my face. When he maintains his silence, I find my voice.

"Was that what you wanted to tell me? About the running schedule?"

He blushes heartily. "Actually, I wanted to ask if you will run by my side tomorrow night."

My jaw lowers at a snail's pace. The same blush that crowds up Atticus's neck and cheeks infiltrates mine, and I shrink back as a wave of shyness hits me.

Why does he have to be so sweet? If he wasn't, then spying on his pack might not hurt as much. My eyelids close as I release a sigh. It would help tremendously if his pack weren't as sweet as him either.

My mother thought this pack wild and uncouth, but they've only proven so far to be lively and amiable.

"All right," I agree.

When my eyes open, he is smiling benevolently down at me. It lights up his entire face, reaching from the high-stretched corners of his lips to the crinkles at the corners of his eyes. I am spellbound by the expression on his face... until my mother's words come back to haunt me.

Should you disappoint us, there will be others who face the consequences of your actions.

His smile fades as I continue to stare at him with my mouth slightly agape. A hand strokes my cheek, and my lashes flutter closed again. *Who had my mother been referring to? Would Atticus be the target of her attack?* I tremble as his thumb runs across my bottom lip and his heat closes in around me. *What—*

My body moves of its own accord to compliment his, and I press my cheek into his open palm. There are hardly any callouses to grace his flesh, but still, I'm able to sense the sure presence of power and strength that lies dormant in his capable hand.

My own comes to rest above his heart, with nimble fingers clutching at the fabric of his shirt. As my pulse beats in time with his, Atticus closes the last inch between us and our lips meet.

We shouldn't, for both our heart's sake. I know it to be true, and yet I can't stop myself. Isn't every woman's wedding supposed to be *hers*? And yet all the details and planning of the night haven't been my own.

I press into Atticus's body. This piece of the night will be mine.

At first, it is a tentative meeting on both sides. We learn one another in gentle caresses and small sighs as we instinctively curl into one another. *Apparently, kissing is in the "moving slow" category.* A hazy pleasure permeates my body.

His tongue drawing past the seam of my lips earns him a shuddering inhalation, and then Atticus's hand dives down my back to anchor me to him.

It is a dangerous move.

The lace backing of my gown allows the pads of his fingers to brush against my flesh between the delicate webbing. His fingers almost touch the three intertwined rings at the small of my back. A phantom spark shatters the spell around us. I jerk away and slam into the door behind me with jarring force.

"I'm sorry—did I do something wrong? Are you okay?" I cradle the back of my head with one hand, using the other to ward him off. "Shit. I'm sorry, I should have asked if you were okay with—are you hurt?"

"I'll be fine," I assure him and begin to grab for the door handle. "It's been a long day and an even longer night. I'd like to sleep now," I tell him as kindly as possible. Atticus's shoulders slump forward, and his hands thrust deeply into his pant pockets as he nods resolutely.

"Of course." He steps back.

I allow my teeth to dig painfully into the inside of my cheek. *What am I doing?* "Good night, Atticus. Sleep well."

"Sweet dreams, Winter."

I steal inside my bedroom before another word can be spoken. The train of my gown almost doesn't make it inside with me, but by some miracle it does.

I slump against the door, my face pressed into the wood as I listen to his reluctant departure. His door shuts with soft persuasion, and I crumble to the floor. Desperately I wish for a different life, one not bound to these damnable curses or my tyrant family.

But if I can keep the man....

My hands close into fists around my skirt. This is my chance to extract myself from my parents' clutches. I only need to discover who they plan on hurting if I fail in their eyes to warn them of my parents' plot... while mollifying my parents' request for information in the meantime. I grind my teeth together as my eyes search the ceiling for a better answer. None comes, and I add a third aim to my list. Don't lose my heart to Atticus in the process, for my chances of success are slim at best.

+++

By morning's end, I decide I must be the only person on the planet who cannot be put at ease by Atticus's charm.

He chatters on and on while making breakfast, filling the space between us with meaningless small talk before it can turn to silence. Unsure of what to say or how to act given the decisions I made last night, I stay quiet for the most part.

Atticus is allotted half smiles from me instead of words. Eventually, my muted airs prompt him to leave. He's to help set up the run base tonight, after all, and he assures me he'll return in no time to fetch me.

I'm thankful for the peace and find solace back on the couch where Atticus set me last night. The long piece of furniture butts up against a sizeable window.

It provides a perfect view of the quaint street and how it curves out of sight. An inch adjustment and my chin rests on the back of the couch cushion as my regard drifts in and out of focus on the snow-laden street and cute little houses decorating it.

I finger the necklace I wear, thoughts treading into territory I know well.

Who will my mother hold over my head to coerce my compliance?

What information can I provide to my parents that will be both meaningful and not at the same time?

How can I possibly ignore and deny the attraction between Atticus and me?

Doubt weighs in my stomach like heavy stones and makes my hangover more pronounced. I just have to keep my head above water and remain calm and collected.

Of course, it doesn't help in the least that these daunting tasks are made more formidable because I must keep them a secret. Should the Adolphus pack learn of my parents' ulterior motives, they will instigate a new war. And if my parents discover my disloyalty... I can't stand to think of what they may do.

My thumb traces the oval moonstone pendant, seeking a sense of comfort and finding none. I lift the moonstone to my inspection. It is nearly perfect, except for the semi-deep crack down its center that is filled with turquoise resin.

The necklace is a family heirloom and my mother's wedding gift to me.

Keep this treasure close to your heart as generations of Blanc's have before you. I know you will not disappoint me. Love, Mother.

Lights flicker to life outside. At ten past four, the sun is well on its course to descend past the horizon. Sometime in the next half hour, it will set, but for now, I enjoy the colors its rays paint across the scattered clouds. As the last of the streetlights flicker on, I pull myself away from the couch.

Atticus will be back soon.

The knowledge fills me with nervous excitement and anxiety.

A pair of lights swing through the living room windows and next through those that frame the front door. Atticus is home. Time to run... and meet the rest of the pack.

+++

Atticus assures me the ride isn't a long one to Xander's, but we'll hit some light traffic due to the snow on the road. I don't mind. The town is bustling though the sun has set. Groups of women navigate their way around precarious patches of ice on the sidewalks, laughing loudly as they slip into the nearest happy hour spot. A few men boisterously shout at one another as they begin to engage in a snowball fight.

An elderly couple sits outside on a bench people watching as they pass a thermos between them.

Emotion thickens in my throat.

"Do they have any idea what's going on? That a war is right at their doorstep?" I ask. My fingers brush away the light condensation on the passenger window as they trail downward. *Do the Adolphus pack realize their campaign to live as they wish is still catching international eyes?*

The air about the SUV changes to something more tenuous. Atticus takes his time answering.

"The Wselfwulf pack hasn't done anything to the people of the town. They won't risk our true nature being found out for it benefits nobody of our kind, let alone the supernatural community. But we've had some difficulties in explaining certain deaths," Atticus tells me seriously. "When we settled here, the Trinity Coven was already settled in the town. They had been for a couple of generations. Before Zoelle and Xander found each other, the Wselfwulfs tried persuading the coven to help them recover their 'lost wolves.' It didn't go over well."

"They did what?" I ask aghast. I round on Atticus, twisting in my seat to stare at him. "But you seceded from their pack. I can't understand why they laid a claim to you. Why did this war begin? Why this need for... *revenge*?" I spit out the word, my own frustration pooling into it effortlessly.

He shrugs, and the car comes to a gentle stop as the streetlight three cars up goes from yellow to red. "Rollins Wselfwulf was not a good man, wolf, or alpha. He pulled heavily on his pack's strength to bolster his own and kept a tight leash on us all. When we left, thirteen of the Wselfwulf pack were killed and twelve of ours, including *our* alpha, Xander's father."

This much I knew. "They wanted to even the count."

"They want us to return. They want our power and numbers. But most of all, they want to see us suffer. Rollins died a little over a year ago, and his daughter ranks as alpha now," Atticus says with a grimace. "She's Xander's half-sister, and about as deranged as her father. At the very least, she's as power hungry as him. Before his death, he revealed his true intentions were to see all of us suffer. He wished for our demise by his hand."

"I didn't know that."

"They're very good at claiming otherwise. I don't know how all of this will end, but I'll always make sure you're safe, Winter. I won't let you be involved in the fight or risk you getting hurt."

Atticus's hand finds mine without trying. Tender emotions rise inside me, and I look away to hide the pleasure blooming on my cheeks.

"I don't think you would want me to fight, anyway," I tell him, trying to work my way away from our previous topic. A solid lump forms in my throat, one I am quick to swallow down. "I'm not a good fighter."

He gives my fingers a squeeze. "Well, I hope you're a good runner."

I nod, struck with sudden bashfulness and attempt to tug my hand away. For a moment, Atticus's grip tightens and time stretches long and thin between us. I know this type of want and longing. It triggers in me as well and amplifies through the reawakened soulmark. How it can tell its other half is near, is entirely unknown to me but it does.

At last, our hands release and retreat back to our sides.

"I'm a fair runner," I acknowledge. "Aren't all she-wolves though?"

Atticus's deep chuckle resonates throughout the car, and it breaks the awkward tension built between us with ease. Or perhaps this is the nature of the *beta.*

"We don't typically start our runs at Xander's place." Traffic lessens as we turn off the main road and onto more residential streets. "We go from my house—our house, sorry." The apology is accompanied by a crooked smile full of uncertainty and embarrassment. "I think it might take a while to get used to the pronoun change."

I bite my bottom lip to hamper my smile. "Agreed," I say in a small voice. Atticus clears his throat.

"Our house is more centrally located in town. Although a decent portion of the pack lives in the subdivision we're headed to, somehow our place became full moon central. We base out of Xander's for more official matters."

"Is there something official happening tonight?"

Atticus reaches over and tugs my braid. "New pack members always have their first pack run at the alpha's." I flush, not particularly liking the idea of being the center of attention. "Don't be nervous. You'll have a great time. Everyone is excited to meet you and get to run with you."

"It won't be the entire pack, will it?"

"No. But you shouldn't expect too many familiar faces tonight. Many of those who attended the wedding won't be running with us so that others get the chance to meet you."

The flush I sport remains on my cheeks. *How many wolves will I meet tonight?* New wolves to the Blanc pack more often than not arrive as newborns. Marriages do occur outside the pack, but only the amount necessary to keep the pack from intertwining their lines too much.

"Our neighbors will be their tonight. Ilene and Ron, he's part of the local police force here but was in the Navy before. They came into the pack a few years ago. Then there's Holly and David. They live in the house to the right of ours. She's an emergency room nurse, which is helpful whenever we have hard-to-explain injuries. Her husband is a teacher at the high school, but you won't see him tonight. He's not a lycan."

I tense as Atticus pulls to a stop on a heavy car-lined street.

"She's married to a human? Is he her soulmark? Like Quinn is for Ryatt."

"Nope." Atticus reaches for his keys to turn off the ignition, but catching my startled expression, stops.

"Does he know?"

"He does."

I don't know what to say, but my reaction is less than affable. Before I can ruin the evening, I direct my gaze at the car parked in front of us. Our lights reflect off the back of the vehicle with a harsh glare, but I can't tear my eyes away.

"Atticus, how could you let this happen? Human counterparts are prohibited unless they bear the wolf's soulmark." My delivery is surprisingly smooth despite the panic rising in my chest like a tsunami. If anyone discovered such blasphemy—

"It isn't prohibited." The firm correction shuts me up. "It *is* frowned upon, but isn't prohibited. We don't run things by the books in this pack, Winter. Truth be told, we're trying to rewrite the book."

A forced laugh makes its way from his throat as the weight of his gaze rests on my cheek.

"You think your pack can rewrite centuries of tradition?" There's no point in hiding my sudden surge of anger. "Our traditions are what keep us connected to one another, no matter how far apart our kind is from one another."

"And some use those traditions to keep their packs in a stranglehold. We're not brushing aside all the old rules, Winter. We're giving them new purpose and meaning." His argument leaves me chafed.

I turn to face him with several lines decorating my brow. "What happens if the she-wolf and her human separate? What then? What's to stop him from telling our secret?"

"Upon their marriage, David vowed loyalty to the pack and, as such, is as much a part of it as you or I. When he made that vow, it was sealed by magic and a potion. If they were to separate, he wouldn't be able to tell another soul." The information does little to appease my irritation.

"What if they have children?"

"At a certain age, they will be told. If the wolf isn't inside of them, the vow will be taken, just as would happen in any other pack. Like I said, we aren't getting rid of all the old rules."

I remain silent, staring at him with my indignation still burning inside me. Albeit, less so after his explanation. In the Blanc pack, no such union would be allowed. Those who did learn of our supernatural secret would be dealt with accordingly to eliminate the threat of exposure. Our ways are... harsh, but I have been taught of their necessity.

"We should head over," Atticus comments, taking my silence as the end of the conversation. He breaks eye contact first, turns off the engine, and enters the cold. I follow suit and hop out of the car cab's cozy heat.

Atticus waits for me to cross the street together. His face holds a pensive pinch to it as he twirls his keys around nimble fingers.

"I didn't really expect our first fight to be so soon," he admits, plunging headfirst into what is sure to be another awkward standoff. I halt my progress, stopping a few feet before him as my eyes shoot toward his. "I was kind of hoping it would be about ice cream or something."

A choked laugh bursts from my lips. "Ice cream?"

Atticus flashes me a charming smile, his eyes twinkling with mirth. He takes a step toward me, his hands going confidently into his leather jacket pockets. My indignation falters as I regard him. He looks much too handsome under the scope of the streetlights.

"I'm a sucker for a rocky road," he confides in me, bending at the waist to lean forward and further into my space. I lean back, fighting the smile that wishes to crop up.

"I like strawberry," I tell him, my heart beating far too fast at his playful nature. Atticus pulls a face wherein his tongue darts out, and his nose scrunches up in disgust.

"Well," he pronounces after righting all of his features into another pleasing smile, "I'm glad that's over. Shall we?"

He offers his arm like a gentleman, and I take it cautiously. All pretense of being cool and aloof in his presence turning to rot. There is something inviting about Atticus that makes it a struggle to stay entirely reserved. My heart gives a flutter. What a dangerous quality my husband owns.

Atticus guides me forward toward a giant house that screams money. Snow crunches beneath our feet with every step, and my earlier nervousness creeps back. I draw my back up straighter. Tonight will be more than just meeting more members of the Adolphus pack. My mother and father will no doubt expect a report on the details for the night.

I sigh, and a cloud of white appears before my eyes. I wish I were strong enough to pull out from under their thumb. I wish I didn't know the harm they were capable of that left me as their pawn, so easy to manipulate with my concern for others.

Instead of walking through the house, we walk around it to the back and head directly to the forest. Once we are several yards deep past the forest line, I spot the scattering of lights in the distance. I check over my shoulder uncertainly to make sure no humans eyes can see us.

"This is purely wolf territory." I scan our surroundings as Atticus continues. "Don't worry, the lights are too far in to be noticed. We've checked a dozen times."

My shoulders relax their rigid posture as we head to the lights. As we close in on the base camp for the run, I begin to slow—not for fear, but in general awe of what is in front of me. Three large canopy tents have been constructed amongst the trees. They're similar to the bridal suite tent I used the other night, but these engulf some of the tree trunks to maximize their space.

Laughter ricochets between tree trunks, and I see more than a dozen people occupying the area in between the tents. They are cast in a glow of lanterns, and several seem to have drinks in their hands.

"Where will the she-wolves run?" I ask, not seeing any other shifting site in the vicinity. My query makes Atticus stop, and I have no choice but to as well with his hand grasping onto my upper arm. A frown sinks his dark eyebrows over his crystal blue eyes.

"What do you mean?" he asks carefully.

I shrug out of his hold with ease and mirror his frown. "Where am I supposed to run?"

"Here." My eyebrows dart up, and Atticus sidesteps in front of me to block the pack's view. He keeps his voice low as he asks his next question. "Where else would you run? I asked you last night to run by my side."

"I thought you meant figuratively," I return hotly, all at once flustered by his assumption. "Of course we wouldn't actually *run* together. Male wolves are too aggressive at the full moon to run with she-wolves. We run separately."

His look of disbelief leaves me doubtful.

"Who told you that?" Atticus asks. He seems genuinely confused and distressed.

"I don't need to be told. I've seen it, Atticus. That's been my life all these years. We don't run together like that in the Blanc pack. It's not safe."

My response stumps Atticus, and my all-American husband's shoulders slump in defeat. I make a move to go around him, but he blocks my way.

"Just wait," he begs, eyes wide as they cast a furtive glance over his shoulder then back at me. His confusion fades to one of determination. "You need to know runs aren't like that here. The full moon is a time to celebrate and let our wolves run free. Just as they were meant to. She-wolves aren't culled from the run for their safety. They're kept *near* so the bigger males can protect them from any outside threat. She-wolves are precious to our pack because they give us strength in their own unique way. You don't have to worry about a wolf being aggressive with you in the Adolphus pack. Ever."

His impassioned speech grows a little louder with each word until I'm sure the pack is privy to every word. I shift uncomfortably, and he shrinks down a bit as he takes a small step toward me. His posturing is submissive and meant to put me at ease. It does, but only by a margin for my embarrassment still strikes me keenly.

"I want you to be comfortable tonight. If you're nervous to run with the guys, there are a couple of women here tonight you can run with instead." Atticus's offer comes in a quiet and placating tone.

I shake my head. I'm unwilling to change the night's agenda to put off my unease. I'll have to trust what Atticus said and hope for the best.

"Are you two finished whispering sweet nothings to each other?" Ryatt calls out from the camp. Atticus stands tall, rolling his eyes as he allows a smile back onto his face. He loops an arm over my shoulder and steers me the remainder of the way into the lantern light.

"Is everyone here?"

Ryatt nods and strides purposefully toward us. He meets us halfway and steals me from Atticus's care. "Come along then, sister." Ryatt pulls me into the very center of the camp with his arm draped over my shoulders.

I cast helpless eyes back to Atticus, but he merely chuckles at my fate.

"I'm afraid he can't help you anymore. You're the property of the pack tonight." His exuberance and excitement are palpable, as is the general consensus across the group. They're all excited for the full moon and, I suppose, for me.

For once, I'm thankful for the cold night air. It better masks the flush filling my cheeks with a rosy hue.

"Ryatt...." The gentle warning comes from none other than the alpha himself. He excuses himself from a couple placed near one of the three canopy tents, and he wears a confident smile. "Do your best not to scare off Atticus's wife tonight."

"Me? Never. If anything, I'm the most fun-loving member of this pack. Aside from the beta himself."

The pack laughs at the gentle ribbing, but Ryatt concedes to releasing me from his hold. Xander approaches, his smile turning warmer. He's dressed in a peacoat and scarf, and his eyes are evergreen in the lighting.

"I hope you're excited for tonight." Xander's voice sounds loud and clear, and the conversation around us stops in deference to the alpha's words. "All of us are. We've been waiting for this night for a long time now. If nothing more than to make Atticus stop counting the days." The group lets out another laugh.

"I wasn't that bad." Atticus shuffles from foot to foot and crosses his arms over his chest.

Xander smirks. "He was."

At this, I let out a small laugh myself. The group's excitement catches and carries inside the few pack bonds I now have with them, thanks to my marriage with Atticus.

Xander's smirk softens to a well-worn smile. "New pack mates are a gift. They're something to be celebrated, especially when those new pack mates are soulmarks, and more so when they are she-wolves. Having you here is like winning the triple crown."

Regardless the corny stature of his words, the sentiment is heartfelt. I sweep my eyes around the group then back to Xander. "I'm happy to be here."

"To make the night better, you aren't the only one we get to celebrate tonight." My eyes widen in surprise. "Matt, Emma, come over here."

The couple who stood by Xander only a minute before approach. Their winter apparel isn't suited well for the current temperature. Their jackets are too thin, and neither wear enough layers beneath to stave off the cold. Yet they smile gayly at their introduction, with familial noses and lips making me rethink my assumption they are a couple.

"Matt and Emma come from the Santa Fe pack. They came in search of a bigger pack to be a part of, and we're happy to accept them. With good tidings, they left their pack and with good tidings enter our own." The wolves around us give a holler and applaud. "If everyone will take their place in rank, we'll allow our newest pack mates to shift first and become familiar with those in attendance."

"Which tent should we use," Emma asks. Xander gestures toward the far left tent.

"Your brother can change in the other, just there." Xander gestures toward the far right tent. "Once we've run, we'll meet back here. Food will be prepared, and we can set up for the next group running."

With our instructions laid out before us, the she-wolf looks to me with expectance. With a jolt, I realize she is waiting for me to go first as rank dictates. I smile kindly and hurry to our designated tent to get her out of the cold.

Emma follows without hesitation. Once we are in the room, she releases a happy noise and claps her hands together.

"Oh, this is so much nicer than what my old pack did for the full moon," she says. I make no immediate reply, heading to the back of the room where two folding screens dominate the back corners of the tent. A small cube unit shelf sits in the middle, with baskets meant to hold our things in while we run.

"What did you do for the full moon?" I ask politely and slip behind one of the screens to undress, two baskets in hand.

"They lacked this... glamor," Emma tells me and follows up the statement with a snort. "We piled up in a few cars and went out to the desert to run. We always fixed up a campfire, and everyone brought food to share as we took turns running. Things get rowdy, but it was always so much fun."

"And you and your brother chose to come up to Montana to be part of a larger pack? There must be larger packs in between here and New Mexico that you could have joined. Why here?"

I'm glad for the screen, the blunt nature of my questioning is not my usual style. My outwear gets piled in one of the baskets and my clothes in the other, then back in the cube shelf. My boots I tuck near the wall, and last, but not least, I unfasten my necklace and place it with my cloths.

"The Adolphus pack is making changes we want to be a part of. Our pack in Santa Fe wasn't happy to see us go, but they were pleased with where our hearts were in making the decision."

Her reasoning makes me pause. Mother would be appalled at her explanation. I shift restlessly as I realize she is waiting for some kind of response from me.

"Let's meet the pack," I say, keeping my words gentle and soothing. "And then let us run."

I hear Emma move to the other corner to change and am grateful that she takes my words to heart. She makes quick work of her clothes because it isn't long until the telltale cracking and shifting of bones fills the room. Emma groans, but that groan swiftly turns to a snarl. I don't flinch at the animalistic sound, but I'm tempted.

Shifting is not a lovely process and one that I have always found to be painful. A soft thud sounds from the corner, then a whine as Emma enters the last phases of her transformation. *My turn.*

A sigh of relief brushes past my lips as I revel in the short moment of tranquility.

Then, with a deep breath to fill my lungs, I will my wolf forward and call upon the moon's favor to see to my request. As always, the Goddess answers, and the very breath I've just taken is stolen from my lungs.

A surge of power and fire races through my veins as the change settles over me. It burns from the inside out. My ligaments stretch. My insides rearrange. I gasp, tilting downward and landing on all fours. A wracking body shudder works its way from head to toe, the wolf stepping forward into its rightful place under the moon's full face.

I pant with the exertion of the final repositioning of my bones and shiver at the odd sensation of fur covering my naked body. I take a moment to adjust to my lycan-heightened senses. The world comes to me now in far more vivid detail and color. A quick scenting of the air reveals the heavy perfume of damp, cold earth and pack amongst what's left of the forest's greenery.

Outside the pack chatters happily—no, excitedly. My keen hearing picks up on every nuance of noise, and I slink out from behind the screen. Emma's soft tread follows behind my own, and looking back I see the small she-wolf. Her fur is a dark sandy color, with patches of brown on her chest and back.

It's a stark contrast to my own coloring: pure white. Like my descendants before me, I retain our namesake as my wolf's coat. Our pack, derived from the northern reach of Canada, are known for our white coats to better camouflage our presence in the Arctic climate.

Emma keeps her head low—submissive—and shuffles a few steps forward before dropping down onto her belly. She releases a soft whine and stretches out onto her side, so both neck and belly are bare to me. I pause before changing course and walking to her. I press my nose into the thick ring of fur around her neck and sniff, taking her scent to memory.

When I begin to pull back, she licks the underside of my jaw in excitement. Her tail wags happily as she scrambles to a stand when I step away. Her playfulness is infectious and reminds me of June's when we are in our wolf forms. I butt Emma with the flat of my head before trotting off outside where the others await.

"Welcome," Xander says, his voice carrying over the excited clamor of the pack in attendance. "Take your time and go down the line to meet your new pack mates."

The alpha takes a knee, and the rest of the pack mirrors his gesture. Everyone wears matching smiles, and through the pack bonds their elation and eagerness slip over me. My tail wags with growing anticipation as I approach first, as is my right by rank.

My ears flatten to the side of my head as I reach out to sniff the side of Xander's outstretched neck. His scent isn't as strong as it would be in wolf form, but the act of staying human is a statement of vulnerability and trust. I can deal a devastating blow to the alpha with ease. The fact that I don't is a mutual act of faith. Xander's hand runs along my neck before he rubs his head against mine.

"Welcome home, Winter," he whispers roughly into my fur and inhales, taking in my scent as well. "Be good to him."

I duck from Xander's tentative hold, bumping into him a fraction as I move onto the next in line: my husband.

"Hey, you." Atticus reaches out a hand to stroke my head. I rock into the touch, my golden eyes studying him. He smiles, and it only grows as I lean forward to capture his scent with a gentle snuff along his neck. "You're beautiful." The words are hushed as he buries his face into the thick fur of my neck. "I can't wait to run beside you, Winter."

A pleased shiver courses over me, but when I attempt to dislodge from Atticus's hold, he grips me tighter. His forehead comes to rest on mine and lingers until we take a breath and exhale as one. Atticus makes a pleased noise in his throat and releases me to finish my greetings.

As we three make our way down the line of pack mates, those who we have met go inside the tents to change. Soon the small clearing is filled with a bundle of wolves who are eager to stretch their legs.

Atticus finds me once I'm done. He is over twice my size, and his coat a dark, muddy brown all over. He licks the side of my face and takes to sniffing me behind my ear in contentment. I shrink at the attention but don't pull away all the way.

The wolf in me couldn't be happier, and it is hard to deny it the pleasure of being in the company of such happy wolves and our soulmark. Tentatively, I lean into Atticus's side, returning his affections gently.

He lets out a happy yip, echoed by several others until the resounding howl of the alpha pierces the air. Xander trots toward the edge of the clearing. He is a fearsome looking wolf, with jet black fur and golden eyes. He lets out a sharp bark and then breaks into a run.

The pack gives chase.

Cold earth and snow fly up from the ground as we scramble after him into the forest. Spirited energy eclipses all other feelings running through the pack bonds. My reaction to the power is instinctive as I dig into the earth for better purchase and fly forward. Atticus keeps pace, his long legs matching my increased gait with little effort.

He bumps into my side, and I cast him a surprised look as my paws stumble over one another before righting. His tongue hangs out as he delivers a wolfish smile in my direction. In his eyes is the same playfulness and kindness I've come to recognize in his human form. I provide a bump back to him, and if possible, I catch his wolfish smile grow.

The ties of the Adolphus pack bonds wind around me further as the run continues. Our high energy gives way to that of love and safety, which draws me in tighter. And I don't mind in the least. This is a wholly different type of bond from that of my old pack—one full of trust and love, not duty and begrudging respect.

As soon as the thought enters my mind, one of the threads that tie me to the Blanc pack relinquishes its hold on me. I almost skid to a stop in sheer astonishment.

I *should* care that this has happened, for my parents will.

I *should* maintain some margin of distrust But I don't.

I feel free.

The notion is selfish, but tonight I can't manage to care. Tonight, I run with my new pack, and I've never felt so alive. Xander stops up ahead atop a large boulder. He thrusts his head toward the sky and releases an earth-quaking howl echoed enthusiastically by the pack and myself.

The night is ours.

II

In a year, two deaths would change the fate of many.

The first was the death of the alpha's heir. Mourned by all, Jean-Marc Blanc was given a warrior's funeral with all the village in attendance.

His death was not entirely unexpected, nor was it unaccompanied. Winter was not a kind season. The hunt for food took the best of the Blanc wolves farther out into the wilderness than usual, and in their search, they'd intercepted another pack.

This pack was not kind either.

They clashed over territory abundant in caribou and white-tailed deer. The scenes that followed their conflicts were witnessed only by blunted and colorless flora and the atrophied branches of towering trees.

But the earth remembered the days it was bathed in lycan blood. And the Moon Goddess mourned her sons.

It was in this time of duress that another death cut deep into the heart of one of the village's residents. A life, come and gone, in the blink of an eye.

Blood stained sheets in the middle of the night, accompanied by a terrible cramping sensation. Merida knew as she stared upon her mess the painful truth—the tiny life inside of her no longer lived.

She mourned alone, and when messengers brought news of the territory wars end, along with Jean-Marc, she mourned with the villagers. Time drifted by slowly as Merida waited for the pack's return. When they did, their numbers far greater than when they departed, the humans left. The careful balance they kept for so long tipped in favor of what they could never truly understand.

Merida felt unease at their departure. She felt unease at the absorption of the defeated pack.

The winds of change blew bitter and cold against Merida's cheeks, but she was a step too gone to notice.

+++

A long-awaited knock at the door brought the witch to weary feet. Several days and nights had passed since the full return of the pack and its newcomers. Days and nights spent in formal ceremony and decadent revelry.

Merida chose to stay away. Her place was not among them. This was a fact she always knew, even with the presence the human villagers to keep the veneer of a modern civilization afloat.

The knock sounded again. "Merida?"

She opened the door. Luc stood close enough to touch. His body was wrapped in protective leather and fur to curb the bite of the wind.

"May I come in?"

She stepped aside and closed the door behind him. There was an ache inside her, one that permeated every inch of her being, and she did not know how to cure herself of her affliction. Merida stared with longing at her lover's turned back. The loss of his brother surely had torn him from the inside out, and responsible as he was to take up his brother's place, there could surely have been no time for him to mourn him.

Merida could not fathom the weight upon his shoulders. Nor could she spare him the ordeal of their loss.

"You are well?" she asked.

"I am worn, but hopeful."

Luc turned to face Merida, his expression bland despite the lofty note at the end of his short statement. Merida thought better of making an approach.

"I am glad to see you back," she confessed, hugging her waist. "I missed you. I missed your warmth."

"Merida...." A cross look spread over his face before his beautiful brown eyes went vacant. "I have come on official business."

The witch stood taller and pushed her fatigue to the side as she examined her lover once more. His garb wasn't just for the sake of the frosty air. No, it was tailored to fit and adorned with jewels and talismans the Blanc's so prized. Even his face bore the markings of recent grooming. Clean-shaven. Combed hair. Washed face.

Familiar unease batted at Merida's insides. She cleared her throat and averted her eyes.

"What does the pack require from my stock?" she asked with genial caution and stepped toward her work table.

Two steps deep and he responded. "You must leave."

"Pardon?" Despite the loftiness of Merida's response, her question fell heavy like a bag of stones between them. A weak smile attempted to frame her face. "Leave?

He gave a solemn nod. "As soon as possible."

Her smile ruptured. "What are you talking about? Why would you ask this of me? What have I done to deserve such scorn?"

At her line of questioning, Luc went mute. His gaze fell upon a distant spot over Merida's shoulder that only proved to enrage the witch. Merida let out a cry of disbelief before she rushed her once lover. Though her fists proved little damage to the solid surface of his chest, they did bring back the emotion in his eyes.

"I ask you to leave for your own sake. For your happiness," he growled back, taking Merida by the shoulders and giving her a rough shake.

"You or the pack?" she snarled back, her unruly curls bouncing in front of her vision.

Luc gave pause. A painful whine emitted from his throat. "Both," he said in a ragged whisper before stepping back.

"Why?"

"I have found her."

"I don't—" Her eyes widened, and Merida swallowed thickly as she repeated his words over and over again in her head. "I'm sure I don't know what you're speaking of. Surely your father must have asked you to come to fetch something from me. Let me grab what elixirs I have to ease the ache of a night's consumption of alcohol."

"You are the most intelligent woman I know," Luc said, his voice low and coarse. "Do not make this harder or more painful than it must be. We cannot be together. With the death of my brother and the discovery of my soulmark among the new arrivals... it would be in your best interest to leave, Merida. Follow the humans south for you will find no love here by my pack or me."

Her hands trembled as she rummaged around the jars and bowls upon her rickety shelves. Never once did an item make it onto her work table. Never once did she turn back to face him.

"This is my home," she said at last, her hands gripping a bundle of feathers.

"Find a new one. My father has claimed this land as his own. You are unwelcome here now," Luc said. His words rode an icy gust of the wind as he fled the little shack.

Merida released a shrill cry at his retreating back. It was filled to the brim with agony. The rickety shelves shook with the force of her emotion until all but a few bottles of precious ingredients tumbled to the ground. Merida glared at the open door. Her angry tears dashed across her cheeks as she watched Luc disappear out of sight. With another cry, the door slammed shut.

She would not leave her home.

+++

Merida had come to the village when she was fifteen. Alone and proudly self-sufficient, she had earned her place in the village with hard work and dedication to her craft. It helped that she was smart as a whip and knew when to be heard and seen, or neither at all.

She knew the people of the village well, better than most realized. Her customers and patients always found themselves to be loose-lipped when paying a call, and Merida never forgot their gossip.

She knew the tenderhearted. She knew who bore keen grudges. She knew the ill-fortuned ones greatest wishes. And she knew the darkest thoughts of those in high power.

Therefore, Merida did not anticipate the tides to turn against her so quickly.

The churning notion in her stomach pleaded with her to leave and forget about this village and these wolves. The witch had other plans, or rather, her pride did.

Winter continued with its harsh lament. Change barreled on.

Where the pack grew strong, the witch did not. Merida found herself being shut out from the little village down the dirt road. They did not like to buy her goods or trade with her. No longer did they seek out her services.

What Merida detested above all was the truth in Luc's final words to her. They did not show her love. Or kindness. Or mercy. And when the other nomadic packs began to arrive and join the Blancs, neither did they.

Their cruelty grew.

Hostile glares turned to heated taunts. Taunts transformed to physical blows. Merida could withstand their loathing and detestation but not his disregard. Spring arrived, and with it, a meager bounty from her garden to sustain her.

It was not enough.

She saw *them*—Luc and his soulmark—and both her heart and spirit broke.

At long last, she conceded to her better senses and began to pack her belongings. She did not know where she would go, but Merida was sure the freedom she sought would be found.

+++

The winds of change came blowing again. This time in the form of a flame.

+++

The pack did not like the witch stalking them from the outskirts of the village. She hovered and persisted among them like a fly with its head cut off. Nor could they fathom why she withstood their scorn. Nor her ability to survive.

Until one day someone saw more than a haggard soul clinging to a piece of land no longer their own, but a woman who looked upon their beta with far too much longing.

They did not like that at all.

When whispered words came of her impending departure, the pack took to the news like a swarm. With the knowledge of her defeat in hand, half of the pack relented in their pursuit of her demise. The other could not have acted faster.

Soon she would go, the first half said, let her be.

No, replied the rest, we will make her flee.

Set in their ways, the latter half devised a simple plan. They knew of only one way to kill a witch—with fire.

And so they came and went in the dead of night, their torches in hand to set ablaze her dwellings and land.

YULETIDE CHEER

- Chapter 4 -

Back home, Christmas is always an intimate affair. The house is perfectly toasty and decorated with glossy baubles and dozens of thick, creamy candles. Dwarf evergreens are set strategically along the hallways and common rooms. My father cooks a delicious ham with a plethora of fixings to accompany it. My mother plays Christmas classics on the piano, and I enjoy curling up before a roaring fire with a new book.

A pang of longing strikes my heart thinking of the simple, yet cozy Christmas tradition kept in my parents' home. Celebrating with Atticus is... different. It is bright and merry. The days between the full moon and Christmas, we decorate the house together with pine garland and sparkling lights. He keeps a marathon of seasonal movies on to fill the peaceful silence between us.

"Ready, Winter?"

I study my reflection in the vanity mirror of my bedroom. We'll spend Christmas at the alpha's home, and I'm uncharacteristically nervous. The new bonds which tie me to the Adolphus pack leave me craving the interaction, but what loyalty remains to my old pack brings my guilt to the surface as I look forward to the celebration. And then there is my "mission" to consider.

I hold no doubts that my mother grows tired of waiting for my call with the details of the full moon run. Today's gathering will also pique her interest.

Just perfect, I lament, fighting the urge to plant my head against the vanity table.

"I'll be down in just a minute!" I shout back from my bedroom.

I've secured my hair into a French twist, with a few choice strands of pearly hair left out to frame my face. I'm dressed far bolder than usual in a cherry red jumpsuit, with minimal accessories to balance the piece. If my parents could see me, they would surely level me with disapproving frowns.

How will Atticus react?

I temper the swell of excitement that stirs from the idea and stand. I can't delay any longer. When I join Atticus downstairs, I spy the look of desire apparent in his eyes. The look alone provokes a spine-tingling rush to skate across my nerves.

"You look phenomenal." Atticus's voice is drawn to a husky whisper. He takes my hand and presses a kiss to the back of it before helping me into my dove gray peacoat.

"Thank you."

We exit to the garage and let synthesized pop carols fill the void of silence between us. It's pleasant, for a time. And then my thoughts warp back to my parents' expectations. Where pleasure coursed only minutes before, dread appears gradually to gnaw it away.

How do I walk this sword's edge? To disobey means dire consequences. To obey means to betray a pack who has never done me harm. I chew the inside of my cheek, keeping my consternation off my face as best I can.

My parents want information… so why not give them knowledge and details they can't possibly make use of?

It won't be the first time I've skimmed the truth about conversations or details to appease my parents' hunger for knowledge. This route doesn't come without its own risks. I have faced the punishment for such leniency before and it came with mild bruises and their version of solitary confinement.

No technology.

No books.

No contact with people outside my parents.

But I have pulled off the feat before too and know how to manipulate my deliveries now to fool my parents.

The more I contemplate the plan, the more it brightens my spirit. This may be the way to assuage my parents' demands without damning the Adolphus pack completely.

"Does your family do anything special for the holidays?" Atticus asks.

I blink in rapid succession, torn from my plotting then glance at my husband. "Nothing too special. If anything, the holidays guarantee a measure of peace in my house. No fighting is allowed. No mischief. Just family time."

"That's nice," Atticus responds. The car turns into the alpha's subdivision with snow crunching noisily beneath the SUV's tires. "I suppose tonight's gathering feels a bit strange to you then, doesn't it?"

I shrug. "Not entirely. Usually on Christmas Eve or the day after Christmas, we spend time with the pack's beta and third, along with their families. This isn't too different than that."

We come to a stop in the long driveway, pulling up close to the house.

"Shall we?" Atticus asks, already unbuckling and exiting the car. I nod and follow.

Entering the large house, we are hit with a blast of heat and a surplus of delicious smells. My mouth waters at the scent of roast beef and buttery garlic in the air.

“Merry Christmas!” Zoelle greets, entering the foyer with a large smile. “Come in and take off your coats. You can hang them just over here.” She points to a coat rack already laden with several items for us to add to its load.

“Merry Christmas,” Atticus says, pulling Zoelle into a quick hug. I’m swept into Zoelle’s embrace next.

“Merry Christmas, Zoelle. Thank you for having us.”

She pulls away, her hand waving off my gratitude. “Of course,” she chirps. “I’m just happy you two could make it. We weren’t sure if you would want to spend your first Christmas alone or not.”

“The more, the merrier, right?” Atticus interjects, a faint blush creeping up on his cheeks at Zoelle’s commentary. The pretty dark-skinned witch laughs. Her dangle earrings chime lightly as her head bobs with the movement of her laughter.

“Everyone is in the Great Room. We’ve got a few appetizers out and *several* drink options, so take your pick. We won’t be eating for a while yet.”

The Great Room is decked in red and gold accents that make the large tree in the far corner stand out further. My eyes draw naturally to the alpha and see him loitering near the liquor cart with Ryatt. They both wear similarly amused expressions and clink their glasses of liquor in comradery. Sitting nearby on an overstuffed couch are two rather serious-looking individuals.

My forehead crinkles as I attempt to recall their names. They had been at the wedding, but I had been introduced to so many people their names slipped my mind.

"Would you like a drink?" Atticus asks. His hand rests in the middle of my back where my skin is still bare. I nod.

"A Pinot Grigio would be lovely if they have it."

Atticus walks off, and coming immediately to take his place is Quinn. The beautiful blonde wears a sparkly midi dress and an impressive pair of heels.

"You look *ah*-mazing," Quinn says, her blues eyes sparkling. She tips her champagne flute in my direction as the corners of her lips tip upward. "No drink?"

"Atticus is grabbing one for me," I respond politely and fuss momentarily with the hair framing my face. Quinn makes a knowing noise in her throat as she sips her drink, and I color unintentionally.

Quinn's personality is hard to forget. She's outgoing and outspoken and delights in making her companions redden. Her soulmark Ryatt is the same, though his mischievous streak stretches farther than Quinn's.

"You might be waiting a while," she says. I glance over to where Atticus stands between the Adolphus brothers, looking pleased as punch… and without my requested drink in hand.

"That's fine," I say.

Quinn's stare is acute, and as it trails over my stiff form, I watch her smirk grow. "What exactly did you rank in your old pack?"

My head snaps to the left to face Quinn straight on. "Excuse me?" I don't mean to bristle—years of etiquette have surely taught me better—but I do. I'm unused to such a question, for I've always been top ranked.

"Your rank?" she repeats politely and takes another sip. Her smirk transforms into an impish smile that lingers around her lips as she waits for my response.

"Fifth," I tell her, though it fluctuated to sixth and seventh at times.

Perhaps I would have been higher, or more likely lower, if my parents hadn't pushed me so hard when I was younger. I came to realize growing up that my wolf spirit was unlike others. Sometimes it barely felt like a presence in my mind, and more of a shade that at times nudged me toward its will.

"Oh." Genuine surprise coats her exclamation. "Is it odd being a beta now?"

Yes, because it begets more power. And yet it isn't really odd at all for I am already "soft," as my parents like to say. June prefers the term empathic, and I would agree with her.

Unconsciously, my eyes go back to Atticus. "No. Not really." I fiddle with the emerald ring on my third finger. "Atticus is a good beta. As long as I follow by his example, I'll do just fine in the role."

"Good plan."

As if he knew his name was just on my tongue, Atticus strides over to us—chilled wine in hand.

"Thank you—" His lips skim my cheek, halting the rest of my thanks with the simple touch.

"You don't mind if I talk to the guys a bit longer, do you?"

I shake my head. Atticus smiles widely and cups my hip to deliver a squeeze. My pulse kicks at the touch, and I swallow thickly as his thumb glides leisurely over the curve of my bone.

"I knew this marriage thing wouldn't be difficult," Atticus teases, earning a laugh from Quinn and a blush from me.

"Apparently!" Quinn says. "Now, get going. We're having girl talk."

His strong fingers contract again around my hip before he retreats. But it is the smile he leaves us with that puts me in a stupor. Or maybe it's his rear end that has me mesmerized. Atticus possesses *fine* assets... assets that lawfully belonged to me.

Assets that I shouldn't be lusting after with the soulmark curse and my parents' plan hanging over my head.

An elbow knocks playfully into my side. "You did good, girl," Quinn says.

"Thanks," I respond automatically before another rush of brilliant scarlet covers my cheeks. My mouth falls agape as I scramble to cover from such an ill-mannered response. "I mean—"

"You don't have to apologize to me," she assures me. Her words are followed by a resounding snort, and Quinn tosses her glossy blonde curls over her shoulder. "I'm all about the appreciation of the male form. While I've made it a habit to solely appreciate *my man*, there is no denying Atticus is a catch. He's got that all-American look going for him with the thick brown hair and blue eyes. And that smile—wow. He could totally star in one of those teeth-whitening commercials."

I can only stare at Quinn as she rambles on. I didn't think it possible, but by the end, she wears a rosy stain upon her cheeks as she watches my unchanging expression of disbelief. She clears her throat and thrusts her shoulders back, regaining some of her lost composure and confidence.

"So, these past few days you and Atticus finally got some alone time. How has that been?"

I lift a shoulder in a half-hearted shrug. "We decorated the house and watched a lot of movies."

Quinn's drink stops halfway to her lips, and a curious expression crosses her face. The space between her brows lessens, and her nose crinkles upward.

"Huh?"

I stem any feeling of embarrassment, for there is nothing to be embarrassed about—even if Quinn's mystified look makes me feel otherwise.

"We're still getting to know each other. Plus, we're taking things slow." And slow involves little touches here and there and drunken kisses.

Her look doesn't retreat at my explanation. "I thought you two have been writing to each other for years. What don't you know about each other?"

"Letters are different than actual face-to-face interactions. You can portray yourself in any way you like in a letter, and the other person would never know if you were lying or not."

"You think he lied to you?" Quinn asks.

I sigh, the only tell of my patience waning. "I'm just trying to say that things aren't as smooth or as easy-going as you think. Atticus and I still have plenty to learn about one another before we move on to anything more physical."

Quinn's eyes go wide, and then a burst of laughter erupts past her mouth. "I'm sorry," she apologizes. There are tears in her eyes. "I'm being rude, aren't I? Again, I apologize. I blame Ryatt. He's a bad influence and is desensitizing me to my loose tongue… not that he minds one bit how loose my tongue can get."

My flush matches my dress, and when Quinn notices, she gives a cringe.

"I did it again, didn't I?" she asks. I nod and take a drink. "So… you've been decorating and watching movies. Have you spoken with anyone from your pack recently? I hope they still aren't upset over Irina and Vrana showing up."

The shift in conversation is welcome, but her choice of topic is less so. I peek through lowered lashes at Quinn's inquisitive gaze and interpret the upward inflection of her tone as not wholly disingenuous… but still, there is something that lingers behind her look and words. *She's fishing for answers*, I realize as I hear her heartbeat spike in anticipation of my response.

The truth, I decide, won't hurt me in this instance. Or my old pack. "I've only spoken with my younger cousin, Juniper."

"Was she one of your bridesmaids?"

I shake my head. "She wasn't able to come. Her parents came instead."

"What did you talk about?" The question is delivered with an impressive nonchalance, and I force myself not to grin at her obvious interrogation.

"We talked a bit yesterday afternoon about the wedding. Except, I skimmed over the ending for her sake. She's a 'happily ever after' at all costs kind of girl, and I didn't want to ruin the illusion for her. We also spoke about her favorite subject: her boyfriend."

Quinn's posture softens. "Ah, young love."

I laugh lightly, thinking fondly of my cousin. "She's pretty great."

"And she's a lycan as well?"

"She is. The Blanc pack is large, and because we live in such a small town, a good fraction of the residents are in the pack."

"Seriously?"

"We're like your pack in many ways. Several of my old pack mates hold positions of power and status within the town—doctors, policemen, and council members. Or they own prominent local shops."

Atticus catches my eye as he moves away from the alpha and the third and over to the couple on the couch. The Native American girl and the surly looking man offer kind smiles to Atticus.

"Who are they again?" I ask quietly.

"Who?" Quinn spies who I am speaking of and gives a knowing nod. "That's Callie and Keenan. They had an interesting start, to say the least."

"Oh?"

"Mm-hmm." Quinn goes to take a drink but frowns down at her empty champagne flute. "Long story short, we sort of stole something from Callie awhile back. She came after it with her brother and a few others, but instead of finding it, she found the love of her life." An entirely too smug expression crosses Quinn's lips.

"You stole something from them?"

"Yep!" Quinn says. She is completely nonplussed by the note of incredulity in my tone. "Oh, don't give me that look, Winter. I used to steal all the time, and I'm not a bad person."

My mouth opens and closes at the blatant contradiction. After a moment, I seal my lips. Quinn doesn't seem the type to be convinced otherwise from her statement. But perhaps I can get her to tell me what they stole… surely that information will satisfy my family.

"What did the pack take from Callie exactly?"

Quinn's sights narrow upon me, and she folds both arms beneath her chest. "Oh, just a piece of jewelry. Irina has it now."

I intend to ask more, but a hearty laugh pulls my attention away from the task. Atticus sits on the couch arm, his head tilted back to release his amusement in broad laughs. Callie and Keenan chuckle along as well, their faces pleasantly flushed from the attention they receive from the beta.

My staring catches Atticus's attention and our eyes draw together like magnets across the room. Goodness, but he is handsome. His skin holds a cool golden color that the winter season can't seem to banish, and it's only more pronounced along the daring line of his clean-shaven jaw.

Unable to tear my eyes away from him, I begin to note the effect my "observations" have on Atticus. His spine straightens ever so slightly with his chest expanding to stretch the cable knit sweater he wears.

The leg he has casually dropped over his knee slips to the ground—ready to move closer should I give a hint of interest.

"I said it once, and I'll repeat it," Quinn remarks. "You did *good*, girl."

I flush and look away. "I'm going to get another drink."

"Great idea!"

We walk together to the drink cart. I take my time searching the wine selection that's out. Everyone seems to have relocated around the seating area, spacing themselves out among the couch and chairs available. A fire roars behind them, the flames reaching high into the chimney and delivering pleasing cracks to chime in with the music playing in the background.

"I can't wait to eat. Zoelle is the best cook, and she's been slow roasting a rump roast for hours now." I glance at Quinn. She stares off into the direction of what I assume to be the kitchen. I might be imagining it, but I swear I see a bit of drool threaten to spill before she eagerly licks her lips.

Quinn closes her eyes and lets out a happy sigh. "Ryatt wants to move out—and Zoelle and Xander want us to as well, even if they're too nice to say it—but we can't cook." Quinn laughs and finishes topping off her champagne with a dramatic touch. "So I keep finding reasons to not move so Zoelle will keep feeding us."

"Clever," I say, plucking the Pinot Grigio from its ice bucket and refilling my glass.

"My sentiments exactly!"

Before another word can be spoken, the doorbell rings. It chimes through the house, bouncing off the high ceilings and against clean walls.

"Coming!" Zoelle shouts. She races from an open doorway at the far end of the room and to the entrance hall.

"It must be the aunts," Quinn comments, sipping casually at her drink.

"Who?" I ask, watching curiously as Zoelle vanishes from sight. Excited exclamations draw from the room moments later. My lycan hearing picks up many footsteps and voices crowding in.

"Zoelle's grandmother and her best friends. Everyone calls them the aunts, Aunt Mo and Aunt Lydia respectively. They're the—"

"Trinity coven matriarchs. The Elder Triad," I finish for her. My mouth sets into a grim line. I know of them, but who doesn't in the supernatural community? A minute later, Zoelle ushers them in further. "I thought tonight we were celebrating with pack only?"

Quinn walks forward toward the three older women when my words bring her to a stop. She casts a winning smile over her shoulder. "They're unofficially officially part of the pack."

The others rise as well to greet the matriarchs, but I find my footsteps heavy. I consider Zoelle an exception to my family's general thoughts on witches—that they are no good troublemakers, and that's the nice way of saying it.

In truth, I find it difficult to look on witches fondly for the curses placed on our kind and my family knowing a witch to be responsible for our plight.

A witch long since dead, a voice in my head reminds me. *Zoelle has been perfectly sweet to you so far... Don't make an enemy out of old fears and superstitions.* It's my simple self-scolding that lifts the weight from my lead feet and brings me to the outskirts of the now gathered group.

And that's when I see her. The creature I've only ever read about in stories—a fairy.

Her startling violet eyes lock on me.

"Oh." My whispered word is swallowed by the rowdy greetings in front of me.

+++

I learn several facts during dinner thanks to the seating arrangements. Though it's hard to tell what parts Quinn exaggerates about. Atticus, who is seated across from me, passes us indiscernible frowns throughout the meal. Whether they are in disapproval or disappointment, I can't tell. I do my best to ignore them all, succeeding for the most part and absorbing every piece of gossip Quinn ushers into my ear.

"Let me get this straight," I say quietly as we all begin to pull away from the table, our bellies full and appetites more than satisfied. Quinn and I keep our gait slow as we follow the others back into the Great Room to congregate. "Lunaria magically appeared when the Crystal of Dan Furth was restored and introduced into the land, but the witches don't know why or how to send her back home?"

Quinn nods solemnly and takes a gentle sip from her red wine. "Correct."

"And last summer not only did the Wselfwulfs attack, but the Wardens of Starlight did as well. The former to hurt the pack and destroy the crystal, and the latter to get back their possessions and destroy the crystal."

"Correct again," Quinn says, herding me toward the side of the room with more urgency than necessary. Then I spot the reason for her haste: Atticus. He's attempting to disengage from a conversation with Keenan and divert toward our twosome. "We lost a couple of witches and wolves. Plus, Callie and Keenan were basically kidnapped and tortured by the wardens. We're lucky they even made it out."

"And Lunaria was hurt too?"

Quinn stops, her palpable concern rests on the quiet fairy who hovers close to the witches. "She was," she whispers to me. "It really messed with her head. Before the battle, you couldn't get Luna to shut up. She was a constant ball of energy with a million and a half questions ready at the tip of her tongue. Plus, there's her whole bit with talking to plants—"

"I'm sorry," I interrupt, my brows coming together. "Talking to plants?"

Plants are a small passion of mine. Their means and measures always a calming act of learning. Not to mention how enthralling and inspiring it is to see what they can endure.

"Fairy, remember? She still does now, but it's not the same. Now... now it's like she lost part of herself. She's withdrawn and doesn't like to talk anymore, let alone with her favorite flowers and trees. I don't think she's ever experienced that kind of violence directly before."

"That's awful," I murmur.

Imagining the violence and pain bestowed upon Luna makes my stomach twist in discomfort. Whether it be from my natural empathy, or the instinctive urge to comfort a fellow pack mate—however unofficial—I find myself angling toward the fairy. I too am familiar with pain.

"Hey."

Atticus's husky greeting draws my pensive gaze away from the fairy. His blue eyes are a mixture of emotions, but I make a note of the tightness lingering around his mouth.

"Hi," Quinn replies. "As you most likely overheard, I've been cluing Winter into all the shenanigans that happened over the summer. Although I've been more than happy to take up the task, don't you think *you* should have been doing it? Talk about a misstep in husbandly duties."

Quinn's ability to turn the tables on Atticus is impressive. The hint of disapproval on his face falters before disappearing entirely with a heavy sigh.

"Thanks, Quinn."

The feisty blonde releases a delicate laugh. "You're welcome. I suppose I'll leave you two be and find my troublemaking boyfriend. Lord knows he can barely survive five minutes without me, let alone however long Winter and I have been chatting."

Her fingers wiggle at us from over her shoulder as she turns tail and—well, not runs—but glides away to said troublemaker.

"So… she told you everything, huh?" Atticus stuffs his hands in his tan trousers. A wrinkle disturbs the plane of his forehead, and I release a little sigh of my own.

"She attempted to," I confirm. I drop my chin a fraction and let my gaze glide back to the fairy's direction. "Perhaps we can compare notes later."

My answer seems to satisfy Atticus as I am rewarded with a soft smile. "Later," he agrees. Atticus clears his throat lightly, casting a look at the others all gathered by the main seating section. "The witches are going to perform a Yule blessing to celebrate the rebirth of light. Although, technically, Yule started on the day of our wedding, the 21st. They'll celebrate Yule all the way to the first of the year."

"I didn't know that."

The group begins to move furniture back and place candles around the room and on every available surface. I watch with keen interest. I grew up learning the supernatural politics, not the practices and traditions of another kind—especially not ones that had cursed us.

"What do they need all the candles for?"

My gray eyes find his sparkling back at me. His cheek gives a telltale twitch before succumbing to a grin.

"You'll see," he says, the playful timbre of his voice drawing the hairs at the back of my neck on end.

His larger hand encapsulates mine, and then Atticus is pulling me along after him to the group. We form into a rough circle, the Elder Triad taking their place at the center. Zoelle makes a more substantial turn of the room to turn off all of the lights before joining our circle's ranks.

The hair at the back of my neck continues to stay on end as everyone passes each other special shared smiles. I fidget with anticipation and uncertainty. I've never experienced an event such as this, but those around me simmer in general excitement. I try to catch onto the feeling and enjoy the experience, but doubt curbs my enthusiasm.

"Tonight we gather to celebrate the rebirth of the day, with family and friends. Thank you, Aleksander, for welcoming us into your home," Zoelle's grandmother, Diana, says.

The witch is somewhere in her late sixties, with her natural hair a pearly gray and white. There is a constant knowing gleam in her eye. I wonder if she knows how enchanting her velvet voice is? Her spoken words exude a strange warmth and coupled with the smooth cadence at which she speaks, I find myself entranced. *Magic.* My nose twitches in slight alarm.

"You're most welcome in our home," Xander replies, bowing his head respectfully to the witch.

I take a calming breath through my mouth as I watch Diana join hands with the two others that make up the Elder Triad, Maureen Claybourne and Lydia Stein.

Diana seeks out her granddaughter's gaze over her shoulder. "Zoelle, the Yule log, please."

Zoelle smiles. She and Xander reach behind them to retrieve a silver stand and a single log owning a dusty white bark.

"We celebrate the Solstice in many ways. Through prayers and gift-giving, and rituals and ceremonies. In honor of the Birch Moon, we humbly offer this birch wood log to be burned," Aunt Mo, the scarred elder, says. Zoelle and Xander submit the objects to the inner circle.

"The Birch Moon is a symbol of rebirth and regeneration," the last of the triad says, her dark eyes heavily hooded as she keeps her voice pitched low. "As we burn this Yule log, we cast our wishes toward blessings endowed in creativity and fertility. As well as that of protection and healing. Let us join hands."

Atticus squeezes my hand, already neatly captured in his own, and I look to my right to see who's hand I must take. Violet eyes blink back solemnly at me. I swallow, offering out my hand for the fairy to take. Her glamours are gone for the evening, Quinn informed me earlier, because the witches hoped to make her happier in her natural state. By the wilted state of the flowers and vines sprawled beneath her skin, I doubt their efforts worked.

"Hello," I greet kindly and stretch my hand out further toward her. "I'm Winter."

The fairy takes my hand with tentative fingers. The slim digits stretch over the width of my palm, then around to cup my hand. As I return her grip and deliver a gentle squeeze, the flowers on the back of her hand begin to bloom up her wrist.

"I'm Lunaria," she whispers back. "I've never met someone with the same hair as me before."

A slow grin creeps across my lips as I lean closer to the fairy. "All of my family has hair the color of snow. They say it happened when the lycan curse took place. So overcome with grief and stress, the members of my family's hair turned white."

The explanation gradually draws Lunaria's mouth open, her jaw dropping at least an inch by the end of my tale.

"Is that true?" she asks. There is a breathless wonder to her voice as she stares me down. I watch the vines and flowers open across her skin as her curiosity grows.

"So some say, but my parents told me our white hair came about to match our white fur coats in our wolf forms. It helps to better camouflage us in our homeland."

The smile returned to me is stunning in its brilliance. Lunaria's iridescent wings glow behind her. "I am *delighted* to hear this," she says. Our hands tighten around one another, and just like that, another thread of the Adolphus pack bonds steal around my heart.

"We shall begin now," Diana announces in her melodious tone. Lunaria and I straighten. It isn't easy to shake the room's attention from us, nor tamper the blush that rises to my cheeks at the attention. Thankfully, the Elder Triad's next words usurp the former.

"The Wheel has turned once more, and
the earth has gone to sleep.
The leaves are gone, the crops have returned to the ground.
On this darkest of nights, we celebrate the light.
Tomorrow, the sun will return,
its journey continuing as it always does.
Welcome back, warmth.
Welcome back, light.
Welcome back, life."

About the room, the candles stir to life. Tiny flames dance tall around us, a pleasant wave of heat blankets the room as we begin to move clockwise around the threesome. Over my skin, a phantom breeze passes, and in its wake resides a glittering sheen that weaves about our persons and tickles our skin. As our steps lead us back to our original positions, the triad speaks again as one.

"Shadows go away, darkness is no more,
as the light of the sun comes back to us.

Warm the earth.
Warm the ground.
Warm the sky.
Warm our hearts.
Welcome back, sun."

One by one, each person offers their token of gratitude to a happening or person in their life. Their words tighten my throat as praise and love are given so freely.

"I am proud to call Winter my wife," Atticus says, his voice loud and clear for the group to hear, though he looks only to me.

A hunger grows in his eyes as they linger on me, and my words become lost. "I am thankful for… a new start."

My words send a ripple of resounding appreciation and affection through the pack bonds. The attention forces my eyes to the ground and another fevered blush to rise to my cheeks.

"I am thankful for new friends," Lunaria says quietly, her fingers press into the back of my hand as she delivers her words.

Once more we walk the circle's path. The triad chants a phrase beneath their breath as we do, and their words evoke that glittering magic to swirl around the Yule log. Stepping into our original places once more—the final act of the ceremony complete—the Yule log catches fire.

The group gives a joyous cheer as another wave of warmth and good tiding burnish everyone with a momentary unearthly glow. I laugh in stilted awe at the parade of power and begin to clap, turning to Atticus with renewed excitement. I don't even mind the way my skin tingles a little too much once all is said and done.

"That was incredible," I say, watching as the golden glow recedes into Atticus's person. "For some reason, I always imagined ceremonies like these performed in black robes with chalices filled with mysterious potions being passed from person to person."

Atticus releases a loud laugh, and even Lunaria giggles from behind me. "It's a lot tamer than that," he assures me, taking a step closer so that I can feel each breath he releases. "Winter, I—"

The chiming of an obnoxious pop song sounds from a distant phone. It causes Atticus to lose focus and tilt his head in question.

"That's my phone," I say, stepping back with a weak smile. "It's June, my cousin."

Atticus rolls his eyes heavenward. "You better move fast if you want to catch her."

I turn and speed to the foyer where my belongings are. "Hello?" I ask, a touch out of breath in worry that I have missed her call.

"Winter! Merry Christmas!" June's cheerful voice brings a broad smile to my face.

"Merry Christmas, Junebird." She laughs at her childhood nickname.

"I can't really talk long," June says. "I just wanted to wish you a Merry Christmas over the phone instead of text. I'm happy you answered, where are you?"

"I'm at the alpha's home celebrating with—"

"Oh shoot, I have to go! Sorry, Winter! I'm not actually supposed to be on the phone at all, and I can hear my mom coming. I'll call you later—bye!"

She hangs up, and a small laugh escapes me. There is little that June can do wrong in my eyes, even hanging up abruptly. I return my phone to my coat pocket with a fond smile.

"Hello, dear," a voice from behind says. I spin around, surprised not to have heard Maureen's approach, although I should have been able to tell by the amount of perfume she wears. Maureen is dosed in a fragrance of rose, amber, and lily of the valley.

"Maureen," I greet with a dimmer smile, my wolf unexpectedly alerting me to a potential threat.

"Call me Aunt Mo, dear. Everyone does." I duck my head in deferment for a moment.

"Of course," I murmur. "I suppose we should be getting back."

"Yes, yes," she responds, waving a scarred hand dismissively at my comment but making no move to go. Our eyes catch in a standoff. "But first, I'm afraid I must pass on a message."

I straighten my spine and angle my head with an inquisitive frown. "From who?"

Aunt Mo smiles serenely. "My tarot cards, dear. You were in my morning reading." I disguise my wariness with a downward tilt of my lips.

"I'm not a believer in such things," I tell her a touch briskly and look past her into the Great Room. Nobody is in sight to make eye contact with and remove me from this suddenly *very*, unwanted conversation.

"Perhaps you should," she suggests with a mysterious laugh. I sweep my eyes over the woman as she loses herself to her amusements. Aunt Mo's alabaster skin is covered in devilish red scars that look remarkably fresh. "After all," she continues, her voice and posture turning solemn, "you're going to get someone killed."

The Reading

- Chapter 5 -

The warm-heartedness that accompanies the Yule ceremony abandons me, and in its place comes a numbing dread as Aunt Mo's words sink in. Me? I will get someone killed? She might as well have hit me with some magic spell—straight in the gut. The color drains from my face. She can't possibly be speaking of my parents' ominous threat, can she?

"That's what your cards told you? That I'll get someone killed?" My voice turns to a harsh whisper as my wolfish temper flares. What is this witch trying to do? Start another war?

Aunt Mo stares back at me before her eyes take on a distant quality. "The winter wolf will break."

My nose twitches at the foreign magic seeping into the air around us. It is a far cry from that of the ceremony. This magic provides no warmth, but a deep chill that slides up my bones.

What terrible beauty magic is. My heart races at the thought.

I jut out my chin and tilt my shoulders back as she comes out of her daze. "And I suppose I am to believe I'm the 'winter wolf' you speak of?"

My short words are not met with agitation or alarm, but sadness. "You cannot outrun your fate," she says simply. I take a breath and step back.

"You're wrong," I clip back. "To my understanding"—what little I have—"tarot cards can be interpreted in multiple ways, and they don't deliver prophecies."

Her eyebrows dip low to my response, and that strange invisible magic solidifies around my bones. "Tarot cards can be interpreted in several ways, my dear. But when the cards turn up the same over and over again after every cut of the deck... you listen."

I want to protest, I intend to when several shouts erupt from the other room. The sudden sound shocks us both, and we pivot in unison to the arched entrance of the Great Room. Exclamations of congratulations draw us in.

"It would seem our conversation is over," Aunt Mo says, her curiosity winning out over my worry. "I'm sure we'll touch on the subject again at another point."

She strides away from me, her strange magic slipping from my bones as she does. Yet I remain, my feet rooted to the floor as my mind devolves to chaos.

What just happened?

Panic strokes the length of my spine before it claws at my ribs and digs between the bone. The air is thinner where I stand, my proof lies in the way I cannot breathe—I can't breathe.

Get a grip, Winter.

The harsh internal scolding is accompanied by a ragged inhalation, but at least it does the trick. Why am I allowing myself to be worked up like this? There is no proof to Aunt Mo's words. They're just cards.

I'm not about to let some pieces of glorified paper dictate my future.

Hearing the celebration continue, I make my way into the room. If I linger any longer, Atticus will come... and how on earth will I explain my distress?

A heavy sigh falls from my lips.

Everything will be fine. I'll put Aunt Mo's moment behind me and go forward with my plan to mollify my parents' need for information with insignificant details. Somehow I'll find out who my parents intend to use against me and warn them... and I won't fall for Atticus.

Oh yes, everything will be just fine.

"Winter! Come in here!" Atticus calls from across the room. I flatten out the nonexistent wrinkles of my jumpsuit and brush aside a swaying curl.

"Coming," I call back, only half as loud.

I walk confidently over, pasting a smile onto my face as I meet the tight-knit circle at the fireplace. Atticus makes room for me to stand by his side, and my eyes widen as I spy the ecstatic faces of those around me.

"What is it? What did I miss?"

Zoelle gives a little laugh, her head ducking in modest excitement. I follow the genial movement with my eyes and further down to naturally rest on Xander's possessive hand around Zoelle's middle. Her dark hands are tucked protectively under his, and before their announcement can be made, I know precisely what news I missed.

"You're—"

"Pregnant."

The group gives another cheer and several exclamations of joy as the news is delivered to me.

"Congratulations!" I step forward and pull both into hugs. "How? When?"

Ryatt barks a laugh. "We all know how," he jokes.

"I'm just about to hit twelve weeks," Zoelle tells me. "But, before the big New Year party, we wanted to let all of you know." A trill of "awws" chase after her reasoning.

"What about your wedding?" Quinn asks. "Will you postpone, or are you still planning for a spring wedding?"

The alpha pair share pleased expressions, a visible manifestation of their love passing between them through the joy in their eyes and broad smiles.

"We're moving the wedding up," Xander tells the group, his eyes never leaving his fiancée.

Excited chatter envelops our group, with questions and comments chiming from every direction. But inside of me turbulent emotions rage. Happiness. Jealousy. Heartache. I push them all down and keep my smile present through it all, just as I was raised to.

+++

We stay far later than I like. I'm not used to extended family and friend gatherings, where drinks and conversation delve long into the night. I do the best I can to stay involved in the discussions around me, but the hands of the clock climb ever forward, and my input lessens dramatically.

After a time, Atticus takes notice of my growing silence first. He makes our excuses to go, and we say our goodbyes. Nothing would make me happier than to make our ride home in silence, but Atticus is bizarrely awake. Perhaps because he stopped drinking well over an hour ago, whereas I maintained a full glass most of the evening to keep my somber thoughts at bay.

Without a glass in hand, I turn tired eyes out the window.

The winter wonderland before me does little to please me now, nor does Atticus's attempt at small talk.

"I think it will be great," he finishes, completing some explanation or story I have entirely missed. I hum accordingly, my eyes never straying from their pointless observation of the scenery.

The slow pumping panic I attempt to curb for the remainder of our evening is creeping back into my body. Like a snake, it winds and winds around each dip and swell of my body and compresses me from all around. Breathing becomes a laborious task again, try as I might to keep it under wraps.

How did I end up in such a Catch-22?

How can I keep the people I care about safe and my relationships intact?

Where does my happiness fit into the equation—or is it a pointless endeavor?

"I'm not going to lie, I really hope they consider me to be the godfather," Atticus announces, his happy gaze turning my way and drawing my attention.

I offer half a smile. "You'd be great."

The enthusiasm on Atticus's face ebbs at my tempered response. "Are you okay?"

"I'm just tired." I allow my gaze to drift back to the snowscape as I shove my acute sensitivities aside. Atticus quiets, and we finish the ride in the worst kind of silence.

When we arrive home, I release a thankful sigh, feeling some of my worry truly wash away as I set foot into the house. I toe my shoes off at the front door, scooting over a step for Atticus to do the same.

"Good night," I murmur, stepping up onto the first step of the stairway.

"Winter, wait." Knuckles rap against my arm, and I turn wide-eyed at the touch. "Are you sure you're all right? I didn't say something wrong, did I?"

My head twists from side to side. "No, of course not. I'm just tired, Atticus. I'm not really used to parties going on that late with family."

He frowns at my response and his lips pursed. "Sometimes I think we were better at talking when all we had were our letters."

Atticus attempts to make the delivery lighthearted, but the touch of melancholy in his voice resonates regardless. My teeth bite down on my lower lip as I contemplate the right response.

"I suppose so," I mumble back, unable to think up anything better in my current state of mind. "Our little messages were always sweet. I suppose it didn't hurt either that all of our letters were monitored and reviewed by our parents to be the perfect response."

The tension that once rode on Atticus's features breaks away as he stares at me in... shock?

"What is it?" I ask. "What did I say?"

"How much of your letters to me were written by your parents, Winter?"

I wind my arms around my middle and shift back against the railing. "I wrote all of the letters, Atticus. My parents just... they just made sure we were making the right impression."

"You didn't have to do anything like that," he argues back. Atticus joins me on the first step. "We're soulmarks. We're meant for each other. There isn't anything you can say or do to make me think ill of you."

I whiten at his words. "Don't put me on a pedestal, Atticus," I warn. "Nobody is perfect, especially not me. And for that matter, no relationship is perfect either. Besides, our relationship isn't just about the soulmark. It's about strengthening the ties between both of our packs through our marriage."

"I see." His words are delivered in a low rumble. A conflict steeps behind his lovely blue eyes—I see it, and my heart cracks when it fades away into quiet disappointment. "Thank you for clearing that up for me. I'll let you go to bed. Good night, Winter."

Atticus steps forward, the warmth of his body reaching mine and causing my breath to catch in my throat. He leans down deliberately slow, and I watch his descent until I can no longer. My lashes flutter closed as his breath skirts across my lips, and then the touch of his kiss lands on my cheek. It lingers and then leaves all too soon.

"Good night," I whisper back, dropping my chin toward my chest as he steps back and walks away upstairs.

Inside the comfort of my bedroom, my fingers dig into my updo to begin the odious process of ridding my hair of the dozen bobby pins that keep it in place. The pins drop onto the countertop of the vanity with subdued clinks, and as I catch my reflection in the mirror, I pause.

With my hair half down, thick chunks frame my delicate jawline, and I imagine their layered pieces as a swan's wings. The frivolous thought leaves my head almost as soon as it comes, my mother's lessons chiding in my head.

Remember, Winter, no one looks kindly upon the vain.

Slate gray eyes harden at me in the mirror as her words draw me back to sobriety. I dig out the rest of my bobby pins with ruthless efficiency. My bed is calling my name, and to deny it would be a crime. I'm intent on doing just that when my phone trills my mother's dedicated ringtone.

I heavily contemplate not answering, but the idea that something could be wrong pushes me to answer.

"Mother? Is something wrong?"

"Why would anything be wrong?" I pause, blinking in a stupor for a moment too long at the perfect mixture of flippant and condescension she is able to convey. "Winter?" The sharp retort brings me back to focus.

"It's nearly midnight," I explain with mild exasperation. Mother hums, unbothered by my tone. And then my lycan hearing picks up the clinking of something against what sounds like glass. A frown tugs my forehead down and my nose up. Did I hear... ice cubes? "Are you drinking?"

The absurdity of the situation strikes me as not only odd but unheard-of. Is Mother drunk dialing me?

"It's called a nightcap, Winter. *Honestly*." Her reprimand would hit harder if I could take her seriously. I roll my eyes and begin to undress. The sooner I can end this call and curl up in my bed—forget the evening's twisted turn of events—the better.

"What do you need, Mother? Calling to wish me a Merry Christmas?"

Silence rings in my ear, but only for a moment. "Merry Christmas, Winter. Tell me, did you prepare a gift for your father and myself? Something in the vein of insights into a certain pack?"

My heart skips a beat. Apparently, she hasn't drank that much if her words can still cut like daggers at will.

"One moment, I'm just slipping out of my Christmas outfit."

I don't give her time to protest. Instead, I toss the phone on the bed and shimmy out of my jumpsuit. Mother's muffled voice sounds against the down comforter at my blatant stalling tactic. A smile curls my lips as her scolding dies off. I would never be able to pull off such a stunt at home in her company... but with such distance between us, the act is liberating.

For a moment, I contemplate taking the time to perform my full nightly routine to extend the wait. *Don't anger her further*, a younger version of myself warns. *You know how she gets*.

Or not.

Pajamas on my person, I retrieve the phone and sit at the edge of my bed. "I'm back. I apologize for making you wait, Mother."

For a tense moment, she keeps her tongue still, and then: "The information, Winter. What do you have to share with your father and me?"

"I celebrated the day with the alpha and his family," I strive to make my words strictly perfunctory. My effort is not met kindly.

"Yes, I'm well aware of your dalliances with that abominable sort. The miles between us dull your pulse in the Blanc pack bonds, but there is something to be said about a mother's tether to her daughter—never mind the fact that I am an alpha. You're creating new ties with the Adolphus pack, Winter... and allowing the bonds of the Blanc pack to slip away. Just what game do you think you're playing at?"

"I'm playing the game *you* asked me to," I reply, my heart pounding away in my chest like a hammer to an anvil. "It will be far more suspicious if after the full moon and the intimate gathering with the alpha family if I didn't strengthen my ties with them. Everything is under control—"

"And yet the only information you have for me is that." I fall quiet, swallowing down the hasty rebuttal at the tip of my tongue. Denial and "excuses" are never the route to go with my mother. I know better than to argue this way.

"I'm sorry, Mother. Please, allow me to elaborate on the night's events."

"Don't carry on too long, Winter. It's well past midnight here at home. We require only important details. What did you learn on your little full moon run and Christmas party?"

Her patronizing tone grates at my nerves, but I say nothing. Instead, a steady stream of air breezes out of my mouth in an attempt to find my well-reserved calm and my shoulders roll forward.

"I wasn't the only new pack mate to run that night."

"Explain."

The curt response is a clear tell of her intrigue, and I waste no time giving the explanation she requires. "Two lycans from a pack in the southwest."

"They fled their previous pack?"

"No." I inch up the bed until I hit the mountain of pillows at the top. "They left with the permission of their alpha."

Mother scoffs. "Then the pack was either too small or too weak to keep them. Both, most likely. What was the name of their pack?"

"I don't know their family name," I reply, and with haste continue before Mother can cut into me. "We were told they hailed from the Santa Fe pack. Their names are Matt and Emma."

She stays quiet for some time, mulling over my words before I hear her raspy chuckle over the earpiece. "Ah, your alpha is more clever than I gave him credit for. Adding another she-wolf to his pack while accepting you so publicly. We attributed the bolster in his strength to your addition solely, though it seemed far-fetched. It makes sense now why the increase was far larger than we expected."

My head knocks back against the cushioned headboard at the casual snub she slips in at the end. "I didn't realize you could recognize his pack's strength and growth, Mother."

"Of course, we can," she scolds. "Alphas can always measure other alphas in such a way. By this ability, we can avoid territorial fights by either ceding to another pack or taking the chance to fight and defend our place. You learned this long ago, Winter. Dear God, it hasn't even been a week, and you already forget so much of what we taught you."

I pinch the bridge of my nose. "I'm sorry to disappoint, Mother."

She shushes me expectantly, dismissing my lackluster apology. "And what of the Christmas party?"

" The Elder Triad attended."

Mother sputters on whatever drink she's consuming, and a coughing fit ensues on the other end of the line. "How despicable. Tell me they didn't perform some ungodly spell for your entertainment."

I color briefly. I want to defend their ceremony and tradition, but doing so will only result in a lecture. "They performed a blessing."

A sound of disgust reaches my ears. "A blessing—unlikely! I would take a scalding hot shower if I were you, Winter, and scrub off their magic by force! Is that all they were there for? To perform their so-called blessing? You didn't garner any other useful pieces of knowledge." Mother pounces on my prolonged pause. "Well? Out with it, Winter. I don't have all night, and what you've divulged so far is hardly worthwhile—"

"They brought a fairy with them." *Sorry, Luna, but it is either you or Zoelle and I can't bring an unborn child into this plot.* Somehow I will find a way to protect Luna from the worst of my parents' attention and make sure she doesn't get hurt. She's been through too much already.

"A real fairy?"

"Yes, with wings and all."

"How on earth are they acquainted with a fairy? What use is she to them? Do not think of withholding information from me now, Winter. You are not the only source of information I have to rely on now when it comes to the Adolphus pack and their witches."

A hollow apprehension unfolds inside of me, Mother's power over me—even from this distance—flexing and reining me to her will. "She boosts the power of the Adolphus pack's barrier."

Silence, one far longer than the last. I shift in my seat, curling my legs under me as my free hand curls into a fist.

"Very good, Winter," Mother finally utters. "Now, tell me everything you learned about her and her relationship with the witches." The tension from my body slips away as I sink submissively back into the pillows.

"Of course, Mother."

Winter Tidings

- Chapter 6 -

Mother's interrogation stalks me days later. Her drill sergeant questions and my robotic responses crop up in my mind whenever I find a moment of peace. It is tiresome and demoralizing to know how easy I fall prey to her authority. My only comfort resides in the remainder of the answers I gave her.

No, the fairy has no other apparent power besides enhancing the border.

A semi-truth told easily enough. Luna does not, to my knowledge, have any other apparent power besides enhancing the magical borderline. The fact that Luna can also speak with plants is trivial and unimportant.

No, the witches didn't perform a spell upon me.

They performed their blessing on everyone, perhaps even on the whole of the pack and coven.

No, the fairy isn't dangerous.

That was my last report to Mother. One I found myself repeating a dozen times until she relented her questioning and hung up. Days later I still can't decide if my response had been correct.

"Hey."

My soft greeting is almost covered by the sound of the faucet running, but Atticus turns and gives me a winning smile.

"Hi," he replies, flicking his eyes back toward the soapy dish in his hand then back to me. "How is your book going?"

"Good. It's been entertaining."

I have buried my nose in a couple of books the past few days to limit my interactions with Atticus. I am fearful of him sensing my anxiety, but I can't avoid my husband forever.

"What are you reading again?"

I hesitate, averting my eyes from the muscles bunching and flexing in his back as he finishes the dishes. "*The Secret Garden*."

My answer must startle Atticus, for he shoots a wide-eyed look my way, his eyebrows raised comically high. "Really?"

I nod. "I'm rereading it actually. It's—"

"One of your top five favorite books," he finishes. My lips part in surprise as I lock eyes with him, but Atticus smiles warmly back at me before I can question his knowledge. "You've told me before. In one of our letters."

I can only manage an owlish blink back at him. But then the slow beginnings of a blush treads up my cheeks as our gazes remain steadfast upon one another.

"You remembered that?" My feet pull me further into the kitchen, and though I typically enjoy letting my gaze wander the beautiful modern decor, I can't tear my eyes away from Atticus. He remembered.

Atticus's answering chuckle reverberates shamelessly down my spine.

"I have the memory of an elephant," he tells me with a wink.

Atticus turns off the water and reaches for one of the tea towels hanging on the stainless-steel range oven handle. As he dries his hands, he tosses me another charming smile. "I'm not sure if I've ever met anyone who reads as much as you. Although, Irina was a bookworm as a kid."

Thank goodness, a topic I can speak on that doesn't make me hesitate.

"Books are worlds all their own," I explain. "I've traveled great distances under the sea with Captain Nemo and courted danger in the opera." Atticus makes his way toward me leisurely, his smile turning serene. When he doesn't respond immediately, I ramble on. "I've probably read every Nora Roberts romance book too."

He stops his approach and leans with casual grace against the edge of the kitchen counter. "Is that so?"

I go to explain further but catch the teasing glint in his eye. The corner of his mouth twitches. "It is. She's a brilliant writer."

"And was romance something lacking in your life before... this." Atticus sweeps his arm out to the side for added effect. I swallow.

"Twenty-five years is a long time to go without romance," I give careful emphasis to each word.

"I agree," Atticus nods and shifts his posturing to something more open and a touch more vulnerable. It shows in the angle of his head and the way it tilts downward along with the slight fall of his shoulders. "I'm certainly in no position to judge, seeing as how I was in the same shoes as you."

He treads the short distance between us with sure steps. The look in his blue eyes is indiscernible, but that doesn't stop them from having an effect on me. Under his regard, the slowest burn stirs in my blood. All of my lycan senses hone in on the wolf before me. His confident but measured gait. His narrowed gaze and hunched shoulders.

Atticus's tongue darts out to wet his bottom lip. There should be no doubt that the movement is innocuous, and yet my eyes won't stray from the gleaning surface of his mouth.

He's hunting me, I realize as he stops only a foot before me.

"But if it's any consolation, I think what we'll have will put all the rest to shame. Even your Nora Roberts," Atticus offers.

His words draw my breath to a stop. I drag my eyes away from his mouth, the hot flare in my blood rising as I chance a glance up to his eyes. A breathy exhalation rushes out of me at what I see. Want. Pure and simple.

So much for taking things slow.

I should speak up, but what can I say that won't end in disaster? Say nothing and my silence may infer a receptiveness I shouldn't give in to, let alone imply. Speak out, and I may make the hunt seem more appealing. Or worse, clue Atticus in on my doubts and troubles... and betrayal.

Fragile darkness looms as my lashes flutter closed, my thoughts clashing in a battle over what to do. I don't notice the gradual decline of Atticus's head closing the distance between us. But the wolf does. I breathe in his scent, and the wolf gives pause to appreciate the top notes of greenery and lavender and base notes of oak moss and musk from his cologne.

"Winter?'

"Yes?" As my lashes draw upward, Atticus's nearness sinks in. My back bends to accommodate his new proximity. A firm hand slides quickly to the soft curve my spine creates, but he doesn't pull me closer. My eyes meet with his dreamy blue ones, and the world around us allows us a quiet moment to take each other in and the possibilities swirling around us.

I place a hand tentatively on his chest, unable to decide whether to push him away or pull him forward.

"I know I've said it before, but I'm *really* happy that you're here." Atticus tilts his head until his forehead rests upon mine. His breath still smells of the cinnamon coffee he had this morning, and I angle my head back to catch the scent a little more. "I want you to be happy here. Whatever I can do to make that happen, don't hesitate to ask."

His hand splays down to my lower back, inching my body closer to his and letting it come to rest above my soulmark. I exhale a touch sharper than intended. My cashmere sweater is the only barrier between our flesh meeting, but knowing it is so close makes me tremble.

"Anything you want... I'll give it to you," he promises, his voice turning husky.

My fingers curl into the fabric of his sweater until the ribbed material is bunched between my fist.

"I—" Atticus's body tenses at my first word, but my tongue feels thick and heavy in my mouth. I'm unable to form a sentence, let alone another word. He draws me in another inch until our bodies are pressing softly into one another. "I want—"

"Yes?"

His heady eagerness cuts through the spell he's cast on me, and my right mind shouts at me to retreat... along with every reason we cannot be together. The soulmark curse that denies us the ability to have a family of our own—not to mention my lying and betrayal.

"I'd like to see Lunaria today," I blurt out. I'm unable to meet his probing stare and direct my gaze instead toward his chest.

"Of course," he murmurs, pulling me into a hug and burying his face into my neck and hair. He inhales long and deep, and the tension that briefly rode high in his body slips away. I too inhale, drawing in his scent to calm my wrought nerves.

Atticus pulls away, the darkened want in his eyes once more subdued. He is reluctant to release me but does so like the gentleman he is.

"I need to make a phone call first," Atticus informs me. "But after that, I'll take you over."

He brushes a kiss upon my temple, and the heat inside me ignites once more at the simple touch. Atticus seems to realize the effect it has on me, his sharp gaze running over me from top to bottom before retreating to his office. I take several steps forward until I reach the black quartz island, my hand reaching out to clutch its cool surface.

There is a storm brewing between us. A shiver of anticipation spider-crawls up my spine. And all my intentions to play it cool are going to be damned... by Atticus's hand.

+++

The day holds an eerie calm to it, a stillness that would be unwise to disturb. I breathe in the cold air and let it fill my lungs.

Standing before the Trinity Coven's front door, my skin and nose itch at the amount of magic surrounding their home. *How bad will it be on the inside?* The thought brings a subtle frown to my brows and my nose crinkles ever so slightly. No going back now.

I give a hearty knock and hear footsteps a few seconds later. The steps grow louder until the noise of the door handle squeaks open. Luna answers. She's bundled up in an oversized turtleneck sweater, and her purple eyes grow wide at the sight of me. I smile back.

"Hello." Luna continues to stare, and I sweep my gaze over her wild white curls. "How are you? May I come in?"

She blinks back at me, nodding with an uncertain air as she allows me in and shuts the door behind me. "What are you doing here?"

I hesitate before slipping off my leather gloves. "Didn't Atticus call?" Luna shakes her head. Then who did Atticus call if not the witches to tell them of my coming?

"Nobody has called all day," Luna explains, still eyeing me with wonder and curiosity. "What are you doing here?"

I tug off my hat but keep my coat on, lifting the corners of my mouth into a bigger smile. "I wanted to see you."

"You wanted to see me?" Her eyebrows dart toward her hairline. "Why?"

"I thought it would be nice to get to know you more."

Lunaria's porcelain cheeks fill with blooming red flowers. "Truly?" her vulnerability softens her posture, and I let my smile mirror the softness.

"Yes."

Lunaria bites her lower lip to stifle the smile on her face before ducking her head. "Oh."

Naturally, my own smile grows larger and far more genuine than before. "I thought we might go for a walk. It's the nicest it's been in days without the wind. What do you say?"

Luna's head snaps up and issues a short succession of nods. "That sounds lovely! Just let me tell the aunts so they can glamour my…." She gestures to the flowers and vines moving leisurely beneath her skin, the bell-shaped sleeve of her turtleneck flopping hazardously over her hand in the process. I nod in return and put back on my hat as she rushes off.

I hope I know what I'm getting myself into.

I have a bad feeling I don't.

+++

The perfume of the forest is dull, even to my lycan senses. The dry winter air and cold temperature cannot effectively trap the aroma of the red cedars and spruce trees that occupy the surrounding area, but trace amounts drift by every now and then.

My breath plumes before me with every exhalation. There one second, gone the next. What a nice change to focus on the peacefulness of the moment and tender silence between us rather than why I have requested this walk with Luna.

The knowledge I shared of the fairy will not sate my parents. Oh no, they will demand more, and so more I will get. The bigger task I'm confronted with is extracting the right information, something that will appease my parents while not compromising Luna's safety.

I glance at the fairy. She walks beside me silently, mittened hands swinging at her sides. Her face is tilted precariously back—almost to an uncomfortable degree—to achieve maximum sun exposure. I'm unsure as to how she doesn't misstep or stumble, but it is she who guides us confidently through the forest.

No longer does she sport a wild garden beneath the surface of her skin, nor are her magnificent wings visible, thanks to Zoelle's grandmother, Diana. There is a peace that exudes from Luna that was not present at Christmas. It's clear she relishes in the act of simply *being* in nature, and it's a trait I can empathize with.

The wolf rouses in my mind to pass along its pleasure. It too likes to be out exploring and learning the territory we now call home. The soft pressure of the wolf's sentiments almost makes me falter, but it circles back to its former resting spot and fades from my thoughts. A shiver dances across my body.

It is strange to hear the wolf's thoughts and sentiments mingle with my own. *Although*, I muse, *not wholly unwelcome.*

Luna stops near a large tree, her hand reaching out to graze the trunk.

"My friend Alekos would love this forest." Luna keeps her back to me as she stares up into the branches and the spindle-like green needles that protrude from them. "He's what you would call a *Tree Runner*."

I open and close my mouth a few times, as my brow furrows with curious confusion. "I'm not very familiar with *Tree Runners.* Would you mind explaining?"

She looks back at me, her glamoured eyes staring straight through me. "Alekos was born of the bark. It's in his blood to know the trees. He speaks with them, and they to him. There aren't too many *Tree Runners* in my... home." Her speech slows as she casts her sights downward. "But I think he is one of the best around. Alekos can even call them to arms. He says it is harder with the old ones with their roots so deep, but he can, even if it's just one."

"That's incredible," I say. Luna hums her agreement, a small smile on her face as she turns an admiring gaze to the tree. "You know, the western red cedar is a popular wood for making furniture. The wood is soft and easy to work with, but it's also durable. They say a piece of furniture made from red cedar can last one hundred years."

"Oh?"

I nod and then point to a different tree in the distance. "That one there—the spruce—its wood is commonly used to make musical instruments, like violins and cellos, even pianos."

"Alekos always told me the trees like to sing, but I can never catch them doing it," she confesses. Her hand falls from the trees side, and we walk on. "How do you know so much about the forest?"

"I'm somewhat of an amateur botanist—heavy on the amateur." Luna casts a shy smile at me. "I've always enjoyed learning about them," I explain further. "There's something about plant life that I find so... satisfying."

"That's lovely, Winter," Luna commends me.

"I used to talk a lot about plants with Atticus in the letters we wrote to one another," I continue, not so certain why I'm revealing the information to her. "I did it more when I was younger. When I was around thirteen, I made a better effort to talk about other things and to learn more about him."

"And for him to learn more about you?"

"Mm-hmm." It's not exactly a lie. In my eyes, Atticus has always been the better writer of us. He captured daily life and personal topics effortlessly. Whereas I discovered a knack for turning the mundane into even more snooze-worthy material, thanks to my parents editing. Anything of substance Atticus might have learned from me will have been from when I was younger and my parents didn't censor our letters so strictly.

"Oh dear." Luna's voice turns hollow with distress.

She stops, frozen in place as she stares at a cedar in distress. We've wandered off the trail meant for hikers and deeper through the trees, but I see nothing out of the ordinary.

I scan the frosted landscape, keeping my lycan senses alert as I take a step closer to Lunaria. "What's wrong?" I ask in a whisper.

Her bottom lip quivers, and try as I might to catch her glossy eyes, they remain locked upon the towering tree.

"Luna, what's wrong?" I ask again, louder this time. Crocodile tears drop down her pinked cheeks, and my concern turns from possible enemies to the fairy in front of me. "Lunaria?"

A soft keening noise drifts from her when her mittens rise to shield her eyes. "I'm sorry," she mumbles past her cupped hands, shoulders quivering.

"It's all right," I assure her and collect her into my arms. She comes willingly, tossing her arms around my neck and sobbing into my scarf. I squeeze her tighter, still keeping an eye out for any interlopers who might intrude on this moment. "Everything is fine, Luna. I promise."

A rush of words floods from her mouth. I can scarcely keep up. Snippets of self-doubt and worries far greater than one person should carry make it to my ears. With great gentleness, I pull her back and lower her hands.

"Luna?"

"They broke me," she rasps, her red-rimmed eyes locking onto the tree again. "They tore me apart, and I was too weak to do anything about it. I can't save her. I can't save... save me."

"Listen to me, Luna," I state with firm authority and squeeze her wrists to draw her attention to me. "You are not broken. Stop selling yourself so short. I know you were hurt that night, but you did what you could. Now tell me, what is this place to you? Is this where it happened?" My voice goes softer at the end seeing the truth to my question fill her eyes.

"I'm supposed to keep them safe. I failed—"

"That responsibility doesn't rest on your shoulders, Luna," I tell her, searching her eyes for acknowledgment. Once found, I continue on. "It rests on the pack and the coven and each and every member to look out for one another. There have been other fights and other casualties, were those your fault too?"

Her struggle shows on her face before she quietly answers. "No. But—"

"No 'buts,' Luna. You have to unbind yourself from this burden you carry. Start accepting it wasn't your fault, because that is the truth. Or you can stay on this path, but you'll only damage yourself further here." I issue a light tap to her temple, easing my lips into a small and reassuring smile. "Don't focus on what is tearing you apart. Focus on what's keeping you together—the friends who are here to support you and this beautiful forest that you nurture."

Though her bottom lip trembles, Luna rolls back her shoulders and wipes her cheeks. Still sniffling, she replies, "I'll try."

"Good." I wrap her up in another hug and direct us back from where we came. If only I could take my own advice.

The quiet between us is like thin ice. Each step we take is made with the utmost caution, and while Luna keeps her eyes glued to the ground in front of her, I stay alert for any unwelcome guests who might disturb us.

"It's not just me who's hurting," Luna whispers as we find the civilian path once more. "The forest hurts too. I want to be out here and comfort them... but their pain combined with my own is sometimes unbearable."

"I can't imagine how difficult that must be for you."

Lunaria releases a heavy sigh and glances up at me. Her wild white hair sways with the passing breeze. "I'm connected to the earth and, in turn, all that seeds from it. Half the forest has fallen to sleep, and the trees only tell the story of when the stone broke. I ask them to tell others, but they won't listen to me."

"But if the trees are of the earth, shouldn't they have to listen?"

Luna shakes her head, lips thinning momentarily. "The earth listens to me and sometimes the lesser flowers, but the trees are not so easily swayed. Alekos could. Perhaps my friend Celosia could, for her spirit burns so brightly."

I begin to chew on my lip, my curiosity rising at her explanations and my conscience along with it. I want to know more, but the thought of potentially turning that knowledge over to my parents makes my stomach clench uncomfortably.

"We should—"

My redirect is cutoff by a loud sneeze, one that causes Luna to stumble back a step. She frowns in frustration, sniffling and patting her nose with her mittens.

"I can't stand the cold! It never gets this way in the Hollow Woods. The aunts say they don't want me to get a 'cold,' but all I ever am when I step outside is cold. I don't understand," she fumes. "And I feel so lonely here... I never felt this way in the Hollow."

I place a gloved hand on her shoulder and squeeze. "You don't have to feel lonely any more. Whenever you need a friend or someone to talk to, just call me. When Atticus returns to work, I'm not sure what I'll do to occupy myself. Maybe we can spend more time together."

"Thank you, Winter. I can see why you're a beta. Atticus once told me betas care for the pack like they care for their own hearts. And you do it well."

I blush at the compliment. "Thank you, and you're welcome, I suppose."

"Do you love him?" she asks. I almost trip over my feet at her blunt, yet innocent question. She looks to me in bewilderment, watching as I right my balance. "Are you all right?"

"I—yes, I mean no. No to the first and yes to the second."

She takes a moment to process. "But... you recently celebrated your union, did you not?"

"Yes."

"Then you are in love?"

"No."

Luna stops, folding her arms around her middle, she sends me a small glare. "I do not understand."

I shuffle to a stop as well but turn my regard to the dull branches of some shrubbery just behind her.

"We have an arranged marriage, Luna. Our families decided it was best we wait until we were older to marry because of the soulmark. All of our communication was done through letters these past twenty years."

I glimpse at Luna's widening eyes and the way her mouth parts with awe. "And after all of these years, you are not in love?"

"There's a part of me that cares for him deeply," I confess, starting to walk again as the cold begins to bite at my nose and cheeks. Up ahead I seek out the line of houses I know to be coming up. A gracious sigh falls from my lips as I spot their shapes in the distance. "But I've been careful to keep my heart at bay all these years. At least, for the most part. Faking perfect or pretending to be someone else is too easy to do when all you have to go by is their written word.

"Every imperfection can be hidden and masked in a letter. A part of me wonders if I ever truly got to know Atticus. I'll only learn if he's the man I met through our letters with time... and that's why I'm not in love with him," I explain, my words soft-spoken.

"But he houses the other half of your soul," Luna argues plainly. "Where in your history has there been a pair who did not fall in love when the sealing, marking, and binding of the soulmark were completed?"

I flush. "The steps to completing the soulmark are very intimate, Luna. And as I've just said, I don't know him."

"But you do know him," she continues on stubbornly. Our eyes meet in twin glares, gray against a glamoured dark blue. "You've known him for twenty years."

"Well, I'm not the type to jump into things headfirst," I snap. "Besides, Atticus and I agreed to take things slowly."

Luna brushes a few wayward curls away from her face, her lips pursing together thoughtfully. I take a moment to do the same. My much longer, snowy hair is in two loose braids on either side of my head, but tendrils free themselves with each passing breeze as the wind picks up.

The fragrance of food from not too far away begins to tease my nose. After a calming breath to soak in the smell, my nose gives an irritated twitch. Food isn't the only thing riding on the wind. Magic is.

We walk in silence, closing in on the fork in the path that will lead us back to the witches' large backyard. I would be perfectly content for it to stay as such, but Luna has other plans.

"If you ask me, there's no reason to delay the inevitable. I think Atticus is wonderful." Her sudden conviction draws my eyebrows high as we turn down the final stretch of path. "He's very handsome and is always nice to me. I think you make a lovely match because you're very handsome, and you've been nice to me too."

Her hand drifts my way, and she toys with the end of one of my braids.

"Thank you."

Atticus's face comes to mind at Luna's compliment. The chiseled jaw and easy smile. His China blue eyes and the physique of a tight end. Another image flashes of him and the way his unruly chestnut hair falls into his line of vision every so often. How he smooths it back without care and his muscles stretch and contract.

"I'm sure you'll fall in love soon enough," she declares, the smile winning.

"It's complicated."

Luna huffs again as we near the house. "Everything is complicated in your world. Especially love, when it's so simple. *Humans*." I don't have to see her eye roll to know that she has done it, and I let out a short laugh at her exasperation.

Luna opens the back door calmly, her earlier spirit receding as we enter the house. I trail in after her, more than prepared to lift her spirits once more when I see who is in the kitchen. It's Aunt Mo and Aunt Lydia, along with a petite Asian woman who looks like she might be still in high school. I stop in my tracks when their eyes remain on me as Luna walks toward the front foyer to hang up her coat.

A sweat develops at the back of my neck as their regard turns frosty. My gaze flicks to Aunt Mo, whose own consideration is less severe than the others, but no less intense. There is no doubt in my mind the other two women are privy to Aunt Mo's Christmas time prediction, and a rush of indignant anger fills me.

Tilting my chin up a fraction, I stride across the kitchen to the foyer, mindful of their judgmental stares following me. Luna's surprise is written on her face when I open up the front door and begin to exit.

"Are you leaving?" Luna's disappointment clear.

"I've just remembered something I need to do," I explain with a casual smile in place. I turn and give Luna a hug, then begin to exit. "How about we meet again soon? Maybe next time you can come over to our house?"

The sentiment makes Luna light up like a star. "Okay," she says a touch bashful. "If you're sure that will be okay with Atticus."

"I'm positive," I reassure her, itching to leave the hostile environment.

"Bye, Winter!" The door closes behind me at Luna's farewell, but I'm already halfway down their driveway. I don't know where to go, or what to do for that matter, but by leaving the witches' house I can breathe again.

III

"You've grown callous, Edmund. What slight have I dealt your pack? What crime have I committed to justify this treatment, as if I'm some venomous crone? They burned my yurt down to the ground. Every medicine and remedy I kept on hand—gone." Merida's eyes flashed with fury at the indifferent alpha. "They burned my *home*, Edmund, with me inside it. Why? How could you allow this?"

The alpha scoffed, a hand absently reaching to stroke his beard as his dark eyes pinned her to the spot. Edmund Blanc was a powerful man, made more so by his lycan ability. Merida held no false hope that her grievance would be acknowledged or accepted, but she refused to stay silent.

"Did not my son ask you to leave our land months ago?" he asked. "What more did you expect, *witch*? In your blatant refusal to vacate our lands, our lycan nature was aroused. From your years spent around us, you should have expected our territorialism. Our aggression."

"Are you not both beast *and* man? What of your human nature? Or has your pack succumbed to your baser instincts and now find your tastes to razing the homes of your peaceful neighbors? What have you to gain from my departure? I have tended half your people for illnesses and eased your bodies of the pain associated with shifting. There has been no crime or act committed on my behalf to earn such ire."

Edmund leaned forward. His top lip furled to reveal stark white teeth that could tear a man or woman—or *witch*—to pieces.

"You stepped outside the bounds of propriety and accrued our wrath when you so wantonly pursued my son."

Merida stared down the alpha even when a telltale prickle irked at the back of her neck. Vibrations carried through the air from growls echoed by the guards in the room.

"I am owed flesh and blood for the crimes committed against me."

"Harlots have faced worse fates than yours," he said and waved a hand dismissively. From behind, rough-sewn hands gripped Merida's arms and pulled her back. She let out an animalistic snarl that roused a laugh from the alpha.

"I will not leave—"

"You will," Edmund snarled, his amusement quick to fade. "Or I'll kill you myself."

Merida's feet stumbled beneath her at the wolves' insistent pulling. She choked out another stunted cry, and an instant later, a palpable current streaked through the room. The wolves at her side quickly leaped back, their teeth bared at the shocking slight.

"You'll regret this," Merida promised.

Her feet continued to blunder beneath her as she made her retreat. The wolves inched their way after her, cautious of the stinging magic that still plagued the air around them. Merida managed to escape the hut unscathed for the most part, though her hip managed to catch the sharp corner of the table near the hut's opening.

But a bruise on her hip was not the only thing she left with.

Clenched tightly in her fist was a small, oval stone that seemed to glow a pale, milky blue. A moonstone. Merida knew how keen the Blancs were to these gemstones thanks to Luc's own cooing over their unique luster.

Soon the Blancs would pay for their greed.

Soon they would pay for the misdeeds against her.

Soon—

"Merida?"

The anger that swelled hot and adamant in her heart of hearts, in her very soul, stopped short of its darkest mark. Merida walked faster, curling around the backends of huts and small cottages cut of both wood and stone.

"Merida, wait."

Who did these wolves think they were to test her power? To test her patience and generosity? *After all of these years…* Merida thought, her malice returning.

"Stop." The voice was closer than Merida anticipated, and when she found herself trapped amongst recognizable arms, she did not fight against them. Steamy, warm breath panted past her ear as the male body guided her to a more private location.

"What do you want?" Merida spat.

"Don't be like this," Luc half pleaded, half scolded. His dark brows hunched over his eyes. He looked down at her as if pained on her behalf, and Merida felt herself falter.

"You did this," she accused brokenly. "You could have stopped them long ago. You could have stopped it with a single word, but you let them persist. Has your heart grown cold for me after only a few short months?"

Luc's jaw clenched. He cast a furtive look over both shoulders before he leaned down. "You will always hold a place in my heart," he admitted. "But my pack would have me believe these traitorous feelings garnered from some potion or spell."

"I would never—"

His palm clamped over her cry. "It matters not," he told her without remorse. "For you must leave now or meet your maker."

Merida shook her head. Luc's gaze hardened.

"Is your heart so shriveled and frozen that you cannot see what your presence has done to me? You parade yourself throughout the village in front of my soulmark and slander my position in the pack with your damnable pride. Can't you see?" he hissed. "You pine away after a man who no longer loves you but another. You insult this packs' generosity with your continued presence upon our lands. I asked you to leave."

His words broke off with a crack, and he shoved away from the witch with disgust.

"You have done this to yourself," he said, repeating the statement once more to reassure himself. When he brought himself to look at his ex-lover again, his wolf prowled forward with dangerous intent.

"Don't be this way," Merida pleaded. "Don't be like *them*. One battle won, and you think yourselves the mightiest pack in the land—"

"Leave, Merida," Luc interrupted. "And do not come back."

Merida thrust her chin high in the air and strode away with a final glare. They both pretended her jaw wasn't trembling at the action.

Merida left. But she planned on returning.

+++

It was difficult for Merida to put into words the deep roots of her pain. Her hatred, on the other hand, bubbled forth like a volcano on the verge of eruption.

They had chased her from the village, wolves whom sweated and howled after a higher rank in the Blanc pack. All ready and willing to do what they thought might please their alpha and beta.

Merida fled to the safety of the forest, calling up the blossoming flora and awakening trees to stall her enemies. They answered, but Merida still found herself far more beaten than when she had stepped foot in the alpha's lair, both literally and figuratively.

It was their physical blows that curbed any forgiveness in her heart. That and the months spent living through their punishing treatment. Now hatred consumed her every waking thought, like a poison. And there was no antidote, except for vengeance.

It was this vengeance that brought about the situation at hand.

Merida thought it poetic her revenge would take place at the spot where she had her first clandestine meeting with her then lover, a beautiful birch tree on the farthest-reaching side of the village. The moon was high and full in the sky with the Goddess's children basking in her glory deep in the woods. All except one.

This wolf was bound by its legs and writhed against its restraints amongst the tree's roots. Its muzzle was bound tightest of them all.

"You forced my hand," she informed the wolf. "You did this to yourselves. There must be reparations, and if your pack is unwilling to give it freely, I must take it for myself," she reasoned.

The wolf struggled against its binds. It comprehended the magic around it different than its human counterpart. Where the human felt the sharp sting of otherness in the air, the wolf felt deep foreboding and danger. Instinct told both to break free by any means possible and run, but it was much too late for that and them.

"It is far past time you and your kind learned your place at the heels of your masters."

Merida's eyes went distant as the fresh spring air turned bitter.

"You must learn, Garret Blanc," she uttered. Memories of her torment by the hands of this wolf among all the others plagued her mind. He was the third son of Edmund Blanc, and the last.

The wolf released a pained whine and that brought the witch back to focus. Its eyes rolled back in its head as it watched blackness seep into her eyes. The wolf's ears flattened against its skull as words arose upon the wind and wrapped around its body and soul.

Merida stepped forward, powerful words dropping from her mouth as she approached the laden wolf with blade and moonstone in hand.

"By all that is powerful and just—hear my blood claim!"

Merida slowed her advance to drag the blade across her palm and raise it high above her head. Blood poured out in copious amounts, more than was natural to the wolf's perception.

"*Brious macab aos;*
Folle d'astalle lios.
Brious macab aos;
Folle d'astalle lios."

The wolf struggled. Within the connection to its human counterpart, darkness was encroaching. The wolf whined and fought further, its fearful gaze lighting upon the haggard witch as she closed in. In its mind, it screamed for its brothers and sisters help and their courage, but there too a dark haze lingered, blocking it from assistance.

"*Brious macab aos;*
Folle d'astalle lios.
Brious macab aos;
Folle d'astalle lios."

Merida's head fell back as she dropped to her knees before the wolf. The wind whipped wildly around her. The wicked seed of hate spread its roots inside her and turned each vein to black. Scoring pain scratched down every limb, but her intent had never been more sincere.

As a pack, they had made her suffer and plotted murder against her.

As a pack, they would face the consequences of their actions.

"*Brious macab aos;*
Folle d'astalle lios."

A force struck back against her magic, making the wolf whine in relief. The dark possession of Merida's magic resisted. *They had come this far... there was no going back.* It would be the wolf or the witch, and Merida had no intention of dying tonight, not when the prospect of their faces torn with grief would finally assuage her need for vengeance.

A different voice appeared on the wind, foreign and just as powerful as the magic pouring out of Merida. This voice was nowhere and everywhere at the same time. Merida did not relent.

Was this sacrifice willing?

"No," Merida proclaimed.

In an instant, her body lurched forward and then back. Unstable magic wreaked havoc across her body, torn in its decision to obey and take life unwilling. But that flare of indecision was crushed by the darkness inside Merida.

So mote it be.

"*Brious macab aos;*
Folle d'astalle lios."

The moonstone rose high in the air.

A symphony of howls ricocheted off towering trees as the blade struck into the heart of the wolf. Merida's eyes remained black, and the hex that tumbled from her mouth was a voice not her own.

"*Tov mal sintave!*"

Magic tainted the air, its noxious fumes culminating in a plume of evergreen smoke that rose from the fallen wolf and spoiled witch.

It is done, Merida thought. Her body slumped forward, drained and aching from her dark spell. The moonstone followed suit. It fell down between the witch and the wolf, its milky-blue luster gone. The witch took the cursed gemstone in hand and rose, then retreated into the shadows of the woods as if a specter.

Echoing through the branches was the thunderous stampede of paws. Of brother and sister calling to arms against a new enemy. Merida did not feel the joy she anticipated... not yet, and so she smiled grimly as she vanished from sight.

Her work was done.

New Acquaintances

- Chapter 7 -

However callous it may sound, I thought myself immune to the heavier hits of guilt when it came to carrying out my parents' wishes. After all, the Adolphus pack isn't the first set of wolves my parents have requested I gather information on or from.

But this request has been different from the start, with doubt plaguing my conscious since my acceptance.

I suppose it's to be expected, this gnawing beast at my gut and nervous system. I did agree to sabotage my happily ever after.

And now there's this on top of it all.

I'm unaware of the quick succession of my steps across the frozen pavement. I'm merely attempting to keep pace with the racing of my heart. It is only when I register the tossed looks I get from the random assortment of townspeople outside that I force myself to a normal gait. This does not, however, stop my heart from beating with its erratic enthusiasm.

They knew.

I come to a halt. My leather-bound hands shoving aside the strands of white curls that fling themselves into my vision.

By their contemptuous glares alone I know this fact to be true. Why else does my presence cause such deep cuts and lines across their aging faces as I step into their home? And who is the third amongst them? She looks young but owns the eyes of a woman who has seen far more than one at her age should.

They knew.

They must have dissected Aunt Mo's reading, and now they too believe I'll get someone killed. But what does that even mean? How will I get someone killed?

What do I do? Tell my parents and face their wrath over my failure?

Or do I tell Atticus the truth and lose what weak ties and trust we've built over the past days? No—not days. Years. *Damn you, Luna, for being right.* I fight the tears that threaten to fall, wiping away the sheen that gathers in my sights.

Remember, Winter, never let them see you weak. You are stone. Nothing can break you.

A woman passes by me, a cordial smile on her lips as I step out of the way for her and her portly dog to walk by. I paste one on as well and take a look at my surroundings. I'm not sure of my location but dread the thought of calling Atticus to come to fetch me.

As if galvanized by my thoughts, the streetlights begin to flicker on. Each dark steel post boasts three orbs, and their warm glow makes the street look calm and enchanting. I relinquish my worries in a long-winded sigh and pull out my phone. The map app kindly shows me I'm a little less than a mile from downtown.

I stride onward. My pace matching that of the passersby I cross. Our intent is all the same: to be out of the cold.

Halfway into my expedition, I'm drawn back to my somewhat rushed pace. I'm not usually one to hurry my wintertime strolls, which begged the question of why I'm driving forward at such a speed.

A frown settles over my brow and tilts my lips downward. The wolf inside me takes note and draws back its ears as its hackles rise in cautious warning.

Something is off.

A twinge of doubt accompanies the goose bumps that run along my arms and chest. Tucking my coat around me tighter, I cast surreptitious looks over either shoulder. The wolf is still on edge, and my heightened senses agree. But where is the threat?

I continue walking so as not to draw attention to myself while I keep my lycan senses on high alert. No definable scents catch on the strong wind attempting to blow me off course. I cast my frown to the sky and cringe at the incoming grim clouds that encroach upon the last rays of the sun.

A short scan up ahead reveals a more concentrated population of shoppers and people milling about. The first batch of local shops just behind them.

Good. Because I now know precisely what provoked my current state: a wolf. And if I had to place my bets on what pack it belonged to, I'd go with my gut and say not the Adolphus pack. Its gaze is too penetrating and heavy, pinned as it is between my shoulder blades.

My stride lengthens.

By the time I reach the outskirts of what is considered downtown, most of the foot traffic I spied earlier is gone. The street is vacant except for two girls who walk on the opposite sidewalk. They huddle close together, then break apart with raucous laughter that bleats down the deserted street. The two are quick to link arms once again as their laughter dies off on the wind.

Then, there is the wolf.

He appears from nowhere. One instant my path is clear. The next he fills the space with his larger-than-life frame. His outfit is inconspicuous—leather jacket, scarf, skull cap, and dark wash jeans. They do nothing to lessen the severity of his size or features. A large Roman nose, its slopping curve heavily scarred and eyes framed with dark circles beneath them.

The stranger's full lips are drawn into a flat line, and his unnaturally dark eyes are half covered by the harsh tilt of his thick eyebrows. I stop in my tracks, picking up the flecks of gold teeming from his glare. My earlier assumption is correct. This wolf is not part of the Adolphus pack.

But this isn't the wolf whose eyes were on my back.

Pinpricks dot up my calves and thighs before converging up my back and down my arms. The pair of eyes between my shoulder blades remains steadfast.

One on one, my odds are better. Two on one, I will need to play it safer and smarter. If I can just get someplace—

"Well, well, what do we have here?" A seedy male voice rumbles from behind me. I stiffen in response, unwilling to turn around and take my eyes off the wolf still several feet in front of me. "Out all by your lonesome, little wolf?"

His footsteps near, until I have no choice but to turn and face him. He's young. Eighteen. Maybe nineteen. He's too young to have such menace in his voice or cruelty in his goading smile.

"What do you say we have a chat someplace quiet?" Unmistakable gold flashes like lightning in the younger one's eyes.

"Who are you?" I demand, keeping my voice firm and low, while I inch back a step. The boy grins widely.

"My name isn't that important," he says. I ready to retort, but a movement from my peripheral vision catches my eye. Across the street and leaning against a lamppost is another towering male. He is tall and thin—wiry, with dirty blond hair that falls in knotted waves to his shoulders. A gust of wind tosses his hair across his face, but his focus on us doesn't waver.

Three wolves to one....

"But you might know the name of my pack," the youth continues.

My odds might as well be nonexistent.

Inside me, I reach for what pack bonds I have with the Adolphus pack but find the pathways somehow blocked. My eyes flick back to the boy as I hide my spike of fear. His smile promises violence, one that I am solely unprepared to meet. I was not been raised to fight. To misdirect and deceive with half-truths, yes.

To be paraded and play hostess, yes.

To risk myself or family honor, never.

I'm sure they can hear the wild canter of my heartbeat. "The Wselfwulf pack."

"Very good, Mrs. Hayes." I flinch at the use of my new name. "Our car is parked a couple of streets back. Why don't you come with us so we can have that chat?"

"No."

My curt response garners a frown from the youth. He takes a step forward, invading my personal space. "It wasn't a request."

"You're not ranked nearly high enough in the Wselfwulf to try and order me around. Only an alpha's will can trump my own," I snarl quietly back, my body angling toward the corner of the street and inadvertently to the wolf in the leather jacket.

There is no place for me to run that is unobstructed by the Wselfwulf lycans unless I count the small alleyway at my back. My heart continues to hammer hard against my chest, thundering in my ears as I stare down the self-imposed leader of their triage.

"Not even two weeks into their precious pack and you've adopted their willful arrogance," he spits, the gold seeping back into his eyes.

"How did you make it past the border?"

He arches a brow at my tone, leaning back on the heels of his feet as he considers me with a growing sneer. "Arrogant and ignorant. You truly are an Adolphus bitch."

"How, Wselfwulf?"

"The crystal was compromised months ago," he says, walking around me in a circle and lingering at my back where I am most vulnerable. I stand my ground, unwilling to bend. "Broken crystal equals broken border."

He stops in front of me once more, his hands stuffed into his coat's pockets. The smile he wears is one of relaxed confidence. It's meant to make me falter, but my experience with men and women who wear the same self-assurance is vast, and I know that kind of bluster happens to be one of their greatest weaknesses.

The boy casts a lazy look over his shoulder at the third wolf still loitering across the street. As his mouth opens to call something out, I take my chance and run.

Overconfident fool.

I flee down the skinny alley, with both elbows and hips bumping into the brick walls on either side of me and random garbage cans. A foul curse follows my dramatic exit. The sound of feet in swift pursuit matches the cadence of my own. Almost.

With each obstacle I maneuver past with nimble footwork, my arm thrusts out to knock them behind me and clog the alleyway. The clatter ricochets off the rough red stone, but it's the lycans' heavy curses and my harried breath that sounds like bombs in my ears.

The alleyway ends as it meets another. I hang a tight left to catapult myself down the next lane, only to run face-first into a different type of wall, one made of muscle and wearing the face of the devil. The leather-clad lycan stares down at me impassively as I stumble back, arms windmilling when I teeter back a step too far.

His hands strike like vipers, his fingers stealing around my upper arms before I can stop him. I hiss in anger, but even that is cut short by the massive man.

No sooner does my breath leave me then I am thrust back against the brick wall. My body is racked with pain as my head bounces off the stone with a dull thud. The lycan removes his hands from my arms, only to ram his forearm against my chest and lock the other around my neck. His fingers squeeze the delicate column almost tenderly.

I stare at him wide-eyed, my hands reaching up to claw at his wrist and fingers to loosen their hold. He stares back with the same impassive regard. There is nothing in his dark eyes. *He's more beast than man*, I realize hazily.

"Did you really think you could outrun us?"

I turn my gaze reluctantly back toward the boy who plays at being a man. "She-wolves are far lighter on their feet than their male counterparts," I say calmly, ceasing my attempts against my attacker. I will not beat him.

Why I don an act of composure, I'm not entirely sure. Can it be my years in the Blanc pack proving useful? How many times over the years has my position in the pack been challenged and questioned? The women of the Blanc pack didn't stoop to brawls to earn their rank. They manipulated and schemed. They maneuvered one another into impossible scenarios, forcing the other to concede to their will and command.

This is just another game of chicken, I tell myself and force myself to relax further against the brute's hold. The last lycan joins us. I can smell him on the wind that passes through. A mixture of tobacco and lead and earth. The one who holds me, with his severe haircut and dead eyes, is no doubt the most significant physical threat I face, but the other is a close second.

How did the boy in front of me gain rank over them?

The boy, with his pretty brown hair, spiked up stylishly, leans forward. His chocolate eyes are filled with loathing.

"We'll keep this short," he promises, a pocketknife appearing in his hand. He twirls it between his fingers before gripping it securely and bringing it to my cheek. I stiffen. My wolf barrels to the surface of my mind with a vicious growl as my eyes bleed to gold. How dare—

"Tell your alpha we've been counting. We know he's been adding to his numbers. Growing the pack." He spits out the last sentence as if his rage isn't palpable enough. The wolf blocking the other entrance lets out an agreeing growl, but the one holding me remains impassive as ever.

"Tell him yourself," I snap back.

The boy chuckles and presses the knife into my skin. It cuts as he does, and the scent of my blood overpowers all others in the alley.

"Tell him he's not the only one." The chirp of a cell phone saves me from any further taunting and message-bearing. With a scowl and sigh, the boy in front of me answers his phone. "What?" he asks, his voice cracking like a whip.

"Head out," a voice rumbles from the other end, and then the line goes dead.

"Consider yourself lucky." I'm told as the blade retreats from my flesh. "Move out. Company is on its way."

I don't witness the third lycan leaving, but his quick exit echoes in my ear. The boy in front follows suit, darting down the same direction as the third. The giant, however, remains.

His fingers curl around my neck, squeezing with practiced ease. I hit and claw at his offending arm once more as my eyes well with tears. It's of little use. The lycan inches me into the air, letting my toes scrap the icy ground beneath us, and then I am slammed back against the brick wall.

Stars burst before my eyes at the impact, but at least the hand about my neck is gone. I crumble to the ground, and my knees smash into the cement as I gulp in the cold winter air. A chill permeates my body, and by the time I have the good sense to scan my surroundings to better see what direction they fled, I am the only one left in sight.

But not for long.

What little of the Adolphus pack bonds tie to me are filled with adrenaline and one burning torch of fear. Why I have been unable to feel any of this before is a mystery to me, but it doesn't matter. My eyes stop on the figure of a man at the other end of the narrow alley, and my stomach gives a nervous flutter as my heart bursts with gratitude. Atticus is here.

+++

"I'm fine," I try insisting for the hundredth time. The cut on my cheek is mended thanks to my lycan healing. The only evidence of the assault is a light pinkness to my left cheek that is not mirrored by the other.

"They attacked you," Atticus seethes.

He's paced the alpha's study for the past ten minutes, while said alpha leans stoically against his desk, his arms folded over his chest. The expression on his face is unreadable, but being so near to him I can feel his emotions clear as day through the pack bonds.

Xander is furious, but his stout anger is directed mostly at himself.

"It was just a scratch."

Atticus stops in his tracks and pins me with a mutinous glare. "And the bruises around your neck? The scratches on your back? There's still blood in your hair!"

Unconsciously, my fingers pat the back of my head. The matting there is less than comforting, but the skin is healed, as have the far more superficial scratches on my back, thanks to the protective barrier of my coat and clothing. My neck, on the other hand, still holds the impression of the beastly lycan's touch, though it fades with each passing minute.

"They could have done far worse, Atticus," I tell him plainly, ignoring the angry growl that tumbles past his lips. He turns his growl to the floor, unable to direct his full anger at me in my state. My fingers curl into fists at my side, and I step forward in his direction. "But they didn't. I'll be *completely* healed within the hour, so we should stop focusing on what they did to me and onto other things."

"Like what?"

I straighten my spine and flick my gaze to the alpha. "Like how they were able to cross your magical border in the first place. And why I couldn't signal for help using the pack bonds."

"It was a coordinated attack." Xander rolls his shoulders back. Before he continues on, he pinches the bridge of his nose with a sigh. As both hand and shoulders fall, he meets my gaze again. With Xander's composure back in place and on display, I find my own soon after. Even Atticus releases a short sigh of relief with the alpha taking charge.

Xander gives us each a short nod. "Ever since the attack at the end of summer, when the Wardens of Starlight broke the crystal, we've encountered tears in the border. They're not easy to find, and we keep a tight patrol to monitor the shifting openings—"

"Shifting openings?" I interrupt as my mouth falls open. "They *move*?"

Xander responds with a much curter nod before going on. "They do. The Trinity Coven is working on making them stationary and mending the Crystal of Dan Furth, but the process has been... limited, even with Luna providing extra amplification to the crystals remaining power. As for why you were unable to access the pack bonds, it seems the Wselfwulfs have made friends with magical means."

"Witches?" Atticus asks, finally finding his voice. I glance at him, but his eyes are steady on Xander, as if by looking at the alpha alone he can anchor his chaotic emotions.

My own turbulent feelings are pushed far away. I'm unwilling to show how shaken the ordeal left me, and how the new information equally does so.

"Maybe sorcerers." The two men share a meaningful look before the alpha breaks their standoff with a heavy-laden sigh. "I'll send word to Irina, see what she might know. After all, Vrana and his family have a history with meddling with the Wselfwulfs."

Atticus softens his posture in a gesture of submission. "That's in the past, man. Things have changed. Even if they don't know anything, I'm sure they'll help us poke around more discreetly than even Ryatt can manage with all his technology."

"And what about their message? They said they've been watching you. The Wselfwulfs are counting how many new wolves you let into your pack," I say. I shift my weight from one foot to the other when I get no immediate response. "They're growing their pack in response to yours," I continue, my voice rising. "That can only mean they're gearing up for something. Something big, Xander. What are we—"

Xander raises a hand. His face is a blank canvas, and I swallow with unease at the hardness in his eyes. Submissively, I duck my chin to my chest and avert my eyes to the floor.

"We'll do better," he says. "An incident like this won't happen again. I swear it."

I nod in response, still unable to meet the alpha's eye. "I only want to do what's best for the pack."

"I know," Xander laments, his voice smoothing out to something low and amiable. I chance a glance at him and find his shoulders hunched forward with a beseeching look in his eyes as he gazes back at me. "You're the beta. Those instincts to protect and care run high in your blood. But it's my job to take care of you too. I want you to take it easy the rest of the day, all right? We'll regroup in a day or two. Keep a low profile until then."

Atticus crosses the room to stand next to me at Xander's orders. His palm finds the middle of my back, rubbing small circles of comfort there that loosens the tension knotted between my shoulders.

"We will," he answers for us. Then we say our goodbyes and go.

+++

I don't know what to say to Atticus that hasn't been hashed out a dozen times at the alpha's house, but it seems, for once, Atticus is of the same mind. We say not a word to each other as we make the journey home, though at times I swear I catch his mouth opening to say something, out from the corner of my eye. Nothing comes out until we are safely inside the house.

"Do you need anything?" he asks, a frown heavy on his brow, his blue eyes shining with concern.

"I think I might lie down for a bit," I say, turning my back to him and shrugging off my coat. Exhaustion hits me like a ton of bricks as soon as my coat rests on its hook. "Actually, I might take a shower. A very long and hot shower. I really want this blood out of my hair."

When I turn back to him, a touch of hurt is added to his expression. He shuffles back to allow me access to the staircase. "I'll make dinner?"

I spare him a thankful smile. "That would be wonderful. Thank you."

For a moment we linger, unsure how to proceed though we've defined our next moves. I notice this happening more between us. This *lingering*, it's as if we can't help but fall into each other's orbits again and again.

"See you in a bit," I finally say, my words coming out far more breathless than anticipated. Atticus nods in return, his eyes darkening as they watch my retreat. As soon as I enter my room, I lock the door behind me and slump against it.

How is it possible one man can make me feel such... longing?

Not ten days in his presence and I can tell the soulmark remembers his touch from so long ago. How long before we give in to temptation and feel its spark again?

I step away from the door, unprepared for my feet to come to a jarring stop when I see the vase of flora on my vanity. My palm jumps to my chest over my racing heart. Thanks to my nerves, it takes almost a minute for me to build the courage to near them.

Closer inspection reveals the vase holds a bundle of holly, and nearby it sits a book I'm somewhat familiar with, *The Language of Flowers*. I spy a small sheet of paper sticking out from its pages and take it out.

We were always better at letters.
Merry (late) Christmas.

-A

A thrill of excitement teems in my blood as I thumb through the thin book to find the meaning of holly. I small smile lights my face as my fingers trace the word. *Hope.*

THE COUNTDOWN

- Chapter 8 -

My mother is *remarkably* good at selective hearing, but she's even better at steamrolling entire conversations. Over the years, I learned the patience needed to insert my voice into the fray, but it's the right words to say that sometimes still evades me.

It was easier with face-to-face conversations. I could read Mothers' moods easier.

Deciphering her motives and emotions over the phone is proving not to be my forte. Mother is too well-versed in weaving traps with her words and lulling you into false senses of security with her cadence and reasons.

Twice she catches me in minor detail changes I make about the fairy's true appearance. I mutter curses under my breath at the scolding that follows each.

On the other hand, speaking with Mother over the phone does allow for some leniency. I am bolder in my responses and don't feel the pressure to give an immediate response. I can think before I speak. Even my wolf appreciates the small liberties.

"Did you listen to what I said?" I ask.

My fingertips stall their drumming on the windowpane as I wait for my mother's response. I catch her in a rare break from her latest rant.

"As I was saying, Winter—"

"I was attacked, Mother. Why are we still on about the witches and this fairy? I told you everything I garnered in the last few days since we last spoke."

Except for a few critical pieces of information here and there... like how the border is compromised and the fairy is more powerful than they let on.

She pauses far too long for comfort, and my pulse speeds at the prospect of her uncanny intuition. My fingers fall to the moonstone necklace and toy with its chain.

"Everything has its place and order, Winter. You assured me you've recovered from what minor injuries you sustained, the time to elaborate on your tale can wait until we finish this conversation. And do remember, when retelling your harrowing ordeal, to spare any dramatics. Facts and timelines do not change due to your emotional state."

A lump forms in my throat as my fingers curl around the moonstone, one that feels so large I'm unsure if I can swallow it down before replying. I manage, croaking out my response in what will undoubtedly earn a reprimand. "Of course."

Mother's scoff hits like a lash at the wound she's just inflicted. "Honestly... may we continue on with our discussion? Or does your need for attention outweigh the task at hand?"

I bite down on my tongue to stop my retort. It is easier now, with such distance between us, to be filled with frustration and disappointment at my mother's tenuous treatment. Whereas before I would sit passively by at each snub.

The wolf echoes my sentiments and releases a restrained growl in the back of my mind, yet it doesn't press further for retaliation. Years of grooming have seen to that.

"I've nothing more to report." The tenor of my voice is as smooth as silk. "The fairy was either lost to her thoughts or in turmoil over her past experiences."

"Yes, as you've said before, but you continue to fail at expanding upon what this 'past experience' of hers was. Do not think to test me here, Winter. I know the effect you have on people. Your empathy and pathos naturally incline those around you to confide in you. Now that you're officially a beta, the instinct is amplified even more so. So tell me, what happened to the fairy."

My stomach knots as I release my stranglehold on the moonstone. With a delicate sigh, too soft for my mother to understand over the phone's receiver, I lean into the window with my head and shoulder. The sharp cold is the anchor I need to carry on.

"She was eaten."

"I beg your pardon? Eaten? By whom?"

"Goblins."

"How on earth did this come about?"

"I told you. I don't know the exact details. The fairy couldn't explain, given her state, and Atticus doesn't want to share another person's story," I lie.

Sort of.

I know details of the battle thanks to Quinn, but her bombastic retelling of events makes me doubt the accuracy of her account. As for Atticus, well, I took his general dislike of my gossip session with Quinn to infer his disapproval of speaking on behalf of others.

My tongue darts out to wet my bottom lip before I continue. "The fairy is still suffering from her memories of the event—"

"And what effect does this have on the towns magically erected border?" Mother cuts in sharply. "Well?"

"I—" I pull from my slack position, sitting upright and alert at the unexpected direction of the questioning.

"I require an answer, Winter."

The order comes through thickly in her voice, and an uncontrollable shiver spider walks down my spine in response. The urge to obey is there, but it is hardly as strong as I've known it to be in the past. Nevertheless, I answer. "I suppose it's weaker, in theory—"

"Just as I thought," Mother announces. "The strength of their border is tied far tighter to this fairy than they have let on to you."

"I didn't say that," I protest, coming to a stand from the windowsill. "I—"

"Then how do you explain how the Wselfwulfs were able to sneak into the town and hurt you? Obviously, the fairy's instability has left a weakness in their touted border."

I shake my head as I reply, curls of snowy white landing in my sights. "We don't know that for certain," I insist, batting away my hair and beginning to pace. "There could be many reasons as to why the lycans were able to get through. Perhaps they have an inside man?"

"Doubtful." Mother's voice drips with arrogance. "We're quite knowledgeable about the Wselfwulfs standings. I assume your new alpha was able to provide an explanation for his failings?"

Once more my teeth clamp down on my tongue. Mother's slight brings an unpredicted wave of protectiveness inside of me. "He assured me it would never happen again." I mildly note the touch of heat to my tone. I know better than to press on, but I can't seem to stop myself. "My ties with the Adolphus pack are still weak, but once the soulmark binding is complete, any of my distress or alarm will be noticed sooner rather than later."

"What a shame you shall never know such comforts," she replies far more cavalierly than I expect.

"I cannot put it off forever—"

"You can," she snaps back, "and you will. We've talked about this, Winter. A hundred times over. Have you no wish for children? For a future unhindered by this curse we suffer so unjustly from? One day soon, I will see you happily matched, Winter... with someone deserving of the honor of our family legacy. Your father and I only ask that you assist us in this effort by being our eyes and ears inside the Adolphus pack for a while longer."

The sound of a car pulling into the driveway momentarily distracts me. I clamber to the window, wiping away the fog that appears at my heavy exhalation. Atticus is home.

"I've been assisting as best I can." The words come out more a growl than polite insistence and Mother retorts accordingly.

"Mind your attitude, Winter," she replies, with her words dripping in condescension. "Your father and I expected far greater from you. It's hard to believe it was just a week or two ago when you so heartily promised your loyalties to this family and this pack."

She *tsks*, but the noise is muffled by the garage door opening and shutting. Next comes the car door.

"I am loyal," I reply hastily, feeling as if the hands of time itself are pressing in on me from all sides. "But I can only achieve so much without integrating more into the pack."

My argument falls on deaf ears, at least that's what I take from Mother's divisive laughter. But it is her next words that strike down my last defenses. "You know, your excuses won't save her."

Another door opens and closes, this one to the house. "Winter?" Atticus's call rings hollow in my ears.

"Save who?" I breathe, my heart caught in my throat.

"Why, Juniper, of course," mother answers calmly. Tears are quick to sting the corners of my eyes, but I'm unable to make a rebuttal for Mother charges on unperturbed. "It's far past time Juniper was dealt with by a firmer hand. She's been babied far too long. Your father and I both agree that she understands her role in this family and in the pack."

"Please, Mother. Don't bring her into this."

Atticus's heavy footfall climbs the stairs.

"Think of this as motivation. We'd hate to have to become more creative in our efforts to ensure your promises are kept. As it is, the distance between us makes monitoring your progress a task in itself." She huffs loudly to express her exasperation. "We shall speak again, and soon."

"Yes, Mother," I reply to the sound of the dial tone. The tears that I held back roll down my cheeks, but there is little time to process what I've been told. A knock sounds at my door.

"Winter?"

"Just a moment," I answer. I move mechanically to the bathroom, running the water in the sink as cold as it will go and before splashing it onto my face.

"There's no rush," he continues quickly. "When you're ready, would you come downstairs? I need to speak with you."

I hesitate, dreading whatever conversation is to be had, but force out a cheery response regardless. "Of course," I chirp back and listen to the sound of his retreat.

Fuck.

I fret in my room for some time, turning over his request in my head until it's nothing more than mush. *He knows*, I tell myself as I go downstairs. *I'm ruined, and so is June*. The witches have finally broken their silence and told him.

"Hi." I strive for casual and latch on to something far more forced and awkward instead.

"Hey!"

Atticus jumps up from the couch in the sitting room. His hand instantly goes to muse his hair as he follows my line of sight to the coffee table before him. My momentum draws short at the bottom step as I stare at the bundle of flowers concealed in brown paper lying on the table. For a glorious second my worries and fears fade, a flutter of butterflies gathering in my stomach at their presence.

"You can open them when we get back." Atticus's voice is laced with delicate hope and a hint of excitement. I sweep my gaze back to him and see his cheeks are a merry red, the product of which isn't from the cold.

His words sink in, and I blink back at him. "Get back from where?"

My eyebrows drift together in confusion, and unconsciously my grip tightens on the banister. Perhaps the flowers are just a decoy to throw me off guard and—

"Dinner."

The wood creaks underneath the persistence of my hold. "Pardon?"

Atticus's cheeks flame brighter at my question, but for the life of me, I can't believe he might be asking me out too—

"Dinner. With me. Tonight. It's New Year's Eve."

We stand in silence for what must be an age before I bob my head in agreement. Atticus breaks out a relieved smile.

"When?"

His smile grows as he walks toward me, answering only when he can lean up against the banister's post. "A couple of hours. I know Xander wants us to lie low, but I figured since it's New Year's Eve we can make an exception. Besides, you won't be out alone this time. You've got me to watch your back."

I'm dumbstruck once more by his thoughtfulness and allure. A shade of darkness creeps into his eyes as we stare at one another. The moment stretches on waiting for my response.

"That sounds lovely."

+++

Dinner is, in fact, lovely. And much to my relief, a lighthearted affair. Atticus proves to be a perfect distraction from thoughts of my mother's threat—even if it lurks in the back of my mind and at times I catch myself debating what to do and who to choose.

Juniper or the Adolphus pack.

My parents' approval or my happiness.

A war, to begin sooner or later.

Atticus catches my eye, and I realize I once again lost track of the conversation. With haste, I piece together the bits I have managed to pick up over the last few minutes and paste on a smile.

"Everyone in the pack seems so close," I comment. His fork is stacked perilously with food that finally makes its way into his mouth. My mouth twitches upward at the sight, and Atticus hums an agreement behind closed lips.

"We're in a rather unique situation," Atticus concedes. "I might be biased, but I think our wolves are closer than most because of what we've been through."

No kidding. "Because of the split?"

His movements slow, but at an almost imperceptible speed. The vigor at which he chews his meal gradually slows. The tick of his pulse stalls a half second too long. He's thinking, mulling over the right words or perhaps what he is allowed to say in front of me.

How often do I do the same? I muse.

"Yes," Atticus responds, at last, "and no."

This time, it's my fork that halts halfway to my mouth. A bite-size portion of rigatoni perched on its end. "I'm not sure I understand what you mean by that," I confess before eating the morsel.

A restless chuckle slips out of Atticus's mouth, one touched with a trace of bitterness if my hearing is correct. He wipes at his mouth with his napkin before placing it back on his lap.

"I suppose I assumed you would understand," he muses. Our gazes catch again. Atticus's voice is soft, but there is something to it that puts me on edge. Is it a spot of criticism? Perhaps it's a grace of contempt dwelling in his tone? Arctic blue eyes study my reaction with keen interest as I dissect his words.

"Why would you say that?"

His lips pull into a firm line, the lighthearted nature of our previous conversation put to rest. "The night we ran together. You said the males were kept separate from the females for the safety of the she-wolves."

A wave of heat flares up my cheeks. "Yes, but—"

Atticus delivers a curt shake of his head, and my explanation runs short. "You said the males were too aggressive. In the Wselfwulf pack, it was like that too, except the females weren't kept separate."

A shiver of disgust rolls up my flesh, raising every hair on my body as the weight of Atticus's implication hits me like a ton of bricks. "What?"

"They keep to the old ways. But it's clear from the past few decades how much harm has been done to keep their *precious* ways."

"And you think my pack keeps to these 'old' ways?" I ask, terse and hurt. Atticus colors faintly around the neck but remains otherwise indifferent to my retort.

"I know they keep to traditions of old."

My hands ball up in my lap. "We keep to traditions that are mindful of our origins, ones that respect our lineage. To those on the outside, it might seem that we're stricter than most, but our namesake carries a certain weight of responsibility that ties us tightly to lycan traditions."

Atticus sighs. "I forget that the 'old ways' I know, aren't synonymous with your 'traditions.' I'm sorry," Atticus says.

I swallow down the rise of anger in my blood and lean back against my chair slightly more deflated. "It's all right. It isn't as though my pack is known for their warmth either."

I reach for my glass of wine and take a long sip before setting it back down. Atticus watches me with rapt attention, and he mirrors my position, slipping back against his chair in a more pronounced slouch. He takes hold of his wine glass as well but doesn't take a drink. Instead, he waits, leaving the opportunity for me to continue, for me to share, wide open.

My mouth opens and closes as I take time to find something to fill the silence.

"This pack is much different than my last," I offer, stealing another sip of courage from the full-bodied Chianti. "It was far more... structured. Everything had an order and place. Everyone played their part. You didn't get ahead by might or strength, though it certainly helped when a move was being played," I continue on, finding my vision peeling off into the distance as I recall what life like was only a few weeks ago. "You had to plan and plot and scheme. And nobody did that better than my parents—does, I should say."

"They are rather brilliant." Atticus catches my gaze and offers me a small smile. I return it weakly.

"They're cunning."

Atticus nods, his small smile growing into a rather infectious grin that is difficult not to mimic. "And you? Are you cunning?"

I know his words are meant in playful jest, but the thought stings. I always thought myself different from my parents, their strive for power and rigid personalities never appealing to me.

But how different can I really be if I'm complacent in their scheming?

Cunning, I am not, but foolhearted... I trace the lines of Atticus's face. That I most certainly am.

"I am something else entirely," I admit. "I had to be to survive my parents."

Atticus chuckles. "I'll take your word for it."

The conversation lulls enough for us to finish dinner. I take my time in doing so, even though my dish lost its heat and appeal. I'm not keen on starting the conversation back up again. Talking about family, especially my own, is not something I'm comfortable with. It also draws my thoughts back to the phone call with my mother.

And all at once, it's clear what I'm going to do.

My hands flatten against my lap. I can't allow my parents to wreak their havoc on June. All I need is to look in the mirror to see every reason why. They'll break her. I suck in a slow, deep breath, attempting to stem my distraught thoughts. I'll have to make a better effort to cater to their curiosity about the pack. Give them more of what they want, even if it cuts straight through to my heart.

My sights flit to Atticus, who is focused on scraping up the last dredges of his meal. *He's strong in body, mind, and heart. He can withstand what I must do.* I hope.

"Can I ask you something?"

I blink back at Atticus, then nod whilst a gentle smirk rises to my face. "It hasn't stopped you yet."

He shoots me a charming smile in return. "True. Your parents... they don't like me, do they?"

Oh. My mouth runs dry, and I silently curse our waiter for not refilling my wine the last time she came around. "If it's any consolation, they don't like most people outside of the pack."

"I figured," he responds coolly, but the sentiment must hurt, for it hurts me.

"It's difficult to earn their respect. Even I struggle with it," I admit, unable to stop my tongue from the Freudian slip. Our eyes meet, and a wave of understanding passes between us.

"I suppose they weren't pleased then when we found each other, what with me being outside the Blanc pack."

A frown falls upon my brow. "I don't know about that." My lips purse together in thought. "You belonged to the Wselfwulf pack at the time, and my parents considered them a strong pack. They still do in several ways, but I doubt they know the true depths of their ways." At least I hope they don't.

He stays silent for a long time, and in the interim, the waitress returns to take our plates.

"It would be nice if they liked me," Atticus says. "Or didn't detest the fact that it's me you're saddled with for the rest of your life. But if they don't... it doesn't matter in the end. I vowed the day I found you I would be the best man I could—for you, Winter. Not your parents. Not your pack or mine. Just you." He lets out a low chuckle, his eyes never leaving mine.

"That's a pretty big vow to make when you're eight."

"I was an ambitious kid," he replies with a grin. "Plus, I was never going to be high ranking in a pack like the Wselfwulfs. When talk of separation came passing by my ears, I knew I needed to convince my parents to leave.

"The Wselfwulf pack was always too cruel for my tastes, even as a kid. But I was lucky enough to be spared most of their tests of loyalty and strength because of my father. He entered the fighting ring to make sure we were safe and to keep us," Atticus tells me.

Dread creeps along my skin. "What do you mean, 'to keep us'? And why did you have a fighting ring?" I ask.

Atticus spins his gaze away in search of our waitress and catches her eye. When she arrives, he asks for two more glasses of wine and the check.

When she's out of earshot, he replies. "Anything could be won in a fight. Possessions. Rank. Money. Rights to mate. Rights for families."

"That's a terrifying way to live."

"It was Xander's father who was brave enough to organize those willing to leave. We all knew what we risked by fleeing, but to stay wasn't an option anymore. He garnered passage for us through a slew of victories in the fighting ring. By the end, Rollins, the alpha of the Wselfwulf pack at the time, had no choice but to agree to the separation. Xander's father had grown strong enough to bring a legitimate challenge to the alpha, so he allowed our party to leave... Of course, he went back on his word. He sent out his men to take us back the night we left."

The waitress returns with fresh glasses of wine and the check, and Atticus takes a moment for a hearty sip. I take the glass and eye him over the rim. His torment is painted clearly across his brow.

When he at last sets down his drink, deep creases remain on his forehead.

"Atticus, you don't have to go on," I tell him with mindful softness. I swallow and reach my hand across the table. He stares at it a long moment before grasping on and giving a shake of his head.

"I want you to know. I think it's important that you know where I came from. Why our pack is willing to do all of this. The night we left, Xander's father must have known Rollin's would try something. So he stayed behind with a handful of others to ward off any who might try to stop us. They killed those men. All thirteen, and paid for it with their lives as well. Now the Wselfwulfs claim fault, even though we lost pack mates too."

"I'm sorry, Atticus."

I'm sorry for all you went through... and for what I'm to put you through. Your pack doesn't deserve my dishonesty, but neither does June deserve my parents' wrath.

The pads of his fingers are smooth as they stroke my hand. They're a contrast to the small calluses rooted at the end of each digit. I lock eyes on the motion and begin to feel what I shouldn't. I shouldn't.

"They can have their old laws and customs." Atticus lowers his volume as he speaks, gaining my regard in a timid raising of my lashes. "The ties that bind the Wselfwulf pack aren't made to last. This pack, our pack, we are. And we'll continue to grow and strengthen."

"Do you really think that?" I ask in earnest. Is this pack strong enough to survive my betrayal?

My query makes him catch his breath, yet he manages to answer not a beat off. "Yes."

Our smiles are candid, though slow to come, and then our tender moment turns to something more as we continue to gaze at one another. A spark ignites between us. It scorches straight from the start and obediently follows the path of Atticus's gaze.

He looks at me as if I'm... *everything.*

Phantom fingertips graze across my back from shoulder to shoulder, drawing my spine up straight along the way. *We keep winding up back here*, I acknowledge, a touch out of breath, *circling each other.* Waiting for the moment, until we both fall off the edge.

Would that be so bad? a velvet voice asks in the back of my head. *What harm can it really cause?* I dare not go through my list of answers. It will take all night. Instead, I finish off my glass of wine in a messy gulp.

"Let's go home," Atticus says. I'm too slow to disagree.

+++

I had too many glasses of wine. This is true because, somehow, the heat of Atticus keeps reaching past our winter coats and stealing across my skin. It becomes worse as we exit the car and head inside. Atticus opens the door and ushers me in first with a hand at the small of my back.

Despite all the layers between us, an insidious shiver walks its way right up my spine.

His hand presses against my soulmark.

Does he know what he's done? Can he hear the rapid rise of my heartbeat at the touch? It is only by flesh-to-flesh contact with the soulmark that its rapturous sensation can be triggered. But this prelude tempts me to think otherwise, for a languid heat sinks low in my belly as his scent perforates my senses.

He smells of leather and anise with hints of some tea leaf that I cannot recall the name of stealing through each inhalation of his cologne.

Too much wine indeed.

Atticus helps me out of my coat and proceeds with his own after hanging mine. I go to the stairs, taking in a steady breath as I sit down on one of the steps to peel off my boots.

"Do you need help?"

I find his eyes in the dark foyer. Even now they burn brightly, a constant light within the darkness.

My teeth find my bottom lip as I weigh the pros and cons of such an action, then scold myself on the foolishness of the act.

"Yes. Thank you."

He kneels before me, and without thought, I scoot up another step to give him more room to work—and me some necessary space. Without delay, Atticus cups my left ankle and stretches my leg out to its full length. The knee-high boots I wear boast daunting laces up their front, though in reality are secured by a zipper that runs the inside length of my calf. Atticus unlatches the small buckle at the top that hides the zipper, his eyes darting up to look at me through thick lashes.

"I hope you enjoyed dinner tonight," he murmurs, eyes slipping back to the task at hand. His fingers pull the zipper down with great patience. "I realize the conversation took a turn toward the end, but I'm glad we spoke about it. It was important to me."

I suck in a breath as he gives a tug to the bottom of my boot. My foot comes free with the help of Atticus's guiding hand at my Achilles. He looks back up at me, his chestnut curls catching what weak streetlight filters through the windows.

"I... I'm glad we could talk too."

"It doesn't always seem to come easy for us," he remarks and sets my foot down. His hand trails up the back of my calf.

"Except for our letters," I murmur.

Atticus pauses just as he takes hold of my right leg. The spark of heat I felt before returns at the smoldering look he passes to me. With a touch more force than the last, he straightens my leg as he did before. This time the act drags me forward an inch, my bottom resting precariously at the edge of the step. My fingers curl around the step's lip as I stare Atticus down, lips parted in mild shock even as a thrill of excitement winds its way through me.

"Except for our letters," he agrees smoothly, the husky tenor of his voice rolling over my skin like a purr.

He takes his time once more. His idle fingers release the buckle with a lazy flick before moving onto the lengthy fastener. The zipper slides down its path at a leisurely pace, but as it does, Atticus leans up. I freeze, watching his predatory movements with wide eyes.

A sharp tug and the boot is removed. It clatters to the wooden floor behind us, but neither of us makes a move. Caught in our standoff, I find myself drowning in the growing streaks of gold in his eyes.

His hand cups my calf, and with a deliberate measure, he pulls me down a step as he continues to close the gap between us. I gasp as I come nose to nose with him, unable to do anything but submit to his wishes.

"Happy New Year's, Winter."

My gray eyes drop to his lips, watching with fascination as his tongue darts out to wet the bottom one. I mirror the response, intentional or not, and I'm greeted with a short groan from the man before me.

"Happy New Year's, Atticus," I whisper back.

The pounding of my heart thunders through my ears as my rational side yells at me to retreat. But the other part of me—the one who longs to finally stretch its wings and throw all caution to the wind—inches me forward.

Our lips meet, but they aren't the only parts of us to do so. In one fluid motion, Atticus surges forward and winds an arm around my back to pull me down. The momentum takes my breath away.

We seize onto each other as if starved, colliding in a sudden and desperate need for each other. *This isn't just the wine*, I acknowledge with a sharp inhalation. *This is fate.* And it burns across my lower back, aching to be delivered.

Atticus's mouth presses hard into mine, his body following suit, rocking against me with a passion that resounds deep in my bones. I find myself adrift, for Atticus is no longer my anchor, but a storm threatening to sweep me away. My legs wind about his waist, cradling him close.

To hell with taking things slow.

With a mind of its own, one hand threads into the soft hairs at the back of Atticus's neck before delving higher for greater hold. The other grips the step digging into my middle back that urges me to arch upward.

His mouth leaves mine in favor of nipping its way across my neck. I moan, boldly careening my head to the side to allow him better access. A hand kneads at my thigh, parting my leg further somehow with its workings before diving under the back of my sweater dress and skimming my—

"Oh!"

My eyes startle open as the world tilts around me. Atticus's hand flattens against the soulmark as he grinds his hips into mine, a growl of pleasure erupting from his throat. Oh God. Oh God. *Oh—*

"Atticus!"

His name breaks past my lips in a hiss as I tug at his hair. I'm unsure whether I do so to pull him away or to find some semblance of ground given the shifting of the earth.

Pleasure spirals across my skin. It whispers in my veins, filling me with want and need. I rock my hips back, unable to stop myself from the wanton act. His hand drifts away from my soulmark, and I'm surprised to hear the whine I emit at the act.

Every inch of my nerves have been set on fire, and it must be because of this that my hands find their way between us to do away with what keeps us separate. Atticus hesitates, his hand sliding away from my soulmark only to grip my hip with a strength that will bruise.

"Are you sure about this?" His question comes through clenched teeth. A strangled noise rises from his throat as his erection falls into the palm of my hand. His shaft is heavy and throbs with a need my core echoes. I wrap my fingers around his width, as much as I can, and stroke. "Fuck."

The coarse expletive makes me shudder and writhe beneath him. Atticus takes his cue, deliberately catching my eye as his hands push my sweater dress above my hips before they fall to the opaque tights I wear.

"I hope you don't like these."

I startle when he tears the delicate fabric down its middle seam, even though I knew full well what his words promised before he delivered. Next to ravage are my panties. When he lingers at the sight of me laid out against the stairs, chest thrust upward and legs spread in reckless abandon, he makes a noise of appreciation deep in his chest. Gold flecks emerge in his blue eyes, and I struggle to swallow down my anticipation.

"You're—"

I cut off his question with a kiss. I'm done with spoken words today... and Atticus's mouth and lips and teeth and tongue are far better suited for other things at the moment. We swallow each other's moans as he poises himself at my wet and waiting entrance.

My lashes flutter closed. "Yes," I breathe as we at last collide.

A hunger rides our movements, which are both desperate and fast. Our panting breaths skim across one another as we make the best of our unique location. I keep an arm slung across his back, gripping at his shoulder with my nails digging through the material of Atticus's shirt. The other holds its position on the edge of the stair, keeping the worst of its blunt angle away from my back.

Atticus's arm helps in this aspect as well.

His straining forearm takes the brunt of his forceful thrusts. My legs tighten on his trim waist when the pace increases and bursts of added pleasure chase our already mounting passion. His arm brushes against my soulmark more and more until Atticus gives into its addicting pull and hooks it around my back to press against the mark totally.

My cry of release pierces the quiet house unashamedly, with Atticus's own following not long after, his appetite undone by my own even as his hips continue to drive into me without restraint.

"Christ," he wheezes, collapsing on top of me. I squirm beneath him, and he slides to my side with an apology.

I'm sweaty and slick beneath what clothes remain on my body. I'm also out of breath.

I can't believe we did that.

My heart continues to slam against my chest as the silence of the house envelops us.

"Winter?" I can feel his eyes on me, but I keep mine directed at the ceiling. What have I done? "Are you all right? I... I didn't really think our first time together would be, well, here."

His breathless chuckles does little to ease the ache swelling in my chest.

"It was fine," I murmur and notice his flinch out of the corner of my eye. I turn to him then, allowing a small but sincere smile onto my face. "More than fine," I reassure him. "A little bumpy though."

My light joke washes away the tension from his face. Too bad it can't do the same for my sudden anxiety. I scoot off the stairs and stand, righting my sweater dress and peeling off what's left of my tights. Atticus rises as well, his attention weighing heavy on my every movement.

I clear my throat as I face him. "I think I'll take a shower and head to bed."

Atticus nods vigorously and rakes a hand through his hair. "Yeah, of course. That's what I was going to do to."

You foolish girl. Look what you've done.

"I'll just... go now," I say, my heart pounding painfully still.

Before my traitorous body can catapult itself into his arms once more, I turn tail and run up the stairs. My bedroom door slams behind me with far more force than I intend.

"Idiot," I scold as I stalk across my room then back toward the door. "This isn't part of the plan."

Before I can criticize myself further, I catch a whiff of something peculiar lingering in my room. Something odd, but familiar. I spot it immediately. A new vase of flowers on my dresser. The ones from earlier.

But how did he get them in my room? I wonder as I approach them.

"Daffodils," I mutter.

The sight of the cheery yellow leaves me in a stupor, and then I see the card leaning up against it.

W.
Narcissus poeticus.
-A

A frown creeps deep onto my brow before my eyebrows jump to my hairline. The book! In a flurry of movement, I cross the room toward my vanity where his gifted book still rests. I thumb through the pages, eyes running over words much too swift to properly catch sight of the ones I want. I miss the page in my frenzied curiosity and thumb back several to reach it.

Narcissus poeticus: *New beginning*.

My heart swells and cracks in the same instant.

How am I ever going to be able to betray him now?

I Spy

- Chapter 9 -

Sex isn't a big deal. I stare at my reflection in the vanity mirror. *Now say it out loud.*

"Sex isn't a big deal," I repeat.

So our lust had gotten the better of us last night, so what? It doesn't change anything between us. Not if I don't let it. And certainly not if I don't pluck up the courage to go downstairs and face Atticus.

Go, the wolf urges, and I fight back a sigh.

Unlike me, the wolf woke refreshed and surprisingly present in my mind. It wants to be at our soulmarks side even if it is only to take in his warmth and scent. At its first insistence this morning, I let out a yelp of surprise, still unused to its voice so long absent from my mind. Plagued by my neuroticism, I shut down its request a tad too hard.

I know I'm overthinking things and lashing out at my wolf, but the truth is I'd rather fret over this than dwell on my mother's threat.

Go, comes its request, this time the word more subdued.

"Fine," I begrudge and fumble with the clasp of the moonstone necklace. "Seriously?" I grumble, giving up the task and marching over to my dresser to tuck the precious gem away in its box.

I leave the safety of my bedroom before my doubts can hold me back any longer and tread down the stairs, only to come to a stop a few steps short of their base.

My hand clutches the railing as I lurch to a stop. The wood beneath my feet and hand give a groan as I remember in detail the night before.

A hot blush stamps itself across my cheeks and neck and further down to my breasts.

His whispered touch along my calf.

The lithe movements of his body as he prowled above me.

My brazen need.

I squeeze my eyes shut tight at the bombardment, but the images only become clearer. How easily he slipped inside of me. The toe-curling pleasure of each thrust.

"I hope you're hungry," Atticus calls from the kitchen, disturbing me from my salacious thoughts. I gasp and trip over my feet to get off the stairs. "I made a big breakfast."

I right myself with wide eyes, before mentally shaking myself. *Get it together, Winter.*

"Coming," I call back and make my way to the kitchen in the back. "Good morning."

"Good morning." Atticus turns and smiles brightly at my entrance. But I'm keen to notice the darker circles that frame his eyes this morning. Little sleep then, for him and me both. He gestures to the table. "Eat up."

I take a seat, eyes greedily scanning the table's contents. Chocolate chip pancakes, bacon, strawberries, whipped cream, butter, and syrup all sit snug against one another to fit at the small circular table. Lashes fluttering closed, I inhale deeply and savor the scents.

New Year's day at the Blanc pack meant goal setting, a customary check-in at every pack mates home starting with the omega, and a feast for the entire pack hosted by the alphas. The latter, as it would seem, is a custom of the Adolphus pack as well. But I doubt theirs ended promptly at eleven like the Blancs.

"Good morning."

The husky greeting is delivered close to my ear, and I jerk back at the sensation of lips grazing my cheek. The blush from earlier assaults my cheeks once more as I process the modest kiss.

"You've said that already," I chide, desperately fighting down my blush and piling food onto my plate.

Atticus hums his response and takes a seat next to me. "Are you excited for today?"

"Is Zoelle cooking?" Atticus chuckles, but nods. "Then yes."

The kitchen steeps with our silence as we begin to eat. I dare not break it or meet Atticus's flickering gaze, even if he looks more delicious than the food this morning in just a Henley and track pants—and tastes it, I recall.

"So, how did you sleep?"

"Fine," I chirp, ignoring the way my hand falters when stabbing at my next piece of pancake. The second attempt does the deed. "And you?"

"It could have been better," he admits.

A noise of acknowledgment leaves my throat as I chew my food. I ignore the fine rasp he hinges on each word as they fall off his tongue in a feign of casual commentary. I know better and so does he.

"When will we leave today for the party?"

I catch Atticus's shrug out of the corner of my vision. "Early evening. We need to go early so I can speak with Xander."

"About what?" With my full attention captured, Atticus sets down his fork and smiles back reassuringly. The comforting weight of his hand falls on my knee and delivers a short squeeze.

"Solutions. New rotations to monitor the border cracks. We don't want what happened to you to happen to anyone else. But there is one more thing I'm hoping to discuss with him."

The warmth of his hand is a distraction that both my wolf and I fall for. I imagine it sliding north to explore when the drop of his voice catches my attention. Atticus smiles somewhat wanly back.

"If you don't mind, I want to share with him a bit of what you told me last night. Explain to him the difference between tradition and old ways. I think it will help us better plan our next move against the Wselfwulfs, or help to anticipate theirs."

This is not what I expect him to say, and judging by the brief flicker of confusion passing by his eyes, it shows on my face. I smooth my features and turn my attention back to my plate.

"I don't mind—" I insist, but he interrupts.

"It's okay if you rather I not. I don't have to, but I would like to. I do think it will help. But yesterday things got... personal." He pauses, hand leaving my knee for his fingers to graze the underside of my chin and turn my regard his way. "I don't want to cut short something that just began, because yesterday felt like a beginning... at least to me it did."

And just like that, his words chase away my doubts and fears of earlier. At least, temporarily. I lose myself in the sea of his eyes and, without thought, I lean into the gentle touch of his fingers. His thumb grazes the slope of my jaw.

"It was for me too," I admit to both him and myself.

Atticus's smile is slow to come, but when it stretches wide across his face, it's as if I'm standing directly under the sun. "Yeah?"

I duck my head and look away, slipping from his tentative grasp and giving a shy nod. What are you doing, Winter? You're only making this harder for yourself. Don't fall for his charm.

"I'm, uh, glad you think so too." I cast him a sidelong glance and follow his hand as it ruffles his hair. "So, about last night...."

"It was nothing," I blurt out, my voice slightly raised. "I mean, not nothing. Just... I don't want to make a big deal out of it or anything. It's just sex, right? And we're married," I ramble on despite the screaming voice in my head yelling at me to stop. "Married people have sex all the time. For babies and also for pleasure. And I'm literally not going to stop talking if you don't step in and shut me up—"

And so he does.

Bending at the waist and rising from his chair, Atticus presses a chaste kiss against my lips. The featherlight touch works. My unruly tongue checks itself, and I release a sigh of relief as he retreats.

"I get the feeling I shouldn't have brought it up," Atticus teases. Though as I open my eyes to see his flush, I also smell his embarrassment.

"Maybe another time?" I offer in consolation, reaching out to pat his hand. "I'm not good at talking." *Not with you, anyway.*

He smiles and captures my hand. "Right. Letters are our things."

"And flowers," I joke and instantly regret it as Atticus's smile lights up the room.

You're leading him on. You're leading yourself on. Stop, Winter.

But I'm not sure I can.

His fingers curl around mine and bring my knuckles to his lips, his smile hardly lessening.

"And flowers," he whispers.

+++

I'm left to my own devices upon arriving at the Adolphus manor with Atticus promising to be no more than fifteen minutes as he heads up the main staircase to meet Xander. Zoelle is there to greet us, but given her flustered state, I shoo her back to whatever task she was handling. She smiles gratefully and dashes off to finish giving notes to the catering staff.

Once everyone is out of earshot and eyesight, I study the house's layout.

Perhaps this information will sate my mother. Doubtful, but my other option consists of sharing my conversation with Atticus about the Wselfwulfs true nature. And while I hope she will be as horrified as me, I wonder how far her sympathies will go.

I begin with the first floor, cataloging each room in a counterclockwise fashion.

"Hey, what are you doing over here?" I spin around, my hand sailing to my heart as I stare at Callie. I close the door I'd been opening.

"Just exploring," I explain. Callie accepts my answer with a smile. Thank goodness she doesn't possess any heightened senses or both my scent and heartbeat would give me away.

"Zoelle asked if we could finish lighting the candles in the open rooms for tonight."

I smile back, the ends of my lips holding more taut than natural. "Of course, let's go."

We tackle the billiard room first where a bartender, waiter, and card dealer are setting up their respective stations and making small talk with one another. Callie gives them all a short passing smile, then brandishes a box of matches at me.

A pretty gold candelabra wound like a winding tree branch is placed in each of the three windows that span the room.

"You look nice," she comments, striking a match.

"Thank you."

My dress is a black fit-and-flare with embellished gold bars streaking down it. The bars stop at various lengths, and for whatever reason, it gives the impression of an upside-down skyline. I secured my hair up for this dress, with a few choice curling tendrils left down to frame my face.

Callie's donned a more casual outfit. Her dress is a midnight blue that bears only her shoulders to the cold. Underneath the short dress, she wears black leather leggings. They go well with her black booties. The entire outfit suits the Inuit woman who comes off as a bit of a tomboy to me. Though her smoky eye makeup and slick ponytail do give her a sultry edge.

"You look nice too. Happy New Year, by the way."

Callie gives a short laugh and finishes lighting the first candelabra. "Happy New Year to you too. Did you two do anything last night?"

I turn and head to the next window, folding my arms around my middle before I answer. "Dinner at Nove."

"Was it nice?" she asks politely.

"It was."

Callie smirks at my short answer. "Zoelle mentioned that Atticus and Xander were talking, do you know what about?"

The question is innocent enough, but there's a touch of too much indifference in the warrior's tone to make me believe it. I coolly take the box of matches from her with a genial smile and walk over to the last candelabra set while she finishes off the middle piece.

Perhaps with Callie, I can scrounge up some information worthy of my mother and father's appetite, something that is more useful than my observations of the alpha's home.

"About the Wselfwulfs."

I let my eyes pass the room surreptitiously, enough so to catch Callie's attention as I intend. She gives a brief nod of acknowledgment, waiting until I finish so we can leave the room together.

"What about the Wselfwulfs?" Callie's voice is all business.

"About solutions and ways to increase the borders patrol." The doorbell rings, announcing a new guest. Callie grabs my arm and pulls me into one of the several closed-off rooms on the first floor.

"Spill," she demands, crossing her arms over her chest and looking every bit the warrior she was bred to be, even all done up like this.

I lick my lips, hesitating as I search for the right words. I don't want Callie to provide me with too much information, but too little and my "loyalties" will be called into question again by my mother.

"When we had dinner, Atticus and I spoke about the differences between the Blanc and Wselfwulf pack."

Callie snorts and arches a brow. "Is there?"

At her derisive delivery, I bristle. "Yes, in fact, there are," I say, my voice crisp. "For starters, we don't allow our wolves to win other people's property or family members in fighting rings. We honor lycan tradition by respecting the established hierarchy and honoring the moon with quarterly feasts. And," I continue, wavering only a half second, "we would never stoop so low as to kill the wolves who wish to leave our pack."

My last statement makes me sick inside, for it isn't true at all. We do hunt down those who dare leave the pack, rationalizing such action by the need for secrecy with our most guarded of secrets. Swallowing past the lump in my throat, I tilt up my nose and raise an eyebrow at Callie.

She doesn't look apologetic, her standoffish posture still in prime form.

"No offense, but as far as I've seen, there isn't a lot of 'gray area' in the lycan world. You're either traditional or not, and those who trend toward the former are getting... desperate. I witnessed firsthand how people react when they fear they're losing the foundation of their life. It isn't kind."

Her brown eyes sharpen on some faraway point. There is no doubt in my mind she recalls said people right now. I glance away, my brow furrowing in response to her words.

"I don't think this is as black and white as you say, but that's a discussion for another time," I tell her.

She turns her solemn regard back to me. A smirk slowly crawls upon her darkly painted lips. "You remind me of Zoelle," Callie says. Her head cocks to the side, and the smirk softens around its edges. "Maybe because of your rank. Being the beta goes hand and hand with a certain type of compassion that's alluring. You're personable without even having to try, which is a lot like Zoelle, except you're far more... diplomatic than her."

Laughter and greetings ring out from the foyer after the doorbell rings again, but we both ignore the jovial commotion.

"And whose qualities do you share as the fifth? Quinn?"

Callie laughs and leans back against the dresser. It jostles at the unexpected force of her movement, but Callie pays the noise no mind. "Yes and no. We're both unafraid to be blunt, but I'm not nearly as colorful as Quinn." Brown eyes narrow in their regard of me. "I see bits of Irina in you too. Although I didn't know her well, there was always an elusive quality to her personality. Something hidden."

I color and once again am relieved that Callie doesn't possess any lycan abilities.

"You think I'm hiding something?"

The breathy quality of Callie's laugh sets my nerves on edge. She regards me thoughtfully, taking her time as she does so. It is the epitome of unnerving.

"I think there's more to you than meets the eye." My muscles lock up at the casual observer and the former warrior notices. "Is there something you're hiding?"

My features draw together in a show of consternation, as I decide to give her a half-truth. "I wasn't raised to be an open book. That's not how you survived in the Blanc pack."

I'm tempted to say more and defend myself, but I bite my tongue. All of this sharing of information is having an unexpected side effect—the Adolphus pack bonds are winding around me once more.

It's a curious thing, for although Callie is a soulmark, she isn't a lycan. Nonetheless, her presence in the pack must be substantial for a non-lycan to summon the pack bonds up like this.

"I get that. More than the others probably do," Callie confesses, her shoulders sagging downward as she frowns at the ground. "When I belonged to the Wardens of Starlight, they taught me to be strong and smart. They taught me to hate the supernatural and how to kill all number of things. But what was most important to the wardens was loyalty. The fact that I left them for Keenan was unacceptable."

I worry my bottom lip, eyeing this more vulnerable side of Callie with veiled astonishment. "But he's your soulmark."

She gives a one-shoulder shrug and meets my eyes again. "I'm sure that made it worse. My decision ruined my father and brought shame to my family, but I think, at the very least, my brother understood. Him and a few close friends. Maybe even my mentor...."

Callie trails off, her gaze going distant once more with that cutting focus. I shift my weight from foot to foot, taking in her story. Then she gives a brisk shake of her head, her long ponytail whipping to one side. Our eyes meet, and a sparkle of something I cannot place twinkles in her chocolate eyes.

"I made my choice, and I wouldn't do it any other way if I had the chance," comes her matter-of-factly response. Callie rolls her shoulders back and crosses one ankle over the other. She's the picture of confidence and self-assurance.

"Which was to join the pack?" I'm uncertain as to why I ask the question with such confusion coating my words.

Callie smirks. "Yep. I like to think of myself as a sort of generic brand she-wolf. I'm a great fighter, and with my bracers on, I'm a real challenge, even to some of the higher-ranking lycans here."

I glance at her bare neck and wrists pointedly, then dip my questioning gaze to her ankles. If she is wearing these "bracers" now, I can't determine where they are.

"Bracers?"

Another chime of the doorbell enters in response. Callie lightens her lean and twists her head in interest to the door.

"Callie?" I ask, drawing her regard back to me. If I can make her to tell me what they are....

"It's a product of the Wardens of Starlight. They're given to our fighters because it enhances our speed and strength, which lets us go up against supernatural opponents more evenly. I don't use them as often now though," she continues, her eyebrows slanting together harshly and her nose wrinkling. "Keenan doesn't like me out in the field because I'm technically human, even if we make a great team."

More laughter sounds from the foyer, and several greetings and cheers arise from the group. Callie steps away from the dresser and passes me a smile.

"We should probably finish that last room," she says.

"You're right," I agree.

This new information for my parents will hopefully appease them, and maybe even draw their focus away from the Adolphus pack for a time as they look into it. Better still is that their ire with me won't be taken out on Juniper.

Not yet at least.

"Winter." My name is quiet on her tongue, and her fingertips brush the back of my arm. I pause midstep in my exit to toss a look over my shoulder. Her arms are dropped to her back pockets, and her features smoothed to something more open and tender. "I just want to say, everyone is happy you're here, and we're all glad to see how happy Atticus is too."

I smile back, my throat bobbing up and down erratically as I swallow the sudden emergence of my guilt. "Thank you."

"About what you said earlier, the information Atticus is bringing Xander? Thanks for sharing that too. I haven't been in the pack long, but I'm not blind. I see what this war—for lack of a better word—has done to the pack. They're really stretched thin here trying to protect the town as a whole, not just the wolves. So, thank you," she rambles on again, a touch of rosy red coming to cross her silky tan skin. "I'm sure the intel will help in some way. Maybe Xander will finally see the light and do things my way after their talk," she jokes.

The hair at the back of my neck comes to stand on end. "And what is 'the light'?"

Callie's smirk cuts across her face. "Bring the fight to them," she says, leaning in as she delivers her words. She laughs at my small recoil, then pats my arm a bit too roughly as she passes me. "Come on, we should go."

She's out of my reach before I can stop her departure. I follow after her, my dread at the news undeniable. If the packs fights, it's clear which side my parents will favor... but that's knowledge only I'm privy to.

People are filing through the front door in pairs and threes, squeezing in past each other and passing off their coats. They're all dressed up for the night and wear eager smiles that reach from ear to ear. The coil of dread in my stomach tightens and spirals up to my lungs.

If the packs fight, my intel will do just as my parents wish and bring down the Adolphus pack.

"Hey!" The masculine voice that sounds behind me does not belong to Atticus. It's far too roughened to match Atticus's smooth cadence.

"Hey yourself," Callie responds, treading up the stairway to meet her soulmark, Keenan, halfway.

I can't take my eyes away from them. The way Keenan's large frame stalks down the steps to meet her. How Callie skips two at a time to reach him.

His hands find her hips, and her lips seek his lips for a sweet kiss.

A couple passes by me, moving confidently down the hall. They break my reverie, but my eyes quickly dart back toward—

Atticus.

Callie and Keenan have swiftly moved down the stairs, and in their place stands Atticus. He looks so handsome with his hair smoothed back in tamed waves and the navy button-down shirt he wears fits like a glove. He smiles, and weakly I return it.

There's no time to dwell on what I'll have to do with Callie's information. The night is meant to be a celebration, and the pack will be looking to its leaders to take their cues from tonight. And with the Adolphus pack bonds continuing to encircle me, I can't afford to let on to my discontent.

"Did you have a good talk?" I ask Atticus as he comes up to me. I push my smile to be a little brighter.

"I did," he says. "Do you want to grab a drink?"

I heave a sigh of relief and am already walking past Atticus when I respond. "God, yes."

+++

My glass isn't empty the entire night. I'm pulled through groups of people, meeting the full breadth of the pack, all the while with Atticus's guiding hand on my back. I've never seen so many happy people at once, who are genuinely pleased to be in each other's presence.

Some lycans leave at the hour, only to be replaced by a new set some fifteen minutes later. Patrols don't stop for the holidays apparently.

I get lost in the good tidings swirling around me and thrumming through me like a second heartbeat through the pack bonds. The wolves aren't just pleased to be in each other's presence. Word of Zoelle's pregnancy has reached their ears, and it causes a far greater celebration among those present.

Atticus tugs me into his side and places a lazy kiss next to my ear before taking in my scent. His smile rises up against the sensitive skin of my temple, and I find myself doing the same. The aroma of his cologne is addictive.

"Are you having a good time?"

I nod and rest my head against his muscular chest, breathing in his scent as well. The wolf inside me revels in a content shiver. Atticus smells of home and pack to my drunken nose, and nothing can be a better distraction than this.

"Yes," I murmur.

The doorbell rings and several heads turn, including mine. It's late, and any lycan arriving at this hour will have surely entered without preamble. A tingle of anticipation darts up my spine.

"Is it the witches?" I ask, turning to meet crystalline blue eyes.

Atticus shrugs and gives my hip a squeeze. "Maybe," he answers and bends down to kiss me.

My heart skips a beat at the sweet pressure, and I lean in with equal measure. A barely there growl of appreciation rumbles from Atticus. His arm drags me up against him, and our kiss becomes far less innocent.

"Ahem!"

I break away, startled to find Quinn standing before us. Her usual cheery disposition is nowhere to be seen. "You have guests. Come to the front door."

Atticus and I spare each other a worrisome glance before he takes my hand in his and leads me to the front door. I suck in a sharp breath upon laying eyes on them. My cousin Lucy and Knox Bernard. Her smile cuts like a knife as she shoves her coat at Ryatt. Two suitcases sit behind them.

"Hello, Winny."

IV

The world had not known magic so dark since the resurrection of the dead… and only the Blanc pack knew the truth behind it.

Across the world, the lycan community howled its outrage and demanded answers from one another. How? Why? Aggression teemed between already squabbling packs, and when no explanation could be provided, they tore at each other's throats.

Such was the pain caused by the hex that brother would fight brother and sister would fight sister in their desperate quest for understanding.

The Blancs stood solemn and resolute throughout the turmoil. They became a pillar of the lycan community, an example of strength and fortitude during the time of crisis. Word spread they planned to seek out the cause of their newfound inabilities.

No matter how far they must travel. No matter how long they must search. They swore it their pack's goal to do so.

Little did the lycan community know they would be searching in their own backyard.

+++

Day in and day out they scoured the forest for Merida.

But the witch became a phantom of the forest. Her scent lingered in places unusual. Her laughter cackled from both near and far. The pack did not relent, but their spirits waned further with their failure.

Their ire turned toward the family in charge.

And in return, the family pressed down their will upon them until they fell to their knees in submission. Edmund Blanc had made known that in order to survive and thrive, meant to *obey* without question.

The fruitless search continued until the winds of change swept by once more on a balmy spring night breeze.

+++

Merida was lost inside of herself. More specifically, she was lost to the Darkness she had invited in.

No longer did she have a grasp on the reality around her. The thoughts and emotions that managed to break through the Darkness left her reeling.

She had done a terrible thing. But what was worse was her enjoyment of the pain she had inflicted upon so many others. *Perhaps*, she thought, in one of her more lucid moments staggering through the forest, *perhaps I deserve this endless torment and wandering.*

Merida had been within the pack's reach upon several occasions, but at the mere inkling of her guilt and willingness to surrender, the Darkness stole her away. They called her a phantom. A ghost. A wicked spirit. Merida agreed on all accounts.

She lost track of time. Until one morning, on the verge of summer's crowing heat, she strayed too close to the village's edge and saw what she should not.

A man on bended knee, his hands reverently upon a woman's belly.

Luc.

Merida shuddered at the sight. This wasn't supposed to be. Merida had not corrupted her body and soul to see this pack move on so lightly. And they would. She could see it. The Darkness swept across her vision like a cloudy film, distorting the figures before her and bringing about a vision—a vision of Merida weakening and the pack capturing her. How they would torture the curse's reverse from her mouth and destroy the moonstone that bound them.

Merida's vision began to clear only to retch at the sight of Luc and his soulmark's tender embrace. Spiteful and hateful notions trickled into her mind like the murmur of a secret lover only to be disturbed by a cool breeze that swirled unnaturally around her ankles.

"Tread carefully, witch," a silken voice commanded. "You have offended me once already with your malevolent spirit and magic."

Merida shuddered anew at the celestial goddess at her side. Whereas the Darkness inside of her stirred to life, tempted by the powerful aura wafting off the goddess.

"Your children should tread carefully," Merida murmured, her eyes unable to leave the sight of her former lover, not that she could withstand to look at the goddess full-on. Her ethereal light would no doubt blind Merida. "Their very presence offends me."

The air thinned as Merida took a breath. She wheezed in her efforts to stay standing.

"You've become arrogant," the goddess mused, "among other things. Sometimes I forget how fickle you mortals can be. How easily you are swayed by your emotions. But you have gone much too far, witch."

The goddess waited for Merida's reply. Her agate eyes swept the terrain. The goddess stood as tall and as immovable as one of this earth's mountains. It was rare that the Moon Goddess set foot among her chosen children's home. Her place was high up in the sky where she could watch and care for them from afar. It was further rare that she interfered in the goings on of her children. But this… this was a heinous crime.

"Or not enough," the witch said.

Merida's words came out sluggish. Her head was clouding with menacing shadows, and the lack of air in her lungs brought on a strong feeling of disorientation. But above all else, there was a stabbing pain in her heart as she continued to study the lycan pair.

The Darkness pressed to take control and confront the goddess. Or better yet, taunt the celestial spirit with its knowledge and the far reaches of its own powers. It was not common for a vessel to so willingly take on its festered roots, but this witch had a wealth of untapped potential that made it the perfect host.

"How is it a witch of your talent could succumb to the clutches of such maleficence?" the goddess mused aloud. Her all-seeing eyes passed over the ragged witch, a wrinkle jointing up her nose at the scent she carried. "It rots you from the inside out. You will not survive much longer, nor can you hide from my children forever."

"Do you think he loves her?" Merida asked. She still grappled for control and the ability to stand—to breathe—and found herself losing the fight on both ends. But this question needed to be answered.

Yes, the Darkness whispered savagely into her mind.

"Of course," the goddess replied. "They're incomplete without the other. Did you truly believe your trifling affair could surmount their destiny?"

The last thought Merida had was that she had… and then the Darkness unfurled in her eyes and veins. Pools of obsidian glanced sideways at the goddess before they sharply spun frontwards at the glaring radiance surrounding her being. A sneer lit upon the witch's face.

"There is still work to be done," the witch wheezed.

"Is your lust for revenge not satisfied?"

The earth beneath them turned gray. "I am insatiable."

"You are a plague."

The witch did not deny it. "Do you intend to interfere with my work?"

The moment stretched long between them, with the goddess closing her eyes in thought. She stayed this way for some time, weighing her decision.

"Mine is not the only agenda to consider," she said, eyes still closed. Then the goddess drifted out of sight as if she was merely an illusion. The atmosphere regained its volume, and Merida sucked in a deep breath, recovering herself.

There was much work to be done before the next full moon. Merida only hoped the moonstone could withstand another curse.

PROVE IT

- Chapter 10 -

For the first time in a long while, I don't know what to do. Staring at Lucy, dressed in killer thigh-high boots and a black, long-sleeve bodycon dress, makes my blood boil. Without thought, I take a step forward, sizing up her attire once more. Her hair is blown out in voluminous curls. Her makeup is worn to entice.

This isn't some paltry house call. This drop-in has been planned. But for how long has it been planned?

At last my gaze shifts to Knox. The dark-haired man only has eyes for me. I tense under his regard, then feel the comforting weight of Atticus's hand curling around my hip. Lucy steps forward. Her most winning smile in place.

Think of this as motivation. We'd hate to have to become more creative in our efforts to ensure your promises are kept.

I take in a steadying breath, pasting on my own gracious smile. *What have you done, Mother?*

"Happy New Year," Lucy greets as she closes the last few feet between us. Her nails dig into my upper arms as she tugs me gently forward and bequeaths a kiss upon each of my cheeks.

"Happy New Year," I reply, far less enthusiastically. Knox inches closer, his eyes darting around the room and taking inventory. "And to you, Knox."

Knox turns his regard to me and tips his chin as he responds. "Happy New Year, Winter."

"To what do we owe the pleasure?" Ryatt remarks.

I almost startle at the sound of his voice, forgetting his presence almost entirely. Ryatt wears an off-putting grin that is stuck someplace between impish and menacing.

Lucy releases me from her talons and brushes past me effortlessly. With her swinging hips, she gently knocks into me on her way to Atticus. I watch her rest a hand on his chest to lean up and brush her lips across each of his cheeks as well. My wolf snarls at her blatant disregard, but I rein back its golden rage before it can enter my vision.

Atticus colors. To the untrained eye, his flush might come across as his embarrassment, but those with a lycan nose can scent his spike of indignation at the slight to me. He takes a full step back, crossing his arms over his broad chest as he regards the two wolves.

"We're here to protect Winter," Knox answers Ryatt.

"What?"

"Excuse me?"

Atticus and I choke out our exclamations in unison, and so it falls to Ryatt to remain the tactful representative.

"Why don't you show the Blancs upstairs to speak privately about this matter?" Ryatt suggests. "I'll fetch Xander and let him know you've gone up."

"You're too kind," Lucy drawls and confidently walks past Atticus and up the stairs. I gape at her manner, then briefly lock my still stunned eyes onto Atticus. He gives the barest of shrugs and follows after her.

I'm about to do the same when Knox's interest in the party catches my attention. All notions of shock are plowed away as a fierce wave of protective instinct floods through me.

"Upstairs," I command as I stride over to him. Knox continues to study the party. "Now."

His lips press minutely together, bringing out the subtle sharpness to his cheekbones and making his hawkish eyes all the more steely. Nevertheless, he accedes to my command and strolls to the bottom of the staircase. Instead of ascending, he stops and turns to face me. I shuffle back a step when he leans forward and holds out an arm to me.

"Shall we?" he asks.

Years of grooming flood through my system, urging me to rest my hand upon the crook of his elbow, but I leave my hand twitching mutinously at my side.

"I'll bring up the rear," I decline, my voice steady and tranquil despite the incandescent anger building up inside of me at my parents' duplicity.

Do they not think the threat against June enough motivation for me? Or are Lucy and Knox here to do more than keep me in check?

There's no denying the friction that rides our group as we climb the stairs and slip away from the party. It builds as the sound of our footsteps outweigh that of the chatter and music below. I wonder who will break the unnerving silence first—Atticus and I with some generic small talk, or Lucy and Knox with some ambiguous comment meant to rile us up.

It happens to be neither.

Footsteps rapidly sound on the staircase behind us, their quick work of the steps amplified in our mute standoff. Xander appears a moment later, striding up to take the lead of our group. His face belays no emotion, but as he passes, I catch the ire in his evergreen eyes.

"Let's chat, shall we?" Xander says. "There's a spare bedroom down the hall that will do perfectly."

I spy Lucy's eye roll and the slight downward tilt of Knox's lips, but neither breathe a word of protest. Atticus takes the lead to hold open the door for each of us to pass through.

"My brother tells me you came here to protect Winter. I assure you that is unnecessary," Xander says once the door is shut behind him. "We have the situation under control."

Lucy snorts. "If you had it under control in the first place, Winter never would have been harmed," she points out, eyes gliding across the room with keen eyes. "My alphas are not pleased."

"Winter's parents and your pack are free to aid us in dissuading the Wselfwulfs from their senseless vendetta. As you can see, their thirst for blood to mend what is only their wounded pride knows no bound."

Knox gives a short shake of his head. "The Blanc pack must stay uninvolved for the sake of the Celestial Court. We can't be seen playing favorites with Winter now connected so intimately to your pack."

"Even when the Wselfwulfs are so clearly in the wrong?" Xander fires back.

Knox smirks. "Are they?"

A snarl comes from Atticus but is cut short abruptly by Xander stepping forward toward the pair of Blanc lycans. Lucy mirrors his movement.

"Settle down, boys. There's no need to get so testy. We're all interested in the same thing after all—the safety and welfare of our dear, Winter." Lucy smile grows as she speaks. "Leave her to us, and you and your capable pack may focus on this... 'misunderstanding' with the Wselfwulfs."

+++

Leaving early will raise the eyebrows of many, so we don't.

Instead, Atticus and I play babysitter to my cousin and Knox. I cut off my drinking, no longer indulging in the high of being in close contact to Atticus or my new pack mates. A headache beats at the back of my head. I fear it won't fade until Lucy and Knox leave.

For a while, the two stick near our side as we introduce them to the pack. Both are on their best behavior, making idle small talk and charming, self-deprecating jokes. The Adolphus pack eats it all up, pleased to think they've made a good impression with wolves from such a renowned pack.

It makes me want to hurl.

The only anchor to my sanity and calm is Atticus by my side. Lingering kisses behind my ear and the heavy pressure of his hand on my hip somehow give me the focus I need to play the role of beta well. At some point, his hand curls further inward to splay possessively across my abdomen.

The action earns ireful looks from both Lucy and Knox. I relish in it. Until the two share a meaningful look and split up.

"Atticus, do you mind keeping Lucy company for a bit?" I ask. My eyes follow Knox's back as he maneuvers through the crowd to the back of the room where a buffet is laid out. "I'm just—"

Smooth lips press against my cheek, cutting off my prepared excuse. They claim my lips next, sucking at the bottom before delivering a tender nip.

"Go," Atticus says, his words pitched low for only me to hear.

I cast my eyes to his own and marvel in their likeness to glacial ice. His eyes are a shade of blue not quickly forgotten— rich in color and bright as the day.

Yet last night they had darkened to a dangerous storm, with lycan lightning spearing down through each iris. At the sight of our unwanted guests, they mirror a tempest at bay.

"You're sure?"

He nods. "I'll make sure Lucy doesn't get into any trouble."

We part, and as I trail Knox my hand drifts to my slightly swollen bottom lip. *You're playing with fire and already getting burned.*

It shouldn't take me as long as it does to reach the buffet table where Knox lingers, but a handful of groups suck me into their conversation as I attempt to weave through the crowd. My frustration builds when I finally manage to disengage and find that Knox is moving on.

With my senses on high alert, I do my best to act natural and keep the rhythm of my heart to a reasonable pace. The last thing I want is to alert anyone of my anxiety and wariness in regards to my old pack.

"Where did you go?" I mutter to myself, pretending to scan the table from end to end while I search for Knox's recognizable dark hair.

"Talking to yourself?"

I nearly jump out of my skin at the teasing lilt of Quinn's voice but settle for a hand over my heart. "Quinn, hi."

"So, what's up with the two newcomers?" To the point, as usual. I put on a smile, one reserved for subterfuge at family functions and soirees.

"They're here on business of a sort," I say, waving a hand dismissively as my wandering gaze treads back over the sea of heads. "And they've passed on seasonal greetings from the Blanc pack—"

Quinn snorts, snagging a glass of champagne from a passing waiter. "Bullshit."

"Excuse me?"

Quinn flips her sunny blonde hair over her shoulder and arches an eyebrow in disbelief. "They brought suitcases to wish our pack a happy new year?" Another snort, this one followed by a rather sharp laugh.

My cheeks deign to flame in response. "I'm sure they view their… extended presence a gift."

"I bet," she replies, sipping from the champagne flute with natural grace. Her eyes flick to something in the crowd, but her clear blue eyes are back on me in a second. "Why are you following him?"

"I'm not—" Her second brow raises, and I let out an irritated huff. "Fine. I'm following him," I hiss and take a step closer to her. With my voice pitched low, almost to a whisper, I fill her in on the circumstances. At least, as much as I'm willing to share. "They found out about the Wselfwulf attack."

"Oh." Quinn's forehead furrows in thought. "I suppose that's cause for a house call," she mutters. "But that doesn't explain why you're following dark-hair guy."

"He's… an old beau."

"An old beau? Who says that?" Before I can defend my choice of words, Quinn barrels on. "Also, don't you think it's going to look weird if you're following around your old boyfriend? You're married. Remember?"

"Yes, I remember," I snap, my patience wearing thin. I swallow, casting a quick look over my shoulder. He's still out of my sights, and my stomach gives an uneasy turn. He could be anywhere in this house. "I don't trust him. He was a suitor my parents had lined up for me in case things with Atticus somehow didn't work out. Knox is the kind who likes to make trouble, and I don't know any other way to keep him under control other than to follow him."

My response comes out more heated than I expect, but the half-truth seems to work. Quinn's eyes widen in understanding before they narrow on some point beyond me.

"I see," she says, her voice like silk. "Don't worry about him. I'll make sure he behaves and keep an eye on him. You said they were staying? Do you know for how long?"

"They are, but I don't know for how long."

A twisted smile slips onto Quinn's rosy lips. "Hmm, I suppose you're taking your cousin in?" At my nod, her smile grows larger. "Well then, Knox should stay here. I've been *dying* to use some of Ryatt's new surveillance equipment. Huh, they really are a present in disguise, aren't they?"

I laugh at the abrupt train of thought Quinn latches onto and watch a mischievous twinkle light up her eyes. "Thank you."

She shrugs. "I wasn't kidding when I said you shouldn't worry about Knox. Your cousin on the other hand…."

My head whips to the direction of Atticus's last position. He's only a couple of yards from his original spot, and hanging on his arm is Lucy. The wolf in me snarls its anger, and I bite my tongue so as not to echo its sentiments.

"You go," Quinn says. "I saw Knox slip out and think he might enjoy some company."

She departs with hips sashing side to side, drawing more than one appreciative glance from several males of the pack. I make my way back into the crowd, avoiding the eyes of those who wish to converse and keeping a polite, thin-lipped smile on as I close the distance between my cousin and me.

"You two look like you're enjoying yourselves," I say, interrupting whatever conversation they were having. Atticus is flushed. Lucy oozes satisfaction. "But I must confess, after last night"—I spare Atticus a not-so-innocent smirk—"I'm too tired to continue. We'd best collect our things and go."

Atticus sighs, his relief palpable, and he attempts to dislodge Lucy from his arm. She doesn't budge, her smile is frozen in place. "Is that so? Well, I don't see why you can't go home and we remain."

I step closer and channel my mother as I stare down my nose at my cousin. "Because I said so."

+++

We catch a ride from a pack mate to get home safely. The journey has all the potential to be awkward, but Atticus remains cool and chatty with our designated driver, Ted. Yet when we pile into our home, the staved-off awkwardness surges forward full force.

"I'll show you to your room," Atticus says once we divest ourselves of our outerwear and shoes. He grabs Lucy's roller suitcase and heads upstairs with us in tow. "You'll be staying in this bedroom," he says, stopping at the far end of the hallway.

It's conveniently the farthest away from his bedroom.

"Thank you," Lucy says, her voice dripping like saccharine honey. "I won't forget your hospitality."

I clear my throat to draw Lucy's sultry regard from Atticus. "I'm sure you're exhausted from your spontaneous trip. Why don't you take a shower and head to bed, you look like you need it."

The smirk she wears so proudly vanishes as she pins me with her chocolate-colored eyes. "How right you are, cousin. I'll just jump in the shower and prepare for bed," she says, pushing the guest room door open. "Once I'm done, you should stop in. It felt like we barely got to talk at the party, and there's so much for us to catch up on."

There's little left to the imagination with her parting words. And by the glint in her eye, she is more than aware of the gauntlet she has thrown down. I issue a stiff nod.

"That sounds lovely. I'll come around in fifteen minutes or so."

An artificial smile lights up Lucy's face. "See you then."

With the door shut in our faces, I release a laden sigh. Atticus's fingers graze my wrist before slipping into my palm. "Are you—"

He doesn't get to finish. The hand he reached so blindly for moves with a mind of its own to cover his mouth. My hair momentarily blocks my vision as I give a sharp shake of my head. Blue eyes widen at me in shock and amusement. Atticus's lips twitch beneath the pressure of my hand just before I remove it.

"Let's go to bed," I say.

Atticus follows the path I mark with my eyes between Lucy's door and the far end of the hall. Both of his eyebrows rise in response, but when I go, he follows. Only when his bedroom door is securely closed behind us, I release a ragged sigh.

I barely give the makeup of his room a second glance, almost immediately turning on the balls of my feet to face him head-on. "We have to sleep together," I say.

The words don't register at first for either of us and then...

"Excuse me?" Atticus blurts out, his face turning scarlet much like mine.

"I mean—no, not like that." A hysterical laugh builds up in my throat, bursting out and urging my blush to extend across my body. "What I meant to say was, we should... sleep *here* together. Not with each other. Not again."

Another laugh, this one earning a grimace in response from Atticus.

"I didn't mean it like that either," I rush on, forcing the wild rampage of my heart to slow to something more reasonable. "I just don't want Lucy to know we don't share a bedroom," I finally manage to get out.

The red recedes from his cheeks, but only a small amount. As I take in a steadying breath, I can't help but note his lingering embarrassment. It stings my sensitive nose.

"You can stay here while your cousin is around," Atticus says, his eyes pinned to some point past my head. "Although, I'm not sure how you'll explain the existence of your room. Your scent's all over it."

I press my hands down my skirt—an old nervous habit of mine—to ease the pressure I feel squeezing around us. "I'll keep it locked after I move some of my things out of it."

We catch each other's eyes and still. "Do you need any help?"

My mouth opens and closes several times before I shake my head. His offer is more than I deserve. "No. I'll make do. And, Atticus?" I reach out tentatively and brush my fingers against the back of his hand. "We can scratch the last of my ramblings from this conversation… sex isn't off the table. Not that I'm putting it on the table, I just…." I swallow thickly and push on. "It's not entirely off the table."

Atticus's fingers entwine with mine, his eyes belying the hunger I know to be seeded inside both of us. Raising our joined hands between us, he bends and presses a kiss against my emerald ring.

"Good," he says, his voice husky. A different heat floods my system as I stare into his eyes. "I'll be here if you need anything."

The kiss that follows is both expected and not. Everything about Atticus is already so familiar to me. The way his hands pull me in closer. How meticulously his lips caress my own. But each union between us, big and small, is never the same, nor is the desire that ensnares me so ruthlessly.

His lips work my mouth open, and tongue and teeth come into play. Goose bumps race across my skin as the memories of last night shift into focus.

Don't do this to your heart, the rational side of my head chimes in as I begin to press into his body.

With regret, the heel of my hand pushes carefully against his sternum in a wordless request for release.

I turn my head just out of reach. "I have to get my things," I whisper against his cheek.

He drags his nose across my jawline before planting a kiss at my temple and nodding. "I'll be here."

I depart with shaky steps and head immediately for my bedroom. I make quick work of it all, shoving an assortment of clothing in a suitcase from my closet and tossing my makeup and toiletries into a large purse. Thankfully, the majority of my most used shoes populate the foyers shoe rack.

With my belongings in hand, I deposit them back in Atticus's room. He's in the en suite bathroom, the shower clearly running. I'll grab the room's key from Atticus later, after I speak with Lucy.

The walk down the hallway feels extraordinarily long, but I'm oddly serene as I gather my resolve. All night I've been left off kilter by Knox and Lucy's presence. I can't afford to be so now in my own home.

I knock before I enter, not giving Lucy the chance to invite me in.

Lucy scowls at my entrance, finishing off tying her robe with a dramatic flare. "You couldn't have waited one more second for me to let you in?"

I ignore her indignation. "You're here to protect *me*?"

A beat of silence passes, and then a small smirk works its way up Lucy's face. "Why, of course. Aunt Adele and Uncle Malcolm were beside themselves with worry—"

"Why are you really here?"

Lucy walks to the room's lone dresser set between a pair of windows. Some toiletries are spread out across its surface, and she takes her time pursuing them before settling on a shiny silver jar.

"You know why we're here," she finally says, not bothering to turn around as she places dots of the jar's contents on her face. A perfume of jasmine fills the room as she rubs the cream into her skin. "Your parents have doubts, Winter. They merely wish us to discover how far gone you really are, or if you've stayed loyal to the pack. Sit."

At this command, she looks over her shoulder to see if I'll obey.

"I'll stand. Atticus doesn't expect me to be long. I assume you have questions to ask on their behalf."

Her eyes narrow, and Lucy turns to face me fully. "Have you consummated your marriage?"

"Yes." I hold her regard, keeping my expression blank and offering no further explanation.

"Have you sealed the soulmark?"

"No."

Lucy arches a brow. "Is that so?"

"Mother would know. The bonds I still keep with the pack would surely break after a commitment like that."

"Maybe," she says, accompanied by a nonchalant lift of one shoulder. "Maybe not. There aren't many cases like yours to go by since nobody in the pack would dare have the gall to spit in the face of our traditions as you have. And if you're already sleeping with him...." Our glares collide, and the room fills with the vibrancy of our angry. I take a step forward as Lucy leans against the dresser.

"You have no idea what you're talking about," I snap.

Lucy bats her lashes at me. "Who knows what sympathies you've gained for this pack by partaking in such an intimate act. You know as well as I, Winter, that intercourse is just another cord that ties us closer to our pack."

I fold my arms across my chest and stand taller. "I suppose not sleeping with my husband wouldn't raise any flags at all," I say, my heavy sarcasm not delivering the desired results. Lucy rolls her eyes.

"Certainly people would understand if you decided to take things slow. After all, you've only ever been pen pals all these years."

"I'm a *beta* now. The entire pack is watching us. So every move I make I do so carefully, so as not to draw suspicion. I certainly can't afford to slip up."

My words strike a nerve, or something close to it. Lucy's jaw clenches as she sharpens her glare. "Yes, poor Juniper. I would hate to be at the mercy of your actions. Which is why we're here. Nothing untoward will happen to her if you follow your parents' next instructions. Check the front pocket of my suitcase."

I hesitate only a moment before striding over to it. Searching inside the front pocket, I find a small metal flask.

"What is it?" I ask, opening the top and sniffing the contents. It barely contains an odor, with only the slightest hint of floral notes to attach to the liquid inside.

"It's for your fairy friend. Put it in her drink."

I snap my head in Lucy's direction, but she wears a bored expression. "What does it do?"

"It won't kill her, if that's what you're worried about. We certainly don't want to have to worry about cleaning up a body. No, this will just… incapacitate her for a period of time. Your parents believe, with the fairy out of the picture for however brief of time, some resolution might finally occur between the Wselfwulf and Adolphus packs."

I glance back at the flask, my grip tightening around the cold metal. "You want me to *drug* her?"

"We want you to prove your loyalties," Lucy corrects softly. "Think of this as your final test. Do this, and the events to follow will bring this silly little war to an end at last. And then you can return home. Right where you belong."

UNDER PRESSURE

- Chapter 11 -

Morning comes, and Atticus is not in bed. My hand combs over the surface of where he last resided. The warmth of his lycan nature still lingers underneath the covers, and I am loath to move. When the heat begins to fade, I roll and grab my phone from the nightstand. It's been too long since my last conversation with June.

Winter: *Happy new year! How are you? Anything new or exciting happen while I've been away?*

To my relief, three little dots appear on June's side of the screen immediately.

June: *Happy NY!*

June: *<<open image>>*

Her image loads after a swift double tap of my thumb, and June in her outfit from last night, a pretty blue A-line dress, smiles back at me.

June: *Have you talked with your parents recently by chance?*

Dread hits me hard as my fingers stall over the keypad.

June: *They're acting weird. And all of a sudden my parents won't let Toby come over.*

June: *I don't know what's changed.*

June: *:(*

Winter: *I spoke with my mother a few days ago. She was in a mood...*

Winter: *You know how she can get sometimes. Just keep your head down and don't complain.*

June: *Okay*

June: *I guess now isn't the time for you to work your magic with them, huh?*

Winter: *Sorry, Junebird. I'll do my best from over here to smooth things over.*

June: *Thx! You're the best!*

June: *BTW how's Atticus and the new pack?*

Such a simple question and yet my body warms at the thought... before going cold. Whatever goodwill and connects I've built with the pack are sure to go up in flames when they learn of my deceit.

Winter: *They're wonderful.*

June: *Good!!!!*

My phone rings, interrupting our conversation. Mother. My thumb hovers over the green button, every muscle in my body tightening as I waver. At the last moment, I hit ignore, pressing the red phone icon with more force than necessary. It's incredible how the tension immediately slips from my body.

I'll deal with her later.

June: *I've got to go. Mom and I are having lunch with Aunt Lydia. I promise to act like a saint. I'll TTYL.*

Winter: *Love you!*

I toss my phone to the other side of the bed and release a groan. *No. No. No.* What more do my parents want from me? I'll do as they asked and bring them the information sought. But why bring June into this?

Laughter reaches my ears from downstairs. When it sounds again, interrupting my train of thought, I rise from the bed. A short trip to the bathroom later and I set off downstairs toward the source of the noise.

"Good morning," I say as I take in the scene.

Atticus at the stove, making breakfast. Lucy is at the table, coffee in hand and a smug smile on her lips. There is also a vase of flowers.

"Morning," Atticus responds. He flips whatever concoction he's making in the skillet then turns down the heat before walking toward me.

I meet his approach halfway, sliding both arms around his neck to greet him with a kiss as if we've done it a hundred times before. My heart constricts with longing.

"Good morning, cousin," Lucy says, her voice far nearer than expected. Atticus and I pull apart from our chaste kiss, only to find Lucy standing right next to us. With a muffled cough, Atticus takes a significant step back.

I offer a stiff smile in return to her greeting, but Lucy persists. She plants a kiss on either side of my cheek, then returns to her seat.

"How long have you two been up?"

They answer at the same time.

"Maybe, fifteen minutes," Atticus says.

"Half an hour, give or take," Lucy says.

My husband shoots Lucy a pointed look. "I believe my estimate to be more accurate," he corrects her. Lucy doesn't bother to rebut his statement.

Whoops, she mouths to me behind Atticus's back.

With breakfast in hand—a ridiculously large omelet—Atticus gestures to the table. "Let's eat," he says.

He portions out the omelet onto all three of our plates, but his regard keeps sweeping back to the flowers in the middle of the table. As do mine.

"Wherever did you get chrysanthemums at this time of year? I thought they were an autumn flower?" Lucy asks. She cuts herself a small piece of the egg dish and eats it like some aristocrat at an extravagant dinner. Her movements are languid, yet precise, and her eyes never stray from Atticus across the table, a fact we're all privy to.

"I know a woman with a very green thumb, as it would happen." A small smile graces Atticus's mouth, but he remains steadfast in looking anywhere but me. The corner of my mouth twitches upward as well.

"The fairy?" Lucy asks just before popping another piece of breakfast into her mouth.

The corner of my mouth drops as my lips chose instead to weld together. Atticus is not so perturbed by the question, but swallows his food faster, so as not to make Lucy wait for an answer.

"No," he replies. "Someone else. I'd say who, but I want to keep my source under the radar so no one else can use her."

He grins at Lucy then winks at me. The combination is rather devastating on my senses.

"How… cute," Lucy states as she sets down her cutlery and leans back in her seat to observe us. "What's on the agenda for today?"

The table grows silent, and Atticus spares me another look, this one laved in doubt. "Uh, well, unfortunately, I have to start preparing to go back to work soon. But we can show you around today."

"That sounds simply splendid! Although I doubt it will take all day," she says, followed by a hollow. "Goodness, how big is this town anyway?"

"Big enough to explore for the afternoon, at least," I say as I grow wise to her motives. Lucy switches her intent regard to me. Her chocolate eyes hold not a hint of kindness to them as she cocks her head an inch to the left.

"Well then, I'll be sure to call Knox and let him know of our plans. He'll be so happy to get to spend time with you… and Atticus, of course. I'm sure he'll want to know all about how you two are getting along." Lucy tosses her hair over her shoulder and rises. "I better go get ready for the day. Let's leave around one?"

"You're finished eating already?" Atticus replies.

Lucy smiles beatifically back at Atticus. "I've never been one for breakfast. I'll see you in a few hours."

Before she can retreat, Atticus speaks again. "How long do you think you and Knox will be around? I want to make sure the house stays stocked properly?" Atticus asks.

She pauses deliberately. "I assume we'll depart once we can be assured that Winter is no longer a threat." Another false laugh tinkles from her throat. "I mean, once Winter is no longer being threatened. That's all her parents really want."

Lucy leaves the room, her stride confident. Once she's out of earshot, I swivel in my seat to face Atticus.

"I'm sorry. Lucy can be a bit much."

He mirrors my position and scoots his chair closer to me as well.

"Is she always like that?" he asks. Within his eyes, I read his frustration and confusion. "She was a little too friendly this morning. She was at our wedding—she *knows* we're married. So what's with her attitude?"

I attempt nonchalance, feigning an act of self-grooming by picking nonexistent lint from my sleeping pants. "Lucy has always craved being the center of attention. It just so happens her favorite way of taking the spotlight is by getting under my skin, for all to see."

"That's pretty messed up."

"She is a product of her upbringing," I say, my tone light despite the topic. "Her parents always made Lucy and her sister compete for their attention and affection. It just so happens that competitiveness and need for validation bled into other aspects of her life."

"But why focus on you? Or is she like this to every she-wolf in the Blanc pack."

"She's been going after the she-wolves higher ranked than her for several years now. Ever since she fine-tuned her *bite*. However... this past year she has focused on me more so than ever. She said I was too weak for my position as fifth, too passive and empathetic."

"She only says that because she doesn't know what strengths lie in both those qualities as a beta," he responds. His hand comes to rest on mine, the one that still fidgets and fusses with my clothing. "Winter, why are they really here?"

The question is pitched far lower than the rest of what our conversation has been. My heart skips a traitorous beat at the direct line of questioning. I wet my lips.

"They just don't want me getting into any more trouble."

He doesn't believe me. I see it in the way lines creep up near the ends of his eyes and the taut line his jawline makes. "Okay."

My sigh of relief doesn't come until I'm able to extract myself from the table and escape to my old bedroom. Striding to my old dresser, I snatch up *The Language of Flowers* and thumb through the pages until I find chrysanthemum.

It means honesty.

+++

Winter typically loses its luster to me come the days following the new year. Now is no exception. Though the downtown square is adorned in picturesque wreaths of pine and red ribbons, and storefronts embellish their windows with festive novelties and glittering lights, they do not enchant me as they once did.

Several people brave the frigid air to enjoy what's left of the holiday spirit. They link arms with each other to fight the wind and snuggle into their coats and scarves with sappy smiles. I examine every person, looking for the faces and figures of my assailants.

A young man with violence in his eyes.

A lanky lackey.

Someone more beast than man.

Lucy turns into another shop. It's the sixth we've been into, and I roll my eyes heavenward to keep from groaning aloud. Entering in behind her, the scent of cinnamon and mulled wine assaults my nose. It's not unpleasant, but the intensity of the perfumed air instantly makes me sneeze. Behind me, Atticus chuckles, his body pressing lightly into my back as he herds me further inside.

Candles and homemade jewelry are displayed on small tables throughout the shop. My fingers grace the edge of a stand as I meander around. I make sure Lucy is in my sights at all times and well within hearing distance, even though Knox does his best to keep me distracted.

It's become a dance between the four of us. Atticus uses his beta prowess to keep our environment calm and Knox in check. I not-so-subtly redirect and politely dodge Lucy's probing questions away from Atticus. Knox trails after me and makes small talk with me every time Atticus's back is turned. And Lucy revels in it all, pumping out question after question to garner information about the Adolphus pack and our relationship.

I'm sorely tempted to knock her over the head with one of the heftier candles, except I can't. For as all of this dancing around is occurring, I must also act as if it's not. As if I don't know Lucy and Knox's true motives. As if I'm not ultimately a part of their plot.

"I'm feeling a bit peckish," Lucy announces, setting a necklace back on its display. "Doesn't Zoelle own a shop of some kind? It would be so lovely to see her."

Atticus and I share a look, and then he responds. "Sure. It's just a few blocks over."

And so we leave, Atticus and I walking hand in hand a couple of feet behind Knox and Lucy. They seem out of place here, even from behind. Their gait suggests arrogance more than confidence, one that comes off as intimidating if the people avoiding their path is any indication.

"Are you okay?" Atticus asks, slowing our pace even more.

I nod and glance up to see his face full of concern. For a moment, I admire the straight line of his nose and the shallow hollow of his cheeks. His brows are drawn in slightly together, the blue of his eyes clouded with worry.

"I just wish they weren't here," I admit, ducking my head to hide the mixture of emotions crossing my face. "It's unnecessary," I continue, my voice gaining some heat. "My mother just wants to make sure I'm—" I pause and glance up to Atticus. He watches me intently, and I tense at my near slip. "—that I'm doing my *duty*."

I color at what I imply. My words aren't truly false. She does wish for me to fulfill my duty but to the Blanc pack. I'm absolutely sure she will prefer my *wifely* duties to be catered to Knox Bernard rather than Atticus.

"Oh." Atticus colors as well, tugging me along to catch the timer on the street post. Lucy and Knox are still ahead, but I catch Lucy throw an inquisitive glance over her shoulder at our delay. "It's straight ahead!" Atticus calls to them.

With the excuse made, we slow our steps in unison once more. "I'm sorry—"

"You don't have to apologize for them," he interrupts. He squeezes my hand in reassurance and smiles softly at me. Rosy red patches begin to appear in earnest across his cheeks. "I'm sure we'll figure out a way to get the point across."

I return his gentle squeeze with one of my own, laughing at the way the tips of his ears begin to go red. "Come on, let's catch up."

We enter Baudelaire Patisserie and Café a few crucial seconds behind Knox and Lucy. They are already calling an obnoxious amount of attention to themselves with Lucy's loud greeting to Zoelle. The witch looks startled at the focus, but upon seeing us, her shoulders sag in relief.

She excuses herself from a customer after finishing their order and heads our way.

"Just take a seat anywhere. I'll be with you—oh!" Zoelle goes wide-eyed as Lucy plants two exaggerated kisses on either side of her face.

"It's so wonderful to see you! Please, finish up what you were doing. We'll just be over here," Lucy prattles on with her patented sickly sweet smile in place. There's no choice but to follow the overexuberant brunette to the table of her choice. I realize the error of our delay as we take our seats. Knox and Lucy place themselves at opposite ends of the table, forcing Atticus and me to do the same.

"Hi," Zoelle says. She's slightly out of breath but wears a beaming smile as she looks down at us. "This is a nice surprise. Can I get you guys anything? Coffee or a pastry?"

We list off our orders, and Zoelle pops off to put them in before returning.

"How have you been feeling?" Atticus asks, wrapping his arm around her waist and tugging her in to give a sort-of hug. Zoelle laughs and rubs his back affectionately.

"I've been better. My morning sickness is only just starting to go away," Zoelle replies.

"Oh, yes," Lucy chimes in, leaning closer to Atticus to address Zoelle. "I heard about the good news at the party. Congratulations. Your pack seems very excited by the news."

Zoelle smiles brighter. "We're lucky to have such a support system behind us," she admits, her hand going to her lower abdomen fondly.

"So," Lucy drawls in a cheerful tone, "tell me everything. When are you due? How long has everyone known? Are you the only one expecting in the pack?"

The smile on Zoelle's face doesn't falter, her excitement superseding what I know to be obvious—Lucy is fishing for information again.

"July ninth. We just started to tell people because we wanted to wait until the end of the first trimester. Just in case," she explains, moving out of the way as one of her employees comes around and places our orders in front of us. "I'm not aware of any others being pregnant, but I think it would be nice. That way I can go through this with someone else."

Lucy lets out a false laugh that dims Zoelle's smile a touch, and Knox speaks next.

"Do you know if your child will be a witch or lycan?" he wonders aloud. "I've never met a lycan and witch who've produced a child, or heard many stories about such a pairing. Your situation is quite… unique, if you don't mind me saying."

Zoelle takes a step back, effectively stepping out of Atticus's embrace. She levels a sharp smile at Knox, and a second later a tingling sensation ripples across the back of my neck.

"We are unique, but that's the beauty of the soulmark. It doesn't discriminate. We like to think of our union as an example to the rest of the supernatural community," she continues, her head held high. "There's no reason why cross-unions like ours shouldn't be the norm."

Knox takes a long sip of his coffee, his eyes drilling into Zoelle as Lucy lets out another laugh. "That's an interesting take on it," he finally says with an equally cutting smile. "I'll have to share it with my alphas."

"You do that," she says, the magical energy palpable in the room, or at least within our vicinity. My nose twitches uncomfortably, but I hold back the urge to sneeze. "Enjoy."

"Well, isn't she something. She has quite the spark, doesn't she?" Lucy comments before sipping her drink as her gaze flits between Atticus and me. "So, when can we expect little ones from you?"

My tea never reaches my throat. Lucy's well-timed question hits just as the aromatic chamomile passes my lips, only to be spat back in the delicate teacup. Atticus fairs little better, his jaw dropping.

"We're not in any rush," he says, looking to me in panic. Knowing the history of our betrothal, most people of the pack held back asking the question, their tact reaching far beyond Lucy's morals.

"Exactly," I chime in. "We don't have any plans for that. What's going on with you and Jeffrey Terreur? When is he going to propose? You've been together for what feels like ages."

A flush creeps up Lucy's face at my question. Her relationship to Jeffrey Terreur is known throughout the Blanc pack as one of convevience, though her parents vie for it to be more. His rank in the pack is high, and his wallet bigger than most. To secure a match with him—despite his *many* flaws—would be seen as the catch of the season.

Yet at my innocent questions, all vestiges of her niceties drop. Her pretty features draw taut as she attempts to keep some remnants of her facade up while looking elsewhere.

"Anything's possible," Knox remarks as he leans back in his chair. He gives little care to the scent of Lucy's embarrassment. Crossing his arms over his muscular chest, he scans the cafe with little interest until his eyes alight upon me. "Aren't you going to ask after my love life, Winter?"

"Got a girlfriend?" Atticus asks in my stead. Knox slants his gaze Atticus's way. *Oh dear.*

"Nah, man," he replies. "Had a girl, but she dropped me for some poser."

The cavalier shrug Knox delivers after his comment is anything but. My hands form fists in my lap at the mocking knowledge written all over Knox's face. It is insufferable, and for the second time today I wish to have one of the large candles to knock the smirk from *his* face. Or perhaps with my fist. Atticus remains cool, but there is something in his movements that reacts to Knox's jibe.

"Lucky guy," he responds, his blue eyes finding me.

Knox runs his tongue across his teeth, head shaking slowly from side to side. "Something like that."

The ambient chatter of the cafe hardly scratches the surface of the sudden curtain of silence that encases our group. And then Lucy's breathy laugh, so full of contempt, cracks it open.

"Well, aren't we all something else? The married couple with no plans to have children—" Lucy spares me a pointed look beneath half-lowered lashes "—and two sad stories of unrequited love."

I direct my gaze at my full cup of tea, unable to meet Atticus's stare. The truth of Lucy's words stings more than they should.

Atticus asked for honesty, but how can I possibly divulge the Blanc pack's darkest secret? My parents worried only of my commitment to spying on the Adolphus pack. What will they threaten if they think the Blancs' soulmark curse came to light?

Another war.

Another punishment.

"Winter?"

My head snaps up at the address, and I find three sets of eyes on me. Only one shows real concern. "Yes?"

"Are you feeling all right?" I hesitate at Atticus's inquiry.

"Actually, I think I'd like to head home."

"That's a good idea. We'll probably want to change before dinner."

Lucy arches an eyebrow and looks between the two of us, lingering on my ill-covered surprise. "Where are we going out to dinner?"

"Winter and I are. You're welcome to whatever food we have in the house. Or if you prefer, you can stay out and explore with Knox. Maybe grab dinner somewhere," Atticus says, rising. He tosses a twenty down on the table and looks at me expectantly. I stand and maneuver around Knox, taking Atticus's proffered hand.

"Well, then, don't have too much fun, you two. I think Knox and I will explore and grab dinner downtown. Don't worry, I'll find my own way back to your place. No need to wait up," she calls after our retreating forms.

+++

We really do go to an early dinner. No matter how early it is, I'm thankful to be out of the near toxic vicinity of Knox and Lucy as it loosens the knot riding between my shoulders.

"I want you to know I completely agree with what you said earlier," Atticus says as he studies the diner's menu. "I want them to leave as soon as possible too."

I choke back a laugh and hide my smile behind the menu. There's a family to my right who keeps catching my eyes, or rather, their son. He stares unabashedly at my hair. The attention brings a light blush to my cheek. Back in my hometown, the residents are used to the sight. Though this isn't the first time I have received looks in Branson Falls, for some reason, the little boy's stare is unnerving.

"You'd think they were made for each other," Atticus continues, his voice trailing off with a suggestive lilt to the end of his words.

I shrug and nibble on my lower lip. "They're different enough to warrant being awful together," I say.

"I was curious about something... you said they were here to protect you, among other things, but why didn't they ask to see the spot you were attacked today? Didn't they know it happened in the downtown area?"

I'm glad for the shield of my menu as the color fades from my cheeks and my pulse dares to quicken. I take a steadying breath, calming my heart before it's too obvious I'm nervous. "Maybe they plan on doing it a different day?"

"Winter," he says with gentle firmness. The smooth measure of his voice coaxes down my shield, and I spare him a glance beneath my lashes. "They didn't even bring up the attack. Not even once."

"I don't know what you want me to say, Atticus. I explained everything in detail to my mother. I assume she told them everything. Just because they didn't inquire about it today, doesn't mean they won't tomorrow. Or even tonight."

"I get the feeling it's not the only reason why they're here."

I swallow but am saved from answering when our waitress comes.

"We need another minute," Atticus says without looking to the plump older woman. She nods with an amiable smile fixed in place and leaves.

"I told you the other reason," I say.

Atticus sighs and leans back against the squeaky cushion of our booth seat. "I think there's more to it than that as well."

"Well, that's all I can imagine it to be."

Silence. It rings loud in my ear as we remain in our standoff. Distrust paints his face by his furrowed brow and downturned lips. This close I can even scent some of his disappointment. I swallow the thick lump forming in my throat and curl my arms around my middle.

"I don't want to pressure you, but something doesn't feel right about this. And you're acting differently. Sometimes I think I glimpse the real you. Or maybe it's who you could be. Still soft and a bit shy, but shining at every moment. But 80 percent of the time you have some shell erected. It's worse now that they're here. I don't know how to get past it. Time, probably," he admits with a forlorn sigh. His expression softens to one of empathetic understanding. He closes his eyes and rests his head back against the high back seat. "I thought, maybe, the sex had changed things. It usually does. I guess I shouldn't have assumed anything."

"Can I take your order, sweethearts?"

We startle as the waitress reappears, and stare numbly at our menus.

"Just an order of fries for me," I say weakly, handing over my menu.

"I'll have the same and a diet coke."

When she's gone, I reluctantly meet Atticus's gaze. Words fall forfeit on my tongue as I search for some reasonable explanation. But what do I say? I wasn't raised to be some open book with my heart on my sleeve. My parents took that from me so long ago. Even now they have their claws in me pursuing their wishes.

"I don't know how to be different," I say, feeling more self-conscious than ever. I re-wrap my arms around my middle, fingernails digging into my sides. "How I act is how I was raised." *How I was bred.*

"And those glimpses I see? Where does that come from? Them?"

I shake my head, but one person comes to mind. The one who I'm doing this all for. "Juniper."

Across the linoleum-covered tabletop, he stretches a hand toward me. I stare intently at it like it's my very doom before reaching out and accepting his warmth and strength. The beta influence is not what I expect to receive through the contact, and my eyes turn to saucers as I stare at him. A rush of acceptance and understanding courses through me.

I attempt to tug back my hand, but he holds fast, shaking his head. "Don't. I get it, okay? She's like a sister to you. It's no wonder you feel you can be so open with her. I guess that means it's only the people you feel safe and comfortable with that get to see those glimpses, huh?"

Again, I'm speechless. "I suppose," I whisper, eyes darting away from Atticus's face and rapidly blinking away the odd wetness that has gathered there.

"Well, then," he says, his voice carrying a teasing note, "I guess I should be happy to have fallen in with such an esteemed group. Even if it's only in bursts."

"Why are you so nice to me?"

Atticus smiles widely and rubs this thumb across my palm. Shivers race up my arm. "Because I know something you don't."

"What?"

"That we'll be everything together. It's not a question of 'if,' but 'when.' I'm just waiting for you to see it too because I don't think your pack has done the soulmark justice. Our souls are meant to be one, Winter. And that's an incredible thing."

My lips part in breathless wonder. Right then and there I almost tell him everything. About the curses. About my parents' intent. About what I've done.

"Here you are, kids. Enjoy."

The fries are set down in the middle of us, and Atticus's coke directly in front of him.

"She is surprisingly quiet," Atticus says good-naturedly and goes for a taste of the fries with a cheeky smile. "Maybe it's her supernatural power?"

I smile weakly back and go for a fry, my confession locked away once more. *Keep quiet, fool,* I berate myself. *Think of June. Will you destroy her future chance at happiness?*

I slump in my seat. Apparently, I'll just destroy my own.

Balance

- Chapter 12 -

Once, when I was eight, I walked the back of a couch like a balance beam. In my imagination, a tumble to the wrong side meant certain death. But to cross meant I would accomplish what none had before. My great act had been performed for the newborn Juniper... who was asleep in her bassinet.

I remember the rush and exhilaration as I took each step, even as the couch gave way to wobbles and rocking. I kept my balance through it all.

The same precarious walk today does not feel like what it did then.

The streetlights pass in a blur on our way home, their luminous glow mingling with the snowfall. It's beautiful in its chaos, but unfortunately not a strong enough diversion from my turmoil.

My parents are not good people.

They are manipulative and self-serving.

They are proud and cruel.

I rest my head against the glass and revel in its icy touch. It is a balm to my growing headache.

And I may be just as bad.

I wish Atticus to be less than he is. It is a terrible thought, but I wish it still. Perhaps if he were, it would be easier to betray him. Maybe it would ease this gnawing guilt pulverizing my insides. Inside my coat pocket rests my phone, clutched ruthlessly within my grip. Text messages from Juniper populate the home screen, all unanswered but seen by me.

Juniper: *Toby broke up with me*

Juniper: *Please call ASAP*

Is this my parents' way of nudging my progress along? Or were their plans to derail Juniper's future always something within their sights?

Will my compliance even help?

This, among all things, feels like the largest betrayal. For I cannot give up on June, because she has never given up on me—*not once*. I bite my tongue to dissuade tears from rising. My emotions are a mess, and I'm not the least bit confident I can keep them in.

"Winter?" The tentative address only makes matters worse.

I sniff and wipe hastily at my eyes. "I'm fine," I insist. "I'm just... feeling a bit lost."

The truth of my statement hurts. It feels as if my heart is being pummeled by some unseen force and there is nothing I can do to stop it. Not until I make a move. Where do I stand? Where? Where? *Where?*

"Hey, hey, don't cry," Atticus croons, quickly pulling the car over a block short of home. "Winter, I—I don't know what's wrong. Why do you feel lost? What's going on? Is it Lucy and Knox?"

Hair sticks to my face as I vehemently shake my head. "No, I—" To my horror a small sob breaks past my defenses.

Remember, Winter, no man likes a blubbering fool. Shed tears for no one.

"Just ignore me. I'm being sensational," I persist. Atticus fumbles with his seat belt, and an instant later I'm doing the same. "I just need some fresh air."

Before he can stop me, I've slipped out the car door. The graze of his fingertips against my back speeding my efforts. I slam the door shut behind me, utterly shocked by my behavior.

I'm having a mental breakdown.

A full-blown panic attack. I haven't had one since I was a little girl.

The world around me doesn't contain enough air. Of this, I am entirely sure. I struggle to capture my breath as some strange physical entity bears down on my rib cage.

"Winter!" Atticus's sharp call does little to break the turbulence wreaking havoc in my mind. Nor does the weight of his hands on my shoulders.

At some point, I've buried my face into my hands. Wheezing and sobbing, I unabashedly hide from the world with my body turning more numb by the second.

I tremble as I latch on to each frantic thought that passes by me.

Juniper will crumble over my parents rough handling.

Atticus will turn me out with the knowledge of my deceit.

And someone will die. Someone will die because of me. That's what the aunt had said. That's what she saw. Because of me.

My hands are pried away from my face with some effort by Atticus. Although his lycan strength is far greater than my own, my desperation fuels a force I've never exerted before.

"Winter, calm down. Talk to me. I can't help if I don't know what's wrong," he pleads. The persuasion of his position challenges the weak points of my panic, and slowly but surely, the betas calming influence drowns out my anxiety. But I still feel hopelessly numb.

"I just need some...." My gaze darts away uselessly as if the answer to all my problems lies somewhere ahead of me.

You're going to get someone killed. That is what the witch had said, and—

"Winter. Look at me."

A knuckle grazes the underside of my chin. The skin-to-skin contact startles me enough to do as he asks. I'm not sure of what's happened to his leather gloves, but the pull of his fixed stare keeps me distracted enough to lose the thought as soon as it come. His blue eyes are dashed with vibrant gold, the lycan in him observing my reactions carefully.

"What do you need?" he asks, his raspy voice pulling at my heartstrings.

"Time," I murmur. *And so much more.* "They won't stop."

Another little cry bursts from me before I resolutely shut my mouth. *Too much*, a voice scolds, *you're saying too much.*

Atticus rests his forehead against mine. Our breath clouds before us, mingling together as it did the night of the full moon. My frayed nerves take to the action like a balm. I nuzzle my tearstained face against him, breathing in his scent and closing my eyes.

"Whatever is happening… whatever is wrong, I can help, Winter. Let me help."

In one fluid motion, he cups my jaw and brings our lips together. They slant across mine in an almost punishing fashion. The drag of his lips consumes my gasp and draws me up onto my toes. Atticus responds in kind, his muscular arm locking around my waist while he presses me up against the side of the car.

I grapple at his neck and back, searching for purchase with a desperateness that makes me quake. Anything to get away from my torturous guilt and anxiety.

We go from zero to sixty when a lurid moan draws past my lips. In the next instant, hands grip the back of my thighs and hoist me into the air. There's no choice but to wind my legs around his waist to aid his effort. My hands find new purchase on the bulging muscle of his biceps.

No second is spared to adjust or think or *breathe* because Atticus's mouth is blazing a trail across my jaw and behind my ear. And—

"Oh *God*."

His growl follows my gasp, and once more his lips assault my own. Panic forgotten, I return his attention with equal fervor. As if kissing him will somehow save me. For that is what I wish for most.

Let me be the damsel that he comes to rescue.

Let him defeat my wicked parents and slay all the enemies at our border.

Let this kiss be true love's and break every curse.

"You can't keep hiding from me forever, Winter," he whispers harshly against my lips. "You can't keep locking yourself away." I've barely the time to inhale before he shows me his frustration in a painfully obvious way. Atticus rolls his hips into mine while his hands head north to knead my ass. He knows exactly what he's doing as the second roll of his hips catches me in just the right place.

"Atticus."

His name is a mere whimper across my lips, and he repeats the motion. Harder this time, earning something close to a whine from me.

"You're mine, Winter," he pants, his hips unrelenting as I squirm against the back of the truck and Atticus's hold. "Anybody who wants to cause trouble with you—they go through me first. Got it?"

I nod helplessly back, stifling a moan as pressure begins to build across my body. Atticus steals another kiss from me, this one, far more thorough than the last. He kisses me as if to prove his point. Nothing can get to me with Atticus as my shield.

Without mercy, the hands that keep me captive slide back down my thighs, only to urge them further apart. My legs tremble at the action but provide no further resistance as his rock-hard arousal grinds against my center.

Though the frigid wind whips the snow against our exposed faces, it melts in seconds to run down our fevered skin. *I'm burning from the inside out*, I think in a daze, my lips chasing Atticus's. I need out of my clothes and most certainly out of my thick down jacket. But I'm going nowhere fast kept prisoner as I am to his ministrations.

The chance of my climax inches higher with each passing minute. The insufferable heat that plagues me builds like an inferno until I'm sure I'll die of heat exhaustion in the blizzard swirling around us.

"Nothing comes between us," he gets out through gritted teeth. My lashes flutter open to stare into his golden eyes. "Nothing." *Nobody*, his eyes insist in silent reprimand.

When his teeth bite down on the corded tendons of my neck, I release another whine, my hips bucking against him to find release. Atticus makes an encouraging noise, his hand slapping against the back of my thigh before his fingers trespass closer to the source of my torture.

I whimper and writhe against the onslaught of sensation, eyes wide as I stare into the flurry of white above us. I close my eyes when the wave of my orgasm takes hold of me, my back arching painfully so. The only means to stifle my cry is by biting down upon my lower lip. Even then my cries of fruition fill the quiet air.

All manner of stress deflates from my body as Atticus slowly sets me down. I feel weightless, yet strangely alive. He presses a hot kiss to my cheek, breathing heavily still.

"You don't have to tell me what's wrong tonight," he says hoarsely. "But you will eventually, Winter."

I barely comprehend the command in his voice, weakly nodding as I catch my breath.

"Oh God," I whimper, tucking my face into his coat. "I can't believe this just happened." My eyes are wide as I stare at him. My meltdown. His assuasive words and touch. A blush covers me from head to toe. "Atticus, we're in a family neighborhood."

Atticus pulls back an inch, and the winter wind sweeps between us to dose us back to reality.

"I guess I got a bit carried away," he admits. "Let's go home before the neighbors come yelling." He presses another kiss to my check and opens the passenger side door for me.

There is little time to feel awkward as we complete the remaining distance to home in less than a minute, and for that I'm grateful. But the feeling swiftly departs at seeing the house lights on.

"I was really hoping she stayed out later," Atticus says, turning off the car and unbuckling once more.

"Me too," I say on the back of a sigh, following him out of the car.

A wave of warmth hits us as we enter through the front door. In the air, scented candles and burning wood mostly mask the underlying note of alcohol about the space. We share a look as we peel off our outer layers.

"Lucy… Knox?" I don't bother to hold back my wince as I creep toward the front sitting room where the fireplace is set to a roar.

"Just me," Lucy says, appearing at first as just a silhouette through the connecting kitchen hallway. As she emerges, I immediately notice her less-than-pristine state. It isn't that she's a mess—not by any means—but her hair is tousled as if from constant musing. And her makeup hasn't been touched up since we last saw her.

Of course, the full glass of wine in her hand leaves little to the imagination of just what Lucy has been doing to pass the time.

"Hi," I say slowly as I step into the room to survey any damage. There is none, but that's no surprise. Lucy isn't the type to cause physical destruction. Her preference lies in barbed words and underhanded manipulations.

"You're back," she drawls, crossing over to the fireplace. "Wine? I can open another bottle."

"Sure," Atticus says as he enters from behind me. He surveys the scene as well. "Why not?"

She saunters back out, arching a brow at me as she goes to the kitchen. I offer a reluctant nod to her.

What's going on? I mouth to Atticus. He shrugs and expresses his own confusion with lifted shoulders and eyebrows. Lucy is back before we have time to mime out more of our perplexity.

"Thanks," I mutter, more out of habit than actual gratitude.

"Thank you," Atticus says, and pulls me over to the couch to sit. Lucy remains standing, plucking her own glass from its temporary position on the glossy mantle of the fireplace. "So... how was the rest of your day?"

Time stretches on for an inordinate amount of time. Long enough that I'm unsure if Lucy will deign to answer. Her sights won't retreat from my face.

I struggle not to squirm. Do the remnants of my panic attack show on my face. Ruined and smudged mascara perhaps? Too red of a nose? Or does the scent of my release waft off me despite the wind's toilsome work?

"Knox left," she says at last.

Lucy brushes her long hair over one shoulder and proceeds to take an extended drink of her wine. What remains is less than half of the dark ruby liquid.

Atticus drapes his arm over the back of the couch, casting me a sidelong glance that I almost don't notice in my shock.

"He *left*?"

"You're not deaf, Winter," Lucy scolds in a near perfect imitation of my mother. So much so my mouth snaps shut at the rebuke. "Yes, he left. We received a call shortly after you two left. He arranged for transportation and had your pack's third escort him through one of your border's little cracks."

"We assumed you two would be around longer," Atticus comments.

"Me as well."

We all take a drink to avoid the silence squeezing in from all around us. As the moment goes on without the sound of our voices to fill it, I realize how unbearably warm it is in the room. I wish to change but fear what subject might be ventured into if I leave the room.

"Who called?" I ask, shooting for nonchalance and failing miserably. Lucy cocks a knowing brow in my direction, along with an answering smirk that is savage. She flicks her gaze away, but not before I catch the bitterness that rises within them. "My mother or father?"

Lucy's stares down into the fire, her hair coming to block the view of her face. I find myself growing annoyed at her upright position. As does my wolf. It does not appreciate her stance, for both Atticus and I rank well above her. To stand above us so literally is a slight, but in her drunken state, I'm unsure if the snub is intentional.

"I don't see why it particularly matters," she finally says, turning her sights back upon me as I begin to fan myself. The bitterness has washed away from her dark eyes and in its place is a mocking cynicism I know well.

I narrow my regard. "If it was my parents, I hope he passed along our obvious greetings and well wishes."

"That hardly seems necessary. You speak with your parents often enough, don't you, Winter?"

Our glares do battle, but far shorter than their usual fare. Lucy scoffs, breaking the intense connection between us and rolls her eyes.

"So...." Atticus clears his throat, his eyes darting between us. "It wasn't Winter's parents, who called Knox back?"

If it wasn't for the dulcet quality of Atticus's voice—a sure signifier of the beta's influence—I doubt the tension between us would have died down. While I lean into Atticus's side and feel my anger dissipate, Lucy visibly fights the calm.

"Spare me your pathetic attempts at coercion," she spits, crossing her arms over her chest. Her wine sloshes precariously up the sides of her glass, but its low content saves her from spilling. "I'm well versed in the tricks and cons wolves of your status use to get their way. I learned long ago not to pay mind to those who pretend to play nice to lull others into a sense of false security. If you want to know, Atticus, ask like a regular person would."

I do not expect... *that.*

The two stare at each other, both frowning but with far different connotations behind each furrowed brow and downturned mouth. I place a hand on Atticus's thigh, letting my own subtle influence reach out to comfort him. A part of me wishes to do the same to Lucy, but I know my empathy will be rejected.

After all, I am the only person in the room who truly understands the truth of her words. If I wasn't the daughter of Blanc pack alphas, there's no doubt in my mind I would have been put through the same gauntlets as Lucy and her sister. As it is, I went through my own minefield.

“Was it Winter’s parents who called for Knox?”

She pauses for an infuriating amount of time, but Atticus withstands her power play. Not once does his body language indicate frustration or annoyance, merely a showing of perplexity in the frown he wears.

“I don’t see who else it could have been, Atticus. After all, they are the alphas. We adhere to all their many whims and desires—isn’t that right, Winter?”

I try not to stiffen, really I do. But there’s no stopping the subtle squaring off of my shoulders at Lucy’s address.

“For all we know, it could have been his parents—”

Lucy snorts and prowls over to the wingback chair nearest to the fireplace. “You know as well as I, Winter, that Knox ranks even higher than his parents in the pack. And he’s not one to be swayed by sentimental familial matters to divert him from his cause. Your mother called,” she drawls, circling to the front of the chair and sinking down into the plush seat cushion. “And like the good lycan he is, went running back.”

“Why weren’t you asked to return?” Atticus asks.

Lucy shrugs, but the bitterness I spotted earlier creeps back into her eyes. “The why doesn’t matter. I wasn’t, and so I’ll remain on guard for Winter here until I am asked to return.”

“You have a lot of faith in your alphas,” Atticus goes on. We watch as Lucy tenses, her eyes set to narrow in a challenge on our persons. “I’m sure they’re very proud to call you, pack mate. Such loyalty and devotion are not easily gained.”

For a moment, Lucy’s rigid guard falters. She swallows and turns her gaze back to the flames. I can’t imagine what goes through her mind at Atticus’s softly spoken words without a single trace of influence in them. When her eyes return to us, they are half concealed by the cover of her chestnut hair.

"And in those who are lesser, it is easily forgotten what we owe to them by right."

Lucy spares me a sidelong glance. I gather a pithy retort to the tip of my tongue, but Atticus speaks instead.

"I'm afraid I have to disagree. It isn't the fault of the wolf if they lose faith or trust in the alpha, but rather the alphas, who have not done enough to prove their worth to the pack. And for that matter, blame may fall on the betas' shoulders as well, for it's their task—our task—to care for the well-being of the pack."

Lucy finishes her drink, her lips smacking together once, then twice after she sets her empty glass on a nearby side table. "Winter, I was wondering… why exactly are your things in two different rooms?"

Bitch.

"Snooping around?"

Lucy leans back in the chair, one leg crossing over the other with practiced ease. "I was bored."

That's what you get for forgetting to lock the room, I scold myself. "You can't just do that, Lucile. This isn't your house, or pack, for that matter, and—"

"Oh really, Winter. Don't get your panties in a twist." Her face is transformed by a wicked smile, and a devious glint twinkles in her eyes, courtesy of the firelight. "Unless it's Atticus doing the twisting of course."

The growl that emits from my mouth is a warning. "Lucy—"

"A toast to the perfect fucking couple." Lucy reaches for her glass, but upon discovering it empty, lets out a massive sigh. "I need more wine."

She goes to stand, but Atticus is faster. "How about water?" he suggests. He's halfway out of the room before Lucy can comprehend and deliver a comeback. In the end, she flops back into a slouch.

"Eager to please, isn't he?" she sneers.

I cast my eyes to Atticus's figure as it turns the corner of the short hallway to reach the kitchen. Then they fall to my cousin without kindness.

"What the hell are you doing?" I hiss.

Her pretty brown eyes still hold their devious glimmer, and she levels a wink at me. "I'm just having a little fun, cousin. Your mother *bids* it."

The sound of rushing water from the kitchen holds half of my attention. I don't have long to question Lucy, especially if Atticus only means to get her water.

"Why was Knox told to return?"

"Certain responsibilities befall certain family members when betrothal contracts are being drawn."

Betrothal contracts? For who? Surely not Juniper... Lucy's sneer returns at my distraught look. "You know this could all be resolved if you merely did as you were told. Do your duty, for the sake of the Goddess. Come to heel like the good girl you've always been."

"Lucy." Panic stirs in the back of my throat and ends up in the delivery of her name. I shoot my eyes deliberately to the hallway where Atticus's footsteps sound. "Don't—"

"Have you even told him, cousin?"

"Told me what?" Atticus asks, mouth downturned as he enters the room. He spears me with a questioning look before crossing to hand Lucy her water.

I can't help but notice the way her fingers reach out to graze the back of his hand. Or the way she bends her neck so submissively to his presence. *Seriously?*

"Oh, everything."

"Lucy, that's enough." I stand, setting down my glass of wine and walking to the far end of the room, lest I become too tempted to smack the smirk off her face. *It serves her right*, my wolf urges.

My cousin's smile is both vicious and rounded in misery. Her glassy eyes focus on me, and only me, as she joins us in standing upon doe-like legs.

"She's told you about her history with Knox, hasn't she, Atticus? Maybe in your many letters. Or while you've been getting to know each other more… intimately?"

Atticus places his hands in his pocket but remains mostly unmoved by Lucy's slurred words. "She hasn't. But that's a conversation we'll have in private."

"There's nothing to tell," I say, surprised at the heat in my voice. "We dated briefly in high school. That's it." I keep my sights on Atticus, watching as his shoulders relax from their rigid line. I'm gifted a tiny smile and breathe a touch easier.

"Apparently you dated long enough to break his heart," Lucy says and takes a step forward. "But even breaking the heart of the pack's golden boy couldn't ruin your reputation, could it? Always little Miss Perfect." Her sharp laugh fills the room, dressed in years of built-up animosity. "How do you compete with perfect?"

Atticus shuffles closer to Lucy, ready to intercede if necessary. "I think it's time we all turned in for the night."

"Well, I think it's time Winter shared with you the big family secret," Lucy announces. She raises her arms out in front of her, like some kind of announcer introducing the next act. "Come on, Winter. Don't you think it's time for a little bit of honesty?"

Her shot hits. So accurately, in fact, she manages to snag two birds with one stone. Atticus stares flabbergasted at Lucy as if taking in the true depth of her character for the first time. I'm equal parts furious and shocked.

"You awful, bi—"

Atticus rushes to stand between us, both arms extended to halt our progress. "Enough," he orders with the full weight of his rank behind his word. "What the hell is she talking about, Winter?"

My mouth opens and closes, unable to fish out the words. After all, how can I be sure of which family secret Lucy eludes to? By the smug look on her face, she's predicted my dilemma accurately. My nails dig into my palm.

Mother didn't send Lucy to protect me. She sent her to act as a ticking time bomb and do what she does best. Cause mayhem. And her fuse had just run out.

"She means the lycan curse," I manage to say even though I can feel my throat closing in on itself. Darkness reigns briefly as I squeeze my eyes tightly shut. "We're the reason for the curse on lycankind. The Blanc pack is."

When I open my eyes, Atticus is staring open-mouthed at me. And Lucy, acting grossly satisfied, smiles softly and bids us goodnight.

+++

Atticus won't make eye contact with me. I hate it. I hate to think that my long-winded confession of my family's sordid past is the source of all lycans' true grief. Unused to this guarded side of him, I leave the room to gather my thoughts and the flower book.

When I return, Atticus is standing in the same place I left him a minute ago, with his back to the door and his head bowed.

He turns to face me slowly, a curious frown on his face when he sees me.

I shuffle my feet awkwardly. "Are you mad at me?"

His eyes widen, but eventually he shakes his head. "No, but I'm… frustrated. At you and myself." A thick lump forms in the back of my throat, and I turn my steel eyes downward. "I thought it would be so much easier than this. That we would have our happily ever after right off the bat. I know it's naive and juvenile… that all relationships take work, even ours.

"I just thought—I hoped it was going to be different. I guess a big part of that came from thinking my enthusiasm would be met more equally. It was on New Year's Eve and tonight. Tonight felt like something big between us too."

I flounder for the right words to say, struck by both his confession and the smolder he wears that darkens from the sparkling ocean to the deep sea. I cannot ignore his challenge—this new line drawn in the sand.

It's his way of drawing me out from behind the wall I've built. If only he knew how badly I wish to tear down that wall myself.

A coarse shiver runs over my body, from the back of my neck down to my toes. Then it dares to race all the way back up as Atticus appreciates my somewhat breathless state with a meaningful look.

And then he peels off his shirt.

How he maintains an ounce of coloring on his skin given the season, I cannot understand. But it does not lessen my appreciation of him. I swallow, eyes lingering on the stacked lines adorning his stomach up to his broad chest where a dark set of intertwined circles rests on his right pectoral. Our soulmark.

As I stand dazed, he prowls forward. "I hoped with all of our recent talks you might be persuaded into making things a bit easier for us," he says, his voice low.

"Oh?"

He smirks, the act is entirely too sinful and tempting. I take in his features. His hooded eyes. The cut of his jaw in the bowed angle of his head. How the dim light catches the warm, natural highlights in his golden-brown hair.

Atticus doesn't stop when he reaches me, but rather stalks around to my back. The stealth of his touch would have me believe his fingertips never graced my hip, but I see them falling out of reach and sight.

"We can move forward, Winter. We can seal the soulmark."

His suggestion draws a gasp from my lips, but it isn't just that. In a bold move, his phantom caress darts across my lower back. I'm entirely too aware of how clammy my skin remains beneath the thick sweater I wear. Tonight's activities have left me sorely in need of a shower to rinse the day and night off my skin.

"Atticus—"

"I know we've talked about taking things slow… but haven't we waited long enough? It's been twenty years of letters. And over the past few days, we've learned each other even more intimately."

He steps up right behind me, his hands gripping my hips. His bare chest and waist cover my back entirely.

"Just think of the ways we can know each other through the sealing," Atticus murmurs in my ear, urging me back against the wall of his chest. "We can be everything together, Winter."

For a moment, I savor it. Savor his scent filling my nose. Savor the strength of his body behind me. Supporting me, as usual. I tip my head back, eyes closed as a new face enters my vision. One of a young, beautiful girl, all alone with no one looking out for her happiness.

My eyes open and Juniper's face vanishes. "No."

WITCHES KNOW BEST

- Chapter 13 -

I'm an expert at avoidance. I've had practice all my life. Whether it be slipping unnoticed into vacant rooms to escape the sycophants panting after my parents' approval, or my parents themselves and the obligations they wish to press down onto my shoulders.

I even put my avoidance skills into practice with Atticus our first few days together. Uncertain how to act and proceed via my parents' wishes while navigating the obligations of wife and soulmark.

I don't expect to be on the receiving end of such avoidance, or it to come from Atticus.

Even if I rightfully deserve it.

By surrendering to his kisses and touch, I'd strung him along. I gave him false hope, when I knew the future between us looked dimmer as the days passed.

Yet, the strange pull of the soulmark grows as we linger in each other's presence. As if it *knows* its other half is in the vicinity and yearns to be reunited. The longer we are together, the more the pull grows.

To put it frankly, I am royally fucked.

The week that follows Lucy's drunken reveal and my rejection of the soulmark is hellish at best, especially with Atticus back to work and Lucy butting her nose into everything I do.

"What are we having for lunch, cousin?"

My eye roll receives no reprimand from the cabinet I stare into. Its contents seem to stare back at me with equal disdain.

"I'm having soup—"

"Do be a dear and make me a bowl as well. Oh, do you know what would go lovely with the soup? A baguette, or perhaps just something to dunk into it."

The cabinet door sounds angry as I shut it with more force than necessary. "I said *I'm* having soup. One can isn't enough for two."

"Then grab another," she retorts, a scoff following her reply. "Honestly, Winter. Is this how you treat all of your guests?"

"I'd hardly call you a guest," I grumble beneath my breath. "More like a parasitic prison guard."

I spy her set down her magazine on the kitchen table. Her eyes narrow lazily on my figure as I stroll about the kitchen. "I'm here to protect you. We mustn't let anything dire happen to the Blanc princess, now can we? What will your mother say when she hears about your abhorrent manners? Surely she taught you better."

I set down the can of soup, my shoulders carrying the weight of my tension as I stride back to the cabinet and take out another can of soup. Check-ins from my parents have been nonexistent with Lucy present. All calls are directed to her, a fact she makes a point of sharing every instance. *My calls and texts to June*, I think with worry, *have gone unanswered.*

"Don't you think you should get rid of these flowers?" Lucy muses as I prepare our lunch.

"No."

Not yet. I can't bear the thought of getting rid of them without new flowers to replace them. However, seeing as Atticus is still avoiding me at all costs, the promise of a fresh bouquet seems slim to none.

"They're dying." A pointed sniff is made in their general direction. Lucy raises her eyebrows at me, leaning back in her chair and picking up her magazine once more. "And they're starting to smell."

"They're staying," I say, my voice underlined in steel.

"Touchy," Lucy comments, drawing out the word to nettle me. It works far better than it should. I turn my back to the brunette, focusing on the trivial task of stirring the soup. "You're in quite the mood this morning, cousin. It isn't because you're no longer sharing your husband's bed, is it?"

My motions cease, though my grip on the wooden spoon tightens considerably. The gentle sound of splintering reaches my ears. "That's none of your business."

"Your mother would say otherwise."

I turn in a flash, the wooden spoon still in hand dripping creamy red on the kitchen floor. "And if my mother told you to jump off a cliff, would you?"

A flash of gold streaks through her gaze. "Of course. Would you?" My hesitation is all the answer she needs. She sends me a shark-like smile. "Why, Winter, don't tell me you would falter in the face of your *true* alphas. Your *true* pack. After all, my aunt tells me the Blanc pack bonds still hold you to a degree, even if you continue to make ties with this pack—as unworthy as they are."

"You're ridiculous," I tell her neatly, making sure no expression crosses my face as she taunts me. I've already played too heavily into her hand and allowed my emotions to be riled. Every day her taunts come. Every day I lash back but not today.

"I'm honest," she croons back. At my unimpressed look, she continues on, but I note the little vein near her temple gives a throb at my nonchalance. "For being the daughter of an alpha pair and the last of her family name—the oldest in lycankind—you sorely lack the esteem and poise of your position."

I take my time to reply, knowing how my aloofness always succeeds in getting under her skin. I wipe the floor of the small mess I've made and tend to the soup once more. It's cooked quickly, but I draw out the process of preparing our bowls.

"Careful, cousin," I finally respond as I set her food in front of her and sit down with my own. "One could argue your words as a challenge for rank. Though what you hope to gain challenging a *beta* not of your own pack, I cannot comprehend."

My eyes bleed gold as I make my remark, and my wolf swiftly rises to my call. Nobody but Lucy can bring out the wolf so quickly, though I have done my best to leash it this past week in response to her goading.

"Yes, one could. Couldn't they?"

We stand on the edge of a new line, our eyes shimmering golden at one another in anticipation of the fall.

There are three ways in which to move rank within a pack—marriage, insisting one's will upon the other in a show of strength, or by the fist, forcing your challenger to submit in a fight.

It is no secret in the Blanc pack that my mother had a heavy hand in my ascension into the top tier of the pack order.

That does not mean females don't try to unseat me. Countless times, I was lured into secluded areas with witnesses at the ready to crow of my defeat. On almost all occasions, my challengers wished to challenge by the fist. But being the challenged, it was my choice... and my choice was by strength of will.

As it happens, enduring my parents' treatment strengthened me. It makes me wonder what my wolf and I could be capable of unhindered.

Lucy's gaze flickers to my necklace. She breaks our standoff and the unofficial prod at my strength of will.

Her jaw ticks.

"You should never have been given that necklace," she informs me. Her golden eyes narrow upon it.

My fingers graze the moonstone resting against my breastbone. *The necklace will be worn by no other than me*, a voice whispers in my mind.

"The necklace is for those who carry the Blanc blood only. Whom else would it go to?"

"Aunt Adele isn't of the Blanc bloodline, and yet she wore it," Lucy snaps back, her ire growing as she folds her arms over her chest.

"The necklace was a gift passed from my father, who is of the blood, to my mother as a wedding gift. She wore it only on ceremonial occasions. Where it lays now is its rightful place."

She works her jaw in a slow grind, glaring at me with profound detestation. A small part of me relishes in it, as our infamous rivalry comes to a head again. A more substantial portion anguishes at the pettiness.

This is not the person I wish to be.

"God, you're insufferable, you know that?" she spits.

I hum my acknowledgment and eat my soup. Lucy does the same with a sneer present on her face. I fight the urge to shake my head in disappointment. My attitude toward Lucy lies somewhere between pity and anger, and now the favor tipped in the balance of the former, as it usually ended up doing.

"I'm only stating what we both know already. Why you insist on being confrontational is beyond me," I say at last. The response is one I know will temper her ire, somewhat, at least.

Lucy far prefers my scorn over my pity.

"You're not even *pack*," she continues on, the heat of her anger still present in her voice. "Not really. Your mother might insist that Blanc bonds still hold you, but I see the way you act with them. I see how you are with him, even if you are fighting now. You don't even realize it," she seethes. "You don't see, but I do. The way you act is disgusting."

"And what is it you think you see?" I ask and begin to clean up, even though my soup remains half eaten.

"Oh, it's not just what I see. It's what I feel. Whatever ties you keep with your mother are quite possibly the only ones that keep you tied to the Blanc pack anymore. Haven't you noticed? The bond between us is nearly nonexistent, cousin."

Her words are like the slow drag of a blade down my flesh. A stir of panic swirls low in my belly as I reach for Lucy through the bonds of the Blanc pack. My heart dares to speed its pace. She's right. What once was ingrained so firmly inside me now feels like a shadow of its former self.

"I'd wager a guess all your *fucking* around with this pack has torn the tether of the Blanc pack bonds from their place. Don't worry, I haven't told your mother the extent of your betrayal," she says, her voice cool as silk. "Not yet, anyway."

"I'm doing as she asks—"

"Are you? Is that what you call all this sitting around doing nothing all day? You call me the prison guard, cousin. But it's you who won't let me out of your sights. What exactly are you afraid of, hmm?"

I set to drying the pot, my hands rubbing its surface with hard, insistent strokes. "We don't have a car," I say. "With Atticus at work, there's no one to take us any place, even if we wanted to."

"Oh, please," she taunts. "You know as well as I that you can easily call one of your new pack mates and they'd come running to aid their beta. Must I remind you of the consequences should you fail to complete your task? Or does Juniper's fate mean so little to you?"

I tense, unprepared to receive such a direct blow. Swallowing, I set the pot on the counter and shake my head. "I—"

"Do you think I want to be here?" she demands, rising from her chair with her palms pressed flat against the table. "Do you think I want to watch you make moon eyes at each other? To pine over each other? It's pathetic, Winter."

A traitorous flush creeps onto my cheeks. "We don't make moon eyes at each other."

Lucy's lips press into a thin line. Then, in a shocking move, she grabs the vase of dying chrysanthemums and thrusts them into the nearby trash can. I watch her violent movements in stunned silence, unable to say a word of protest or block her rash decision by physical means.

"What the hell are you doing!" I finally deign to cry, striding over to where she hovers breathlessly over the trash can. Its lid closes over the pruned petals of the chrysanthemums in mocking softness. "I told you I don't want to get rid of them."

"Do you want to know the real reason Knox went back?" she asks, her frame trembling with emotion as her eyes glaze over with tears. "Because he got the brilliant idea after our conversation at the cafe to help Juniper secure a better betrothal. Of course, his younger brother, Daniel, will be devastated to lose out on our pretty little cousin, but Knox will set him straight. After all, who can deny what a fine match Juniper and Jeffrey Terreur make?"

Another direct hit. I careen back a step in shock and confusion. Lucy's brown eyes follow with sick satisfaction. "But... but you and Jeffrey—"

"Not anymore, cousin. Why I would have expected Juniper to have delivered the good news of her betrothal contract to you herself already. I wonder why she hasn't confided in you yet?"

I swallow the stone in my throat with difficulty and fight for some semblance of calm. It's little use. A few tears escape Lucy's determined glare, and she hastily wipes them away. This time, it is she who turns her back to me, heading straight for the hallway to make her exit.

"He's in his sixties, Lucy," I manage to choke out, still dumbstruck with horror. "She's barely of age as it is."

Lucy stops in the kitchen doorway, her hand gripping the frame with white knuckles. "Juniper understands and accepts the expectations of her family. Perhaps you should take notes from our young cousin?" And with her parting shot delivered in the most serene of voices, she walks away.

+++

With my world so neatly put on its end, I can think of nothing better to do than flee as well. In the bare essentials of what I need to trek outside, I find my feet guiding me into the center of town rather than the forest where I would typically take refuge. The chance of encountering a pack mate, or several, for that matter, sours the place of my most wanted retreat.

The chance of running into a Wselfwulf anywhere makes me *ill.*

And yet, despite these fears, I've inadvertently directed my feet in the direction of Zoelle's patisserie and cafe.

I'm standing before the cafe cheerfully decorated windows before I know it. My walk is a blur in my mind, but my ears and nose ache with the stinging cold of the journey. I rake my eyes over the window paint, seeing past the swirls and shapes to the figures that patron her space.

There aren't too many inside—only three to be exact, a couple and a lone woman who sits at the table nearest the window. Her ambivalent gaze falls upon me, clearly questioning my odd stature before the store. And then I see Zoelle, or rather, she sees me.

A smile lights up her face, and she motions for me to come inside. I hesitate, but in the end, I shuffle inside.

Warm, sugary concoctions and flavored coffee perfume the air heavily. A deeper inhalation reveals the fragrance of dark chocolates and loaves of bread. It's a comfort, and one the patrons seem to bask in.

"This is a surprise," Zoelle greets, pulling me into a hug. "Did you walk here? Where's your hat and scarf? Did your cousin leave?"

Her questions are entirely innocent, but my response falls short. Zoelle's regard sharpens on the way my brows draw lightly together, and finally I find my reply.

"Can I sit over there?" I point in the general direction of the back tables, and Zoelle nods.

"Let me take your coat. You go sit, and I'll grab us some coffee, or would you prefer tea?"

"Tea would be great." I shrug off my coat, handing it to her with a small smile and brushing my windswept hair back. I long for a hair tie or some headband to rule over the mess it has become, but all I've taken is my coat and phone. Not even my wallet made the trip.

I cringe internally as I sit. Zoelle is already back behind the counter fixing up our drinks. Every now and then her hand strays to her abdomen, a fond smile appearing on her lips as she does so. A pain strikes my heart, one induced by jealousy. I steer my gaze away to dampen it before she returns.

"So, what brings you around?" Zoelle asks and wipes her hands on her little black apron before taking a seat across from me.

"I just needed to get out of the house," I say, combing my fingers through the end of my snowy hair.

"Bored out of your mind?" she asks jokingly. The corner of my lips tilts downward as I sink back into my seat.

"More like annoyed out of my mind."

Zoelle's dark caramel eyes spy at me through lowered lashes, her hands busy pouring the ceramic teapot's contents into our cups. "I take it your cousin is still around." I rub my eyes, inhaling deeply and relaxing at the familiar scent of chamomile. "Honey?" she asks.

"No, thank you."

We lapse into a peaceful silence, but I'm quite aware of Zoelle's subtle regard. I can't find the energy to care, letting the warmth of the tea seep into my veins and warm my chilled hands.

"Penny for your thoughts?" she muses aloud.

My teeth dig in to the tip of my tongue as I search for an excuse to give. "I just feel...."

The fragmented words of my panic attack earlier this week surfaces. Lost isn't quite what I feel anymore. Trapped is far more accurate. The only way I know to potentially save June means harming Luna, and the fairy has been through so much already. "Tired," I say with a resigned sigh.

Tired of fighting my parents.

Tired of walking the sword's edge.

So damn tired.

"I can't imagine how strange this whole situation must be for you, even knowing you and Atticus have been acquainted for so long. One day your pen pals. The next, you're married," she states.

"Strange somehow doesn't do it justice," I murmur. "Surreal might be better."

"Surreal it is," she agrees and reaches out with her teacup to clink against mine. I smile weakly back at her attempt to break me from my stagnation. "Have you and Atticus—" Zoelle makes a vague gesture with her hands, her cheeks turning pink.

I sputter around my tea, setting my cup on the table between us to busy my hands. "That's a bit personal, don't you think?"

She lets out a nervous laugh. "Sorry, I think I might spend a little too much time with Quinn. She's very… personal." Our cheeks redden in unison. "It's just, Atticus has come over a few times to chat with Xander and Ryatt. But not about the Wselfwulfs."

"He's talking about our relationship with them?" I squeak. My eyes slam shut as embarrassment floods my system. "Perfect," I practically wheeze, taking up my teacup again and finishing its contents like a shot. "As if we don't have enough problems."

Zoelle worries her bottom lip between her teeth before topping both our cups off. "Problems?" She broaches the subject with a frown creasing her pretty, smooth brown skin.

My mouth opens and shuts an inordinate amount of times with guilt and misplaced loyalty struggling heartily with one another. *If Lucy can force you to spill a family secret to Atticus, you can confide in your alpha, surely?* Except I learned the day after Lucy's drunken antics, it had been our mother's orders. The why behind it had—frustratingly—not been explained to me, a fact that may also be contributed to my mother's orders.

"It's my fault," I say, the words coming out of my mouth in a rush. "I've been awful lately. We've been… *intimate*, but not in the way you might think."

Her frown deepens with newly set confusion. "I'm afraid I have no idea what you think I might be thinking," she murmurs.

I brush my hair back, my fingers getting tangled in a few choice knots that are hell to break free. When I finish my stalling, I can't help the forlorn sigh that peels out of me.

"We've had sex," I say, the familiar rush of blood racing up my neck to my cheeks and ears. "But we haven't done anything else, if you get what I mean."

"Oh."

Genuine surprise alights her face as she leans back in her chair to contemplate my words.

"I'm sorry, but why does that make you awful?" Zoelle asks.

I blink back at her. "Don't you think I'm being a—" I stammer to a brief stop, coloring more brightly "—a tease?"

"No. But you clearly do, and I can't fathom why."

I duck my head at her soft reply. "We're married because of our soulmarks… but I don't want to be sealed." I look up sharply to catch Zoelle's reaction to my words, but she doesn't seem offended. "Not yet, anyway."

Not ever.

And Atticus will never want to stay bound to a woman he can't conceive with, let alone one who is working with another pack behind his back.

"There's nothing wrong with that," she insists. "No one is going to begrudge you wanting to have something akin to a normal relationship with Atticus before diving into that kind of commitment."

"Except Atticus."

Zoelle is momentarily stunned by my grumbled response. "Is he pressuring you into sealing the soulmark?" she asks, her voice holding a dangerous lilt to it, like a mother ready to defend its child. "Because if he is, I'll spike his next drink with some potion to teach him a lesson."

I soften at her automatic defense, immensely grateful to have someone on my side. "Atticus wants to be sealed," I admit. "But… he's not pressuring me for it. I understand why he wants to move in that direction. I'm tempted to, but—"

"You're scared?" she fills in.

I know better. I avert my eyes.

"It's just… not the right time."

Zoelle's eyes scan her customers until they alight on someone behind me. "Excuse me a moment."

She makes the rounds as is her job, and when they're satisfied with her service, she comes back to sit with me.

"Sorry about that," she says, a gentle smile on her lips.

"Don't be," I reply, fiddling with the napkin underneath my tiny spoon. "I probably should head out soon, so I don't keep you from your work."

"No," she insists, reaching out and placing her hand atop mine. "You're not bothering me or disturbing my work. Stay as long as you like, especially if you need a break from your cousin."

A knot forms in my chest at her unbound kindness. "Thank you."

Zoelle pauses, her features rewriting themselves back to confused concern. "So you and Atticus are in a weird in-between," she surmises carefully. "Your cousin is probably a pain, and… is there something else, Winter? I can't help but feel like there's more."

The knot tightens.

"It's just," Zoelle continues with a tender smile, "well, maybe it's because I'm the alpha and you're the beta, or maybe it's my witchy instincts kicking in, but something doesn't *feel* right. There's something more, isn't there?"

Her words come out just above a whisper. For a moment it's as if we are the only two in this cafe and I can bare my soul to Zoelle. I don't notice my hand in her own resting in the middle of the table until the comforting brush of her thumb over the back of mine comes into focus. With a fair amount of ruthlessness, I bite down on the inside of my cheek to try and keep myself in check.

"Winter?"

My slate gray eyes flash to her honey brown ones. "You're right... about being the alpha and beta. We carry a special connection between us, because it's only the beta's strength that can buoy the alpha's in times of distress when all else fails around them. The pack can rally... but every alpha needs a beta."

Zoelle softens. "Winter, you can talk to me, especially if whatever is weighing you down you don't feel like you can talk to Atticus about." She smiles wistfully. "The perks of being an alpha, no one can order me to break your confidence. I promise, Winter, I won't breathe a word to Atticus or Xander. Tell me," she urges. "Get it off your chest so you can breathe."

And because she's the alpha—because she's even more empathetic than me—the words begin to stumble past my lips until they are crashing out of me like a waterfall.

"My youngest cousin is in trouble," I say hoarsely as goose bumps erupt across my skin. "My parents are going to make her marry a man three times her age."

Her hand tightens around mine. "Why?" she asks, eyes wide and lips parted in a mimic of my horror.

"Because... because it's advantageous for her family. Because it will give Juniper a higher rank in the pack. She's too delicate to rise up the ranks through strength of will, or strength period. Because of—" *me*. Because I have coddled and protected her all my life. June has never known the harsher aspects of pack life because of my interference.

The world begins to fall around me as a dull ache throbs at the base of my skull and traverses its way up to dig into my head.

"Winter, breathe," Zoelle commands. She lowers her voice and leans across the table. "I'm going to make some more tea. It's going to help you relax and give you some peace of mind, all right? Chin up and bear this feeling just a few minutes more. Okay? I'll make this better. I promise."

She dashes away from the table behind the counter. Without her hand to ground me, a numbness begins to creep into my body through my fingertips and toes. I release a shaky breath and curl my arms around my middle, trying to do exactly as she's said. Just breathe.

But even this simple instruction is a task when the eyes of the room are on me. Their judgment pierces my weak armor, and the numbness threatens to grow. *What am I doing?* The frantic thought makes me catch my breath. *Am I really about to betray my parents? Am I ready to forsake Juniper?*

Another voice, far softer and less manic chimes in. *Can I go on living like this?*

"Here."

My eyes snap to Zoelle ,who returns in a breathless state. She pours a new tea into my cup, steam billowing from the liquid to warn of its temperature.

"Give it a minute or so to cool down, or you'll burn your tongue...."

It does burn. My lips and tongue and throat immediately protest my decision, but in a desperate need to end my warring thoughts, there is no other choice for me. The teacup rattles against its dainty saucer when I set it down.

"Winter?"

"I just need a moment," I rasp, pressing my fingertips to my lips.

She frowns but nods. "I'll grab some water and let Veronica know to cover the store for a bit." My eyebrows raise in question. "She's my employee," Zoelle explains.

Again she departs, but this time around, my anxiety is wrangled down to a manageable level. And all it took was a single sip and a burnt mouth. She places a glass of ice water in front of me upon her return.

"Thank you," I breathe, taking a large drink of cold water and soothing the worst of the burn.

"Maybe you should put a couple of ice cubes in the tea," she suggests wryly. "It won't dilute my—uh—special ingredient."

I do as she suggests, conscious of my compliance in her magical methods of calming me. Mother would be incensed. A smile touches my lips at the thought.

"Are you feeling better?" Zoelle asks after allowing me another minute to compose myself. I bob my head as my fingers dash away any tears that have slipped past my notice in my panic. They are few, but they are there. I drag my fingers under my eyes to disturb and displace any that dare linger.

"Yes," I say, shocked at the amount of relief in my voice. I dare to take another sip, pleased when the heat isn't nearly as scalding as before. "How did you…?"

"It's a gift," she tells me. "I can impart my emotions into the things I make, or in this case, brew. To a higher degree, I can will an emotion to be in the things I make so that those who consume it feel what I want them to."

"That's a powerful gift to have."

Understanding flashes across her eyes as she sinks back into her seat. "It is. Now, I believe you were telling me about the rather unfortunate circumstances of your cousin." A severe scowl hunches her brows, partially obscuring her regard. "I'm sure you've been trying to figure out a way to help all this time. Have you considered extending a formal invitation to your cousin to join our pack?"

My world flips on its head for the second time, but this time, my feet find their rightful place under me. "I… I hadn't thought of that." Hope flares to life inside of me. "I—" And then it is dashed. How will I ever get Juniper out? And if Juniper came, Toby would need to be extracted too.

"I'm sure we can figure something out," Zoelle says, latching on to the idea as she studies my reaction. "Xander can speak with your parents and—"

"No!"

The room comes to a pointed still at my outcry. I swallow sharply and reach out to grab Zoelle's hand, trying to find a smile of reassurance to give her.

"No," I say again in a tamer tone. "My parents will never allow it," I tell her with a sad smile. The tea keeps my heart at a steady pace even as reality settles back in place. "You don't just... leave the Blanc pack."

"You did," Zoelle counters, giving my hand a squeeze.

"I'm different," I explain calmly, though a faraway part of me wanes with sadness at the statement. "I have the soulmark as my allowance."

Zoelle sighs, pouring herself a cup of her magical tea as well. She blows on its steamy surface before taking a tentative sip and wincing. "We don't have to inform your parents of her departure...."

Our eyes lock, Zoelle's meaning quite apparent even in its unspoken state. I give a slow shake of my head.

"You'd be starting an altogether different war," I tell her plainly. Zoelle's shoulders sag, but I can still see the gears whirling in her head as she searches calmly for a solution.

"I don't suppose you can speak to your parents about her predicament?"

"They support the match."

"Oh," she mutters. Her teeth sink into her bottom lip momentarily. "Surely there's a better match to be made with the man other than your cousin. Maybe another offer can be brought to the table?"

I squirm in my seat and take another sip of the tea when my anxiety tries to poke its head up. "There... might be a way to help her, but there's no guarantee it will work."

Zoelle ponders my statement, twirling a curly strand of ebony hair between her fingers. “You love her a lot, don’t you?”

“I don’t know if I would have survived back home without her,” I confess. Or without my correspondence with Atticus, and the hope it brought of freedom.

“Then you have to try. Try, and if it fails, we’ll figure out a new plan.” Zoelle smiles brightly. “We'll find a way to help your cousin, Winter.”

Her hope is infectious, and that dreary dark spot in my conscious begins to lighten. “There’s one more thing, Zoelle. I was hoping you might be able to help me with a small project I have in mind.”

She cocks a brow, sipping her tea more comfortably now as she awaits my proposal.

“It has to do with flowers.”

V

Her name was Arlette, and the only thing mildly important about her was that she carried Luc's child.

Merida regarded her with keen eyes. The witch could not fathom what love Luc held for this woman other than the aforementioned fact. She was not particularly pretty, but she had peculiar features that made her stand out in the pack of wolves.

Brown hair that looked like spun copper when in the sun.

Hazel eyes set a touch too far apart.

A smile too wide by any reasonable standard.

Merida pursed her lips until they became a hard line during her study. *Arlette isn't smiling now.* But neither was Merida. Bringing the she-wolf to the golden birch tree had been a challenge, one that had taken up precious energy she couldn't afford to lose.

Merida blamed the Moon Goddess.

For all of Merida's gloating in the weeks following her curse, she had assumed her hex had worked and the Blanc pack would no longer be able to shift to their wolf selves.

After, she had been immensely pleased to learn how far-reaching her hex was. Not only had she leashed the wolf spirits of the Blanc pack, but it appeared all of lycankind. She had laughed endlessly with glee, filling the forest with the cackling sound.

For these reasons, she assumed her plot for the night would go seamlessly… until she learned, along with the rest of the pack, they could shift into their wolf form under the protection of the full moon. Merida had seethed and raged from her concealed position in the wood. The trees trembled and the ground withered beneath the weight of her anger.

Even now, Merida simmered with it as she stared at her prize nestled in the roots of the golden birch tree. She had expended a great deal of magical energy to suppress Arlette's wolf spirit and secure her with wolfsbane-soaked ropes. *Too much energy*, Merida and the Darkness ruminated. Perhaps not leaving enough to execute the hex.

A growl curdled at the back of Merida's throat as she turned her back to her unconscious prisoner. It was essential that everything from this point forward go on without a hitch. After all, the only totem she had of the Blancs to bind the hex was the moonstone, which already bound the previous hex.

Another could fatally compromise the first, or ruin both efforts entirely.

Which meant no mistakes. The cursed moonstone currently rested inconspicuously around the she-wolf's neck lost among the several others she wore that befit Arlette's station.

The Darkness sank into possession of the witch's body. No mistakes meant allowing the festering presence to lead their efforts, and it took control with ease. Merida became a mere bystander to the events about to unfold, her true spirit waned and shriveled beyond repair.

Breaking the quiet of the night was a piercing howl followed by several others.

The haunted witch looked to the moon above and gave a menacing sneer. Upon arriving at her chosen altar with she-wolf in tow, the witch had erected a ward. The ward concealed the two women and further confounded the sight and noses of those who sought them.

Another desperate howl, closer but not enough to cause worry. The witch had no reason to doubt the ward's ability, for it had performed adequately for her thus far.

She turned back to the she-wolf and snapped bony fingers to awaken her.

Arlette awakened sluggishly at first and then snapped to focus with a jolt. Her body hurt, and there was something very wrong inside of her. The wolf inside her mind was a hollow presence, being somehow there and not at the same time.

Fear scored through her veins along with adrenaline as Arlette spotted the ragged figure of Merida several feet in front of her. She jerked in her bounds and gasped against her gag as the binds that tied her cut through her flesh.

"It should please you to know that I've no intention of killing you tonight," the witch said and began to pace.

Arlette watched the witch stumble back and forth with wary intensity. She was no stranger to the battlefront, and such an admission by her enemy was not in the least bit comforting—not when Merida clutched a jagged dagger at her side.

"It is not for lack of want," the witch continued, dragging pitch-black eyes to the she-wolf. "But for you to truly suffer as I have, I must go another way."

The two regarded one another stoically until the witch's hand drifted absently to her middle. Arlette froze. Her gaze could not be moved from that wayward hand, even if she had tried.

"*Mmph!*"

Arlette's fear doubled, then tripled as the witch's lips grimaced into the form of a smile.

"More than anything, I wish for you to live a long life, accompanied by the knowledge that you will never bear your soulmark a child."

Arlette wrestled with her bonds, her back arching and bones building with the pressure to shift. But she could not. Try as she might, she could not. She collapsed against the earth with a body-wrecking sob.

The witch clucked her tongue and stopped before the she-wolf. She crouched before her, dagger held leisurely in hand. "I too know the pain of losing a child," she said, her smoky voice without inflection. "We shall be sisters in this… along with all the other soulmarks in the Blanc pack, for I am not so cruel as to make you suffer alone."

"*Argh!*"

The stunted cry was guttural and followed by a distant howl. The Darkness shivered with perverse delight at the sounds. They would be too late.

"Hush now," the witch cooed, stroking the blade's edge along the stern line of the she-wolf's jaw. "The time has come."

The dagger's point dropped down to the multitude of necklaces adorning Arlette's neck. It made a pleasant tinkling noise as it glided over jewel and ornament alike.

"Now is the time," the witch muttered once more as black veins began to spiderweb across her skin.

In a violent strike, Arlette was pinned to the ground by the witch's body. Her struggle was futile, and her pain inconsequential to the witch as she was positioned for her demise.

"*Mmph!*"

"I said, hush."

The hissed words were soaked in magic and stung sharply as they willed themselves upon the she-wolf. The witch wheezed with excitement and slashed the blade over Arlette's cheek. Dark red spilled across her whitened pallor. Now was the time.

Unholy energy festered around Merida as she walked away from the broken woman. Her body trembled with anticipation as she dropped the wards.

"Come back to me," the witch murmured, staring out into the dark recesses of the forest. "Come back to me, Luc."

+++

He did not understand how he came upon them. Only that in one instant he was searching for Arlette at the lake's edge, his nose hunting for her scent in the sand, and the next he was here, at the old golden birch tree where they had found his younger brother Garret's body last month.

Merida smiled at the sight of him. He was stunning in wolf form. His dark coat was thick and lustrous. His golden eyes were mesmerizing.

"You came," Merida breathed.

Luc growled low in his throat, a warning to the witch that held his soulmark captive with a dagger against her neck. The scent of his soulmark's blood in the air was close to driving him mad, and it was with great restraint that he did not make a move against the witch. His soulmark was not only in pain but drenched in fear that polluted the air with its sour stench.

"Change," Merida commanded with lazy authority, the darkness in her eyes visibly gleaming as he failed to comply. The dagger pressed harder against Arlette's neck. "Change."

He did.

"If you release her to me now, I will kill you quickly," he promised.

Merida produced another blade from behind her back and tossed it to him. The blade was small and dull—an added act of petty vengeance to the blow she was primed to strike.

"You are in no position to make demands of me," a malefic voice spoke in place of Merida's husky tone. "I shall not kill her," it continued, "if you remove the soulmark upon your skin and give it to me."

Arlette snarled a warning at her beloved and pressed forward toward him despite the blade's keen touch. Luc responded with a growl of his own, his golden eyes ablaze as they darted between the pair.

"Release her!"

The witch's smile fell. As did the dagger, until its wicked point caressed the she-wolf's abdomen. Luc let out a snarl, so fierce his body shook with its release. But the witch stared impassively back, heedless to the parade of howls that followed the alpha's son's anger.

"Don't!" he shouted as the long edge of the blade ran softly along Arlette's belly.

Several wolves appeared in the background, pawing frantically at the strange magical barrier that kept them from their leader's son. The witch's ward was erected once more.

"What have you done?" Luc demanded.

"Remove the mark, and I shall tell you."

With great reluctance, he complied. His eyes locked upon the pair as he bent and plucked the small blade from the ground. He made short work of his task, though his face revealed what pain it caused him to do so. The wolves surrounding them barked and howled, stirred to a frenzy at the act.

Merida knocked Arlette to the side, one hand outstretched to catch her former lover's soulmark as it soared through the air into her palm. Luc lunged forward but crumpled as Merida's fingers curled possessively around his stolen flesh.

"Defiant until the end," Merida seethed, a sneer curling her upper lip to reveal discolored teeth.

"Nevertheless, a sacrifice no matter how unwilling is still a sacrifice."

The pack cried out as one. It as a horrific and skull-splitting sound as Merida presented the pieces of flesh to the earth. The flesh quivered in her outstretched palm before rising. Merida's lips parted and spoke.

"*Ovræ playus outum! Viest tocrum o sath vorce. Alst om duay cultost, nallem!*"

Both Luc and Arlette grew taut at the first utterings of the archaic hex. It raked along the base of their necks and ignited a fire. In Luc, the fire blackened his heart. In Arlette, the fire blackened her womb.

"*Ovræ playus outum! Viest tocrum o sath vorce. Alst om duay cultost, nallem!*"

The earth protested as did the stars and her altar tree. The witch's body caved at the backlash, her bones crunching in protest. But the Darkness forged on, its will stronger than the forces of nature anticipated.

"*Ovræ playus outum! Viest tocrum o sath vorce. Alst om duay cultost, nallem!*"

Arlette cried out against her gag in agony, the toxic touch of the fire spreading to her womb. The soulmark began to char in its levitated state while Luc watched on in frozen horror.

"*Ovræ playus outum. Viest tocrum o sath vorce. Alst om duay cultost, nallem.*"

The last stance was all but whispered by the witch as she snatched the soulmark from the air. Her bony fingers squeezed tight around it as a snarl bared her stained teeth to the gathered pack.

"*Ovræ playus outum. Viest tocrum o sath vorce. Alst om duay cultost, nallem—duem raste lorem!*"

A brilliant light eclipsed the gathering, followed by the mournful howls and keens of the pack stricken by the hex. The witch convulsed as the words continued to tumble past her brittle lips. A dangerous power poured from her body, leaving only ruin in its wake.

Merida's grip relaxed and from her palm poured the ashes rendered from the soulmark. Luc's poignant anguish seized the pack bonds at the sight.

"No!"

Luc's roared protest rebounded against the surrounding trees. With blade in hand and the strength of the Moon Goddess behind him, he ripped away from Merida's enchantment and sprang forward. A terrible growl ripped from his chest as he slammed his once lover into the tree with his knife firmly planted in the center of her chest.

The witch gave a tremulous groan. Glassy black eyes slipping to pale blue.

"And with my final breath let it be done," Merida croaked. *It was done. Their pride and prejudice will forever be their downfall.* "Sealed, marked, and bound by my words. Farewell, my love." Blood smattered across her lips and cheeks as what little life held in her body fled out her wound.

As her body slumped against the tree trunk, Luc abandoned her corpse for his wife. The binds that held her captive burned his hands, but he cared not. The magical wall had crumbled along with the witch, and his pack was here to help.

"Arlette! Arlette!" Luc dragged her into his chest, unabashedly crying his relief as she sobbed into his chest.

It was over.

THE CALM

- Chapter 14 -

I drink my coffee in small sips, keeping the mug close to my lips as I stare past the flowers placed in the center of the table and into the nothingness of the beyond. On the inside, my patience is reaching its breaking point.

Not that I let it show with Lucy watching me so intently.

Out of my peripheral vision, her brown eyes simmer with interest at my placid trace.

Of course, Lucy looks absolutely pristine today. Her hair is done up in a high ponytail to better show off her lithe neck in her off-the-shoulder sweater dress. There's little doubt she's dressed to impress as the weekend is finally upon us, which means Atticus is home all day.

But apparently not this morning.

My gaze flickers to the clock. It reads ten past nine. From the weeks that have passed, I know Atticus to be an earlier riser. His absence leaves me pondering the possibilities of his unusual tardiness. If it weren't for hearing him arrive late last night, I would question his very presence in the house.

"Did you sleep well without your husband warming your bed, cousin?"

Lucy bats her lashes at me. The very picture of innocence… if one didn't know a viper when they saw one.

"He snores," I murmur as if I can't be bothered to entertain Lucy.

With a tender sigh, I perch my elbows on the table and take another sip of coffee. *Patience*, I remind myself, *he'll come*.

"Tell me, Winny"—my eyes roll sharply upward—"when will you see your little fairy friend again? I hoped after our conversation yesterday you'd be properly motivated to prove your loyalty."

My soft hum is the only reply that I offer to Lucy, but it only spurs her on. She deposits her coffee onto the table to lean closer to me.

"Don't forget, the tonic we wish you to provide the fairy with will do her *no* harm. It will merely take her out of play for a few short days. Honestly, Winter. All of this—" Lucy twirls her hand in the air "—can be resolved come next week! Wouldn't that be lovely?"

I set down my coffee as well, reluctantly turning my regard to Lucy. Her smile is benign, but her eyes hold a secret. "The witches will know something is wrong with her. Something unnatural."

"Will they?" she counters. "How much do they *really* know about the way fairies act and behave?"

I have no response. Lucy's smile remains the same.

"The witches will know there's been foul play," I argue back quietly. "It won't take them long to turn their eyes to me."

"By the time they realize the depths of your betrayal, Winter, you'll be far gone. I already told you we'll return home once the task is finished. You do want to go home, don't you?"

I force myself to keep her stare. "This is a dangerous hand to play, Lucy," I warn her and attempt to steer the conversation away from my contested loyalties. "The Blancs threaten war with such an act."

"Must I repeat myself again?" she hisses. "The tonic won't hurt the little fool. However, it will ensure she can't bolster the precious border of your new pack. Your parents aren't interested in a war with the Trinity Coven. We all fully remember what happened last time our pack scorned a witch, do we not?"

Footsteps creak along the ceiling above, and our conversation comes to an immediate stop. We store away our sharp glares as the steps draw closer.

"Morning," Atticus announces. He enters the room with closed eyes and a stretch. He's shirtless, with sweatpants slung low on his trim waist. I can't help but stare while his muscles unfold to accommodate the pull of his arms above his head.

I'm not the only one staring. My wolf rears its head, and a low growl tumbles past my throat as I direct a pointed look at Lucy. She raises both brows in response and leans back into her chair, averting her eyes reluctantly from Atticus broad-boned chest.

Atticus clears his throat, and I hastily return my gaze to him. His blue eyes flicker between the new vase of flowers on the table and me.

"Good morning," I say, standing slowly and inching toward the kitchen. "Can I make you breakfast? Coffee?"

He nods, his gaze still drifting back and forth between the flowers and myself. He completely ignores Lucy's own greeting, and I bite back a smile.

"That would be great," Atticus finally says. A hand breezes through his already mussed hair, making the chestnut hair stand on end. This time my smile wins out. "What, uh, what kind of flowers are they?"

As he takes a seat at the table, I hurry to get him a cup of coffee, my sights darting between the figures at the table. Lucy's arms are crossed over her chest, an unimpressed look on her face.

"They're purple hyacinth," I tell him, setting his hot beverage in front of him.

"Anyone with eyes can see they're purple," Lucy mutters.

But Atticus and I share a smile. His hand grazes my hip as I step away and back to the kitchen, and our eyes catch once more. My heart flutters like mad in my chest at the look in his eyes. It's forgiveness, of a sort, and something promising a reconciliation. I hope.

I blush and duck my head.

Purple hyacinths mean an apology, and they've worked far better than I could have hoped.

"Would you like eggs?"

He nods and takes a long drink. "And a few pieces of toast, please. And another coffee?"

I toss a curious look over my shoulder as I fetch the necessary items for his breakfast. His usually glowing complexion is lackluster, and it looks as if he hasn't shaved in a day or two. The sight is odd considering how well-kept he likes to keep his appearance.

Atticus takes another long drag of his coffee, his hand absently scratching at his chest. My movements come to a slow stop to watch the course of his hand, only to be caught seconds later in my admiration by twinkling blue eyes. Tired, he might be, but he still has his wits about him.

"You look a bit worse for wear, Atticus," Lucy claims. "Trouble sleeping?"

I make no illusion of my interest in their conversation, keeping my body open in their direction, even if it meant cooking his eggs at an awkward angle.

"You could say that. I got home pretty late last night."

Lucy hums her acknowledgment. "I heard," she empathizes. "I hope it wasn't anything too serious keeping you up."

He hesitates, and Lucy pounces.

"Don't tell me it was the Wselfwulfs?" Another silence, Lucy hides her pleasure well with a furrowed brow and downturned lips. She toys with her mug, pretending at consternation as Atticus stares down into his dark coffee. "They're certainly getting bold."

"They're getting presumptuous," Atticus corrects, his voice darker than normal as his face morphs into a frown. "They slipped past the borders again. Got into town and had some fun with the locals at a bar."

I miss Lucy's reaction, my sights pinned to Atticus in shock. "What?"

He nods grimly and tilts his mug in my direction. I shake myself from my momentary daze, tending to the scrambled eggs briefly before turning down the heat beneath them. Seconds later, I'm refilling Atticus mug. My regard is full of concern.

"How? Where did they get through?" I ask quietly.

He gives a slow shake of his head and captures my gaze to relay a silent message: *Later.* I give what I hope to be a subtle nod and head back to the stove.

"It doesn't matter how or where. What matters is that they did. The Wselfwulfs aren't just going after the pack. They're going after the town. If this isn't a clear indication that what they seek is far beyond their supposed 'blood debt,' then I don't know what will be."

I'm busy plating the eggs when Lucy chimes in again. "Indeed. Their actions are a direct violation of our laws. Human blood and flesh are not ours to take."

I turn with Atticus's plate in hand to see Lucy give a short shake of her head. I have trouble reading the consternation on her face. Is it real or false?

"The Celestial Court—"

"Has had its say," Lucy interrupts rather blandly. "This is your fight to resolve. No other pack will intervene."

Liar.

Atticus is too busy gulping down his second coffee to notice the fierce glare I shoot Lucy and her smirking rebut.

"I'm beginning to think Callie is right," he remarks, his exhaustion showing as he runs his hand over his hair again. The muscles in his back bunch and stretch as he bends with the action. When I return and set down his plate, I run my hand carefully over the taut muscles in comfort. Atticus peeks up at me through dark lashes, looping his arm around my waist and tugging me into a side hug. "Thank you for breakfast."

"Of course," I murmur, softening against him immediately.

I hadn't realized how much I missed his touch. My hand lies tentatively against his back still, enjoying the sheer warmth of him.

Lucy clears her throat. "And what does this 'Callie' suggest?" This time it is Lucy and Atticus who pass a meaningful look between them. I can't stand it.

"More coffee anyone?" I ask. Their connection breaks, and I let out a small, thankful sigh.

"No, but thank you," Atticus responds, squeezing my hip fondly.

Lucy holds out her mug, a smug smile on her face. "Yes."

Forced to fetch her another coffee, I move with speed, loathe as I am to keep my back to them for even a second. I accomplish the task quickly my teeth as I pour, before striding back over and setting the drink in front of her. Then at long last, I take my place by Atticus's side.

"I—" The vibration of a phone sounds, and Atticus reaches into his pocket with haste. "I need to take this," he murmurs, then excuses himself from the table.

His footsteps sound through the hall, then up the stairs. His husky voice is a mere whisper to my lycan hearing with the sound of his heavy steps muffling his words.

"You see, cousin," Lucy begins, her voice soft and alluring. "Everything is already falling into place."

I pause at her words. Lucy examines me through lowered lashes, a smile of satisfaction curling the ends of her lips. The sight does more to aggravate me than anything else. Seeing her so relaxed and confident in *my* home... it ignites in me a wave of anger only Lucy can muster.

"You can't be so ignorant as to think the Blancs will support the Adolphus pack regarding this unseemly ordeal," she says. My lips form into a line, and in an insufferably patronizing move, Lucy reaches out to pat my arm. "Oh dear, did you think your marriage secured an unbreakable alliance between our pack and the Adolphus'? Winter, *honestly*."

I grit my teeth to keep from snapping back, but the wolf prowls forward in my mind regardless to speckle gold across my gray eyes. *How will Lucy treat me if she knows the wolf and I are becoming closer with every passing day?*

"A simple divorce will put everything right, and really, after they learn what you've done, the odds of one occurring are startlingly high. Don't you think? Thank goodness you've not sealed the mark," she says, her voice suddenly filled with exasperation. "It's the one thing you've managed to do right."

I am dumbstruck, not merely at Lucy's heartless behavior, but at my own nativity that somehow, after everything, things will be all right. The gold specks fade. There will be consequences no matter what hand I play.

I stall a moment longer, taking a sip of my coffee to contemplate what response I can give. "After hearing what Atticus said, I doubt any intervention will be needed to provoke the packs into a final confrontation," I say.

"Indeed," Lucy replies, back to her poised nonchalance. "But your parents—the alphas of your rightful pack—want this tricky little magical curtain surrounding the town felled."

"You heard what happened last night," I argue. "The Wselfwulfs aren't just going after the pack. They're going after the humans of this town. Deactivating the border will put them at risk. Besides, we don't even know if giving the tonic to Luna will make any real difference in the border's stability. What's the point—"

Lucy lets out a cruel laugh, her head tilting back and her glossy ponytail swaying back and forth. The sound almost covers the pacing occurring overhead.

"I knew it," she says, at last, her brown eyes pinning me in place. "You've completely assimilated here, haven't you? God, why your parents even tried to bother with keeping the Blanc pack bonds around you is beyond me. I always knew you would falter. I knew you would leave us the second the opportunity presented itself. It was only a matter of time."

My throat tightens. "That isn't—"

Lucy scoffs, the sound harsh and grating. "Please. Your pathetic excuses will not sway me, cousin. Besides, your disloyalty is of no real consequence in the end. I'll be taking up the cause in your stead."

"What?"

She hums. The glint that's in her eyes is insidious. "Your parents must have had their doubts too. Why else would they make such a contingency plan? And cousin—" she leans in once more, her wicked smile still in place "—the tonic they gave me isn't nearly as forgiving as yours."

"No," I say, my voice firm. "You are not hurting Luna."

"Then do it yourself with the tonic you've been allotted. Or else I'll do the deed with mine."

I clench my jaw, glaring daggers at my cousin. "I could have you confined with a single phone call."

"Oh, cousin, you don't think we haven't planned for that, do you? All eventualities have been accounted for. If the Wselfwulfs can get past your precious wolves and magical border, what makes you think I can't give you the slip? I told you. Everything is in place. Even if I'm held back, there will be another to take my place. The fairy still enjoys walks in the forest, no?"

"You said my parents don't want a war with the Adolphus pack."

Lucy slips her hand behind her back, and a moment later she is sliding a silver flask across the table to me. Her smile cuts.

"I lied," she says with a laugh. "It's your choice, Winter. Will the fairy live or die?"

A thick silence overwhelms the kitchen. My fingers clutch the coffee cup in my hand, but my tension and fury cannot be contained to the simple action.

"Tick tock, cousin. Your beau will be down soon enough. I wonder what news he'll have to share with us." Lucy's expression forgoes any attempt at concealment. Her glee at knowing something I do not is unbearable.

My hand snatches up the flask.

+++

Somehow, I am able to leash the tears that beg to fall for the long walk to the Trinity Coven's house. I expect my feet to drag the entire way, but my trepidation seems to have the opposite effect.

At the very least, I'm more prepared for the trek than my last into town. I'm bundled up against the harsh batting of the wind. Atticus caught me at the front door, an expression of surprise on his face with his phone at his ear.

I waved my own phone at him, mouthing my cousin's name as my excuse, then left.

When I reach the witches block, I am surprised—and somewhat disappointed—that Atticus has made no attempt to come after me. My throat tightens unexpectedly as I suck in a sharp breath of cold air. That he didn't come to rescue me, I correct myself.

But it isn't me who needs to be rescued. It's Luna.

You're going to get someone killed.

Aunt Mo's words whisper like a ghost past my ear. In my mind's eye, she follows each step I make. Never in my wildest dreams would I have imagined myself in such a role. Nor that Luna and Juniper would play the part of my potential victims.

At the end of their driveway, I stand. An odd sensation tingles across my skin, but it is one I am familiar with. Magic. My wolf comes to the surface and wishes us to be careful in the witches' territory.

My rabbit heartbeat cannot be slowed as I inch closer to the house. It is still decked in Yuletide cheer, with wreaths of evergreen and pops of holly. The sight of the bright red berries makes my stomach twist as I recall Atticus's first attempt at communicating with me through the language of flowers.

Holly meant hope, but their message couldn't be further from the truth to me now.

I curve my path to take the shoveled walkway to the front door. I don't expect it to open halfway as I near nor Aunt Mo to be standing there. I shuffle to a stop, staring with wide eyes at her unexpected presence.

"I've been expecting you," she says. Her hair, as white as my own, is braided in a thick plait and hangs over her chest. "Why don't you come in out of the cold."

But I can't. Not when my boots have suddenly frozen to the ground, and the flask in my back pocket weighs as much as a brick. "I—"

"Yes, I know," Aunt Mo says kindly, though a sadness lingers plainly at the corners of her soft smile and wrinkles near her eyes. "I don't have long to chat. Diana and Lydia are expecting me, as is my daughter at the clinic. Well, child?"

She moves to the side, leaving the door open wide as she fetches a long wool coat from nearby. I take a step forward, my lungs emptying out in a large cloud of white before me.

Aunt Mo watches my cautious approach with a knowing gleam. "Don't fret, child. Your journey is nearing its end. Though the road is treacherous, your sacrifice won't be forgotten."

I stop before ascending the small porch. "I don't think sacrifice is the right word," I say, my voice brittle. Or maybe it is considering I'm about to sacrifice Luna for Juniper.

"You'll see," she counters as she wraps a technicolor scarf around her neck. The action doles out a strong waft of her perfume, and rose, amber, and lily of the valley fill my nose. "We all have our parts to play in the grand design. Even I."

Aunt Mo dons an equally bright hat and slips out the door to stand in front of me. I swallow and avert my eyes, before I dab at the bottom of my nose with a little sniff.

"Does the cut of your deck continue to repeat itself in my regard?" I ask, surprised at how level my voice is.

She places a hand on my shoulder as she goes to pass, her mittened hands giving an affectionate squeeze. "For you and me both. It seems our paths are unavoidable."

"What do you—"

Aunt Mo uses me to steady herself as she steps down off the porch, a weary sigh flying past her lips.

"Remember, Winter. You're stronger than you give yourself credit."

I watch her go, dismay swelling inside my chest as my retort lodges itself in my throat. Her words, no doubt meant to provide comfort, do not hit their mark. How can she be so calm and collected knowing what I'm about to do? Why doesn't she banish me from the house with some spell? Or warn Luna of my approach?

"Hello?" a curious voice calls from inside. "Is someone there?" Footsteps pad lightly from afar, nearing at a reluctant rate. I take another step forward and scan the interior of the house, my eyes colliding with Luna's figure.

"Hi, Luna," I say, a weak smile in place.

"Winter!" A large smile splits her face, and she reaches me in three large strides. "Come in. It's too cold to be outside." Taking my wrist in her hand, she tugs me past the door's threshold and eagerly shuts the door behind me.

"I… I hope I'm not interrupting anything."

"Oh, no," she replies, bobbing on the balls of her feet as she watches me shed my outwear. "I've had a very nice day today. Much better than yesterday, or the day before. This morning I took a long walk, and when I returned, Zoelle was here! She took off work today to spend time with me, and we've been baking cookies."

My smile falters. "Zoelle is here?"

She nods, her strange purple eyes regard me with an intensity I'm unused to. "She used to live here. She comes by quite a lot," she tells me matter-of-factly and cocks her head to the side. "Are you feeling all right? You look… ill."

Luna takes a step back, her eagerness swiftly waning.

"I am feeling a bit under the weather," I confess, stripping off the last of my winter wear and patting down my hair. A terrible knot forms in my stomach. "I'm sure it's nothing a spot of tea can't fix."

"You came for medicinal tea?" she asks. With a little sniff, I nod. Luna stills eyes me cautiously. "Are you contagious?"

My mouth opens and closes as I stare back at her. "No," I finally say, confused and uneasy by her line of questioning. "Why do you ask?"

She shrugs. "The aunts don't want me to catch my death of a cold. You probably shouldn't walk around outside so much," she prattles on. "You might catch your death too."

"Luna? Who are you talking to?"

Before I can answer, Luna turns about-face and begins skipping off in the direction of the kitchen. "Winter came to visit! She's sick and needs tea."

I blanch, but with little reason not to, I follow. My hands fuss with the bottom of my sweater. I'm glad for its thick nature as it better covers the flask's bump in my back pocket.

"Hi," I greet Zoelle with a small wave and force a smile onto my lips.

She's leaning over an open oven, two tattered oven mitts on either hand. The room smells of chocolate and sugar, with traces of lavender and eucalyptus in the air. I eye the steaming kettle placed at the back of the stove and Luna's perched position on the kitchen table's end.

Her blunt ivory hair sways as she rocks along to the music playing softly from the radio. But it's the gentle fluttering from her iridescent wings that steals my attention. Luna pays no mind to my study, but the weight of Zoelle's gaze rests heavy on my figure.

"You're still not feeling well?" she inquires, straightening with a tray of cookies in hand. The oven door closes softly without aid from Zoelle. Magic. It tickles beneath my nose, and I give another sniff.

"Yes, but this is a more standard affair," I lie. "If you have anything to help fend off a cold, I'd be grateful."

Zoelle smiles back, but I see the wane edge to it. "I'll check the cupboard. I'm sure we have something."

I stand awkwardly near the kitchen's entrance, taking my fill of the cozy atmosphere.

"Can I help?"

Zoelle looks over her shoulder at me and gives a nod. "That would be great! I need to get the cookies off the tray and onto the cooling rack. Gran requested a batch for the coven meeting tomorrow, but I'm not sure if they'll last the night here. Use two scoops of this"—Zoelle waves a jar full of dried leaves and other bits at me—"and half a scoop of this." The second bottle is a glittering navy powder.

"What is it?"

"The first is a mixture of ginger, lemon, and clove. And the other is, well, some magic really. It will give the tea a real boost. If you like honey, it's in the cabinet just there." Zoelle sets a third jar full of green leaves and little white feather-like strands on the counter. "And if you can make some of this jasmine for Luna and me, I'd appreciate it."

I'm lucky Zoelle and Luna are absorbed in their own worlds. They don't notice my mechanical movements as I make my way toward the far end of the kitchen island. Zoelle hums along to the song on the radio as she transfers the cookies from the sheet pan to her cooling rack. Luna's eyes have flutter closed as she continues to sway to the music, her feet kicking absentmindedly in the air.

"Do I need to put on a new kettle?" I ask, my tongue heavy in my mouth as I force the words out.

"Hmm." Zoelle spins around and picks up the kettle, giving it a little shake. "It can do with some more water."

I tame the tremble that dares rise as I take the kettle and place it beneath the faucet. My gaze slants surreptitiously back over to Zoelle, who is finishing up her task.

Can I do this? Drug Luna, right under Zoelle's nose?

Do I have a choice?

I thought I had it all figured out. I thought I would be able to ask for help and avoid this measure altogether. A lump forms in my throat, one I struggle to swallow down as I turn off the faucet and place the kettle back on the stove. The flame flickers to life underneath its black belly.

I can't afford to take Lucy's threat idly. *I'm sorry, Luna,* I think with great remorse.

Zoelle sits at the table when she's done, stretching her feet out onto a spare chair. "I think this afternoon I'll take a nap. I was up so early this morning," Zoelle comments. "What are your plans for the rest of the afternoon, Winter?"

Digging my own grave. And Luna's.

I keep my back to the two, searching the cabinets for three mugs. "Making sure my cousin doesn't stir up trouble," I reply.

I hope they can't hear the hoarse quality to my voice as I try to keep my emotions in check. Grim anticipation snakes through my veins, coursing through my body mercilessly. The color drains from my face as I square my shoulders and turn back around to gather the tea leaves.

Zoelle and Luna pay me no mind. While Luna's indifference does not surprise me, Zoelle's does. Surely she can feel my unease through the pack bonds? Either she makes no mention of the fact for the sake of my privacy or other issues must occupy her mind.

I wait impatiently for the whistle of the kettle. My fingernails find purchase in my palm, flexing and unflexing with nervous energy.

"Can I have a cookie, Zoelle?"

The witch laughs at Luna's question. "I told you they wouldn't last," she says. I force out a chuckle in response. "Sure, Luna. Bring me one too, would you?"

"Do you want a cookie too, Winter? Zoelle makes the best chocolate chip cookies."

"No thanks," I reply, tensing as I hear Luna's approach. "I just ate."

For whatever reason, their lack of suspicion only makes my nerves worse. When the kettle sounds, I nearly jump out of my skin. I place a hand to my heart, my bottom lip trembling as I turn off the heat.

I can't do this.

"This is so good. Are you sure you don't want one, Winter?"

I shake my head as I hunch over the countertop to dole out the tea leaves. "Positive," I reply breathlessly.

"I was going to call you today, Winter," Zoelle says from her seat. "I wanted to know if the tea you had at the cafe yesterday helped you figure out how to help your cousin?"

The spoon I use to measure out the leaves falls from my grasp. Its clatter sounds like the crash of broken glass in my ears. I hold my breath, slamming the spoon down to stop it before it can bounce off the counter.

"Sorry," I mumble. "I've worked things out. Sort of," I say more loudly.

Remember, Winter. You're doing this for Juniper. And if you don't... Lucy will.

I take a deep breath and force myself to focus on the superficial task at hand. A faint buzzing-like static begins to sound in my head as I slip the flask from my back pocket and hurriedly splash its content into a turquoise mug.

"That's good," Zoelle replies, her words slightly jumbled from her chewing.

The flask returns to my back pocket, and the rest of what occurs is like something out-of-body experience. I see myself reach for the tea kettle and pour the steaming liquid into each mug. The purple for Zoelle. The green and white striped one for myself. The turquoise with the tonic for Luna.

"Let me help!" Luna chirps.

Her enthusiastic reply breaks me from my spell. Before I can dissuade her, she is at my side, plucking two of the hot mugs from out in front of me as I scramble to set the kettle back down.

"The turquoise mug is for you," I spit out. "The purple is for Zoelle."

"Okay!" she responds, sparing me a happy smile. "Isn't this nice. I like having visitors. A lot of the witches come around, but they don't stay for long. Plus, they all look at me funny still. The pack doesn't like to visit because they don't like magic. Do you like magic? I've been told it bothers the lycans?"

I stare dumbstruck at her back, her wings fluttering more vigorously with her excited chatter. "Pardon?"

"The magic doesn't bother me, but that's because Gran says I'm made of magic. Like her and Zoelle! And Aunt Lydia and Mo! We're all magic, so it doesn't bother us."

I don't know how to respond, let alone react. Luna stretches forward, and Zoelle leans forward to meet her reach halfway. A sharp prickle of apprehension crawls down my spine.

"Remember, the turquoise is for Luna and—"

"Do you think the witches like me?" Luna asks Zoelle, slipping back up onto the table and finally turning to face me.

My breath catches in my throat before a startled cry makes its way out. I dart forward, and Luna lets out an indignant squeak as I barrel toward her.

Her jasmine tea sloshes over the pretty purple ceramic. "What's wrong?" she cries out.

Zoelle makes a noise. The sound like a hum of an acknowledgment. Her head pops around Luna's body, the turquoise mug poised at her lips. Zoelle's brown eyes grow wide at my frantic approach.

Again I seem to slip out of my body, watching in horror as Luna slides off the table into my path. I barely stop myself from colliding into her, and even Zoelle lets out a shriek.

"Don't drink that!" I get out, grabbing Luna by the shoulders and jerking her to the side.

Luna lets out a startled cry, swinging far too easily in the air as she tucks her legs up and her wings beat rapidly behind her. "Ow!" She passes the purple mug back and forth between her hands before dropping it and skirting backward—*flying* backward.

It's a momentary distraction as I stare at her in astonishment, my mouth hanging open like a goon.

"What's wrong with it?" Luna asks, practically hysterical as her eyes dart between the tea and me.

"No—I…." My gaze darts to Zoelle, whose posture has changed only marginally to her feet planted on the floor instead of propped up on the chair next to her in case she needs to move as well. "Don't drink that," I tell her, holding out a hand in warning.

"It tastes fine," she reassures me, a smile on her face. "What's—"

No. No. No.

Not this. Not Zoelle. *The baby….*

A rush of blood shoots to my head. The dizzying sensation makes me falter. The world around me begins to dull, and though Zoelle's mouth moves, clear lines of concern drawing her brows together, the sound is muffled. A hand wraps around my waist, tugging me backward and I stumble.

"Winter!"

The sharp cry pierces the fog walling up around me, but only for a moment. In an instant, a sense of foreboding envelopes me as my vision escapes me.

"Get the water. Winter? Winter, are you all right?"

My senses come to me gradually, but the panic hits me full force. "What happened?" I breathe, arching up. My hands scramble for balance, only to meet the hard floor. "Why am I on the floor?"

Zoelle shushes me, helping me to sit upright slowly. "You fainted," she says calmly. "You're fine. You didn't hit your head. Luna caught you."

I slant my eyes away from Zoelle to watch Luna's quick return. A glass of water clutched in her hand. She's still flying, her feet inches from the ground. Her wings help to lower her to the ground, in a move so graceful my breath catches once more. She passes me the water wordlessly, her face pale and purple eyes glimmering with unshed tears.

"Are you okay?" Luna asks.

"The tea!"

Zoelle's grip on my upper arm tightens. "Winter… why didn't you want me to drink the tea?"

I slam my eyes shut, thick self-hatred crawling up the back of my throat with an acidic taste to it. "Please tell me you didn't drink it, Zoelle. Please."

When I open my eyes to examine her expression, I am met with her startled expression. "Winter," her voice belays her fear.

"I'm sorry—I'm so sorry. It wasn't meant for you. It was—Zoelle? Zoelle!"

The dark-skinned witch's eyes flutter, her rigid posture growing lax. "What did you do?" she whispers.

Her grip on me falls away as she places a steadying hand on the ground and the other to her temple. My full facilities come racing back to me.

"I don't know," I confess. "It's supposed to temporarily incapacitate a person." Shame floods my system as tears rapidly make their way down my cheeks. I catch Zoelle as her arm buckles, pulling her into my lap. "I'll fix it," I ramble, a hand stroking her cheek. "I promise. I swear it. I'll fix it. This wasn't meant to happen to you."

I see the whites of her eyes briefly before she succumbs to oblivion. I squeeze my eyes shut, a panicked sob wrenching from my throat. There is no escaping my guilt. Her fear and disappointment brand themselves across the back of my eyelids like a tattoo.

"What did you do?" Luna demands, her voice quivering with disgust.

The consequences of my actions crumble down upon me like a pile of bricks as I twist my head slowly to observe Luna. Though her skin is devoid of color, the vines and flowers that slither beneath her skin now writhe and whip in agitation. I suck in a steady breath, eyeing the fairy warily.

"I made a mistake, Luna. I—"

Her expression turns dark. "Don't touch her," she snaps, pointing a finger at me. "You *hurt* her! You were going to hurt me!"

With great care, I maneuver Zoelle's sleeping form off my lap and onto the ground. She's breathing—*thank God*—but the fear of not knowing precisely what the tonic will do puts me on edge. What if it kills the baby? What if it kills both of them?

"You don't understand," I plead, raising my hands in a placating manner as I stand on shaky legs. "I had no choice, Luna. She was going to do something irreversible to you. This… this can be fixed. She won't stay like this forever."

The cut of Luna's glare is powerful, but it is the simmering electricity filling the air that worries me more.

"I'm sorry," I beg through tears. "I didn't want anyone to be hurt, but I didn't have a choice. They made me. My—"

A cry erupts from Luna's lips, but not just any cry, one that promises war. Her hands thrust forward, and I am tossed back by an unseen force. Her blistering magic scorches my skin, ending only when I hit the ground and rebound into the formal dining room table.

"You chose wrong," she says. Her voice is utterly devoid of emotion as she makes another sweeping motion with her hand.

The magic thrusts me back once more, plucking me from my spot and forcing me from the dining room into the adjacent hallway until I am forced into the entryway. I scramble for breath against the onslaught of burning energy.

"Luna, wait!"

But my desperate plea is of no use. The front door slams open behind me, and I'm tossed outside like some rag doll. All the air dislodges from my lungs at the brutal impact with the ground. Tumbling like some fool, I barely manage to stop myself from being hurtled to the end of the yard.

When I manage to stand, my body is trembling. Luna stands in the doorway entrance, her eyes glossy with tears and hate before the door slams shut.

"No," I whisper. "No, no, no."

It's difficult to place my feet under me when they shake so terribly. My nerves are shot, and my skin still feels ablaze from Luna's dangerous outburst. What have I done? *Oh, God.* I reach the door breathlessly, banging my fist against it in a desperate attempt to reenter.

"Luna! Luna, please open the door!"

There is no answer from inside. I bang my fist once more, gasping for breath as tears continue to ruin my vision.

"Please, Luna!" I cry. "I'm sorry."

In my state of shock, I don't comprehend the sound of tires squealing to a sudden stop until it is too late. My body turns frozen as the slamming of a car door reverberates through the air.

"Zoelle!"

Knees buckling, I palm the door to find balance. It's Xander.

"Zoelle!"

I barely move out of the way in time as he slams into the door. His body forcing the door open with wild authority. He doesn't spare me a glance as he rushes inside. When his howl of pain and rage fill the house, the countless threads of the Adolphus pack bonds constrict. My knees hit the ground a second later under the force of the alpha's unbound emotions.

What have I done?

THE STORM

- Chapter 15 -

Whatever magic Luna has performed bars me from entering the house. The magic burns the pads of my fingers as I reach out a tentative hand against the wall. Inside, Xander's desperate cries echo clear and aching in the house.

The sound of another car's rapid approach reaches my ear. Its tires skid to a halt as the engine is abruptly cut off. I spare a look over my shoulder, my dread building all over again.

It's Atticus.

"Winter? What's going on? What's wrong with Zoelle." He races over to my side, faster than he should in such a public space. "Are you hurt? Who did this to you?"

Atticus drops to his knees in front of me, pulling me into his chest like a bear trap. Selfishly, I breathe in his scent and take a moment's comfort in his embrace. *This will be the last of us.* Tears momentarily blur my vision.

"Atticus...."

"Atticus!" Xander's competing cry trumps my own. Both our heads snap in the direction of the house, peering down the long hallway that takes guests and occupants alike to the sizeable back kitchen.

Strong hands help me up, then rest on the last few vertebrae of my spine to urge me inside. I resist.

"What is it?" Atticus asks breathlessly, stepping around me and past the invisible border that denies me entrance.

"I shouldn't go in there," I mumble back, head shaking resolutely from side to side. "I can't."

Deep lines crease his forehead, but before Atticus can offer a rebuttal, Xander gives another shout. "Okay, just… just stay here." He whips off his coat and thrusts it into my arms. "Put this on. You'll catch your death out here," he says in parting.

I watch, chin wobbling in distress as he goes to see my handiwork. Like an addict, I bury my face in his coat and breath in his scent. It soothes me in a way I cannot begin to understand. Even the agitated state of my wolf takes comfort in the act.

Damp moss.

Rosemary and other green notes.

Warm musk.

Atticus.

All of these scents have come to mean so much more to me than I've anticipated. Safety. Security. Home. Hope. A harsh wind beats at my back, and though I long to stay just as I am, my clothes provide no protection from the elements, not after I have been tossed so ruthlessly in the snow.

I slip on his jacket, my body aching as I do. Luna's magic still spasms across my muscles as I stretch my arms through each sleeve with a hiss.

I had no idea Luna was so powerful.

Does anyone else?

Voices from inside are muffled and fast paced. They're too low for me to keep up with, and I distantly wonder if the buzzing sound in my ear is the byproduct of Luna's magic. My fingertips press hesitantly against the magical border once again.

"Ouch," I mutter and bring the offended fingers to my lips. It might as well be an electric fence.

Minutes begin to trickle by. I wish desperately for my phone or a watch to study the hand as it inches past each tick mark on the clocks face. What is taking them so long?

I reach for the flask and give it a shake. I had only added a splash to the drink... maybe that meant the tonic won't be as potent? I gulp. I can only hope.

My teeth bite down savagely into my bottom lip. What are they going to do to me when they find out? A coarse shiver races across my skin. Will they send me back to my parents? Lock me up in some cell? Take their retribution with my flesh?

Another shiver trounces my body as the wind whirls around me. Will they be as unforgiving as this winter wind?

I'm too lost in my thought to notice him at first. But when the distinctive creak of a floorboard gives under the weight of a body, I shoot my gaze in its direction. Atticus stands in the hallway, his phone clutched in his palm tightly and his face pale.

"Winter...." He steps forward, then stops. The floor creaks again, and a shadow emerges from behind him. Luna's dark face stares back at me. "Winter, what did you do?"

+++

I'm passed off to Keenan—the fifth-ranked wolf in the Adolphus pack—in the end. He drives me to the alpha's house, a ferocious scowl upon his face. When we pull up to the house, he escorts me inside and upstairs to one of the guest bedrooms. I don't protest when he locks the door behind me.

My "cell" is bright and warm. Why I haven't been detained to more deserving quarters, I can't begin to understand. And then I wait, left with my thoughts and guilt.

My bones ache. The blood in my body runs cold despite my lycan nature. Every other thought in my head berates my actions for the day, while the other part shouts its excuses and protests.

It was for Juniper.

My nails dig into my thigh. *Was it though?* A soft voice persists. *Or was it for you?*

Footsteps weigh across the hallway floor outside along with hushed voices. When the lock rolls over to its proper key, it is Keenan who enters my cell.

"I need you to come with me now, Winter," he says gruffly. There is little emotion on his face, but what I can read turns my stomach violently. Disappointment. Shame. Anger.

All deserved.

"Okay," I whisper, finding my voice rough. Still wrapped in Atticus's coat, I shuffle after Keenan's imposing figure as he makes his way down the hallway. We reach a room with two large doors. Keenan gives a single sharp rap against the wood before pushing forward inside.

Xander and Atticus occupy the large study. They wear matching frowns, though their eyes convey far different messages to me. I duck my head as Keenan leads me to a chair placed deliberately before their stoic forms.

"Leave us," Xander orders. Keenan obeys, the door opens and closes softly behind him.

Silence hangs over us like a heavy blanket to slowly smother us with its tension. I dare not utter the first word. I know well enough that it is not my place to do so. Not when their emotions are directed so poignantly at me through the pack bonds.

There's little more that I can do than bend my head to the side, fully exposing my neck as their displeasure weighs me down. A soft whine escapes my throat at their persistence. This... this is far worse than any punishment my parents have doled out to me.

The alpha and beta's disappointment resonates through every cell in my body. It forces the wolf to roll onto its back, exposing its vulnerable belly to them in tandem with the exposure of my neck.

"Why?" Xander asks, voice cracking painfully on the single word.

My lips press into a hard line. A dangerous lump forms in my throat as a sob threatens to surface. But my hysterics will have to wait. The command in Xander's voice is unavoidable.

"My parents," I say, attempting to find the right explanation. "They gave me an ultimatum. Help them, or see my cousin put in her place. They're going to marry her off—"

A vicious growl tears from Xander's throat, and I flinch in response and snap my mouth closed. My eyes grow wide in shock and fear as Atticus steps into Xander's path. His palm presses firmly against the alpha's chest.

"You'd risk the life of Zoelle, of your alpha, to—to avoid your cousin getting married? Do you understand how absurd that sounds? Explain to me how you compared the two and determined who faired more important."

"You don't understand. June is practically a child. She's seventeen, and he's sixty-three and widowed twice through questionable means. If she marries him, she's signing her own death certificate. Not to mention whatever other plans my parents have in mind to make sure she's up to the task." Terrible gnawing guilt eats away at my insides at their expressionless faces. "They said if I helped... she'd be spared."

Xander jerks back with a growl. A tanned hand spears through his dark hair in frustration. "Why? Why did they want you to hurt Zoelle?"

My mouth opens and closes as I sink into my seat. "My parents didn't want me to hurt Zoelle," I confess hoarsely. "They wanted me to give their tonic to Luna. To take her out of the game. It was never meant—"

"If it was meant for Luna, then why the *fuck* is my fiancée the one who's unconscious?"

I shudder under the intensity of his rage. "She took the wrong mug."

Xander curses and spins to the lone desk in the room. A single swipe of his arm and the contents it keeps on display crash to the floor. I flinch back.

This I'm used to and have seen before. Next, a well-placed hit against my cheek will occur. Or maybe the stomach. The familiarity of my situation provides little comfort, but at least in knowing what will happen next, I can—

A hand comes to rest on my thigh. The touch is surprisingly intimate, and as I look into Atticus's blue eyes, I hesitate. His mouth is set in a grim line, and his cheeks are drawn in to suppress more emotions.

"Why do they want to hurt Luna?"

"To bring down the barrier around the town. My parents think Luna is the key," I whisper back.

Atticus squeezes my thigh in reassurance. He takes a deep breath through his nose that I unconsciously mimic. "Why would they think Luna is the key?"

My chin falls to my collarbone as I struggle to answer. With my steel eyes averted to my lap, I reply. "Because I've been giving my mother updates on the pack. I stopped when Lucy came, but only because she took over the task."

For a moment, the grip on my thigh intensifies. My heart skips a beat as anticipation runs through my body. This is it. I clench my jaw and stiffen, prepared for whatever blow is to be delivered at the announcement of my treachery, but none come.

Peeking through my lashes, I see the look of revulsion painted across his face at me. There's no reason to bat away the tears that trickle down the side of my cheeks. The hot droplets run freely, stopped only when they reach the fabric of my—

His palm gingerly cups my cheek, for his thumb to wipe away the traces of my distress. "I'm not going to hit you," he tells me gruffly. Atticus's hand drops, and he walks back several steps.

I let out a harsh breath, one that I didn't know I was holding so tightly in my chest. "You're not?" I blurt out.

My eyes dart between the beta and alpha. It's well within their rights to dole out punishment as they see fit. Something of this caliber would call for a public shaming of some kind at home. But upon reexamining the wary horror that skirts across Xander's face as he examines my tense form and the hunch of Atticus's back, I realize their revulsion isn't directed at me. It is directed at my clear expectation of their reaction.

"No," Atticus says, his voice abrasive. He keeps his back to me, and for some time we stay in contemplative silence.

When Xander breathes a heavy-winded sigh and leans against the desk with arms folded tightly over his muscle-bound chest, I relax. Somewhat.

"Tell me everything," he commands. "Start to finish."

And so I do. Taking in a shaky breath, I confess to it all.

"They never wanted me to leave the pack. I'm the last of the Blanc line, with my father being the last male heir to our namesake and tie to the original pack line. At first, they tolerated our betrothal, but then...."

I trail off as I remember when news arrived that the Adolphus pack had been formed. My parents nearly called off our betrothal, because they were so incensed at the scandal.

"Then we split from the Wselfwulfs," Xander fills in.

I find his jasper-green eyes across the room and give a shallow nod. "Yes."

"What next?" he asks.

"It was obvious their attitude toward the betrothal changed. They didn't approve of your separation. They still don't. I thought my parents might withdraw from our contract with the Hayes all together when your feud came to a head last year, but the opposite happened. They became more invested in it.

"I didn't know then what I do now," I say after a deep breath. "That my parents want to ruin you from the inside out, using me as the tool to do so. They believe your feud can only be resolved with bloodshed." I swallow thickly and dash my tongue across my bottom lip. "Preferably yours."

The men share a look, one I cannot begin to fathom as they communicate soundlessly with one another.

I shift restlessly in my seat, clearing my throat softly before I continue. "My parents asked me to report on the pack's 'goings on' and to learn your plans against the Wselfwulfs. So I gave them bits and pieces of information that hedged on important or could at least be made to seem as such. They latched onto Luna."

"What else did you tell them?" Xander asks, his voice too calm for comfort. Heartbeat quickening, my fingers begin to toy restlessly with each other.

"My parents know your pack is large, far larger than they originally thought. They didn't realize you had wolves coming from across the country to join your pack. Truthfully, I never got to tell them much more outside of Luna's existence and the pack size before they sent Lucy and Knox." My fingers curl into my palm, the strain turning my knuckles white. "Apparently, I needed motivation."

Dark lashes hood Xander's cutting regard as he stares in contemplation at the ground. When he begins to straighten, his features stoic, the room relieves itself of some of the tension it carries. He walks forward confidently across the room, clasping Atticus on the shoulder as he passes.

"Sit, brother," he commands, his voice no longer void of emotion.

A shudder ripples over the banks of Atticus's shoulder, and my heart gives a painful lurch. Atticus does as his alpha commands, perching on the arm of a chair, but he continues to provide us with his back. *Not us*, I scold myself, *me*.

"Winter?" Xander comes to sit on the end of the coffee table before me. His feet are splayed far apart as he leans forward. "What was in the tonic you gave, Zoelle?"

"I don't know." I bite the inside of my cheek in frustration. "Mother and Lucy said it would only keep Luna incapacitated for a few days. They didn't want to do any permanent damage."

I see his jaw work as a glimmer of fear spots his eye. But Xander takes a deep breath to quell his baser emotions. I watch his control with awe, my lips parting in fascination as he leashes his greater impulses.

"Lest they start a war with the coven, no doubt," he states. "What do they think they'll gain through this kind of sabotage?"

"Mother and Father believe the fairy contributes heavily to the structure and stability of your wall. If she were taken out of the equation, it would allow for a final confrontation to occur. They want the dispute between the packs settled, once and for all."

"And they favor the Wselfwulfs?"

I hesitate. "Yes. Though Mother has never said it outright to me. There's little doubt in my mind that they wish to see the Wselfwulfs as the victor. Their… ideals and attitudes on how a pack should be maintained run in the same vein of thought, I'm afraid. Mother said your separation has caused too many waves in the lycan community, as well. My reports on the growth of your pack surely didn't help in curbing her thinking."

The scent of my shame must saturate the air, for Xander's nose crinkles in distaste.

"Is there anything else I should know?" he asks seriously.

Anything else? Only everything.

How can I possibly detail the power my parents held over me? The conditioning I went through to be the perfect daughter and tool for their gains. What of our family curses? The Blancs stand at the root of the lycan curse, and then there is the delicate subject of the soulmark curse cast upon my pack alone.

Unwittingly, my eyes trace over Atticus's stooped spine. How can I tell him I'll never bare his children?

"Winter?"

I wish not to take my eyes from Atticus, but my attention and cooperation are the very least I can offer my alpha. I bow my head, a sigh tumbling from my lips as one final vicious thought lashes me. Atticus will never wish to be with me after this—even if I could offer him a family.

"Yes?"

"Is there anything else I should know? Are your parents planning anything else? Do you know anything of the Wselfwulfs plans? Would Lucy?"

With a furrowed brow, I begin to shake my head, only to stop mid-turn. What about Lucy and her special tonic? Do I dare speak of Aunt Mo's prediction? My treacherous heart leaps into my throat.

"Lucy… she has another tonic," I tell him. My eyes dart up to lock onto his jasper-green eyes. They stare back solemnly, the only hint of his unease in the tightness at the corners of his eyes. "When I refused to follow through with their plan and threatened to expose her, she delivered a different threat.

"Lucy was given a different tonic to administer if I failed. Something more… toxic, I guess—" my voice wavers at the flash of gold in Xander's eye "—and that if she was compromised or hampered, there was another to take up the task in her place."

Another strike of gold lights his eyes. But this time the wolf inside him holds, completely alert. "Who exactly will be here to take her place?" he asks tightly. "The other wolf from your pack left. We had eyes on him all the way to the border of Canada to make sure of it. Who else is here?"

I shrug helplessly. "I don't know. I have no idea, I swear."

A growl of frustration and anger stirs in his throat. He stands and begins to pace the room. The respite from the thick tension ends as we wait for Xander's next words.

I feel his presence stir the air behind me as he passes, and I stiffen.

"Your cousin attempted to leave Branson Falls—"

"What?" I spin in my seat to look at Xander. "She tried to leave?"

My body shakes with unadulterated fury. *That deceitful bitch.* Of course, she would abandon me here to face the consequences of my parents' plan alone.

"I said, 'attempted,'" Xander murmurs, clearly studying my reaction. My shoulders sag with some relief, but ire still floods my system. "She's being questioned downstairs in the basement as we speak."

"She is?"

Xander nods, and I press my nails into my palm to force myself to hold his gaze. "Good."

As I turn to face forward, letting my thoughts come at me in a whirlwind, I catch Atticus attempting to turn himself away from us before we notice. *Away from me*, I correct myself. A tight fist clenches my gut at the slight.

He can't even look at me... and how can I possibly blame him?

"Do you know if she kept this other tonic on her? Or if it's among her things back at your house?"

My mouth feels dry. In the interim of my speechlessness, I manage to shake my head.

"I'm not sure where she kept it," I answer at last. Then my hand goes fumbling to my back pocket to produce the silver flask. "This is what I put in the tea. I only put a small amount in. You can tell by its weight," I say, thrusting it in Xander's direction.

He takes it, a flare of hope igniting in his cheeks and eyes. "I'll make sure this gets to Zoelle's grandmother and the others of the Elder Triad immediately. Hopefully, they can deduce what it is and make the antidote."

"And if they can't?" Atticus voices.

Both Xander and I turn our attention to Atticus. His body is held tight, even as he stands and turns to face us. His expression is the darkest I've ever seen. It is a mixture of despair and disappointment, along with traces of anger that draw his jaw into a staunch line.

Xander folds his arms across his chest, his lips pulling downward. "We *will* find a way to wake her."

"But what if—"

"There are no 'buts.' No 'what-ifs,'" Xander snarls. "I don't care what we have to do to wake her. We will. Even if it means going after the Blancs."

I suck in a breath and earn both wolves' scowls.

"Do you have a problem with that, Winter?" Atticus asks coldly. "Still sitting on the fence about where your loyalties lie?"

His words are like a slap in the face. "I...." I don't know what to say. What *can* I say? "I won't support my parents any longer," I say, my voice gone small. "I'll do whatever is necessary to revive, Zoelle. I'll do whatever you ask."

I flick my gaze between the two men with uncertainness, but only one spares me a look of semi-approval. And it isn't the one I want. Atticus looks away, his glare striking the wall with vicious intent.

"Good," Xander tells me and walks my way. "We'll need all the help we can get if the Blancs are set on our demise. Atticus, go downstairs and have Keenan bring up Lucy. Then set Quinn to fetch the concentrated lunaria serum."

I want to reach out as he passes, but Atticus takes the long way around the room. He makes his way around several pieces of furniture to avoid being in my near vicinity. I watch him go, fighting off tears that are determined to fall despite my best efforts. A headache shudders to a throbbing start as the door slams shut behind him, and Xander's strong hand comes to rest on my shoulder.

"I'm sorry," I whisper harshly, tears spilling over my cheeks. "I swear I'll fix this. I'll fix everything."

His grip tightens momentarily before releasing me. "You'll forgive me if I don't place too much of the responsibility on your shoulders," he says, his voice remarkably steady and composed. It is such a change from his earlier temper, I spare him a wide-eyed once-over.

"Are you going to send me back?" A seed of sincere doubt enters my mind, taking hold of my imagination with grim aim and showing me visions of my parents' wrath.

The space between his brows pinches together. "Send you where?"

"To my parents?"

His eyes widen in alarm. "No," he tells me harshly. "Why don't you take a seat on the couch, Winter. I plan on Lucy sitting there."

I move, shrinking instinctively as I cross the distance to the nearest couch. As I sit, my heart thunders in my ears, and I brush my hair behind my ear.

"What are you going to do with me? And what if Atticus is right? What if she—" *Never wakes up? What if I killed her?* The words die in my throat as a panicked sob erupts from my throat. "Do you hate me?" *I would. I do.*

Xander pinches the bridge of his nose, a roughened sigh escaping him.

"I… I'm having trouble identifying just what I feel at the moment." I watch his Adam's apple bob and his brows hunch over his eyes. "I can't *feel* her. I keep fluctuating between anger and grief and this gut-wrenching panic that I can't feel her anymore because of the tonic. To be perfectly honest, I haven't spared you a thought other than trying to wrap my head around what your actions have done."

I release a tremulous breath, torn between semi-relief and despair. At least it isn't hate. Xander rakes a hand through his hair, his features smoothing to marble.

"I can't afford to dwell on any of those emotions, not with knowing how involved your parents have been in our pack's affairs and the Wselfwulfs waiting to strike." Xander pins me with a hard stare. "You will not dwell on this either, Winter. I want you rational and collected—that's an order."

I submit willingly to his heavy-handed command, a short whine crawling up my throat as I nod and bend my neck submissively. Faster than I anticipate, my fraught nerves and guilt slip away from me. Replacing them is a cool sense of detachment at my actions.

Vaguely I compare Zoelle's tea to Xander's alpha order. Her touch and manipulation are by far gentler, but Xander's is no less effective.

"The pack will look to us to see how they should react," Xander explains. "We cannot, above all, show weakness to them. We need to be strong, Winter."

I inhale calmly, folding my hands across my lap. "I understand."

Xander nods curtly, then begins to pace once more. "What are the chances your cousin sent word to your parents about tonight?"

"High," I reply, voice soft but steady. "If you caught Lucy attempting to leave, she will have informed my parents of her departure immediately. Or contacted someone to retrieve her."

"Would she have relayed any other information other than needing to be retrieved?"

I frown as I think. "Depending on where she was caught, Lucy will have attempted to convey the status of the border surrounding the town. If it was down or still up," I explain. "If she didn't, then whatever scouts they might have in the area—be it Wselfwulf or Blanc—will no doubt be checking to report the border's status."

Xander stops, his head cocking minutely to the side. "When they arrive, I don't want you to say a word, Winter," he commands. My throat tightens involuntarily at the order.

A long moment passes. I hear multiple sets of feet climbing the stairs. My heart kicks in my chest at the approach, but soon enough a forcible calm settles it down per the alpha's wishes.

"I don't hate you, Winter," Xander says quietly as he catches my eye. "But you've broken the trust of the pack, and that will have consequences I cannot begin to fathom. You'll have the whole pack to make amends with for hurting their alpha."

Holding his gaze, I give a tight nod and swallow thickly again. A wave of unnatural apathy helps it go down. "Of course," I murmur and then drop my gaze back to the floor just as a knock sounds on the door.

Rolling his shoulders back, Xander clasps both hands behind his back. A mask of indifference slides over his features as he peers at the door.

"Come in."

Lucy all but stumbles through the door. She shoots a vicious growl over her shoulder at Keenan, whose hand remains outstretched from his firm guidance. Callie trails after her muscle-bound soulmark, and I cannot help but notice the thick metal bands encircling her wrists. They look to be engraved with tribal markings.

My curiosity is hampered by Atticus entering and closing the door behind the others. Our eyes meet briefly.

A flash of something lingers in his gaze, but it is a look I can't possibly decipher for so many emotions flit across his arctic eyes. I dare to hope one might be an ounce of understanding.

"Don't touch me," Lucy snarls, righting herself and glaring at each occupant of the room with equal fervor. "When my alphas hear of this, they'll—"

"Enough," Xander commands with languid authority. Lucy's mouth snaps shut, her gaze narrowing on Xander. "Sit."

If her hands weren't bound behind her back, they'd be folded defiantly across her chest. Instead, she arches a brow in a challenge. Her feet remain steadfast in place.

"I'll stand."

I watch, half twisted in my seat as Xander nods to Callie. The once-warrior wears no expression as she walks past her beau toward Lucy. The engravings on her bracelets fill with an unearthly blue light as she nears her target.

"Don't—" Lucy's protest ends in a snarl as Callie roughly maneuvers her forward. My eyes alight in recognition as Lucy's struggles are countered with surprising ease from Callie. Those aren't just bracelets Callie wears—they're her *bracers,* the ones she spoke of at New Year's.

Lucy lands roughly in my previous seat. Redness encroaches upon her smooth complexion. Then, finally, her eyes settle on me. I stare back impassively.

"Cousin," she seethes. I dip my head a fraction in acknowledgment to her hostile greeting. "I see you followed through with your threat. I always knew you'd turn your back on us. Just wait until the pack learns of your disloyalty. They'll eat you alive."

The room stays quiet a moment too long for comfort, all eyes of the room darting between the two of us. My lips thin at Lucy's words, but I offer nothing in return. *Not that I could if I wanted to.*

"Did she give you anything useful?" Xander directs his question to Keenan.

The large man gives a resolute shake of her head. "No, just the same kind of bullshit she's spitting now," he answers brusquely. "Empty threats."

Lucy's head whips to the side to pin Keenan with her icy glare. "They aren't empty. My pack will seek retribution for this barbaric treatment."

Xander snorts. "As will mine. Though while I imagine your pack favoring more of its underhanded power plays, we'll be seeking justice more formally with the Moon Order."

The color slowly leeches from Lucy's face even as she thrusts her nose up into the air. The Moon Order is comprised of the oldest and most prominent packs across the world. They convened only in matters of great urgency or when the lycan community faces a great disturbance from within that threatens all. The only reason the Wselfwulf and Adolphus dispute had not been brought before the court was because of the witches' involvement.

"The Moon Order won't convene over a fairy," she finally spits, her eyes gleaming victoriously. "And the Celestial Court has already ruled on the matter."

"You're right," Xander responds coolly, "they won't convene over a fairy. But they will for an alpha."

Lucy's brows pinch together. "No amount of bitching and whining to the Order will—"

Xander holds up a hand, halting Lucy's speech. "If you cooperate and help us in reversing the effects of the tonic, I may be inclined to reconcile the matter directly with your alpha."

"She's just a fairy," Lucy snaps, shaking her head. "She'll wake up… eventually." Lucy ends her statement with a smirk.

The first traces of Xander's anger slip past his carefully built mask. I shift uncomfortably in my seat as the anger rolls through the pack bonds.

"You weren't listening carefully enough before," he tells her. His voice is dangerously soft. "Your attack wasn't carried out against a fairy but an alpha."

Lucy sucks in a sharp breath with realization, her eyes snapping to me. "You had one job, Winter. How could you possibly manage to fuck it up? How?"

She lurches toward me, but she doesn't make it out of her seat with Callie standing behind her at the ready. Lucy grunts as she is slammed back into her chair.

"Well?" Lucy snarls, still looking to me for an explanation.

I redirect my sights to the other side of the room, feeling more than just Lucy's glare digging into the side of my face. I tremble at the urge to speak, but bite my tongue instead.

"The 'how' isn't important, because the fact remains that my fiancée is in some supernatural coma—and it's your pack's fault."

Lucy doesn't answer. She lets the minutes pass by until I can no longer ignore making some assessment of her features. When I turn my regard back her way, I instantly encounter her dark eyes. A slow smile curves across her lips at my reaction.

"I'd argue the blame lies on Winter's shoulders. After all, she didn't have to deliver the tonic."

"Nor did you have to deliver the tonic to Winter, unless your alphas commanded you to do so. In which case, the blame rests solely on your alphas' shoulders," Xander replies. "Now tell me," he commands, plowing forward when Lucy opens her mouth to speak. "How do we reverse the effects of the tonic? Why do your alphas seek to tear down our territories borders and side with the Wselfwulfs?"

Lucy's chin quivers as she clenches her jaw. Xander's questions are thick with the commanding power of the alpha, but Lucy valiantly fights against it. My parents must have their own stringent orders in place to keep their motives secret.

"I'll take this as your decision not to cooperate. Atticus, get the serum." Atticus doesn't hesitate to obey the command and exits the room. "Do you know what *lunaria* is, Lucy?" Xander asks.

The she-wolf remains steadfast in her silence. Xander smiles grimly.

"It's a plant that when broken down to extract its essence can be used as a truth serum. Thanks to our friends in the Trinity Coven, we are well stocked and know how to use it. Under different circumstance, I might offer you the choice to ingest it through food or drink… but your combative behavior leaves me no other option than the other, more direct option. Atticus is fetching the syringe now."

"You can't do this to me," Lucy snarls at him, her eyes wild with fury and a touch of fear.

"I can."

Lucy turns to me. "Winter, are you seriously going to let them go through with this? Do you have any idea what your parents will do when they find out you were complicit in this?"

My jaw ticks in restraint, and my gaze darts to Xander in dismay. Unable to speak out or act as I wish is torture, but whispers in my mind tell me the punishment is deserved, even if it hurts. The dark thoughts smooth away as the alpha's orders replay in my head.

Don't dwell on your emotions... I want you rational and collected—that's an order.

My eyes shutter closed as I sink back into the couch.

"Selfish until the very end," she spits. "Don't worry, Winter. I'm sure Juniper will last at least a year or two with Jeffrey."

My eyes snap open at the threat, the wolf pushing past Xander's orders long enough to deliver a strangled growl before retreating.

"Winter," Xander barks. I shake as his earlier orders curl over me like some fist.

I'm sure Xander intends to say more, but the door to the study opens. Atticus enters, pausing a moment as the door closes behind him to assess the room. A concerned frown graces his brow as he looks between my taut figure and Xander's strict form.

"Keenan, make sure she doesn't move. Atticus, administer the serum."

Neither wolf hesitates. Lucy puts up a struggle, enough so that Callie wordlessly joins the fray to pin down her legs as Keenan keeps her in her seat. After the serum is delivered, Lucy is left panting.

Hatred and resentment come off of her person in palpable waves. Xander waits a full minute before he begins his interrogation, letting the lunaria seep into her system fully.

"Have you made contact with your pack since fleeing Hayes' house?"

"Yes."

"Who?"

Lucy attempts to fight the effects of the serum, her mouth opening and closing in rapid succession before she concedes to its effects. "Knox."

"What was in the tonic?"

"I don't know," she says.

"How do we reverse it?"

Lucy shoots daggers at Xander, but a gleam of vengeance sparks in her eyes. "I don't know," she responds.

Xander's stoic facade flickers. His green eyes narrow on my cousin. "Who will know?"

"My alphas."

Her answer makes Xander give a short growl. "Of course they will," he all but seethes. Xander takes in a deep breath before he settles down. "Do they realize the full ramifications of such an act? This was a premeditated act of violence on our allies in an attempt to eliminate our border."

Lucy gives a shrug, but it doesn't come off as nonchalant, as I'm sure she would like. "They wouldn't have gone through with it if they didn't consider all of the ramifications."

"Jesus Christ," Kennan mutters. I watch as he spares Xander a brief, incredulous look. Then the burly man crosses his arms over his chest and glares at the back of Lucy's head. "Your pack has no honor."

The words are harsh enough that even I recoil.

"Why are they willing to risk a war?" Xander asks, trace amounts of genuine curiosity peeking through his voice. Lucy scoffs, her eyes rolling up.

"Why would I know? That's the alphas' business—not mine."

"Tell me why you think they're willing to risk going to war."

Lucy stares back in confusion, her eyes dart nervously to me and back to Xander's imposing figure. I arch a brow back, keeping my face otherwise neutral.

"I… I don't know," she says with mild exasperation. "Probably because you're set to ruin the entire foundation of lycankind. You're so determined to be different and buck tradition that you don't see the ripples your actions have had on the rest of the packs who've heard of your disobedience. Well-ordered and maintained packs are breaking up. Wolves aren't respecting the hierarchy—"

"Change is inevitable. If we are the catalyst, so be it."

Lucy eyes him with contempt. Her silky hair falls half in front of her face as she leans forward. "So arrogant… it *will* be your downfall."

Xander ignores her commentary, plowing on. "How long will the effects of the tonic last?"

Lucy shrugs, another snark smile making its way onto her lips. "A few days… maybe longer. The tonic was meant for the fairy, you imbecile. Not a witch. Hopefully, she'll never come to—"

Xander's hand wraps around Lucy's throat. Her words cut off with a choking noise as she attempts to jerk out of his hold. Xander only bares his teeth.

"Xander." Atticus steps forward. He places a placating hand on his shoulder to urge him back. Xander goes reluctantly, eyes speared with gold as he glares at my coughing cousin.

"Get her out of my sight."

Keenan and Callie rush to obey, hustling Lucy out from her chair. Triumph reigns her features, but when her eyes land on me they gain a dangerous gleam.

"Oh, Atticus," she simpers mockingly. "Don't forget to ask my cousin about the other little curse. I'd hate for you to hold out hope for some kind of happily ever after."

They haul her out, and I dare not look back at the men behind me.

"What the hell is that supposed to mean?" Atticus barks.

ALL IS FAIR

- Chapter 16 -

There is something far worse to a deliberate measure of silence than one of awkward strain. The air becomes stretched thin between the occupants inhabiting the space and somehow riddled with electricity.

Knowing it's only a matter of time before the silence breaks—erupts—is a different kind of torture. And yet, knowing there is nothing that can be done to stop or deter the breaking leaves one feeling oddly at peace. Because if nothing else you know the silence will come to an end.

My eyes stay glued to the scenery outside the passenger window. They lock onto some far-off point until all that registers in my vision are stretches of white and blurs of the streetlights. A soft exhalation is driven from my mouth. It clouds the window momentarily and has the unpleasant side effect of refocusing my gaze upon my reflection as the condensation slowly fades.

At least I'm no longer walking the sword's edge.

I allow my gaze to shutter momentarily. I might not be walking the sword's edge anymore, trying to decide what to do and who to hurt, but now I'm deep into the fall. The talk at Xander's makes my perilous descent even more pronounced. Now there is nothing for me to reach out and grab on to. There is nothing and no one to support me.

The replay alone makes me ill.

"What the hell is that supposed to mean?" Atticus barks.

The door closes with a bang. I startle at the sound and take a step away from Atticus's hostile regard. My mouth runs dry as it opens to explain.

"What other curse?" Atticus demands. My mouth snaps shut.

Why the hell *did Lucy say that? First, she corners me into revealing the lycan curse origin, apparently on my mother's behest, and now this? I cannot* believe *my mother would allow her to make me expose one curse let alone* both.

Least of all to a pack my parents deemed dogs.

"Winter," Xander says, "answer him."

I whimper in retort as I continue to struggle to speak. My eyes dart nervously from alpha to beta. I will not be able to withhold my tongue much longer. But why—why would Lucy do this? Those who know of our curses and attempt to leave the Blanc pack are... taken care of.

"Oh God," I say under my breath. The men stiffen before me, but my eyes drill past them into some distant point. They must not expect the Adolphus pack to survive to spill their secrets.

"Winter." I break from my daze and look to Xander. "Explain. Now."

I swallow and lick my lips. My fingers knot themselves together as I rock back on my heels. "The Blanc pack suffers from a second curse. A soulmark curse." I bite the inside of my cheek and close my eyes.

"It denies us the privilege of conception with our soulmark."

"It denies...." Atticus voice trails off, and I open my eyes to see the color drain from his face. "You mean we can't—we can never?"

I shake my head. "If your wife was anyone else, then you could bring a child into this world, as many as you want, but not with me."

"And this curse affects your entire pack? Not just your bloodline?"

"That's correct," I answer Xander. The alpha runs his hands over his face and curses.

"Why didn't you say anything?" Atticus asks. His voice is oddly hollow.

Hastily, I wipe at the tears that threaten my vision. "The cost of my confession would have cost us both our lives." Both men share a look of horror. "It's the Blanc packs greatest secret and weakness. For if any were to find out—"

"They would be attacked," Xander finishes solemnly. "What pack wouldn't wish to be known as the one to supersede the Blancs? Is this why there has been resistance with your betrothal?"

I nod.

Atticus takes a few steps toward me. His hands are balled into fists at his side. "We can never have children?"

My tears return and spill down my cheeks. "Never."

Anxiety crawls under my skin as we pull into the driveway of our home. *Of his home*, I correct dismally. It was never really ours.

The engine rumbles to a stop, and somehow our silence grows louder without it. A quick glance at Atticus in the yellow overhead light displays the cut of his jaw and nose in sharp relief. He doesn't bat an eyelash at my short study. The frown on his face is still in place after the entire length of our drive. Nothing has changed.

I exit the car without further ado, and Atticus follows suit. He trails close behind me as we walk inside. The tempo of my pulse kicks up at his nearness and the promise of another collision.

"How long have you known?" he asks once we're in the foyer. "How long have you known we'd never be able to have children?"

My movements are mechanical as I peel off the coat. I bite my lip, anticipation thrums through my veins as I place it on its rightful hook.

"I've known since I was young," I tell him, my fingers unable to relinquish their hold. "They don't officially tell you until you're thirteen, but rumors and stories always end up circulating between the kids before that. Since we found each other so young, they had no choice but to explain the curse to me."

"Your parents knew when making the formal betrothal contract with mine that we would never...." Atticus lets out a noise of frustration. My fingers release their hold to turn and observe him. His face is pitched in grief and anger. "How is it that nobody else in the lycan community is aware of it? Do they really keep that tight of a leash on you?"

I jerk back at his harsh delivery but nod with reluctance. "I told you what they do to us, Atticus. They can't afford to let outsiders know. There are orders in place. But for those who would defy them, safeguards have been put in place."

"What kind of safeguards?"

"They have watchdogs. Pack mates who spy on others to make sure everyone is toeing the line. Those who pose a concern are reeducated. As for the ones who are considered more likely to put the pack at jeopardy, they are simply taken care of."

"They would kill their own to keep their secret?"

A spike of defensiveness rallies through me. "The Blanc pack would have been eradicated centuries ago if they dealt with the situation differently. And if not that, then shunned by the community. It's difficult enough that the pack has the weight of the entire lycan curse to weigh upon our shoulders. But this? It's humiliating," I explain, surprised to hear my words delivered with such rough passion.

A war rages within Atticus's mind. I can see it through his eyes and the scrunching of his forehead and lips.

"So instead your pack chose to become elitist pricks that fear monger their own pack into submission? Instead of asking for help?" His gaze drags over me before he starts walking to the front sitting room. "Yeah, I guess that explains a lot."

He might as well have slapped me. His tirade effectively shuts me up as I stare at the spot he once occupied in a daze. It takes a long moment for me to find my nerve, and my tongue, and then my feet make me stride after him.

"You don't understand, Atticus," I hamper on. "It was either the Adolphus pack or—"

"Your pack. I get it," Atticus interrupts smoothly, not bothering to turn around and face me as he heads for the kitchen.

"No. Not the pack. Just Juniper."

My voice cracks on her name, but I force myself to forge on as I stop at the kitchen table. His back muscles bunch together as he grips the kitchen counter in front of him. His head is ducked down and out of view entirely.

"They'll destroy her. She's not as strong as you or this pack. She's just a kid."

His lack of response makes my stomach clench uncomfortably as I wait in the mounting silence for him to give me something. Anything.

"I get it," he says at last. "You've told me enough times how much she means to you. You grew up by her side. You share countless experiences with her... of course, she would win your loyalty. The Adolphus pack can't compete with that. I sure as hell can't either."

"Atticus." His name falls out in a whisper. "I'm sorry."

He sighs, and the muscles across his back release their rigid posture as he turns to face me. "I understand why you did it, Winter," he concedes again, but there is an undercurrent of discontent. "What I don't understand is why you didn't ask any of us for help. I thought there was at least something growing between us. Something real—"

"It was real. It is real. I swear."

"Then why didn't you say something?"

The sudden rise of his voice startles both of us. Wide-eyed, I approach him with careful steps.

"I was afraid," I admit. "Just because I was out of my parents' and the pack's reach didn't mean I was safe from their wrath or the consequence if I didn't obey. I thought... I thought they were going to hurt you at first. Mother didn't say exactly who would suffer if I failed, and I assumed it would be you."

Atticus studies me with an intensity I'm unused to but makes no comment.

"I'll find some way to fix this. I swear I will," I say.

He shudders a sigh at my vow, his hand reaching to grapple the back of his neck. He pins his sights up to the ceiling above, his Adam's apple bobbing. The broad line of his shoulders drops as his grip grows lax and his stare remains true.

"I dreamed of you. Of us." An ache resonates in Atticus's voice, one that is bone deep. I pull in a tight breath, blinking away the surge of guilt that wells in my eyes. "I don't know how you can fix this, Winter. I don't even know how to begin to forgive you."

A rough laugh barks from him as he sets his sights back on me. My gut gives another painful clench.

"Do you realize the position you've put me in?" he asks.

My retort lives a short life on the tip of my tongue. Searching his face, I capture all of the frustration and anger and disappointment in the strain that lines his eyes and mouth. I shake my head slowly, inching forward regardless of the danger that comes with such an action.

"We're the *betas*. We're supposed to be the heart of this pack, and you went and stabbed all of us in the back. Not just me or Zoelle and Xander. All of us. But it's me who will need to provide an example of forgiveness for the pack… to present ways for you to earn back everyone's trust. And I don't know if I can do either of those," he says, voice low and rough.

"I said I'll fix this, and I will. There has to be something Lucy knows about the tonic. Something she's not saying. Let me talk to her and I can—"

Atticus gives a sharp shake of his head, and when his phone buzzes, he lets out a grateful sigh. "No," he tells me, not sparing a glance in my direction as he reads the message sent to him. "I have to go. They need me. With Xander in the state he is, we need our strongest wolves to pull together. The pack can't afford to be weak, not with the Wselfwulfs pounding at the border."

His walls come slamming down around him as he shoves his phone back in his pocket and makes his way back to the foyer. He keeps his eyes straight ahead. Those crystal blue eyes of his not bothering to see me standing there, flush with disappointment.

And then… "Not with your parents plotting our downfall from within," Atticus mutters just as he passes.

I can only stand and gape in response, watching his strides lengthen down the short hallway.

"What did you just say?"

The words spill past my lips before I can stop them. Being as they are drenched in indignation, Atticus stops. With a shaky exhale, I give chase, following after him with a frown so severe it pushes away some of my numbing guilt.

"Nobody knows how closely my parents have been working with the Wselfwulfs," I say in an even voice. "Yes, they support their cause, but they would never dare play such an active hand in aiding them, not with their position on the Celestial Court. And they would *never* support an attack against their own daughter."

Even as I say the words, they ring false inside of me. Defending my parents leaves a terrible taste in my mouth, but the action comes second nature after all these years. I wish to take them back as soon as I say them, but Atticus rounds on me as I reach the end of the hallway. He is ready for this particular fight.

"Are you sure about that, Winter? Because targeting you seems like a great way to entice a war. Threaten the last of the Blanc line? Do you know what *hell* Xander got from your parents after they sent your cousin and Knox down? They demanded full retribution on their daughter's behalf… They wanted us to go after the Wselfwulfs."

My world has the audacity to flip upside down.

"What?"

He takes a step forward, his finger raising to point accusingly at me before he releases a frustrated growl and rakes his hand over his face instead. His expression is torn between ire and great reluctance.

"They wanted us to 'defend your honor' by *attacking* them. They tried to order Xander—"

"No," I protest, shuffling forward. "No, they wouldn't do that. My parents wouldn't send out enemy wolves to attack me. They wouldn't demand… they wouldn't."

I swallow thickly, unable to look at him as thoughts collide in my head. *They wouldn't... would they?* And yet, the truth of the matter is undeniable. My mother's nonchalance at the entire event on the phone makes horrifying sense to me now.

But still, I can't bear to admit it.

"They wouldn't do that to their daughter." I tell him hotly, even as traitorous wetness begins to stain my cheeks. Even when I know I should be apologizing and begging forgiveness for breaking his trust. It all keeps coming back to my parents and this senseless need to justify their actions.

His jaw clenches, and his tone remains stern. "*Winter.*"

"You don't know what you're talking about!" I shout, my finger jabbing in the air as I brush past him, ready to march up the stairs and hideout in my old bedroom. *Apologize you idiot!* a voice inside me screams. *It's not about you!* "They wouldn't—"

His hand hooks around my upper arm and twirls me back. I barely stop myself from slamming into his chest. Our gazes clash in a maelstrom of emotion, and our heavy breathing drives at one another without remorse.

"Don't do this, Winter," Atticus growls back, his frustration and anger out in full force. "You just told us they're holding your cousin hostage and plan on making her marry some way older guy. A man you not-so-subtly implied abuses his wives. Why is it that you can't fathom the idea that your parents would collude with the Wselfwulfs?

"Why are you still defending them after everything they've done? You don't think they'd rough up their own daughter to push their agenda? You're a pawn in their game, just like June. Stop making excuses for them. Stop defending them!"

I'm ready to go on, but my arguments lose wind as I see his genuine perplexity at my adamance. I shudder a breath and squeeze my eyes tightly shut.

"I'm not defending them. I just...." My words briefly stall as I search for the right words. "I just can't believe it, Atticus. I'm their *daughter*. Their *only* daughter. I'm sorry, okay? I'm sorry for everything they've done and everything I've done for them."

Doubt and pain eat away at my resolve, and my tears come faster as I lean toward his body. What kind of people use their children in such a way?

And what does that make me for going along with it?

A monster, a horrible voice whispers in my head. *You're just as bad as them.*

"I can see the wheels turning in your head, Winter," he murmurs, the worst of his anger ebbing from his voice. Atticus takes a hesitant step back and releases my arm. I sniff and rub away what wetness remains on my face. "You aren't them," he says with a tiredness that speaks volumes.

I bite my tongue to hold back a refrain and opt for a curt shake of my head instead.

"Winter...."

I drop my chip until it almost brushes my collarbone. A terrible laugh tries to curdle its way up and out of me. "You don't have to try and make me feel better, Atticus. I'm the one in the wrong. I'm the one who messed up and put lives at risk."

The words stall on my tongue as my throat suddenly constricts. The hoarse laugh I attempt to hold back breaks loose. I sound insane. Mad. Maybe I am to follow my parents so blindly.

"You can say whatever you want," I tell him, eyes drifting closed as I swallow past the constriction. "You can do whatever you feel is necessary for my punishment. I won't utter a single complaint."

"There are more important matters at hand than deciding a punishment for you. Besides, I think you're doling out your punishment harshly enough for yourself," he says somberly.

I wrap my arms around my middle—not for comfort, but to hold myself together. "Some would argue against it."

For a moment, I dare to think Atticus is tempted to reach out to me. I hold my breath and watch the tremble that runs through him, lips parting gently. When our eyes meet, the world falls still around us.

I exhale a tremulous breath, scared to remove my sight from him. "I'm sorry," I say. "For everything."

There is a softening in his eyes as he gazes back at me, and then what must be a thousand emotions flutter across his face. It dawns on me that though we are only a few feet apart, a vast chasm lies between us. I long to cross the distance to be in his arms once again, for it is the only place I've ever felt safe.

I'm not sure what he sees dart across my own expression, but it's enough to make him look away.

"I have to go," he tells me again and brushes past me to fetch his coat.

I trail behind him, unable to stop myself. I find myself irrevocably drawn into his orbit—soulmark or not. Maybe that's what makes everything hurt worse—knowing the feelings between us in this short amount of time have been real and strong and true.

"Will you come back?" I whisper.

He pauses. "Always," he responds quietly. "Can I trust you to stay here while I'm gone."

"Of course." That he must ask makes the hurt sink deeper.

Atticus gives a curt nod. "I'll be back."

The house feels colder without him. A minute passes me by, and then another, and it is all I can think. It's cold without him near. Exhaustion weighs upon every inch of my body, and my hands seek to curl themselves around me farther.

Shuffling further into the front sitting room, I steer toward the couch. I slump down into my favorite corner spot.

How do I fix the mess I made?

The chances of my parents exchanging the information about how to release Zoelle from her magical sleep are slim… unless Xander is willing to pay the price for it. It is a fact that my parents might already be counting on.

Without thought, I curl my legs up to my chest, my arms slipping to wrap around them as I lose myself to each path I can take.

Dealing with my parents will have to be a last resort. The price for Zoelle is too compelling of an argument for the Adolphus pack's surrender to the Wselfwulfs. My teeth dig in to my bottom lip at the thought.

I can't let my mistake be the pack's downfall.

Somehow I'll find a way to fix this mess. I'll do whatever it takes, no matter the cost. The Adolphus pack deserves this from me. As for June… I will find a way to save her too. Somehow.

My wolf provides a soft echo of an agreement.

It's an odd moment to feel the pressure of its thoughts among my own, but I'm thankful for its support and strength regardless. I'll need it.

Bright lights stain the sitting room for a brief time. Headlights. I squint out the window, heart thumping madly as only one thought or rather, person enters my mind. *Atticus*. I rush to the front door when I hear the slam of the car door.

"What is it? What's wrong?" I ask as I swing the door open wide. It slams against the wall with the force of my pull and the added aid of the wind. I put a hand up to block the glaring yellow of the headlights, trying to squint past my fingers in an attempt to adjust.

"Nothing's wrong… not unless you refuse to cooperate." My arm drops at the familiar voice.

A shard of ice pierces my heart as I recall it with aching clarity. The voice is on the cusp of manhood and far too confident to leave one at ease.

I react a split second faster than the fearsome youth I encountered weeks ago and slam the door shut before he can barge in. It's a struggle to lock the door, between his jarring insistence and my shaky hands, but I manage.

Taking a wary step away from the door, I eye it with distrust. How long will the lock hold? Is the Wselfwulf lycan willing to force it open and alert the neighborhood to his actions?

Will he have to?

I race off to the back of the house when the dangerous thought springs to mind. Mentally, I count off all the entrances to the house: the garage, the back door, any of the windows. There are too many to cover if he's brought more wolves with him.

The back door is locked, so seldom in use, especially during the winter. I breathe a quick sigh of relief. It is short-lived. The doorbell goes off in a crazed set of repetitious chimes. I make my way back to the front door, heart hammering in my chest, and a butcher's knife clutched in my hand.

"Come on, Winter. We just want to chat. We never got to finish our conversation from before."

I say nothing. Instead, I move toward the window I so love to sit next to and pull its curtains shut.

"Is that really necessary?" he asks, then drills at the doorbell again.

His attempt to distract and unnerve me through his actions only half works. With swift feet, I make short work of closing all the blinds and curtains on the first-floor windows.

"Let us in, Winter. No one is going to come to fetch you.... Your packs a bit preoccupied at the moment with other matters."

I suck in a sharp breath and glare at the door. "What did you do?"

His laughter makes my blood boil. "Open up."

"No."

That puts a stop to his infuriating laughter. "Then I'll huff, and I'll puff," he says, his voice pitched to a dangerous rumble. "And I'll blow your house down."

Knowing it's coming doesn't lessen the poignant force of his entry. The door *cracks* against the wall and the pair take a step forward. The young man who led my assault before stands with one of his sidekick: the hulking beast, with severe features and dark eyes. I stumble back a step, my knife held out low in front of me, and my lips pulled back in a snarl.

The beastly man regards me with little interest but prowls forward nevertheless. I shift back several steps to match each of his own and barely register the sound of the door closing.

"Heel, Adrian," the younger commands, walking up behind the intimidating man with feigned leisure. His eyes gleam with wicked excitement as he runs his gaze over me. "Put down the knife, Winter. You'll only hurt yourself."

"Get out of my house."

"Or what? You'll come after us with your big, scary knife?" His condescending tone is unbearable. A soft chuckle preempts his next words. "You know, I don't think we were properly introduced before. I'm Jason."

"Get out of my house, *Jason*. And take your lapdog with you." The lapdog in question—Adrian—lets loose a low growl that seems to shake the entire house, but he makes no move against me for the slur.

"I wouldn't get him mad," Jason advises. "He's barely trained as it is."

I eye them both, taking in their positions and plotting my best chance at escape. Jason's disturbing smile halts my thought process.

"Don't get any ideas of running. Adrian here loves to give chase. Besides, there's no need for any more destruction. We're just here to pick up something. A necklace."

Though I make no outward indication of how the word brings to mind the moonstone necklace in my dresser drawer, it's my heart that gives me away. It provides a mad thump at his words, one I've no hope of controlling.

He smiles slowly. "That's right. I believe it's a moonstone. Every pack knows from here to England how much your family adores them." With a leer, he rakes his eyes across my chest, then lower. "You wouldn't happen to have it on you, would you? My own alpha hasn't received the agreed upon compensation from your pack, and she's always been a bit keen on the finer things in life."

"The necklace belongs to me," I say, voice low.

"And now it belongs to my alpha."

Our synchronization would be impressive in any other circumstance with Jason shooting forward and me darting back. I sprint down the hallway through the kitchen, aiming for the back door. Jason is hot on my heels and gaining. As I scramble past the kitchen table, he inches past me to skid to a halt in front of the back door. Panting, Jason's eyes shoot past me briefly to the lycan I know to be at my back before returning to me.

I stop a mere arm's length away from Jason and shift my stance in an attempt to keep both men in my sights. Adrian closes in slowly from the hallway entrance, ready to herd me into Jason's clutches.

Not good.

"What did you say the last time we met? Something about she-wolves being light-footed?"

He releases a merry laugh as I make a second attempt to flee. It's only by luck that I dodge Jason's groping hands and duck into the formal dining room off of the kitchen. My knife makes its presence known in a vicious swipe as Adrian joins the fray. The more massive wolf stumbles back a step or two with his dark eyes bleeding red for a second.

Red? *What the hell?*

I almost stop, my shock and fear grappling for the right to guide my next move. Fear wins out. I push through the room, tossing chairs behind me to hinder their pursuit and sprint around to the entryway. The sound of competing footsteps resonates loudly in my ear.

My eyes scan the wide entryway of the living room, anticipating a lycan to appear and thwart my escape and trap me in the room.

Despite my fear boosting my speed, I manage to reach the foyer at the same time as Jason. He pants with excitement as he skids to another stop, this time before the front door.

"Nice try—"

His taunt cuts short as I throw myself up and over the stairway banister and launch myself up the stairs. Seconds later, a hand clamps around my ankle and yanks with vicious intent. My cry pierces the air. I struggle to find purchase as I fight against the second harder pull at my person.

"And here I thought your parents taught you to behave," Jason says menacingly, his fingernails digging into my ankle. I turn myself around on his next assault, my free foot using the momentum to smash into his face.

He howls and rears back, tumbling down the stairs with several curses. I don't bother to admire my handiwork with the threat of Adrian lurking in the corner of my vision. Instead, I scramble up the stairs to my bedroom.

Shutting and locking the door behind me, I move to the nearest piece of furniture—a low dresser—and begin to push it in front of the door. The sound of their approach flays at my nerves, for it is done deliberately slow, yet loud enough for me to hear. I shuffle back until I hit the opposite end of the room.

I should have stabbed him—not kicked him.

I gnash my teeth and attempt to slow the racing of my heart. The scent of blood does little to calm me. I stare down at the knife. It's painted with crimson, but it's not the only thing. The palm of my hand is cut open—most likely from my fall on the stairs. But the sting of it barely registers. Even now.

Adrenaline ushers about my next move. I move swiftly to my dresser and retrieve the moonstone pendant necklace. With shaking hands, I place it around my neck and tuck it under my shirt.

The only way these thugs will take the necklace is from my dead body.

A crash from downstairs startles me from my state of shock. It's followed by various shouts, and I dart to the window to peer outside. A new car haunts the end of the driveway.

The voices below continue to rage on as a strange electricity seeps into the air. I hesitate for half a second before pushing aside my barricade and opening my bedroom door. Another loud crash sounds from downstairs, followed by a piteous moan.

The air vibrates with tension. It makes the hair at the back of my neck stand on end as I creep forward. With my heart in my throat and wolf at the ready, I tread close to the wall and toward the commotion below.

"You can come out now!" a feminine voice calls from below.

Startled, I continue my approach just as cautiously, peeking only my head out from around the corner of the stairs. Three women stand, each holding a different item in their hand—*a different weapon*, I correct myself—and all in black.

"You, Winter?" the shortest asks. She has her dark hair pulled up into a ponytail and tugs down the odd piece of cloth covering her mouth and nose. Without the garment in place, I see how young she is.

"Yes… and you are?"

The three share a brief, unreadable look. "One of our seers foresaw the intrusion, and the Elder Triad commanded us to assist."

Relief floods my body, and I slump against the wall. Thank God.

"The big one got away. He tore past our enchantment somehow," the dark-haired girl continues. "We'll be taking this one into our custody instead. Do you know who he is?"

I meander around the corner and down the first step of the staircase, eyeing the Wselfwulf lycan with disgust. "Only that his name is Jason. He attacked me a couple of weeks ago. Along with the one who got away."

She nods, then her sights narrow on me. "Got it. Grab him, ladies."

The other two witches move with confidence toward the fallen lycan, tucking away their weapons into side holsters. With their hands outstretched, strange green shimmers tint the air and his unconscious body rises. I hold back the sneeze that threatens as their magic permeates the air and press a hand against my nose just in case.

The dark-haired witch mutters something foreign under her breath as the two walk past, and they slowly begin to disappear from sight. By the time they are out the door, they're no longer visible at all.

"Thank you," I say, taking another step and surveying the damage.

The coffee table is cracked and flipped on its side. The couch has a scorch mark slashed across it and indecently displays its stuffing around crisp fabric edges. Other bits and pieces from the sitting room are scattered and broken across the floor as well. Even the stairs aren't spared. The front right railing is broke and hangs by a few precious wooden strands.

"Whatever," she says and delivers a scoff.

My eyes widen at her sudden callous nature. But as a pretty sneer snakes its way across her lips, I'm no longer confused about her sudden hostility. Zoelle.

"Let's go. You're coming with us too." I swallow but nod, noting the way she clutches a long, thin knife in her hand.

"Okay."

ACES ALL THE WAY

- Chapter 17 -

The car ride is particularly hostile and grabbing a parking spot near the Elder Triad's home is no picnic either. At least a dozen cars take up the street parking, and as a tingling sensation grows across my body with each car we pass, I can only assume more witches are in my immediate future.

Perfect.

"Don't drag your feet," the dark-haired witch commands, prodding me in the back with her hand after we exit the car.

My lips thin, but I refrain from making a retort. I don't need to provide any more reasons for them to hate me. The leader of the trio makes her way around me once we are halfway up the drive and opens the door for us. Unsure of where the other two witches and unconscious lycan stand due to their invisibility, I scurry ahead but stop before the door.

"Well?" the witch asks impatiently.

I grimace, reaching out a hand tentatively to feel for the magical barrier that barred me earlier. No electricity spikes violently out at me, and I breathe a sigh of relief as I step inside.

The magic bustling around inside is too much to withstand. An unnatural heat fills every inch of the air, and it gently burns me from the inside out with each breath. An iridescent haze trails after an older woman who walks by with her nose in a book.

My nose gives a telltale twitch before I erupt into a sneezing fit. I crowd up against the nearest wall in the hopes of being out of the way. The witch behind me snorts at my reaction, then proceeds to unveil the other three with more muttered words and an elegant motion of her wrist. The air waves in front of her, like a ripple of water, and slowly the others come into view.

My awe is momentary, for I am quickly hit with two matching glares from the revealed witches. I duck my head, my fingers pinching my nose to halt my sneezing fit.

"Stay there," the dark-haired girl commands. She shuts the front door with a flick of her wrist and marches off.

I wish I could sink into the wall. Too many witches mill about. They dash upstairs or around to the kitchen, all of them with their own streaks and currents of magic dogging them. They vanish this way and that, but the ones who hurry into the room on the other side of the entryway capture my attention the most. I try my hardest not to stare, but my curiosity and unease make it difficult.

It's clear some know who I am. Their glares and body language keep my wolf on edge. Others merely allot me a cursory glance. It's a day and an age—or so it seems—before the dark-haired witch returns. Her face is carefully blank as she points toward the kitchen. She leans against the staircase railing with a knowing look in her eyes.

"Mo will see you now. The others can't be bothered to deal with the villainous bitch who went turncoat on her allies." I'm left with a parting smirk before she takes the stairs two at a time.

My stomach twists. I'm unsure if my feet will obey and take me farther into the household. I last set my feet inside this house hours ago, only to be zapped out of it. I scan the near vicinity for the fairy but see no sign of her pearly hair or glittering wings.

I mutter to myself the worst pep talk ever. "Just get it over with." *You'll have to face them sooner or later*, I add silently to myself as I force one foot in front of the other.

When I enter the room, it quiets with eerie synchronicity. Maureen is studying a hefty tome on the dining room table. She wears thick glasses that tread dangerously to the tip of her nose.

"Leave us," she commands absentmindedly. She flips a page, the action only adding to the odd air in the room as the witches stare me down. "Now," she adds politely.

The witches in the room file out, only one of them daring to exit through the doorway I stand under. Her shoulder knocks into me, delivering a fiery pain along with it. I grit my teeth and release a hiss but say nothing.

Maureen spares me a glance, her eyes traveling knowingly to the offended body part. "Jessie has a bit of a temper," Maureen explains, returning to her tome. "She's a brewer like Zoelle. She's very talented and works closely with Zoelle on potions for the coven."

"Noted," I mutter, rubbing at the strange and painful heat radiating down my arm.

"Sit."

I do, and with each step feel irrevocably more uncomfortable. It's not just the witches' magic anymore. It's potions brewing on the stovetop. Their fizzling and smoky discharge fill the air with supernatural energy that makes me cringe.

"Apologizes, dear," Maureen says, pushing aside her book and taking off her glasses. She rubs the bridge of her nose, eyes shuttering as she continues. "I realize being around magic like this is not a pleasant experience for your kind."

My jaw sinks open. "Maureen… you don't have to apologize. I should be—"

She interrupts me with a tsking noise. "Call me, Aunt Mo. Haven't we had this conversation before, dear? I can't quite recall."

My dumbfounded state continues on a second longer. "Aunt Mo… it wasn't supposed to be Zoelle," I say, my voice soft. "She isn't dead, is she?"

Her eyebrows shoot up. "If that were the case, we wouldn't be here right now. Or rather, you wouldn't."

A touch of resentment stirs in my stomach at her nonchalance. "*You're* the one who said I'd get someone killed. Besides, Lucy said the tonic was intended for a fairy, not a witch. What if it affects her differently? What if—"

"Hush, now," Aunt Mo says sternly. "As it happens, and quite unfortunately at that, it does seem as though the tonic is having a strange effect on Zoelle. To curb any other unwanted side effects that might crop up, they've spelled her into a kind of suspended animation. It will stall the tonic and ensure her and the baby's safety, but it also cuts deeper into the connection of the soulmark."

I work my jaw a moment before speaking. "What do you mean? Xander said before it wasn't working properly… is it *worse*?"

Aunt Mo's shoulders sink a fraction.

"In its own way, yes. The spell we've put Zoelle under, in addition to the tonic, has dulled the bond between them further. While we suspect Zoelle able to feel Xander while incapacitated, we no longer believe so. It must be excruciating for them."

I slump back into my chair as the words settle in. "That's…." *Unbearable.*

And it's all my fault.

"Is there anything else you can do? Surely there's a way to reverse the tonic's effects," I ask.

Aunt Mo stands slowly, both hands flat on the table to steady herself. "It is true that all magic done can be undone," she states. "Would you like some tea, dear?"

I balk. "No, thank you."

She ignores my reaction and shuffles over to a long cabinet, rummaging inside its contents to pull out a single jar. "We are doing our best to identify the components and enchantments put in the tonic to make a remedy. But it will be far easier to do if we can speak with the witch or warlock who concocted it."

"I don't know who my parents would have contracted to have the tonic created. They don't exactly like to… mix with other supernaturals. I'm sorry."

The kettle lands on the grates of the stove with a light clatter. Aunt Mo nods along as I speak.

"It's all right. We'll figure something out. We have very talented witches among us. If we cannot learn directly from the source the means by which Zoelle was incapacitated, we'll figure it out ourselves."

Her short speech doesn't sit well with me. How long will it take them to find a way to reverse the effects of the tonic? A week? A month? If it does take long, how will it affect the pack and the coven?

"Maybe they'll be able to get more information out of Lucy," I suggest, though my skepticism shows in both my voice and the downward tilt of my lips. "I offered to help, but they didn't think that was a good idea. At least, Atticus didn't. I'm assuming he speaks for Xander."

At the sag of my shoulders, Aunt Mo makes another tsking noise. This one is far more exasperated in nature.

"You must realize the position this incident has placed both pack and coven in. Though your plan to subdue Luna went awry, you've no less managed to deal a blow to the pack. We cannot afford to let our enemies on the outside know what happened."

"And I'm the enemy," I reply, voice thick with emotion. I inhale deeply, biting back the dreaded guilt that surfaces. "No wonder they don't want me near a phone."

"You're not the enemy, Winter," she scolds sharply. "It is paramount for us *all* to remain silent on the events of today."

Aunt Mo rejoins me at the table, each hand carrying a mug of piping hot tea. She sets one down in front of me and then one on her own spot before winding down carefully into her seat. I eye her with worry. When she notices, she waves away my concern.

"I'm doing just fine. Don't concern yourself with me."

I avert my gaze to the tea before me—the one I said I do not want. Studying the liquid does little to change my mind for its murky depths are far from appetizing. Peeking through my lowered lashes at Aunt Mo, I catch her pointed look and feel a prickle of apprehension.

"Is it...?"

"Poisoned?" she asks. I bow my head an inch. "No. Just a little something to ease your mind."

I frown. "I don't know if that's appropriate," I mutter, fingering the bulbous curve of the mug. "I doubt anyone wishes me to be at ease, given my hand in the events of today. They probably wish it *was* poisoned."

"Nonsense. Drink up."

I take a reluctant sip, the tip of my tongue scalded from the taste. But a taste is all it takes. The tea's magic flows effortlessly through my veins to chase away the harsh grip of guilt. I sniffle and rub my agitated nose.

"Aunt Mo, you told me at Christmas I would get somebody killed. If it's not Zoelle, then who?" I raise my gaze to her and meet her frown with one of my own. "Please, I don't want to hurt anyone."

"The cards do not relate to me who, only a certainty that death will occur by your hands."

She might as well have slapped me with her placid delivery. The color drains from my face, and instinctively I take another sip of the tea. The relief it delivers is far more than I deserve, but it doesn't wash away my anxiety completely.

"I want to see for myself," I say. My fingers curl tightly around the mug as I tense in anticipation for her rejection. "I want to see you draw the cards yourself."

Her eyes narrow, but after a moment she bends her head in my direction. "Very well. Bella!"

It takes a moment for my lycan hearing to hone in on the sudden rush of footsteps that race our way. I hold my breath in anticipation. Seconds later, footsteps thunder down the steps and a figure comes rushing down the hallway. Bella slides across the kitchen floor in her socks, her hip colliding with the table's edge as she stops. Tea sloshes over the side of my mug.

"Yes, Aunt Mo?"

The girl can't be older than eight or nine. Her almond-shaped eyes are the color of warm caramel, and her voice holds a note of reverence as she addresses Aunt Mo.

"Bring my cards, child." The little Asian girl's hair swings happily as she gives an enthusiastic nod. Then she spins and races off. "Bella is Kimberly Moon's younger sister. She's a seer, just like Moon."

"Oh," I murmur, my eyes tracking the girl's movements until she's out of sight.

"She's the one who saw you were in trouble."

"*Oh.*"

"It quite frightened her," Aunt Mo admits. Her lips thin.

I don't know what to say to her confession, but it's clear she doesn't expect a response from me, not with the way her eyes seek out something far in the distance behind me, where only a wall resides.

The harried sound of footsteps comes back into range. When Bella reemerges, I'm prepared for her turbulent landing. The table rattles with her collision, but my mug is in hand and out of the danger zone.

"Here," she pants, thrusting out a thin arm.

Aunt Mo takes the worn deck and gives the girl a smile. "Tell the ladies upstairs I don't wish to be disturbed."

The girl's brown eyes wander my way as Aunt Mo delivers her instructions. I stay as still as possible, getting an eye full of Bella's short stature.

"Does that hurt?" she asks, her eyes flickering to my bloodstained hand. My mouth opens and closes, and I look down at my wounded hand as well.

"No," I tell her. "It's already healed in fact, thanks to my lycan abilities. The cut wasn't deep to begin with."

Aunt Mo clears her throat pointedly, but Bella continues to stare at me unabashedly.

"Everybody's mad at you," she says rather matter-of-factly, but without any genuine malice.

I smile sadly back at her. "Yes, I know."

"Bella." There is a warning lilt to Aunt Mo's voice, but the child ignores her, choosing instead to rock back and forth on her feet.

"It doesn't matter what you do," she says, eyes roaming the ceiling in favor of looking at either Aunt Mo or me. "They're not going to forgive you."

"Go," Aunt Mo says sharply, her hand slapping the table. The little girl startles back, a sour expression on her face.

"Fine," she snaps, folding her arms over her chest and marching out of the room.

"Don't mind, Bella. She has no finesse when it comes to abstract readings."

"That was a reading?" I choke out.

Aunt Mo passes along a grim smile to me as she slides the deck from its casing and begins to shuffle the cards.

"In its own way. Now, cut the deck." There's no masking my sudden hesitation, but with Bella's eerie prediction, my conviction dims. "Don't go shy on me now, Winter. Cut the deck."

I do. The stack I pull from the top is far thinner than what I leave on the bottom. I place it to the side, and Aunt Mo restacks them.

"Pull the top three cards," she instructs, folding her hands over her lap and closing her eyes.

Tension fills the air, one drawn thick by anticipation and fear, if not the smallest dash of curiosity. "Aren't you the one who should be drawing the cards?" I ask, unsure of her methods.

She doesn't bother opening her eyes when she replies. "The cards will not change for the hand which draws them."

Nervous fingers caress the soft edges of the dark cards. They hesitate in their task, and no amount of willing their cooperation works. My gaze darts to the serene picture of Aunt Mo. Her long white hair holds several small beads, and from her ears hang a daring set of turquoise hoop earrings.

Aunt Mo's scars come across more vividly in the soft lighting of the kitchen. It's difficult to tear my regard away, but as my fingers finally obey, I'm drawn to the deck.

The first turn of the velvety card reveals artfully arranged swords, nine in all. In clear, bold black the words *Nine of Swords* is written. The second turn reveals a gangly skeleton. It leans heavily against a scythe that is larger than its body. *Death* is printed below the image.

With my heart skipping a beat, my fingers linger along the soft edge of the last card I am to turn.

I exhale slowly and flip the last card. A pentacle stares back at me. The star and circle are simple in design, but surrounding the pentacle are embossed flowerlike shapes, connected through winding lines. The *Ace of Pentacles*.

"Finished?" Aunt Mo asks.

"Yes."

"And did you turn the nine of swords, death, and the ace of pentacles. In that order."

I swallow and lick my lips. "Yes." My pulse thumps loudly in my ears as I seek out the last card. The ace of pentacles is eerily mesmerizing with its pearly white lines so stark against the velvety black surface of the card. "What does this one mean?"

Aunt Mo's lashes sweep open, and dull blue eyes stare back at me. "In due time. We begin with the swords. From the start, I found it peculiar that it should be dealt first."

"Why?" I ask anxiously. Aunt Mo smiles back at me, taking a sip of her tea.

"I've beheld it many a time as a companion to death. As a symbol of mourning and grief to the period of time after someone is lost. But to start the reading, it gives a different impression. It means the reader hosts concerns about death. They have it on their mind. And if this is the case, then it is on the mind for a good reason."

My gaze darts nervously around the room, expecting to find some eavesdropper. No one is there.

"Before you came to me, I didn't have it on my mind. What do you make of that?" I ask.

"Didn't you?" she retorts coolly. "Perhaps not death, but a punishment worse than it?"

I inhale quickly with a gentle hiss accompanying the action. Our eyes colliding. Desperately, I wish to lash back as fear spikes through me at her strange magic and insight. *How can she possibly know such things about me? Hadn't I thought of the worst with my mother's threat?*

"Fine," I relent, albeit shakily. I jab the middle card with an accusatory finger. "And this? This represents someone's death?"

"It does, but it is the ace which speaks of its truer meaning. Always look to the card following death to read it correctly. If the card following is positive, it represents a new beginning. A metaphorical death."

"And if it's not?" I ask, already knowing the answer as a hollow feeling grows inside of me. I finger the soft surface, a shiver dancing up my spine.

"If the card is negative in nature, the card will represent a physical death." Aunt Mo reaches out across the table, her hand reaching for death's card before shifting sideways to the ace of pentacles. "The ace of pentacles is highly regarded as a positive card, Winter."

A sob of relief bursts past my lips but ends almost as quickly as it arrives. Aunt Mo's eyes hold a distinct sadness to them as she peers at me and not the card beneath her withered and scarred hand.

"We must not read the cards as a whole. The swords represent the coming of death, confirmed by the card itself, and reinforced by the ace of pentacles."

My jaw drops open. "But you said it's a positive card. You said it represents a metaphorical death."

Her hand stretches out further until it encompasses my own. "Though the death of a loved one is a heartbreaking experience, not all that is rote from it is bad. Good may come from death. At times the ace of pentacles represents inheritance. You may find yourself in possession of your loved ones most treasured possession—"

"I don't want that!"

I jerk my hand out of her empathetic touch and topple my chair backward in my hasty retreat. Standing on shaky legs, I hold my hand protectively to my chest.

"I don't want an inheritance. I don't want anyone to die." My voice cracks, and I struggle to hold back the new wash of tears that surges to block my vision. Aunt Mo's tea is losing out to my turbulent emotions.

"It will all be over soon," Aunt Mo soothes.

For a moment I do nothing. Then a keening noise breaks the tenuous silence between us. My lashes shutter closed as my lament ends.

"How soon?"

Her hesitation draws my questioning gaze. I watch as a shudder ripples over her body, her eyes lost to some void beyond once more.

"The full moon will bring the packs suffering to an end," she says. Her words come out as little more than a husky rasp. It brings my own turmoil out of focus as I take in the next raking shudder that overcomes her body.

"Maureen?" I question gently, shuffling to her side and taking a knee as she sucks in a ragged breath. "Are you all right?"

She pats my hand, the movement providing little comfort as it's intended. "Aunt Mo, dear, call me Aunt Mo."

"Aunt Mo… should I go fetch someone? You don't seem well," I say carefully.

Her ivory hair accentuates her sudden pallor. And if I'm not mistaken, her eyes remain slightly out of focus, even as she continues to steady her breathing.

"No, child. I've merely exerted too much energy. We are not meant to see all, only blessed to see what is meant to be."

"And you see a death caused by my hand," I murmur. Her hand squeezes mine. I cannot help but stare at the vivid red scars that decorate it. "Do they hurt?"

"Ah… yes. Pain is my constant companion." She grimaces as her sight clears and focuses on my deferential form. Though she makes a motion to usher me up and back to my seat, I remain. This time, it is my hand that squeezes hers.

The scent of magic still lies heavily in the air, but there is so much more to detect from the room beside this unearthly energy. A waft of something unpleasant drifts past my nose. It bites at my olfactory epithelium and makes my nose wrinkle at the smell of musty mothball and sour rot.

It takes a long minute for me to realize the smell comes from Aunt Mo. Aunt Mo who typically wears her obnoxiously heavy perfume. Aunt Mo who seems to be in a constant state of fatigue.

"You're sick," I say. She scoffs. This time it is Aunt Mo who tugs her hand away, but I remain bent at the knee and study her sudden scowl. "I can smell it. There's no point in trying to deny it."

"Oh, sit down, child. You make me feel old when you pose like that. Go on now, sit."

I do so reluctantly and without taking my eyes off her once. Her features have lost their severe cut and are rearranged into something far more tired. It drags down her cheeks and the corners of her soft pink lips.

"How long have you been this way?" I ask, eyes roaming freely over what scarring shows. "What happened?"

She lets out a plaintive sigh. "A deal gone wrong is the sole reason for my state. That, and my slow feet. I'm not as spry as I once was. These scars are the aftereffects of a curse I was unable to dodge. One day they'll be the death of me, but I don't need the cards to tell me this."

My hands curl to fists in my lap. "Aren't you afraid?"

Aunt Mo smiles softly back at me but makes no reply otherwise.

"How can you be so calm about it?" I ask, unnerved by her acceptance. "After what I did today, I can barely stand to look at myself in the mirror. And now these stupid cards are saying I'm going to get someone killed? I won't be able to live with myself if it comes true."

"There is good that comes from death," she reminds me, reaching out to tap the ace of pentacles. "Don't forget that."

We sit quietly for a long time. Aunt Mo's worrying gaze drills into me from across the table as I stare at the cards.

"What's on your mind, child?"

My lashes fall to rest against my cheeks. "What isn't?" I respond weakly. "What I want most at the moment is to find some way to fix what I've done to Zoelle, but each idea I come up with is pointless. If I ask my parents, they'll only use the circumstances as leverage against us. They don't want me speaking or questioning Lucy—not that she'd be of great help anyway because it's clear my parents deliberately gave her a limited amount of information.

"I don't know where to go from here. Sometimes I wish Atticus and I had never met. If I had never come here, I wouldn't have had to split my loyalties between the packs—"

Her loud snort stops my lament. My eyes snap open to see her bemused expression.

"If one thing is clear about this mess, it is not in concern to what pack has your loyalty, but what person. Your soulmark or the girl whom you so clearly love like a mother would a daughter. Your parents were very clever in pitting you against your heart. And very cruel."

I duck my head, and my hair comes down to shield my face from the world. "I don't think that's how people will see it." *No matter how right her words are.*

"In time they will."

In time they will… I release a hollow laugh and shake my head from side to side as I raise my gaze back to the elderly witch. Letting my shoulders drop back, I rest against the back of the chair. A laden sigh follows my odd burst of laughter.

"Time isn't exactly on my side. The full moon is in ten days. Ten days, and then someone is going to die because of me." My hands cup my face as a noise of frustration gurgles up in my throat. I am completely fucked. "If I don't manage to fix Zoelle by then, I'll have another person's blood on my hands. And I don't think any amount of time can fix that."

"Good can come—"

"From death," I finish. Aunt Mo arches a brow at me as I finish her sentence. With my insides twisting and bunching in indecision, I snatch up the ace of pentacles. My forefinger traces the lines of the star.

"You worry far too much for things that lie out of your control," Aunt Mo tells me. "We'll discover the means to reverse the tonic's effects in due time. Right now, we must celebrate and acknowledge of our small victories. We have one of theirs and can question him about his knowledge, such as why they came after you again."

I frown and set down the card. "I don't know how much information you'll be able to get out of the Wselfwulf. At least not in regards to the tonic," I reply with a frown. "They wanted my necklace."

Aunt Mo stares inquisitively back at me. "What necklace, dear?"

I pull the necklace out from my shirt, tipping my head down slightly as I raise the long chain over my head and place it on the table beneath us. The moonstone is not out of place among the tarot cards. Indeed, it seems to fit right in with the witch's tools.

"It's a family heirloom. My mother gave it to me as a gift for my wedding. We've had it for ages."

A hum of interest purrs from Aunt Mo's throat. She reaches for the necklace, then pauses. "May I?"

I nod and fold my arms over my chest, looking thoughtfully at the opalescent surface. "They said something about payment, but I—Maureen!"

The older woman's fingers grace the moonstone's smooth surface, and she instantly goes still. Her eyes roll back in her head, and a delirious moan erupts from her lips.

I dart to her side, knocking the necklace away from her tentative touch. She slumps against me, and I cast a furtive look over my shoulder. No. Not Aunt Mo. I can't kill her.

"Please don't die. Please, please, please don't die," I beg as I gently shake her.

"Oh, tosh, child," she mutters. "My tea," she croaks, trying to right herself.

I fuss about her, helping her to sit upright even though my hands shake. When I've successfully passed the tea into her hands, my shaking subsides… some.

"What just happened?" I ask breathlessly after she downs her tea.

Aunt Mo takes a long minute to respond. "I'm not entirely certain," she responds. "But one thing is clear. That necklace is far more important than you give it credit for. I've never felt such magic from a singular object before. And never one so well cloaked."

My breath catches. "What?"

"You family necklace is more than it seems," she continues, eyeing the jewelry with a wary eye. "We'll need Diana to look at it. I've not the strength for the task."

We're too busy taking in the enormity of the moment to notice the goings-on around us. In the time it takes for Aunt Mo to gather her wits, and me to calm my racing heart, a throat clears noisily from the hallway entryway. I spin to face the witch in question... and Atticus. Both wear matching frowns at our figures.

"Need me for what, exactly?" Diana asks, her brows pinching even more tightly together.

Warrior's Words

- Chapter 18 -

Aunt Mo and I share a look, our consternation shared at being interrupted. Heaving a sigh, Aunt Mo hauls herself up. At my vantage point, I see the way her hands strain with the action. I'm tempted to help, but I catch the subtle shake of her head just before she tilts her chin up.

"There's been a development," Aunt Mo says. Diana takes a step into the kitchen, the bell-shaped ends of her peasant top sleeves billowing as they move to cross over her chest. She doesn't take her eyes off me when she answers.

"Do we have another comatose witch on our hands?"

"Diana." Aunt Mo's rebuke is far sharper than I expect. Diana's dark eyes shift to her cohort, and the harsh lines about her face soften. "Be thankful it wasn't lesser hands who attempted to deliver the tonic, for the situation we are in would be far less manageable."

Diana gives a stiff nod. It is clear she is unused to such reprimands and tries to regain her imposing stance.

"What is it then?" she asks, instead of offering an apology. I step out of Aunt Mo's way as she edges forward from the table to stand at my side.

"The girl's necklace. It hosts powerful magic. One I've never felt before," Aunt Mo explains.

Both Atticus and Diana's eyes widen at the revelation, but only Diana comes forward to inspect the piece of jewelry lying precariously at the tables end.

"Don't touch it!" I warn as Diana reaches out. She glares at me but stops at my warning. "Aunt Mo did and… and it did something to her." I look back to the other witch for confirmation of my statement, and she nods.

Aunt Mo sends the necklace a hearty glare.

"The magic is well masked by dark intent. I barely touched the moonstone, when it reacted. It caused momentary paralysis, and a pain inside that made every nerve ending feel as if it was being seared. Yet, when Winter knocked away the necklace, it was clear the pain had been an illusion." Aunt Mo touches her temple tentatively. "I've not had a headache this terrible since my antics in the 70s."

"You need to rest. You've pushed yourself too hard today," Diana says, her frown back in place. Although this one holds a motherly edge to it.

"I know my limits," Aunt Mo gripes and hobbles forward. "Which is why I'm going to bed. Don't let anyone touch that necklace… no witch at least. You've never felt pain while wearing the necklace, have you, Winter?"

I shake my head. "No. Although, I don't always feel comfortable wearing it," I admit. "It's difficult to explain the feeling, but perhaps it was the magic?"

My skepticism shows in the high-pitched tone I take, but Diane and Aunt Mo give an acknowledging nod at my thought process.

"I'll make sure the necessary precautions are taken. It might be best to take it to a different location for examination. In case anything were to go wrong, I don't want Zoelle and my grandbaby to be in the near vicinity."

"Diana, I'm—" Her scowl almost stops me, but I plow forward, faltering only slightly "—sorry. I'm so sorry. I'll do everything I can to help make this right."

"We'll see," she says tersely. Diana's nose thrusts up into the air as she places a protective hand on her friends back and guides her away. "You two know where the door is."

I watch them go with a sigh. My energy is fading from the long day's events. But the weight of Atticus's regard draws my spine up straight. I turn my gray eyes to him. His face is carefully blank as he looks me over.

"I'm sorry," I say, shifting my weight to my other foot under his scrutiny. "I didn't plan on leaving—"

"You're hurt."

I freeze at his interruption, then nod dumbly in return. Blinking owlishly at him, I soon set my sights to my offended hand. "It's healed now," I tell him mechanically. "I just haven't had the chance to clean it up yet."

"You're all right?"

My eyebrows shoot up as my heart gives an unexpected jump at his concern. An undeniable longing strikes at my center, urging me to say no. Because nothing is all right and absolutely everything is wrong. But maybe if he would just hold me in his arms—

I shake away the thought and the hot flush that stains my cheeks at my impractical thoughts. *Get a grip, Winter.*

“Just a bit shaken, is all,” I mumble and give a cracked smile.

My weak smile slips away as his eyes stay steadfast on my bloodied hand. I itch to place it out of view—behind my back or in my pants’ pocket perhaps—but instinct tells me the idea is foolish. Instead, I clench the hand into a tight fist, hiding the worst of the dried blood. Atticus’s nose flares, and his stormy eyes drill into me. Their depths are unfathomable.

“Atticus, I—”

He approaches with a suddenness that makes me take a step back. My shocked gasp sounds loudly in my ears I eye him with slight dismay. Atticus's dark gaze tapers under the slant of his eyebrows. I swallow.

There is something animalistic in his approach, and so I don’t expect him to wrap an arm around my waist and pull me into him. His other hand roughly dives up the back of my neck to grab a fist full of hair. With another tremulous gasp, I allow him to tilt my head back, and his lips take mine.

The act is hard and demanding.

I whimper at the connection. The taut anger displayed in Atticus's initial arrival is still present throughout his body as he crushes me into his chest. Tension rides through the quaking of his muscles as he drags his lips across mine. A heavy pant falls from my mouth due to his rough ministrations.

It is evident with the next bruising onslaught of his lips and teeth that this is no mere kiss, but a reprimand in itself. It’s in the way his hands guide my every movement. The pressure of his embrace. The coiled tension that rides so high across his body.

There is a desperation to our connection, and I am only too willing to yield to his guidance.

I place my hands tentatively against his chest, reaching upward to curl my arms around his neck. If this is to be our last kiss, I will make the most of it.

With equal fervor, I kiss him back. Our tongues duel in battle, fighting for dominance that I've no hope of winning.

His hand clenches harder in my hair and a hint of pleasure-pain triggers at the sensation as Atticus drags my head to the side to kiss me deeper. Teeth bite down on my bottom lip, the pointed assault doing far more than show me his turmoil. A heat ignites between my thighs and, pressed against his body as tightly as I am without room to move, only makes the burn brighter.

When he pulls back, a sharp intake of breath steals through the air between us.

"I didn't know what happened," Atticus pants, resting his forehead against mine. "The house was a mess, and I thought...."

I shake my head and tilt my lips upward, intending to soothe instead of claim. But Atticus twists his head at the last second. I swallow down the hurt and attempt to step back, but the steel band of his arm does not relent. My eyes squeeze shut in confusion.

"I just need a minute," he mutters.

Atticus's hold tightens minutely as he gathers himself while I stay plaintively still in his arms.

"Sorry." His arm drops, and Atticus takes a step back, running both hands through his hair and making the hair stand on end. "We didn't know what happened. We didn't know you were even in trouble," he says, his anger directed somehow at himself.

I would question the "we" he speaks of, but it's clear he speaks of himself and his wolf. There are streaks of gold in his eye, after all, and my own wolf presses forward to study its mate.

My lips part to speak, but there are no words I can think of to say. Because as clear as it is to me that he is speaking for himself and his wolf, it's equally apparent that his frustrations lie in the current state of our soulmark bond.

If we were at least sealed, he would have come running. He would have known something was wrong.

"Let's go home," Atticus says, and so we do.

+++

I awake alone in bed. The fact isn't as much unexpected as it is disappointing and unwanted. Besides the rampart of events from the other day keeping me up all night, it is the scorching kiss Atticus delivered to me that won't stay out of my mind.

Why? Why did he have to kiss me?

I'm more than prepared for the backlash my actions have brought me, but this strange circling of Atticus and me drives me insane. As much as I long for him to hold me close and help pull me from the grave I have dug for myself, I know my hopes will go unfulfilled. At least I thought, but now, I'm not so sure.

The shutting of the front door startles me from my reverie. I lurch from the bed, tossing the comforting warmth of the blankets away as I dash to the window. Pulling the curtains roughly aside, I watch Atticus stride toward his car. He catches my eye as he enters the front driver seat.

I don't realize I've leaned forward to gaze at him too far until my nose and forehead bump the cold glass. I startle back, eyes wide, but manage to catch the sharp bark of laughter from outside before it's stifled by the car door closing.

Where is he going?

There isn't time to dwell on his sudden departure, for the unexpected sound of the television turning on captures my attention. My lycan senses alight as I tread softly to my bedroom door. Pressing an ear to its surface, I linger until I hear equally soft footsteps downstairs.

My brow furrows in response. Surely Atticus knew someone had been inside before he left? But who?

Slipping on an oversized sweater over my thin camisole and swapping my sleep shorts for some joggers, I pad downstairs. A quick perusal of the entryway reveals a new coat and pair of snow boots next to ours. A woman's jacket and shoes, if size and style are anything to go by.

"Winter?" a familiar voice calls.

It takes me a moment to place it, then my frown softens. "Callie?" I call back, making my way to the family room where the television resides.

She's made herself at home on the couch. A plate of crumbs sits on the coffee table before her.

"Hi," I say, albeit hesitantly.

Callie doesn't bother to turn around, but she does toss up her hand in a half-hearted greeting. Her bracer is fastened around her wrist.

"I'm here to help ward off any surprise visitors and sound the proverbial alarm via the soulmark connection," she says, eyes glued to the morning news. "Not that I think it's *completely* necessary. They've got a couple of wolves watching the house from different spots on the cul de sac."

"Great," I mutter sarcastically. Wolves and a warrior to keep watch… or are they here to follow me?

"Did you say something?" Callie asks, passing me an inquisitive look over her shoulder.

"No," I refute, and lean against the large entryway. "Did Atticus make you that?"

She hums an agreement before speaking. "Just some microwave waffles."

I place a hand over my stomach. "I'm just going to make myself something to eat," I say, and take my leave.

Something to eat turns out to be coffee and buttered toast. One cup of coffee turns into two as I stare mindlessly at the back door, running back through yesterday's chaotic confrontation. How had the Wselfwulfs managed to get through the border again and so deep into town? They must have more help on the inside, but with Lucy out of the mix, who could it be?

Jason's wild eyes and that hulking beast of a man—Adrian, I remind myself—had navigated the house with ease. Realization hits me gradually, but when it does, a low groan pushes itself out of my body. Lucy.

And Knox no doubt made a thorough search of the Adolphus house. My gut clenches at the thought, unless Quinn and Ryatt had been able to thwart his investigation.

"Hey...."

I startle, my coffee sloshing dangerously up the side of my mug. "Hi."

"Sorry, I didn't mean to scare you."

"You didn't," I insist, and set the drink on the counter behind me. "Did you need something?"

She gestures to the empty plate and then walks over to the sink. Our gazes cross paths several times, but neither of us speaks. When the silence becomes too much to bear, I force myself to talk.

"I'm going to clean up the living room," I tell her, winding my way around the long end of the kitchen island. "It's—"

"I'll help," Callie offers.

I stop and stare. "No, that's not necessary."

"I don't mind," she says and with long strides walks ahead of me and down the hallway to the room in question. I follow quickly at her heels.

"Really, you don't have to help."

She shrugs. "You look like you could use the help."

The short statement knocks me short. I stare at her back, watching as Callie places her hands on her hips to survey the damage. All the while, I try and gather what meager pride I have left.

"I thought you were just supposed to be watching me," I comment.

Another shrug, this time without the accompaniment of an actual response. Instead, the Inuit girl begins to collect shards of woods from the floor.

"We're going to need some trash bags," she says, not stopping once in her chore.

We clean the room together. Most of the smaller debris can be vacuumed away—the bits of glass and splinters of wood—but the rest cannot, such as my furniture. Those pieces end up on the curb. The couch, coffee table, two lamps, and one of the chairs.

The sitting room is a shell without it all, I note with grim remorse.

Callie is busy tidying up the surface of the mantel, rubbing a wet cloth over a stubborn scorch-like mark on one of the corners. Her hair is half up in a messy bun, while the rest falls far down her back.

The casual wear she dons seems far more her personality than the outfit she wore on Christmas and New Year's. Even from behind she looks to be a formidable woman, her muscles clearly working beneath the thin long-sleeve top she wears. Though no longer a warrior, she apparently still trains like one.

"Is there a reason you're staring at my butt?"

My eyes widen on her rear end before snapping up to her smirking face. A flush brightens my dull cheeks as I stammer an apology.

"Like what you see?" she asks dryly, though her amusement is evident. She gives her butt a little shake from side to side and laughs at my mortified expression.

"Sorry," I repeat, my flush growing stronger as I focus back on the simple task at hand. "I was staring off into space. Just ignore me."

Callie turns to face me, her shoulder bumping up against the chimney as she leans against it. There's an appraising look on her face, all of her amusement is gone.

"It's kind of hard to ignore you when it's my job to watch over you," Callie says.

The embarrassment I felt moments ago flees for a different kind. This embarrassment couples with my ever-present guilt, and I busy myself with tying off the few bags we've filled. As I grab the filled bags to bring to the garage, the telltale sound of scratching and ripping sounds. The bottom of a bag splits open and pointed glass shards litter the floor once more, along with the rest of the bag's contents.

"Seriously," I groan, shoving the other bag back on the floor away from the new mess. Callie is at my side in a second, her half-full bag there to accept the garbage.

The air around us is disturbed only by the rustle of plastic and the clamor of glasses, wood, and other debris piling up against one another. Each small collision sounds louder than the last. I'm nervous I'll start to develop a tick as it builds, my fingers grabbing more roughly at the pieces than necessary until we reach the final layer.

"Hey." A soft tan hand wraps around my wrist before I can snatch up a piece of glass. "Be careful," she scolds me lightly.

The attempt I make to pull myself free of her grasp is met with resistance, but my second attempt is a much neater extraction. There is a tightening at the corner of Callie's eyes at my action, one I mirror with the edges of my lips. Then, just like that, the tension slips from her face.

"I get it," Callie says softly, her eyes flickering down to the broken glass then back up to me. "I get why you did it."

I swallow and stand, dusting my hands off on my pants as she makes to rise as well.

"We should be using a dustpan," I tell her after clearing my throat, hoping my change of subject will stick. With my recent luck, I should know better.

"I know what it's like, Winter. I've been in the same position as you.... My family, they disowned me. They wanted to break my spirit and put me in my place, or rather, the place they deemed fit for me. They asked too much of me," Callie says, her voice low and earnest. "I know that now, but back then it was all blurred."

My head moves to-and-fro.

"I *get it*," she insists, stepping over the pile of glass and into my personal space. Her hand rests against my shoulder. "Our positions aren't entirely the same, but I do understand the pressure your family put on you. I understand the impossible choice you had to make."

I suck in a sharp breath, willing the sheen of liquid that clouds my vision to vanish. "Why are you telling me this?"

Brief confusion flits across her face before a kind of pity overtakes it. I try not to flinch. At least I succeed in this.

"I remember you telling me about your cousin before. June, right?" I nod and wipe hastily at my eyes with the heels of my palm. "You did this for her. Is she... is she going to be all right?"

Between Callie's tone and the empathy laid bare in her body language, I crack. Hot tears spill down my cheeks. She is the first person to ask.

"I don't know. Probably not." The words are hard to get up my throat, let alone off my tongue and past my lips. They are thick like concrete, and pushing them out doesn't release me from their weight. "I don't know how much my parents know. And I don't know what to make of the Wselfwulfs' attempt yesterday. But I'm pretty positive no good will come out of the silence. They'll make her suffer for it," I say, trailing off at the end.

They will indeed, though perhaps not so obviously at first. My parents will start with small things to build up her tolerance before the more significant blows. The final will be passing June off to Jeffrey.

"Would it help if you spoke to them? Your parents?"

"No," I say with regret. A clench of my jaw does little to relieve my tension. "The only way to help June is to get her out of there… and Toby too, if June were to have any say in it. He's her boyfriend—*was* her boyfriend."

A hoarse laugh drags itself out of my chest, and Callie passes me a raised brow.

"June would probably think of it as the ultimate romance, escaping away with her boyfriend," I explain. And this thought, amazingly, does lessen the heaviness from my chest.

Callie processes my comment. "So what are you going to do?"

Great question. I chew on my lip for an inordinate amount of time. What do I do now?

"Help wake Zoelle up," I say. "I can feel the loss of her more today. Like there's a piece missing from the pack bonds that keep it running smoothly, but without her, there's a kink in the line. Atticus and Xander are doing their best to cover it up, but with their attention scattered, it's slipping through more and more. I can feel it. As if it's an ache in my bones."

"Me too," Callie confesses.

One arm wraps around her middle, while her other hand finds a place at the back of her neck. The disconcerted action reminds me that Callie's place in the pack is high. She's fifth, as I was in the Blanc pack, which means she's high enough to feel the loss of Zoelle more keenly.

"They're trying to keep it under wraps for as long as they can so as not to scare the pack. But it's only a matter of time until they find out what happened. They can't keep it up it forever," Callie says.

I nod. "Hopefully the witches can get the Wselfwulf to talk. I wouldn't mind if they figured out what the hell is going on with my necklace too, though I know that's obviously not the priority."

"What necklace?" Callie asks as she squats back down.

The tinkling and scraping of glass is a gentle backdrop to my explanation. Callie's gaze darts between her task and myself, until I kneel down across from her and begin to help once more.

"It's a moonstone necklace. My mother passed it on to me as a wedding gift. Apparently, it hosts dark magic inside of it, the likes of which Aunt Mo has never seen or felt before. It... did something to her. Hurt her," I explain with a growing frown. "She said the magic it holds was expertly cloaked."

"That must be some strong magic for you and your family not to notice. Aren't wolves sensitive to works of magic? Every time Keenan has to meet with the coven, he complains about how it makes him itch."

An impish grin works its way onto my lips.

"It makes me itch too," I admit, then sober. "But you're right. The magic inside the necklace and the magic hiding it must be incredibly strong. I don't know why I couldn't detect it, being as sensitive as I am to magic. Yet, when I think back to each instance I wore the necklace, I suppose I felt a certain level of discomfort."

The times are few and far in between, but each time I can recall those days feeling worse than others. Callie stands, the last bits of trash put away. This time around, neither of us attempt to remove the garbage from the room.

"I'm sorry," she says, wiping her hands together to free them of any dust and dirt. "You lost me. You felt discomfort wearing the necklace?"

I flush and rise as well. "It wasn't exactly discomfort," I try to explain again, "but I was uncomfortable to an extent. As if my worries were heightened."

"Strange...," Callie says before she peers about the room. "I think this is as good as it's going to get."

With a sigh, I survey our work as well. The room will need some good TLC, but whether or not I'd have a hand in its makeup is questionable. I clear my throat. "Do you want some coffee?"

"Nah," Callie replies, walking with me to the kitchen as I reclaim my mug and toss it in the microwave for half a minute. "Hey, do you think the necklace will be able to wake her up? Maybe the coven can siphon its magic, or whatever they do, and use it to wake her."

My astonishment comes in a widening of my eyes. "I don't know," I reply honestly. "Maybe? But probably not if it's dark magic, right?" Callie shrugs helplessly. "Regardless, if it can't help wake her up, that doesn't make it any less useful to us."

"What do you mean?"

The microwave beeps its completion, and I remove the mug gingerly as I quickly run over my thoughts.

"I mean, if the Wselfwulfs wanted the necklace badly enough to come after it, it means something to not only them—"

"But the Blanc pack," she finishes.

"Exactly."

Her eyes spark with growing recognition. "You think we can use the necklace as leverage."

My coffee pauses halfway on its journey to my lips. A trickle of excitement and hope wrap around me. "I do. If my parents somehow got wind of the necklace being in the coven's possession, they might be more inclined to share what they know about the tonic in favor of its return."

"That's not a bad idea," Callie says, her tone a touch impressed. My chest puffs up an inch at the praise but deflates when reality sets in.

"It might be a decent idea, but that doesn't mean the pack or witches will go along with, especially if they know it was me who came up with it. Notwithstanding my current position in the pack, my last suggestion didn't go over well."

Callie shrugs, her hip bumping against one of the kitchen chairs. "Then I'll pass it off as my idea."

I blink. "Really?"

"Yeah, it's a good idea, especially if nothing comes out of the interrogations."

The coffee, still only lukewarm despite its time in the microwave, brings with it a modicum of comfort. "Thank you," I say around the mug's rim, my eyes meet Callie's across the room.

She tips her head, her hickory-colored eyes narrowing on me. "Now let's talk about your cousin. How do you plan on helping her?"

Her question catches me off guard, and rightly so. I've managed to make June's fate second to the needs of my new pack, and giving her attention now seems unfaithful—no matter how absurd it sounds. After all, it's my loyalty to her that brought us to this scenario in the first place.

"I don't know," I tell her, fighting off the panic that comes with the unknown valiantly. "I just have to wait and see what happens with Zoelle and the necklace. Maybe after I can convince Xander to send a team up to negotiate for her."

The chair scrapes loudly against the floor as Callie turns it about-face to sit backward in it. "How much time do you think you have to get to her? Realistically?"

I shift uncomfortably at that, not liking one bit the thought of the immediate dangers she faces in my parents' venture to spur this war to its conclusion, no matter what the cost is.

"Best-case scenario?" Callie nods. "My parents will drag out the engagement. They'll make June go through all of our packs sacred ceremonies and make a public showing of it. She'll be made an example of to the pack to prove that when one wolf steps out of line, they endanger the whole of the pack."

"And the worst-case scenario?"

The room remains thick with silence as I will myself to say the words.

"They don't drag it out at all. They rush June through the ceremonies without giving her time to heal before handing over her leash to Jeffrey."

Calliope's eyes go flat. "What kind of sacred ceremonies does your pack play host to that it harms your members?"

I turn my gaze away from her hard stare. My throat constricts as I set aside the coffee and grip the counter behind me instead.

"A fair few, as it happens," I murmur, "but it's the last that hurts the most."

Callie waits patiently for me to continue, crossing her arms over the top of the chair's back and resting her chin there.

"They'll strip her of her soulmark," I say.

"What?"

Heat sprawls across my neck and cheeks. "It's considered a testament to one's commitment to the Blanc pack. The physical removal of the soulmark implies the dedication to the Blanc pack's survival. You can't bond with your soulmark if you don't have one... or so the sentiment goes."

"That is... so fucked up."

Begrudgingly, I nod, not expecting her to continue.

"The Wardens of Starlight have their own fucked-up practices," Callie says, her eyes going distant as she no doubt recalls them. "But why is it that one hurts the most?"

"They say the sensation is akin to ripping out your heart's hope. It sounds sadder than it does painful, but I've heard the screams that tear out of the men and women who do it." I tremble.

"How exactly is it for the survival of the pack?"

I smile sadly. "Haven't you heard?" I attempt to joke. "The Blanc pack is the reason for the lycan curse, but we were also saddled with a separate curse. The second denies us the ability to conceive a child with our soulmark."

Callie reacts as predicted. Her face pales and her lips part in astonishment.

"That's terrible." I can only hum my acknowledgment back. "The information on the lycan curse was somewhat limited at the Banks Facility where the wardens base out of, but I never knew of your soulmark curse. There has to be a reverse, right? Every curse and spell and potion or tonic—they all have a workaround, a back door to undo what's been done."

My sad smile stays firmly in place, though it becomes strained at its edges. "Nobody knows the parameters of the curses. Anyone with substantial knowledge didn't bother to pass on their thoughts or findings, and now they're long past dead. Without the knowledge, they can't be undone."

Callie slumps in her seat.

"It's too bad the coven's seers can only look to the future and not the past. I mean, I know the curses aren't high on the priority list right now, but that would be a real game changer."

"I guess," I all but mumble. "But you're right. It isn't high on the priority list. I don't think Xander or the witches will want to devote any sort of time to something like that. Everyone is focused on Zoelle right now and finding the reverse for her tonic."

Callie stands and spins the chair around about-face. She swings her leg over the seat and sits once more.

"Everyone?" she asks, raising her voice at the end along with an eyebrow. My eyes widen in mild alarm at her tone. "Every single witch is working on it? They couldn't spare a just a few?"

I gape. "Why would they want to?" My head moves side to side. "The pack is in bad standing with the coven because of me. They're not going to want to help."

"Probably," she admits with a shrug and a growing grin. "But why not just ask? The worst that happens is what we expect—they refuse. On the other hand, they could decide to keep the matter on their radar or on the back burner."

My heart skips a beat. "Why are you pushing this?" I ask tentatively as my confusion grows. "The chances of it working at all are slim to none."

"Grandiose plans are kinda my thing," Callie says, and then she softens. "We aren't going to accomplish anything just sitting here. We should take action when the opportunity presents itself."

"Callie, I—"

"Let's go now."

My spine snaps straight at the bold suggestion.

"We can't go. We're not supposed to go anywhere."

"There's no time like the present," she says and stands. "Besides, I'll be with you to make sure you're safe. We can check in on the coven's progress with the necklace and the Wselfwulf too."

My heart starts to speed. I lick my lips in anticipation.

"Okay. Let's go."

A New Order

- Chapter 19 -

They are glaring. All three of the Elder Triad are glaring—at me.

It comes as no surprise, but I can't help but wonder if my presence was subtracted from the equation if they would sport such looks for Callie. Her delivery of the idea is the perfect mixture of thoughtfulness, persuasion, and tact. The idea comes across as the next course of action rather than a suggestion.

Callie's proposal certainly intrigues the witches, but their hesitation is evident.

"Does the coven have a seer with that kind of ability?" Callie asks.

She stands in front of the three seated witches, her arms folded over her chest and chin held high. The witches share a look, but it's Aunt Lydia who responds for the group. Her hair is pulled back into a tight chignon, and her cat-like eyes narrow upon our pair.

"There is one," she says begrudgingly. Her sights shift not-so-subtly to the witch at the other end of their semicircle of chairs. With an unhurried air about her, Aunt Lydia's cat-like eyes move back to us. "But we will not risk her energy and spirit to such a powerful spell. What you ask for is a profound act of retrocognition. To perform such a spell will require the aid of our best seers."

"All of whom," Diana adds with deceptive calm, "are working diligently to wake my granddaughter."

The room spikes with latent hostility. Diana's piercing gaze never once leaves my seated form behind Callie. I show no outward sign of discomfort as the air thickens with biting static, except for the occasional flinch when said static breaks against my skin.

"Not all of them," Aunt Mo corrects. "Other tasks are taking up the coven's energy as well, Diana."

For a brief moment, Diana's heated gaze is directed at someone other than me.

"Are you talking about the necklace?"

The question tumbles past my lips before I can stop them. It is the first time I have spoken since arriving, and from their looks, my question isn't exactly welcome. Regardless, Aunt Mo answers.

"Yes."

"Honestly, Maureen," Diana snaps.

"Don't start, Diana," Lydia warns right on the heel of Diana's remark.

The Elder Triad passes measured looks to one another. An entire silent conversation traverses between the three, but it is unclear what decision they come to. Aunt Lydia rolls her eyes with a huff of frustration as Aunt Mo and Diana continue to stare each other down.

Finally... finally, Aunt Mo turns her regard back to us.

"Some might call it a coincidence that you came seeking answers to curses long since left untouched and unknown. Yet, after an interesting turn of events around three this morning, I'd safely call it fate."

Callie dares a look over her shoulder at me, her eyebrows raise conspicuously high before drawing back down to look at the witches.

"What the hell is that supposed to mean?" she asks, sans-tact.

Diana makes a growling noise low in her throat, spearing Aunt Mo with one of her potent glares. The lights in the room flicker. A sneeze threatens at the tip of my nose.

"Not another word, Maureen."

"It's meant to be, Diana," she argues back, unfazed. There is a fire that blazes in her murky blue eyes as she glares back at her friend. "Let us not fight, and work instead toward the inevitable end. I can perform the spell."

Diana stands, a visible tremor running over her body. "This isn't a discussion, Maureen Clybourne. Our focus will remain on reversing the tonic. There will be no talk of this nonsense, and you most certainly will not be performing any spells after yesterday."

Aunt Mo bristles, her spine straightening as rigid as the chair she sits in.

"As I recall, the decisions that guide the triad are made by the majority."

Diana flushes, her dark cheeks taking on redness. "You are not strong enough. Besides, the pursuits of the coven need to be targeted at one project, not split. What you deem so recklessly as fate is nothing but a wild goose chase."

"What say you, Lydia?" Aunt Mo asks, leaning forward to peer around Diana's imposing figure. Her long silver-white hair cascades over her shoulder, hanging so long that it almost touches the ground.

Aunt Lydia's features tighten in thought. Her silence clearly rankles Diana who stands akimbo. When Aunt Lydia sighs, brushing imaginary dust from her gray velvet sweater, the bangles dressing her wrists jingle merrily.

"She's right, Maureen. You cannot do the spell."

Diana puffs up in smugness. Then Aunt Lydia continues.

"You'll need a small collective to do it. Have Moon lead the efforts—she's our most promising seer. And your daughter, Charity, should oversee the collective. She needs to start—"

"You cannot be serious, Lydia!" Diana exclaims, rounding on the other dark-skinned witch.

"You know I have no fondness for jokes, least of all in times such as these. Fate cannot be fought, Diana," Aunt Lydia says.

Unrest rides the friction between them. It makes me shift uncomfortably in my seat.

A lightbulb shatters from a nearby lamp, and Aunt Mo rolls her eyes. A scoff is halfway out of her mouth when Diana speaks again.

"So be it," Diana says darkly. "But do not expect any help from me."

She storms from the room. The lamps and light fixtures she passes breaking in succinct bursts as she goes by. The room, now considerably dimmer, is also quite thankfully relieved of its most prominent source of tension. Aunt Lydia and Mo watch her go with varying levels of concern.

"I'm sorry," I say, licking my lips nervously. "This doesn't need to take precedent over Zoelle. We can wait—"

"We've made our decision," Aunt Lydia tells me tartly. "There's no going back now."

Aunt Mo surveys us in quiet contemplation before another tired sigh issues from her. "Pull up a seat, Calliope, and don't dawdle over there, Winter. Scoot your chair in closer so we can speak more comfortably. Lydia, the lights, if you please."

As Callie grabs a wooden chair from the neighboring room, and I pull mine closer to the witches, Lydia begins to lift her hand. Her fingers, which started as a tight fist, slowly uncurl as they rise higher. I spare the broken lighting my attention, watching in wonder as the fractured pieces go back to their original state.

By the time Lydia's hand is well above her head, her hand is closed once more, and I've sneezed three times.

Callie looks at me in mild amusement before she directs her attention back to the room's power duo. "What exactly happened with last night? Did it involve the necklace?"

Aunt Lydia snorts, a wry smirk curling over her lips as she stares with half-lidded eyes at us. "It did involve the necklace. We made quite the discovery... your necklace is the vessel for a curse, girl."

"Lydia," Aunt Mo's tone very clearly indicates a warning.

"My apologies," she says without any sincerity. "Your necklace is a vessel for two curses." By Aunt Mo's cross look, she is unimpressed by Lydia's delivery. Callie, on the other hand, is thoroughly enjoying it.

"You've got to be kidding," Callie asks, her disbelief radiating off her. "How the hell can it be cursed and Winter and her family never knew? Did you *not* just witness her sneezing fit? Magic and wolves don't exactly vibe well."

Aunt Lydia cocks a brow, unimpressed at Callie's attitude.

"Well?" Callie prods.

The two remain in their stare off for a painfully long time. Until Aunt Mo gently coughs to break the tension. We share a tired look, and I clear my throat as well to gain their attention.

"Callie does make a fair point. Magic leaves a palpable trace in the air. I'm fairly certain I'll start to get hives if I keep coming over," I say.

"It's *dark* magic." Aunt Lydia's says with exasperation as if it explains everything. "It leaves a different trace, child," she continues patiently. "Think of dark magic as a shadow—"

"A corrupt shadow," Aunt Mo adds.

Aunt Lydia nods, unperturbed at the interruption. "It's far more malevolent than the tickling of your senses. It disturbs you. Even a human can recognize the feeling and steer clear of cursed items. And as Winter witnessed last night, the magic is far more violent. We do not practice the darker arts of magic because of how uncontrollable it can be."

"Right," Callie says, drawing out the I. "But that still doesn't explain why Winter and her family never knew it was cursed. If anything, they should have known right away."

"You do realize your questions would be answered by now if you would allow me to finish?"

Another standoff between the two formidable women occurs. Callie's stubborn nature is almost an equal match to Aunt Lydia's. In the end, Callie concedes. Her shoulders sink an inch submissively as she tilts her head a fraction in Aunt Lydia's direction.

Satisfied, Aunt Lydia continues. "The only spell strong enough to conceal and constrain the curses attached to the moonstone is with a soul sacrifice."

I scan Lydia and Aunt Mo's faces, both are drawn into somber expressions. Squirming slightly in my seat, I cast my gaze to the tufted rug on the ground to keep from looking at their faces.

"Something tells me that's not good."

Aunt Mo makes a noise of agreement in her throat at my small comment. "Soul sacrifices are powerful things, whether done willingly or not."

"And was this soul's sacrifice willing?" I ask. "Can you even tell?"

Raising my eyes to Aunt Mo, I catch her slight nod. Neither witch makes a move to say more. Instead, they look to one another and partake in another round of silent conversation. Callie looks to me in the meantime, her eyebrows doing a dance as if to communicate to me as well. Our efforts are admirable, but all I can garner from Callie is a general feeling of unease and frustration. Both are feelings I can relate too.

"Go on then, Mo," Aunt Lydia says at last. "We're already this far into it. No turning back now."

Aunt Mo heaves a sigh fit for a battle-worn soldier on their last front. "It's complicated," she confesses, brushing her hair over her shoulder as she leans forward. "From what our witches can gather, the soul sacrifice connected with the concealment was willing—albeit tainted."

"What does that mean?" I ask, beating Callie to the question.

"The soul was tainted. Weak. Sullied. There's no way to tell why, only that it was. It explains the imperfection in the moonstone. The crack that rides its center. The soul was barely strong enough to conceal the curses," Aunt Mo explains.

"Oh."

My flat response goes unacknowledged as Aunt Mo forges on.

"As to the other soul sacrifices—"

"Whoa, whoa, whoa!" Callie exclaims, hands shooting up and shaking. "Just how many soul sacrifices are contained in that thing?"

"Three," Lydia replies. "The first and second sacrifices were unwillingly given, and the third—no doubt given by the witch who cast the curses—was given willingly. For the third to contain the other two… she must have given away all her power as well."

"I didn't know that was possible," I murmur.

"Because it is not done. Rarely in our history has a witch gone to such lengths to tap into such dark magic," Aunt Lydia explains.

Silence, thick and worrisome, blossoms in the quaint sitting room we find ourselves in.

"Let me get this straight," Callie says. "All of this time there have been *two* curses sealed into the moonstone necklace by the caster sacrificing their own soul?"

Aunt Lydia tips her head in Callie's direction, her dark eyes are half-hooded by dark lashes. "You are correct."

"And what does this have to do with our proposal—*oh*." Callie's eyes widen comically as she rocks back in her seat. "Oh, you have got to be kidding me," she mutters. "It's the lycan and soulmark curse, isn't it?"

I snap my head in Callie's direction and then to the witches. "That can't be," I say hoarsely, rising from my seat only to stand behind it. My feet are unwilling to take me further, and so I grip onto the chair without remorse. "What kind of—pardon my French—*fucked*-up person makes their victims wear their condemnation like some prized jewel?"

"A very angry witch, apparently."

"Lydia!" Aunt Mo balks.

Anger and disbelief whirl into a storm inside of me. Callie casts me a worried look.

"How can this be possible?" I ramble on. "How can we not have known? For centuries we've had this necklace—*centuries*. Yet, all this time and no one figured it out?"

"Stranger things have happened," Aunt Lydia tells me kindly. "If the necklace was left mostly undisturbed and unworn, then how and why would your pack investigate it? Curses are not always contained to an object, and furthermore, back in those times, magic wasn't as well understood by other supernaturals. Even now it is not. We all tend to keep our secrets close."

"No kidding," Callie says on a scoff. Both her tone and scrunched nose attesting perhaps to previous experiences.

My mind is too abuzz to contemplate what they could be. Instead, I reach back into my memories of seeing my mother or grandmother wear the necklace. But only special occasions come to mind.

"I know this information is startling,"—I guffaw loudly, but my outburst does not stop Aunt Mo's words—"but this is a good thing, child. Can't you see?"

"No," I snap. "I can't."

Because at this very instant it is impossible to even grasp at the revelation. For centuries lycankind has been plagued with this abominable curse... and all along we've had the very abomination in our possession. The ancient witch had indeed been cruel and devious to have my family flaunt and parade the very thing that kept our wolf spirits leashed this entire time.

I glance Aunt Lydia's way and notice her tense at my sudden regard. Her spine goes rigid, and she delivers a cool look back.

"Don't go wolf on us now of all times," she says.

I don't register the press of the wolf near the forefront of my mind. It takes in the information with stoic silence, but there's no denying its obvious interest in the turn of the conversation.

Rarely does the wolf press its will against me, but in acknowledging its presence, it lunges at the opportunity. The wolf wants to be free. Truly free, as it was always meant to be. The curse that binds it to the moon is like a shackle, one that has strained its spirit more than most.

"My apologies," I manage to get out through gritted teeth. Shouldering back the wolf's presence takes more effort than has ever been necessary before, and still its will and want wraps around the core of my being. It is a plea, more than anything else.

Callie clears her throat. "Do you think the Wselfwulfs knew about the necklace?"

I am a touch out of breath as I smooth back my hair with an agitated hand, but at least my wolf is back in its place. "I don't know. I don't think so. If my family never knew, then how could the Wselfwulfs?"

In unison, the three women form a variation of the same doubtful expression. Their cheeks pulling in. Their lips thinning. Their brows tugging together.

My heart gives a strange flutter at their doubt.

"They didn't know," I snap, casting them all a glare. "My parents would have tried whatever they could to reverse the curse. The Blancs bear the soulmark curse as well, atop the moon curse, or have you forgotten? Lifting the curses would have brought the Blanc pack honor."

Callie flushes and holds up her hands in defense. "Okay," she says. "It just seems a little strange that they wanted it so badly...."

"It was probably just an excuse they used to justify the attack," I argue back. I tame my voice into something more subdued but no less firm. "Lucy dropped hints about the necklace while staying with us. Maybe she's the one who passed along the idea to my parents or the Wselfwulfs themselves."

"Motives aside... this discovery is pivotal in our ability to determine the components of the curses," Aunt Lydia says. "The effort will be exceptionally taxing, so rather than attempt something now, we will wait until tomorrow's witching hour."

Aunt Mo hums her agreement, then gives an additional nod of affirmation. "The strength of the waxing moon will be behind us. With it we can draw what we want most to us—information."

The two witches go off on a tangent at that, listing off supplies and names of people. They rise slowly from their chairs, and Callie and I look to one another, unsure if this is a dismissal or not.

"So tomorrow at the... witching hour?" Callie asks, breaking into their conversation when they both mean to take a breath.

The witches look surprised to see us still standing there. Aunt Lydia frowns at us.

"Yes." Aunt Lydia looks to Aunt Mo in exasperation and walks from the sitting room, muttering under her breath choice words. Aunt Mo lingers, her eyes tired but holding a flicker of anticipation.

"There's nothing for you to do here today, but get in our way," she teases kindly and ushers us toward the front of the house. "I'll call your alpha and let him know what we intend to do. None of us can afford to be left out of the loop. Besides, I have a feeling he will take the news better coming from me."

A frown decorates my forehead. "Are you sure that's best? It might come better from Callie."

"I'm sure," she states. "Now, off you go. There's much work to be done in a very small amount of time, and we may require you in the next day or so. You don't need anything else, do you?"

We shake our heads, going obediently to the door and putting on our things. Aunt Mo waits patiently near the door, ready to see us out when an idea strikes me.

"Aunt Mo, there is one thing you might be able to help me with... if it's not too much to ask."

Both women look at me expectantly, and I do my best to keep the flush of red off my cheeks.

"Of course, what is it?"

"I need some flowers."

+++

The bouquet Aunt Mo conjures for me prickles my palms the entire way home. Callie drops me off, but she doesn't bother to follow me inside for Atticus will be back soon, and there are wolves still on watch.

By the time I deposit the flowers into a vase of cold water and scrub my hands pink, the crunching of snow under car tires reaches my ears. I'm tempted to run and hide—more than tempted if I am being honest. Facing Atticus after he left without a word this morning makes me nervous.

What if he chooses not to face me at all?

I'm still at the sink when the door to the garage opens, and the distinct sound of boots tapping the doorframe rings familiar in my ear. Even with the subdued bang of the door shutting and the soft sliding of fabric reaching my nuanced lycan hearing, I almost hear none of it due to the erratic beating of my heart.

For a lingering moment, the house seems so still.

Can he hear my heartbeat? Can he smell my anxiety? What of the magic and flowers?

Will he come?

The floor creaks with the pressure of his approach. I dry my hands with a dishtowel nearby, searching for my courage only to find it long gone. Atticus stops, the floorboards holding back their predicted groan, and I turn to face him.

I expect to see him lingering in the kitchen's entryway. He's not.

"Atticus?"

The footsteps continue until he fills the entryway. I inhale deeply and catch his scent, greenery with touches of lavender, oakmoss, and musk. The scent fills my lungs and acts as a balm to my nerves—at least what is left of them.

Atticus doesn't look my way.

It might be for the best. I take in his profile from half-lowered lashes and drag my gaze over the lines of his face caught in shadows and meager light. He didn't shave this morning.

I can see the stretch of dark stubble hugging his strong jawline and over the cleft of his chin. My sights linger on his lips. They hold no tension to them. A long, slow breath passes from my mouth as I relax minutely. Atticus is completely composed. There is no hint of a wrinkle or crease to betray outward feeling near his eyes or across his forehead.

But if I could see into his eyes, would it be different?

"Where did you get these?"

Just breathe, Winter. "Maureen Clybourne."

A drawn out beat and then his curt response. "How?"

"Callie and I went to the Elder Triad's house," I say carefully. His jaw clenches in the dim light, but still, his eyes remain forward. I rush on to explain. "When Callie and I were cleaning up, we came up with a sort of crazy idea that turned out to be not so crazy at all."

His silence prompts my continuation.

"My necklace, or rather, the moonstone, is cursed," I tell him. "But it's not just any curse—it's *our* curse. The one that holds our kind to the moon's whim and the plague on the soulmark for the Blanc pack."

"We're supposed to be focusing on Zoelle," Atticus says. "Xander is shutting himself off to all emotions just to keep going and resting more and more responsibilities on my shoulders to carry the pack. We can't have our attention split like this," he finishes, managing a biting tone regardless of the fatigue that so clearly plagues him.

"The aunts think it's meant to be," I murmur.

"They don't know everything."

I squeeze my eyes shut, opening them only once I've captured a lungful of air. Breathing it out entirely, I take a step toward Atticus. His gaze flickers, and for the first time, he tenses visibly. My fingers curl into my palm at the slight, steadying my resolve.

"They're wallflowers," I tell him.

The cherry red and orange petals are out of place among the cold and callous tension riding the walls of the home. But their presence and meaning will override it—at least I hope they will.

Another step forward and I begin to curl around the kitchen island. Atticus's spine goes rigid.

"They mean faithful. I know the sentiment might be too little too late, but I need you to know. I'm going to make this right. All of this. And I swear to you that from this moment on, I'll be faithful to you and to this pack. I won't let myself be misguided by my family anymore."

Nothing.

No twitch. No sound. No reaction.

But he doesn't leave either, and that alone stifles the awful ache ticking in my heart. Slowly, Atticus turns his head in my direction. The weight of his regard halts my advance.

As I succumb to the depth of emotion swirling in his eyes, a familiar tugging pulls at my center. The need to be closer to him rouses inside of me. Something far beyond the soulmark's will, but one I now know of as my own true want. I want to be in the circle of his arms and never leave.

With or without the soulmark tying us together, I know without a doubt I will always be drawn to Atticus.

And I dare to think I see in his eyes the same recognition of the undeniable force between us. Slivers of gold emerge in his gaze, and my own wolf draws forward to meet its match. The floor does not creak or whine as I shuffle forward, but the world around us comes back into dizzying focus when I do.

My movement shatters the spell.

The gold vanishes from his eyes, and Atticus fights to rearrange his features into something bland and unrecognizable. He leaves once the look is mastered, and pain lashes out at my heart.

I will make everything right, I vow vehemently as hot tears rush down my cheeks. *I will.*

The Witching Hour

- Chapter 20 -

The peak witching hour is at three in the morning.

It is a fact I learn over the phone late the following evening with Atticus. Aunt Lydia laughs merrily at my ignorance after I confess my assumption that the witching hour is at midnight.

Atticus's displeasure about the upcoming night's events is evident, but it softens when Xander arrives to pick us up.

"Lucy said the tonic would only last a few days, right?" Xander asks as I reach for my seat belt. My movements slow exponentially, and I nod as I catch his green eyes in the rearview mirror.

"That's what she said," I confirm.

"Good, good," he mutters under his breath.

Xander tosses an arm over the back of the front passenger seat, where Atticus resides, and backs out of the driveway. Swiveling his gaze from front to back, he glides the car out into the street without a hitch. Xander changes gears, his movements less fluid and more abrupt.

"One of Diana's brewers thinks they have something to wake Zoelle sooner. They're trying it tonight as well."

"That's good news, man," Atticus rumbles, his hand claps onto Xander's shoulder and gives it a squeeze. Xander nods. His intent focus on the road is undisturbed by his beta's reassurance.

"I'll drop you two off at Lydia's sister's house and pick you up after it's all done. Just give me a call, Atticus. I'm going to see Zoelle and speak with Diana about my talk with Irina."

The steady drum of fingers against the steering wheel is an odd noise to coalesce with Xander's bizarre tone. His words come across with their usual strength weaved about them, but there's an unnatural cadence to them. His fingers continue to *tap-tap-tap-tap.*

"Sounds like a plan," Atticus remarks, passing his closest friend and alpha a sidelong glance. "When did you talk to your sister?"

Tap-tap-tap-tap

"After Maureen called me yesterday to let me know your plans." Xander's eyes flicker to the rearview mirror to find mine. "I asked her for a favor."

His eyes dart back to the road, and he releases a somewhat shaky sigh. When the car rolls to a stop at the next intersection, Atticus squeezes Xander's shoulder again. The drumming stops, and Xander turns his attention to Atticus.

"What'd you ask for? You gotta keep me in the loop here, Xander. We can't afford to be out of sync."

Xander nods, the movement echoing down his body as it rocks slightly forward. The car plugs onward, but at a far slower pace than necessary. At least there is no worry of causing traffic with our slow speed at this hour.

"Jax is coming."

Atticus frowns, his regard still trained on his friend. "The sorcerer?"

"Yes." The clipped response makes Atticus flinch, but Xander doesn't seem to notice for he barrels on. "I want the coven's focus entirely on Zoelle, tonight is a one-time exception."

Well then... I turn my eyes out the window, avoiding whatever looks either man might deem to send me.

"You sure that's a good idea? Isn't he associated with the Stormrow clan of sorcerers?"

"He is."

"I don't think Diana is going to appreciate having a Stormrow sorcerer on their turf. Not after what happened last year."

Xander remains silent, and for a time, I do too. And then my curiosity wins out.

"What happened last year?"

Atticus cranes his neck over his shoulder to look at me. His lips are set into a firm line, and I can see the argument he has with himself mentally. To share or not to share?

He sighs. "The coven attempted a trade last year with the Stormrows. To say it didn't go as planned would be an understatement. You've seen Maureen's scars?" I nod reluctantly, stomach twisting. "I'll give you one guess where she got them from."

I suck in a sharp breath even as Xander shoots a glare at his beta.

"He might be from the Stormrow clan originally, but he's a Vrana now. If Irina says he can help and she trusts him, then I do. She says he can get on a flight within the next day or two."

"But Diana—"

"We'll deal with it," Xander cuts in savagely. "We both want what is best for Zoelle and the baby, and that means having the entire coven attending to her. Tonight the witches will look into the past as much as they can... but when Jax arrives, he takes over this project. No questions asked."

The underlying steel in Xander's voice leaves no room for argument, and the rest of our drive is conducted in painful silence. Being so near the two top wolves in the pack as they butt heads is uncomfortable, but I make no attempt to complain.

"Remember to call me when it's over, and I'll come to pick you up," Xander says as he pulls up in front of a small two-story house.

"Of course," Atticus replies easily, the tension evaporating from the car as he reaches over and gives Xander a one-armed hug. "Everything's going to go over well tonight, man. Breathe easy, brother. With all of us working toward a solution, we'll make one happen."

Xander claps his hand roughly on Atticus's back, and the two stay locked for a moment longer in their embrace. When Atticus pulls back, the nervous energy thrumming through Xander lessens.

"Thanks, man," Xander says quietly. Seeming to have gathered himself, Xander looks to the both of us with firm resolve. "Make tonight count."

The air is particularly crisp at this time of night. Every breath clouds in front of my face, and the cold immediately bites at my cheeks and nose. The car drives away once Atticus, and I are on the sidewalk.

"Ready?" he asks. My mouth opens and closes, but I merely nod.

We walk side by side up to the house, and with every step closer, a feeling of great unease grips my insides.

"I don't like this," I mutter, voicing my thoughts as an ominous influence begins to grow in the air. "It feels...." I look up to him and watch his brows hunch over his eyes in consideration. "It feels like a warning. Maybe I should call—"

The door to the house opens, and in its frame is Aunt Lydia. She's dressed in all white and eyes us superiorly from her vantage point.

"*Astrus mosta.*" Her words ring out against the night air with authority, and the house appears to shiver. "Come," she says, sweeping her hand out behind her. "Hurry, before it closes."

We move into the house, but I cannot shake my uncertainty, and crossing into the household only worsens my unease. A quick look at Atticus and I'm assured the feeling is mutual.

"I'm afraid you'll have to suffer through your discomfort. This is no ordinary magic we are dealing with, and so we've had to dip into more powerful magic ourselves," Aunt Lydia says, her eyes hovering over the tense line of our shoulders and rigid postures. "You can go to the open office upstairs. It overlooks the room here"—Lydia gestures to the room to her left as we strip out of our coats—"where we will perform the ceremony."

I look at our designated area. The open office reminds me of an interior balcony, as it hangs a quarter way over the room below it overlooks.

"Off you go, it's almost time to begin."

Aunt Lydia spins around, her long white dress fanning out with the motion. A warm weight settles on the small of my back, urging me away from the room next door full of witches in white.

"Come on." Atticus's breath stirs the hair tucked behind my ear and sends a shiver down my spine.

We climb the steps slowly, both of our attention drawn to the scene below. The room is clear of what furniture it used to host. Only imprints remain in scattered squares or circles. *A chair here... a table there*, I note.

The only objects that remain are three standing mirrors. They are equal distance apart from one another and act as tips of a triangle, facing inward toward each other. Just looking at them makes the uncertainty of tonight's activities even more pronounced.

Atticus guides us to the middle of the banister once we are upstairs. We stand hip to hip as we watch the witches organize themselves below. Aunt Mo speaks to three witches in the far corner of the room. I cannot see her face, but her hands move about wildly to explain something to them. The witches opposite her are rapt in attention.

Meanwhile, Aunt Lydia's instructions ring the loudest in the room.

"Eldritch witches, take your place," Aunt Lydia commands with a clap of her hands.

Atticus tenses beside me and stands straighter as we watch six witches gather around the set of mirrors. In each of their hands is a broom, and upon finding their places, they hold them horizontally, waist high. They adjust, closing their ranks a step tighter until every broom is nearly touching from handle to base.

"*Brisium*," they say in unison.

The wooden broomsticks make a distinct *clink* as they snap forcefully together and begin to gently vibrate in the air of their own accord. The Eldritch witches take three steps back, their hands kept out in front of them as if the action alone keeps the brooms held up in the air.

"That's… interesting," Atticus mumbles.

I grimace in response, not liking the reverberation of magic in the air. The magic is more powerful and painful, even more so than Luna's outburst. Whatever energy powers this magic is concentrated and hangs densely in the air. It pinches and pricks at my skin. Every breath I take leaves my insides feeling irritated and rubbed *raw*.

"I have a feeling it's going to get a lot more interesting," I say lightly back as I shift my weight from foot to foot and wrap my arms around my middle.

Aunt Lydia circles the perimeter they have created and eyes it critically for any weak points. When she is satisfied, she shuffles over to Aunt Mo and places a hand on her shoulder.

"It's time," she says too lowly for human ears to catch, but for lycan hearing in an abnormally quiet room... it's as if she's speaking right to us.

Aunt Mo nods. "All right, ladies, take your positions." They do as they're ordered and stand in the spaces between each mirror, a mere foot away from the broom-circle's circumference. "Charity?" Aunt Mo calls.

From beneath our private mezzanine, another witch enters the room. Her hair is long and blonde, and her willowy frame drowns in the white cloth gown she dons. Similar to the Eldritch witches, her hands are held out in front of her. But instead of thrusting her palms forward, she enters with her hands cupped.

A whisper reaches my lycan hearing. Words I cannot begin to decipher prickle at the delicate curve of my ear and make me twitch uncomfortably. Atticus grunts, unable to resist the urge to scratch and rub at his ears. I catch his eye, and we stare at one another in quiet trepidation.

"You okay?" he asks, his eyes running over my form. "Doesn't it bother you?"

My eyes widen comically. "I feel ill," I tell him a touch breathlessly. "I wish we didn't have to be here."

Atticus frowns sympathetically. "They need witnesses from the pack."

"I know," I say, turning my gaze reluctantly back to the proceedings below. Aunt Mo and Aunt Lydia are pouring some dark matter out onto the ground to encase the three witches in another ring. This dark ring creates a divide with the Eldritch witches standing behind them.

I'm so engrossed in the goings on of the witches, I jump when Atticus's hand brushes against my own. I stare down at the offending appendage and my heart races. Atticus says nothing, and he doesn't move his hand. I dare not risk looking up at his face and slip back into my earlier stance with our hands now touching.

"What are you doing?" I whisper.

Atticus's warm breath fans my neck as he ducks his head beside me. "Watching a magic show," he says seriously, though I just make out his twitching lips out of my peripheral vision. It never fully forms. "I think we're better off facing this together," he concedes after a moment. "If it bothers you—"

I shake my head faster than I can voice my response. "It doesn't."

He stiffens momentarily and breathes in deeply before straightening. My heart beats a little faster at the motion, and despite knowing better, I lean closer to him. There *is* a comfort in our closeness. It rides through the pack bonds, looping around us as the witches carry on.

Charity walks forward, past the two sets of witches and up to the broom ring. From her cupped hands lifts an object. It's the necklace. I jolt at seeing it, although why I cannot say. After all, this is what we came here for—to use the jewelry to look into the past, and maybe, just maybe, garner something useful about our curses' origins.

As a clock somewhere inside the house begins to strike three, the lights dim and candlelight flickers to life. And then, the witches start.

"In the witching hour, this darkest time, we call upon your sacred power."

Aunt Mo's voice is husky, sedate, and full of power.

"I call upon the sands of time! *Vio doxin, sareth.*"

The three witches nearest Charity respond. "*Vio doxin, sareth.*" Their voices echo through the room, dying off in a whispered wind before Aunt Mo continues. She tilts her head back, and an unearthly wind dances through her hair.

"By the power of three,

grant unto thee,
the gift of second sight!"

"*Vio doxin, sareth,*" the eldritch witches repeat. The room swells with heat, dry and blistering.

"To see the truth,
to know the way,
I cast this spell in every way!"

"*Vio doxin, sareth. Abrath malox. Vitume clos.*"

The chanting of the last line brings about a new energy to the room. The unnatural heat cracks like heat lightning, and I let out a yelp as the candle flames shoot upward. Atticus shifts to wrap an arm around my back before his hand settles on my waist. As he does, the air begins to glimmer with golden streaks.

The necklace is propelled into the middle of the triangle, and so follows the glimmering light. My breath catches in my throat as I watch the magic run through the air, leaving behind dust-like particles that shine on brightly. I dimly register grasping onto Atticus's arm as if he is the only thing to keep me afloat. Atticus shivers and moves to stand behind me, his hands coming to grip the banister as his arms continue to shake.

"Just breathe, Winter," Atticus says, exhaling loudly as if to show me how. I follow suit, trying my best to focus on the rise and fall of his chest at my back.

But the air is thick with magic, and every drag of air burns painfully on the way down.

"Look," he rasps as his grip tightens.

The golden light circles around the set of mirrors like a cyclone and the mirrors' surfaces begin to ripple.

"Oh."

The three witches chant something new that is indistinguishable and full of magic.

Three things become clear to me very suddenly as images begin to play out in the mirrors' surfaces.

First, if Atticus weren't here to support me, I'd be in a crumpled ball on the floor. Second, there isn't just magic in the air but evil and sickness and malice. The glittering light whips out of its self-contained cyclone only to snap at dark, smoky tendrils that escape the necklace.

And last, it's working.

It's not just images that string themselves across the mirror's surfaces but moving pictures. Like flashes of memory playing out against a screen, they play out in flickering bursts.

It is mesmerizing, and soon enough, the pain that accompanies the magic fades and dulls. I am saturated in its energy and completely inundated to its will—whatever it may be.

"What are you doing?" Atticus asks, squeezing me back unbearably tight against his front.

I stumble back a step, shocked to find that I have moved forward at all. But both of my hands now grip the banister and strain to pull me closer. I gulp at the air, but there is no satisfying my lungs.

"Atticus? Are you feeling this?" This lightheaded, dizzying, *madness*. A woman's voice rasps in my ears, growing louder and louder until I am a whimpering mess. My legs collapse beneath me, but Atticus is there to catch me.

"Yes," he responds gruffly. He lifts me and presses my body between his and the banister to support me completely. "Just hold out a little longer."

But a little longer is almost too much to bear. Below the magic builds to a crescendo slowly. A throbbing builds at the back of my head as I watch. The scenes continue to play out along the mirrors, growing in speed. They flicker and jump around until I think I might be sick.

I wish to look away, really I do, but there is no hope of turning my gaze away. Whatever magic guides this spell has us both enchanted as well. The wolf in my mind is eerily silent. Its presence muted. And yet, the feeling isn't quite as awful as I imagined it to be.

The spell ends with Aunt Mo dropping to her knees and the scent of blood cutting through the air. She gives a hacking cough as the spell breaks apart and the magic dissipates from the room in angry sparks.

Lydia rushes to her side, helping the older woman to her feet. I note, with a gasp, that red droplets streak down her cheeks.

"Maureen."

Her name ushers from me almost soundlessly. I push away from Atticus's hold, or try to.

"Not yet," Atticus says in a low voice. His body trembles against mine as he tries to regain his equilibrium. A low groan issues from his large frame, and he turns his head into the crook of my neck. Inhaling deeply, he calms himself.

"Are you all right?" I ask.

His head moves against my neck. Up and down.

"We should go down," I say, anticipation crawling up my body and chasing away the magic zipping through my veins.

"Don't you think we should give them a moment to collect themselves?" he asks.

Down below, the witches pull together around Aunt Mo. A seat has been brought out from another room for her to sit on, and though she attempts to laugh off their concern, there is no hiding her relief in the action. Someone brings out a glass of water, and the other witches flutter out of the way of the delivery. It's Charity. She presents the water to her mother on bended knee.

I squirm in Atticus's hold, and he releases me with a scowl marring his beautiful face. I peer at him beneath half-lowered lashes then flick my gaze back downstairs.

"What's so important that you can't wait to get out of here?"

"I—" A thrill of excitement races through me. "—I recognized something in the mirror."

Atticus stares at me dumbfounded.

"What?"

"The tree. I know that tree, Atticus." His scowl returns, but I don't wait to face his skepticism. I escape from his hold and head down the stairs as fast as my feet can carry me.

The witches glare as I intrude upon their space, but an unseen force pushes me through their small ranks. I kneel beside Charity and place a hand on Aunt Mo's knee.

"I know those places," I say.

Murky blue eyes, so much hazier than the day before, stare straight through me. Aunt Mo's lips thin to two lines. "Yes," she murmurs. "You saw?"

I nod, unsure if she can see the action. "I did. The paths they walked are our roads now. The river bend with its boulders is the same as where I played as a child. And the tree...." The large birch with its golden autumnal leaves. "I grew up climbing in that tree. We hold festivals nearby throughout the year. Couples carve their name into its trunk."

"Good."

A moment of silence passes, and then Charity rises. "What did you gather?" she asks of the witches who stood closest to the mirrors.

The three share a look, and then a girl with glossy dark hair and pretty almond eyes steps forward.

"Not enough," she replies. "The sacrifices took place at the same tree and on a full moon in each instance. To undo what has been done, the reverses of the hexes will need to be done at the same tree and on a full moon. The problem is the hexes themselves. They were difficult to decipher and determining what hex belongs to which curse will take time."

“Make a record of what you witness while it’s still fresh in your mind, then go home. Take the bath salts we made earlier and soak yourselves for at least an hour among them. We don’t want the darkness staining your souls.”

The three girls nod and hustle off to another part of the house. The eldritch witches begin to whisper among themselves, no doubt waiting for their own instructions. Charity dismisses them, directing them to use the set of oils in the kitchen to cleanse themselves. When they depart, Charity drops to a knee once more before her mother.

Her blue eyes shine like sapphires. “What would you have me do?”

“We will wait to contact Diana until the girls give us their record,” she responds, exhaustion in her voice.

“And then?”

The floor creaks beneath tentative feet, and a look over my shoulder reveals Atticus. He stands nearby, hands tucked into his pockets. He stares at Aunt Mo with a solemn expression haunting his face.

“Thank you,” he says, his gaze flickering over her depleted form.

Aunt Mo summons a brilliant smile. “All is well, and the end is near,” she professes with relief.

“Is it?” Charity inquires, reaching out and taking her mother’s hands.

Aunt Mo nods, but her smile dims. “I have a feeling there is an element to our efforts we have forgotten,” she confesses. “But I cannot fathom what.”

Charity takes a moment to ponder her mother’s words. “You’re right,” Charity says. A frown tugs her lips down. “It will take precious time to decipher the order and words used to compose the hexes.”

“Go home,” Lydia says, joining the conversation and eyeing Atticus and me with thinly veiled interest. “We’ve still much to do tonight, including recording tonight’s events.”

Atticus comes to my side, holding out a hand for me to take. I do so and rise with a small hiss. The throbbing at the back of my head grows more substantial, but there is a comfort to be found in the simple skin-to-skin contact with him.

"We'll be in touch," Atticus says and pulls me toward the front door, leaving the three witches to quietly converse.

I don't mean to eavesdrop, but the circumstances make it somewhat unavoidable. Even as I process what has just happened and the ache pulsing in my body, their words reach my lycan hearing.

"We need a direct bloodline," I hear Charity insist. "You know exactly what we should do—"

"Hush, now," Aunt Mo snaps before a small, pained moan escapes her. "That path lacks the proper strength behind it. Besides, there are more ways than this to achieve our goal."

Aunt Lydia snorts, but it is Charity's voice that speaks next. "Yes, Mother," she says somewhat caustically. "All we need is someone who can speak to trees. Then we'll get the account word for word."

A dose of cold hits me in the face as Atticus opens the door. His hand has once more found mine, and he tugs me forward, but my feet dig in to the ground. I turn to the witches, my face losing all its color.

"I know someone who can speak to trees," I say, my words louder than I anticipated. Three sets of eyes pin me in place, but only two of them widen in acknowledgment.

Atticus brushes past me with a single step. His frame half blocks me from view. His blue eyes peek over his shoulder at me briefly, and then back to the trio of witches.

"Who?" he asks.

The clock begins to chime from one of the other rooms in lieu of our hush. The docile noise strikes four times, and in the process, knocks me back a step. *Has an hour really passed?* The spell couldn't have been longer than ten minutes or so.

"Who?" Atticus repeats.

"Luna," I respond along with Aunt Lydia and Mo. Magic tickles down my forearms and across the back of my neck at the innocent act.

With a gentle shake, I rid myself of the feeling. But magic still taints the air, making it thick and uncomfortable to be in. I move closer to Atticus's side.

"She told me a while back that she could speak to plants and trees," I elaborate. "Whether or not those trees and plants could remember that far back...."

"You really think she could talk to the tree and get the full story?" Atticus's disbelief is only mildly softened by the touch of wonder in his voice at the revelation. He looks to me for the answer, but it is Aunt Lydia who responds.

"In most cases, I wouldn't expect such an ancient being to remember all of the details, let alone any one event, but the circumstances are different. Such a marked experience is not easily forgotten by those who survive it."

Aunt Mo's chair squeaks as she readjusts herself. She looks about to speak as well, but one of the three inner circle witches comes back into the room. She keeps a small bundle tucked beneath one arm, only to briefly set it down in the corner of the room in favor of the kitchen broom and dustpan in her hands. Her brown eyes find mine with alarming speed.

"Shouldn't you be helping your sister and Monica, Bella?" Charity asks, standing and giving the girl a pointed look.

Bella smiles, though it doesn't reach her eyes. "I didn't see anything during the ceremony, so they sent me in to start cleaning up. But I did end up amplifying their experiences."

Charity and Aunt Lydia give an approving nod to Bella as she breaks the circle of brooms carefully on the ground, and then the second drawn circle with her broom. As the dark material scatters across the floor, I realize it is dirt, of all things. Atticus nudges me with his elbow. His eyes draw back and forth between the witches and me.

"Is there anything we can do at the moment?" I ask.

The witches ponder my question, murmuring more fervidly amongst themselves now that the opportunity with Luna has been broached. I let my sights drift back to Bella. She is careful not to stand in the line of the mirrors as she inverts one 45 degrees and breaks their triangular symmetry.

In an instant, the sting of magic lessens. Atticus's sigh of relief sounds loud, my own mingling in with his. We share a grateful glance toward one another, still waiting for the witches to decide what they will have us do—if anything at all.

Sage, cedar, and a hint of spice begin to taper into the air, dispelling and covering what magical residue remains. Bella walks the perimeter of the room. Her arm is held high above her head, waving the small bundle of smoldering dried plants to smudge the room.

"She could speak to her," Aunt Mo says quietly. I glance back to the women, who now take to shooting us looks as if we can't hear every single word with perfect clarity. "Make amends."

Aunt Lydia snorts, her voice rising to a reasonable level as she acknowledges our regard. "The fairy hasn't come out of her room since the incident with Zoelle, Maureen. And let's be realistic, our goodwill with her is fading. You know how desperately she wishes to return to her plane of existence. No doubt, all she sees in us now is false promises."

The two elders share a meaningful look. Then Aunt Mo's resolve hardens.

"We must exhaust all other options before resorting to the last," she says in a firm voice. "Go with them back to the house and tell Diana to expect the Moon sisters and Monica for a briefing. She might say she wants to be kept out of the loop, but it's important for her to know."

Aunt Lydia rolls her eyes, hands planting on her hips as she glares softly at her friend. "Fine, Mo, but don't get in the habit of trying to boss me around, you hear?"

The women smirk at one another.

"Go."

+++

Although the sky begins to turn the horizon a humbler shade of dark blue, the Elder Triad's home is bustling. Aunt Lydia takes one look at the witches clamoring from room to room and scowls.

"Either something went right," she says, "or wrong."

Seeing my struggle with one of the arms of my coat, Atticus helps me tug free from it. I cast a shy glance over my shoulder, unable to stop the way my heart skips a beat at the small action. But I utterly freeze when his hand reaches out to brush away the snowflakes that stick to my hair.

"Thank you," I murmur. I catch Atticus's eyes and stall further at the calculating slant of his regard.

He nods solemnly, his hand falling away as he directs his attention over to Aunt Lydia who watches our interaction with a raised brow. "Where are they?" Atticus asks.

"Downstairs," she says and looks pointedly down the hallway to the door located beneath the stairway. He nods and walks off, but I swear the pressure of his hand rests at my hip for the briefest of seconds.

I watch Atticus go, heart stuck in my throat. I don't understand what has prompted all of the small touches and gestures. I doubt it to be the flowers from last night for he had walked so stiffly away from them. Perhaps it is the magic of tonight?

The need for *pack* is too difficult to resist in such a chaotic climate.

I make a weak attempt to reach out to his retreating form, but my hand falls uselessly to my side as the door to the basement closes softly behind him.

The witches continue to scamper around us, though now they seem to finally take notice of the most recent occupants of the house. While Aunt Lydia receives respectful nods and shy smiles, their expressions turn slightly darker once they reach me. I sigh, the sting of magic tingling down my throat no more than a mild annoyance by now.

My wolf stirs, shaking itself from its unusual slumber, and its thoughts graze my own. No good magic is here. *We are too vulnerable....*

Aunt Lydia says something to which I absently nod my head. My eyes drift back toward the basement door. I doubt my wolf and I would feel as vulnerable if Atticus stayed by our side.

"You'll have to do more than make moon eyes at his back and some flowers to earn your way back into his good graces," she tells me dryly.

I wear my mortification and anger hotly on my cheeks. "Excuse me?"

"It's not enough," she says, an eyebrow cocking pointedly. "Now, I'm going to make up some tea for Atticus and yourself to cleanse you of the negative energy tonight. You head on upstairs and see to Luna."

She walks away before I can protest. My shoulders slump in defeat as I'm left alone in a house full of witches that despise me... and a fairy who attempted to kill me. I grimace as I tread up the stairs.

"I don't even know what room is hers," I mutter to myself with a growing frown. But when I reach the second-floor landing and look down both ends of the hallway, it isn't hard to decipher which room is Luna's.

I turn right, toward the door with leafy vines crawling out of the crack at the bottom of the door and hugging the frame.

Make amends, Aunt Mo had said, but what if Luna refuses to see me? What if she tosses me out of the house again?

My hand is poised to knock, but indecision makes me falter.

About a dozen more what-ifs storm through my mind. In the end, it's Aunt Lydia's condescending words from minutes ago that brings my hand down against the door's surface in a timid rap.

"Luna?"

Where once a subdued rustling and slithering touched my sensitive hearing, now nothing comes into range. It is a noise I don't notice until it is gone. Several voices chatter on down below and threaten to steal my focus.

"Luna?" I try again, rapping once more. "It's Winter… I came to apologize… to make amends."

The vines hugging the door frame give an agitated rustle. I jump back a step, my heart suddenly racing.

"Luna—"

I stop myself. Instead, I watch with growing disappointment as the vines wind across the door and lock me out. They entwine, curling around each other and forming knots as their leaves quiver with the movement. Upon closer expectation, it isn't the only movement they shudder at, but the buds hiding behind them that wish to bloom.

The sight of the flowers dry my mouth, as I remember all those passed between Atticus and me.

Holly for hope.

Daffodils for new beginnings.

Chrysanthemums for honesty.

Purple hyacinth for apologies given.

Wallflowers for faithfulness.

I stand before a supernatural creature who had been led on by false promises for too long and preparing to sweet talk her with apologies only to use her once more. I slump back against the opposite wall, staring forlornly at her door. After all I have done, the thought of pressing this task onto her shoulders feels wrong.

My eyes slip closed.

"I'm sorry," I say softly, uncertain if she can hear my words through the door. "I'm sorry for lying to you and scaring you. But I need your help because there's a chance you can fix… *everything*."

When I open my eyes, the vines have gone still. A flower here and there have opened as well, their dark centers eyeing me boldly.

"I know I'm in no position to ask, but I have to… I *have* to at least try."

My head knocks rather painfully against the wall as I wait in silence for a response I know won't—

"Kind of like you *had* to poison me?" The fairy adds a remarkable amount of scorn to her words.

"Yes," I reply, unable to cover my astonishment. "I mean, no, but yes. It's not that simple, to be honest. Maybe I can come in and explain?" I ask, the pitch of my voice rising at the end.

The vines stiffen at my request, and each bloom snaps shut. Well, that answered my question.

"Okay," Luna says, almost too quietly for me and my lycan hearing to catch.

The greenery retreats back to its position of sentry duty, and the door opens a crack, but no more than that. Curbing my fear, I force my feet forward and enter the room.

AMENDS

- Chapter 21 -

Luna's room isn't so much a room as it is a *jungle*.

The door closes behind me with a soft snick, but not by my hand. Luna sits in a nest of blankets on a raised platform that resembles a bed.

No, that *is* a bed.

Only it is shrouded in thick vines—or perhaps they are roots. After all, there is a tree in the far-left corner of the room. It is wedged in place with its branches spidering out across the ceiling and walls with lush green leaves hanging from them.

I take another step forward, examining how plant life covers almost every inch of the room. Almost, because I can still see the frame of the bed, and the dresser and mirror on the opposite wall have been left mostly untouched.

"You did this?"

There's no need for her to respond, I know the answer is yes—we both do—but I don't wish to hide my amazement.

"They said it was my room to do with as I wished… for as long as I was here," she tells me, a hint of steel underlying her words.

"It's spectacular. I've never seen plants like these before," I breathe.

Losing all sense of former hesitation and fear, I walk over the dirt-laden and gnarled-root floor to the other far corner of the room. What used to be a place to showcase books and knickknacks now proudly houses several dreamy-looking plants, the likes of which I have never seen or heard of.

The flowers are teal with creamy white spots that spear out intermittently along their petals. Each petal flares out and turns back *just so* at the very end. Several black stamens jut out from its white eye, bobbing gently along a nonexistent breeze, as if they're waving hello. I step closer, entranced by the motion and its citrusy smell.

"They're poisonous," Luna comments idly from the bed. I halt in my tracks, unaware as to how close I had come to the plant. "Although, there is a certain justice to you ingesting them…."

Her calm voice trails off from behind as I summon the strength to tear my eyes away from the alluring plant.

"I wasn't going to eat them," I tell her, feeling my nerves pulsate behind my eyes. I rub my temples and eyes to attempt to dislodge the foreign ache.

"Weren't you?"

The sincerity of her question leaves me speechless. *Was I?* A foreboding sense of discomfort is all the answer I need.

"Thanks for the warning," I say and step back toward the middle of the room. Luna leans back against the cocoon of blankets and pillows she amasses on her bed, eyeing me with distrust. "I know you didn't have to," I add, saddling up to the side of the dresser.

Luna sniffs and raises her chin. She says nothing.

"Why?" I ask, unwilling to keep the silence.

Her dignified demeanor softens a touch due to her curiosity. "Why what?"

"Why did you warn me?"

Luna casts her gaze elsewhere. Her face is carefully blank, but the flora around us react to her emotions. They twist and weave amongst themselves almost in contemplation.

"I don't like to hurt people," she murmurs at last, turning her violet eyes my way. "I can't stand it when people treat each other so cruelly. I don't understand this war," she continues on, a frown wrinkling her nose and forehead. "I don't understand why you would want to hurt me. I thought we were friends."

Her voice is brittle at the end and incredibly soft. Taking a deep breath, I lower myself onto bended knee, letting Luna take the higher and more dominant position.

"We were… I know after all I've done that we aren't now, but I would like to be again in the future. I am sorry, Luna. I issued the tonic in the hopes of protecting someone I love back home in my old pack."

"I don't see how," she mumbles.

Dropping my gaze to the foot of her bed, I respond. The words come out flat, almost robotic. "My parents wish to see the Adolphus pack ruined." I pause to swallow. *They wish to see the Adolphus pack defeated, broken, and eradicated as well as their new ways.* "They used me as a means to gain information, and upon sharing my experiences with you, they decided you were a threat. The tonic was meant to subtract you from the situation temporarily and allow the fight between the packs to go unhampered."

"Who?" Luna asks. "Who were you protecting? Did it work?"

My throat tightens, and I tuck my hair behind my ear. "I did it for my cousin. Her name is Juniper. I don't know if it worked. I haven't spoken with my parents or her in days."

"Why would your parents want something like that?"

"Because they're scared." The answer is the closest to the truth I've ever gotten.

My parents are scared. They're scared of a newer, stronger pack cultivating the idea that there is more to life than the traditional ways. The Adolphus pack gives wolves hope for a future not strictly dictated by an alpha's law. But mostly, I assume, they are scared of change.

"I'm worried she won't wake up," Luna confesses. She sits up and catches my eye. "The witches tried something about an hour ago, and I don't think it went well. Xander was shouting a lot, and the witches have been running around like crazy. It woke me up."

Her words feel like a physical blow.

"Just great," I mutter to myself, raking a hand back through my hair and wincing when it catches in some knots. "I know they want Zoelle to wake as soon as possible, but if Lucy was telling the truth, then she will be awake in a day or two." *If she was telling the truth*, I think dismally. "How can I help wake her if they keep using new magic on her? What if what they're doing to her now is making everything worse?"

"Do you think they would do the same for me?"

I rock back onto my heel at her question. "Of course they would."

Luna ducks her head, her colorless hair hiding her face. "Do you really think so?"

"Yes, Luna," I tell her firmly. The fairy sighs, dragging her gaze back to mine. They are filled with sadness and uncertainty.

"What did you want my help with?"

My mouth opens and closes a few times before I process her question correctly. "You'll help me?" She nods, and the ability to speak is lost to me again.

"I don't have to hurt anyone, do I?"

"No," I say quickly. "No, not at all. I hoped you might speak to a, uh,"—heat suffuses my cheeks—"a tree for me."

Luna perks up. She edges herself closer to the end of the bed. "I love talking to trees," she says. "They have the best stories."

In a reflection of Luna's interest, the room's plant life swells to be nearer to her. And me. I shift back, trying not to show my sudden fear, just in case they can sense it.

"I bet…." I agree with a nervous laugh. "The thing is, the tree is back in my hometown, in Alma, Quebec, and we need to know a specific story from the tree. A few stories, actually. Ones that took place a long time ago."

"I see."

The vines and roots wind together as Luna's contemplation manifests around her. She begins to nibble on her lip and looks down in thought only to steal glances at me. The movement beneath my knelt form nearly unseats me, but with my grip on the dresser edge, I remain grounded. Somewhat.

"I'll help," she says carefully, her eyes hardening. "But I won't help for nothing. Not any longer."

Though my gut clenches, I nod. "What do you want in return for your help?"

"I want to leave."

The clenching sensation releases, but what takes its place is a sickening feeling. "Leave?"

"I want to go home," she reiterates. "They've told me a hundred times they will help me get home, but something always comes up. And when they do try, well, it doesn't seem like they're trying very hard at all."

"I see," I breathe, taking a dizzying moment to decipher my own plan of action. "I'll try and help you,

Luna, I swear I will, but I don't know what I can do. I can't perform any magic."

Her lips thin. "If you can't promise to return me home, then I won't help you."

"But I don't know if I can even keep that promise!"

"Promise or I won't help!" she shouts back.

Something wraps around my shin and yanks it back, so I am on both knees before her. I stare in shock at the fairy. My wolf snarls and pushes to the forefront of my mind as Luna's temper flares. But it's not just her temper... Luna's eyes shine with unshed tears.

It takes a moment for me to leash the wolf's anger, taking special care to examine her. I'm sure if it weren't for the heavy perfume of flowers, I would be able to scent her real emotions.

"Luna... I can't promise to find you a way home," I tell her with regret.

Like a child who has not gotten their way, she spins herself around. The tips of her fingers are visible from the back as they reach around her middle. Her crying fills the air, but instead of the attack I'm sure is to come, the plants converge onto Luna. They wrap around her protectively, and she leans on them for support.

"It's not fair," I hear her say. "Nobody will help me go home. Nobody cares."

Her tear-ridden words tug at my heartstrings. Tentatively, I rise, my knees shaking as I step to the bed and reach for her. Her skin is surprisingly cool to the touch, and it is evident in the way she jumps she does not expect my approach or hear it.

"What?" she bites out, wiping furiously at her cheeks even as her tears continue.

"I can't promise to find you a way home, but I vow to you, Luna, I will help you however I can in your efforts to get home. But not before Zoelle is awoken. I've already given my word to the coven and Xander that I would—that I will help them fix this mess."

She sniffs, and suddenly the vines and roots push and pull me forward until I'm right next to Luna. I almost tumble into her from the force of nature and stare at her wide-eyed and nose to nose. Her violet eyes widen in a similar fashion as my slate gray ones, but it's the gentle mingling of our equally snowy white hair that draws her regard away. Her fingers reach up, touching the ends of my long hair.

"Okay," she whispers, voice sullen but sound. "I'll help."

"You will?"

She nods, then turns watery eyes back to me. "And you promise to help me after?"

I capture her hand in mine and press it over my heart. "I swear I will help you after all of this is done. When Zoelle and her baby are safe and we've learned what we can from the yellow birch tree, I'll be your faithful companion and help you find your way home."

Luna smiles weakly back at me.

+++

Atticus is waiting at the bottom of the stairs for me. He casts anxious glances at his phone, then up the stairs. When they land on me, I still.

"We need to go," he says. His voice is clipped.

"Is everything all right?" I ask, scurrying down the stairs and letting him usher me into my coat and straight out the door. A black SUV is waiting at the end of the driveway; Xander's scowling face peers out at us through the passenger side. "What's going on?"

Atticus urges me on faster. His hand at the small of my back guides me firmly forward.

"I'll tell you at home."

I dig my heels into the ground. "*Nooo*," I say, head moving quickly back and forth, knowing all too well that Xander can hear. I round on Atticus, keeping my voice as low as possible. "Tell me now. I'm not going in there with a fuming mad alpha, who is already furious with me."

"It's either in there with him or inside with a coven of witches, who just found out we're bringing in an outside sorcerer."

I gulp. "Car it is," I breathe, already back to speeding toward it.

Once we are fastened up inside, Atticus peels out of the driveway and down the road. I hold back the urge to counsel Atticus on his speed, even as the residential homes go past us in a blur. Xander is barely able to contain the low growl rumbling continuously out of him.

I shrink back in my seat, catching Atticus's gaze in the rearview mirror.

"I can't believe they have the gall to scold me. As if I'm a child who doesn't know what they're doing—that I'm unreasonable and rash. They're the ones who messed up tonight." A snarl rocks the inside of the car followed by a loud bang.

My heart jumps in my chest as I slam myself back against the seat. It is only Atticus's voice that keeps me from leaping into the trunk to get away from the alpha's anger.

"You knew the risks, Xander. You knew what they were going to try, and you supported it. Don't get this way," he says with vehemently. "We talked about this, man. We *knew*."

A disheartening feeling rides through the pack bonds, and so close to the source, my stomach clenches painfully. A small whimper eeks past my lips, but the men ignore my discomfort.

"Fine," Xander replies tersely.

In the passenger side window, I glean a bit of Xander's reflection. His face is drawn, and his eyes stare out the window bleakly as his hand winds up around the back of his neck. Then, I watch as his top lip curls back, another snarl of fury releasing.

"They can't keep me away from her," he says harshly. "And they sure as hell won't keep Jax away from her. She's *my* soulmark. She's carrying *my* child. If I discover they've tried another of their worthless spells without my consent, I'll—"

"Don't go there, man," Atticus interrupts, pulling to a stop on an empty street. He stays put, turning to Xander more fully. "All anyone wants is to wake Zoelle and set things right."

Thick tension enters the car as Xander remains quiet. I still, all too aware of the implicating silence, and clench my jaw tightly shut. When their gazes search mine out in the back seat, my head is already ducked submissively. My eyes are glued to my lap.

"As already proved, we don't all have the same wants," Xander says frightfully composed.

I hunch a bit further, feeling the alpha's displeasure directed my way. Tilting my head to the side, I present my neck in an offering of apology.

Atticus growls lightly. "Be careful with your words, brother." The warning draws both sets of eyes away from me, and I breathe a sigh of relief as their tenuous weight lifts. Peeking at them, I note both sport rosy-hued cheeks and stern frowns.

"She—"

"Is not the enemy," Atticus cuts in sharply. "She was just a pawn used by her own fucking parents. You can't sit and steep in this anger. We need to be focused and alert for the pack because the real enemy is out there waiting. And *stop* riling things up with the witches. You had to know they'd be offended by you calling in Jax. Come on, man. He's a *Stormrow*. You know their history."

Xander deflates. Though his cheeks still remain colored from both embarrassment and a touch of shame, the rest of his face remains ashen as his gaze turns somber.

“I can’t stand going on like this without her,” he confesses, his voice hoarse.

Atticus claps a hand onto his shoulder, leaning in. “You have too.”

With his ability to manipulate the pack bonds, Atticus pulls at the support and love spread out among the pack and directs it toward the alpha. His brow furrows in concentration as he bolsters Xander back to a reasonable state.

Xander shuts his eyes with a grateful shudder, his head bowing an inch in gratitude. Without thought, my hand rises and rests upon Atticus’s. His blue eyes flit to me, but only momentarily. For the first time since joining the pack as the female beta, I attempt to manipulate the pack bonds as well and draw from myself heavily.

A sweat builds at the back of my neck almost instantly. Being the beta might allow me this special privilege, but without any practice, there is a strain to my efforts. I squeeze my eyes tightly shut and *concentrate.*

I send Xander my love, gratefulness, and admiration.

Love, because he so desperately needs to feel it without Zoelle to fill that space in his heart.

Gratefulness, because his pack has shown me what it means to live and be happy.

Admiration, because his sheer strength and power awe me. Because he doesn’t use either to force his pack to submit to his will and uses it to empower them.

A warm hand rests atop my own. It pulls me from my work as I open my eyes in a daze. Two sets of eyes are back upon me, as well as the alpha's hand.

“Thank you, Winter,” Xander says sincerely. “But you’re giving too much. You’ll pass out at this rate.”

He gently moves my hand away onto the back of his chair instead, and I slump forward with a wave of exhaustion. A hand briefly touches my cheek, or so I think. When I have sense enough to look, I cannot determine which man showed the small affection.

"Let's get going," Xander says. "All of us need rest after the night we just had."

"I'll drop off Winter and go back with you," Atticus says, pulling out of park and back into the street. Early risers begin to enter the road as well, commuting out of the quaint town to another for work. Our speed this time is to the law.

"No," Xander states after a minute of silence. "Go home with Winter. Take the day off work and rest. We need to be at the top of our game, and your boost helped—both of yours—but I know how much it took out of both of you. Our planning can wait until this afternoon."

We say no more, although I couldn't even if I wanted to. The magic and tiresome task of boosting the alpha leaves me drained. And yet, some spark of promise keeps me wide awake as I stare at Atticus unabashedly.

He had come to my defense. He had stuck by my side all through the night. *What does that mean?*

Atticus parks in the curve of the cul de sac in front of our house and hops out of the car, leaving it running for Xander. When I exit, I don't expect Xander to wrap me up in a brief hug and place a kiss atop my head. A little quiver racks my body when he pulls away and gives Atticus an even larger hug.

Xander eyes us both when he reaches the driver side. "Be good to each other," he commands.

I nod, then follow Atticus up and into the house. He makes no attempt at conversation as he shrugs off his coat and hangs it up. His lips stay sealed as he takes my coat from me and hangs it as well.

Anticipation sweeps up in my chest as words creep up my throat to the tip of my tongue. Locking eyes with Atticus, I take a deep breath.

"I think we should talk."

"I'm going upstairs to call work and go to bed."

Our sentences clash together just like our eyes. An awkward moment passes, and Atticus shifts uncomfortably under my disappointed look.

"You should get to bed too," he recommends and slips up the stairs with nothing more to be said.

I stand in silence with tiny fissures of hurt splitting my heart as I watch him go. Minutes later I am still in the foyer staring up at the upstairs hallway. Indecision leaves me paralyzed. Part of me sullenly accepts his rejection, thinking it is more than deserved. But another part wonders at how he can turn his back upon me so easily. How, when there is a magnetism drawing us together time and time again?

I tried to ignore the draw and push it aside, but I don't want to fight it anymore.

I don't want to fight with him anymore.

I drag my feet in the direction of the kitchen, intent on getting a glass of water, when the sight of the wallflowers steals my attention. *Faithfulness.* The last conversation in the kitchen dashes through my mind. All those promises I made to Atticus… only to be slighted with his indifference.

Hurt pierces my heart, along with one of deep frustration and remorse.

I'm trying, dammit.

I allow my teeth to sink into my bottom lip. The pain it causes diverts my attention momentarily, but not enough to keep my lament from repeating. *I'm trying.* No matter how many times I get rebuffed, I will *keep* trying. My wolf rumbles its agreement.

My newfound determination forces me back the few steps I have taken, and I stare hard at the stairs.

I take them two at a time, breathing fast and hard as my courage builds. We are going to talk because this limbo we stand in, this perilous line we walk, is too much. One of us—maybe both of us—are at risk of a fatal misstep. If that happens, we won't be the only ones to suffer, and I can't summon the selfishness necessary for such a careless act.

Even if it hurts... try.

I open his door.

"Atticus, we need—" *We need to close our mouths*, I think belatedly as I stare at his crouched form near the gas fireplace.

The curtains are closed, and the room is bathed in soft light from the bright flames and the few candles that decorate his long dresser. Lavender and sage perfume the air, innately calming me.

Atticus rises, his bare chest gleaming in the swaying and flickering firelight. Dully, I note his shirt tossed haphazardly near the wicker laundry basket.

"What are you doing in here?" he asks.

I continue to stare for my speech is forgotten. After all, his pants are unbuttoned, and the sight alone makes a hot flush rise to my cheeks. Atticus places his phone on the mantle perched above the fireplace, then crosses his arms over his chest.

"Well?"

I swallow thickly. "I wanted to talk...." But the damn speech I had in my head is still nowhere to be found, and as it happens, the sight of the soulmark on Atticus's chest is distracting. I marvel at the three small, intertwined rings that are the symbol of our souls.

"I'm tired, Winter," Atticus says softly. "You should go."

Should, not must.

"I don't want to. I want to be here with you and make sure you're okay. I want to talk about where we stand and how to move forward after tonight."

He shakes his head firmly, lips thinning minutely. "I don't want you here."

Ouch.

Atticus casts his gaze quickly away after saying the words and walks over to the dresser. I follow his movements with my eyes, glued to the spot. The fine needle of hurt pierces my heart again. Just as I'm accepting tonight's attempt as a failure, my lycan hearing picks up on the slight increase of Atticus's heartbeat, and I feel my own go still. I assess the scene once more. Between his furtive look and pulse, his words hold considerably less bite... and far more interest.

I step further into the room, making sure to close the door behind me as I take in a steadying breath.

"I don't believe you," I say, my words shaking.

Atticus stills with his back to me but says nothing. I take another step. *Try. Make amends.*

"These past few days have been hell, and I know it's my fault, but the only times I've felt even remotely okay and as if there is an end in sight to this terrible mess… it's been with you at my side."

He gives another shake of his head, this one is delayed. "You feel that way because of my rank and because the nearness of *pack* is comforting on some level to every wolf. For the record, that feeling of being okay goes only one way. Thanks for asking how I feel—oh, that's right, you didn't."

My cheeks flare red as shame slaps me in the face. In the moment, I am prepared to snap back when I see the glint of gold in his eyes, but my retort dies at the back of my mouth when his shoulders drop.

"You're right," I say, closing my eyes and balling my hands into fists at my side. "I didn't ask, and I should have." I open my eyes and take a slow breath. "How are you?"

His eyes blaze.

"I'm pissed. And hurt. You betrayed us for a pack that clearly doesn't value you… but worse is that I get why you did all this. I know you did all of this to protect June, but it still *hurts*."

"I'm sorry, Atticus," I whisper and shuffle back a step. "I'll never stop being sorry for this, but I hope one day it will hurt you and the pack a little less. Until one day the hurt scars over and no longer causes you pain. But I'm not going to stop trying," I tell him, my last sentence firm yet choked with emotion.

Atticus remains stoic, but his heartbeat is a thunderous sound in the quiet room.

"I'll do whatever it takes to make things right with you and the pack to earn back your trust and heal this wound, but you need to know that I'm not going to stop fighting for you or us."

I slip forward with care. The race of my heartbeat joins Atticus's.

"You said my feelings were one-sided, and that's fine"—even if it hurts like hell—"because you are still the light at the end of the tunnel for me. You've been it for me since the moment we met."

Atticus turns. His blue eyes are stricken with golden lightning as he takes me in. I halt all of my movements, unable to read the expression in his eyes or the carefully smooth facade he wears. The hair on my arms and neck rise as his gaze narrows.

"I love you," I insist and take a shaky step forward. "I tried not to because I thought it would make everything easier, but choosing between you and June was the hardest decision I've ever had to make. I convinced myself you would be strong enough to handle my betrayal, but that was foolish and selfish of me. You have every right to be mad and hurt. I'm just… I'm so sorry I did this to you and the pack. I'm sorry I did this to us."

The gold in his eyes flares.

"Do you mean it?" he asks roughly.

"Every word," I respond back, my voice just as unpolished as his own. I shuffle forward and concentrate as I did before in the car to push my love and remorse through the pack bonds for Atticus to feel. *Please feel it*, I pray. "Can't you tell?" I ask breathlessly.

Atticus prowls forward, each calculated step making my breath come in panicked pants. Will he reject me again? Or will—

"Say it again," he demands, his voice pitched low with heat that doesn't hold its predicted measure of anger. I nearly sob in relief.

"I love you," I say, and am quick to wipe away the tears that break loose. "Atticus, I vow to you I'll do whatever it takes to earn back your trusts and the pack's."

Atticus closes the distance between us. His wolfish advance makes me tremble as I take in the loose sway of his arms at his side and his slightly hunched back.

He looks as if he is ready to pounce at any moment.

"Whatever it takes?" he rumbles, stopping before me.

My eyes widen, and I swallow down my nerves. "Yes."

His thick arm wraps around my waist and tugs me forward. I place a hand tentatively on his chest and inhale rather sharply. His scent surrounds me. The familiar aroma of lush greenery along with musky notes of oakmoss and amber is a welcome assault on my senses. I swallow thickly once more as Atticus's fingers brush the underside of my chin and bring our eyes into contact.

"Ever since the night you were first attacked, all I've been able to think about is our soulmark. How much of this would have ever come to pass if we were together as we were meant to be? I would have felt your guilt and indecision. I would have been keen to all of your worries and doubts." Atticus takes a deep breath, his eyes boring down into mine. "I can't say how long it will take you to earn back the pack's trust, but I know *exactly* what I need from you to start."

My mouth runs dry at the serious tilt of his brow and firm line of his jaw. His smoldering gaze, on the other hand, entices my breathless reply.

"You want to complete the soulmark."

Atticus nods firmly.

"Even though we can't—"

"I dreamed of a future with *you*, Winter," Atticus says. His words ending the conversation at hand.

Tears storm past my defenses, and I duck my head to bat them away. A warm hand cups my jaw and tilts my chin up. When my weak attempt to turn away is blocked, Atticus sighs and ducks his head until our foreheads are almost touching.

"You should have told me," he scolds. His voice is hard but filled to the brim with emotion.

I nod as tears continue to slip down my cheeks.

The arm around my waist tightens.

"Doing this won't make everything right," Atticus says, his tone still hard and low. "It's going to take a lot of work to find a place where we can stand on equal footing again. But if we're both willing to try, and you consent to the binding, it will be a step in the right direction."

"I do." A shaky breath brushes past my lips as my nerves coalesce. I clear my throat gently, forcing myself to maintain eye contact. "I consent."

Atticus's lips take mine in a bruising kiss. Pent-up emotion and energy surge between us and draw us impossibly closer.

The hand at my chin makes a home at the base of my neck. It drags my head this way and a little ways that until the angle is just right for his plunder. A guttural moan rocks through me as I wrap both arms around his neck and pull myself onto the tips of my toes. His approval comes in nips and long strokes of his tongue against mine. All the while, his other hand roams my hips to my backside.

It matters not that there is a perfectly good bed a few feet away from us, for it is the fireplace that Atticus leads us toward. The action leaves the muscles at the junction of my thighs squeezing tight with desire.

It's a miracle we make it to the floor without either one of us hurting ourselves. As it is, our legs entangle with one another too far, and we go down less than gracefully, our kiss breaking into small gasps. I find myself on top after the act is complete. One leg stuck between his own, and my hands framing either side of his face as he grips my hips.

For a time, we stare into each other's eyes. The shock of our fall gives way to our lust.

The second meeting of our lips is just as urgent as the last, but this time, our hands move with a frenzy over one another. Strong hands slid up my rib cage, taking my sweater with it. I rock back to rip off the offending garment. Desperate to feel hot flesh against my own, even as the fire drenches us in heat nearby.

Shaking hands unclasp my bra, and once I'm finished with the task, I bring them down upon Atticus's firm chest. Equal in states of undress, Atticus perks up on one elbow to lavish attention to each of my breasts. The intense focus he applies to my nipples leaves me mewling in constant desire, my hips rocking back and forth to rub against his thigh.

Breath hitching, I throw back my head and cup the back of his head to curl my fingers into his hair. Atticus's touch chases away all feelings of doubt and uncertainty. The hot rush he entices leaves little thought in my mind other than *more, more, more.*

I breathe his name and am forced to arch against him further in pursuit of his nipping, biting, and suckling.

"Please," I whimper, riding his thigh with little abandon.

A large hand tugs at my thigh, pulling it over to the other side of his hips and reminding me of his own confined arousal. The moan that Atticus releases when I rub against his hard-on leaves me quivering. Stormy blue eyes, with several streaks of gold, stare up at me. Their smoldering regard floods my body like hot lava.

Atticus's hand crawls up my thigh to my hip, then reaches around to my lower back with clear intent.

"Ready?"

The voice that says the word sounds so unlike the Atticus I know—one full of passion and fervor, and dark desire. I take his other hand that rests underneath my breast and maneuver it to my other hip. Atticus half purrs and growls his approval of my acceptance.

Although I know it is coming, the stretch of his fingers solely spanning my lower back leaves me breathless. When the edges of his digits grace either end of my soulmark, I go rigid with the stunning amount of pleasure that accompanies it.

I release a small cry and grind down against his erection to increase the flames that consume us. I shake with the strain to stay above him. Planting my hands back upon his chest, I bend at the waist with a moan, dragging my hips down his hard member and arching my chest as his hand smooths my mark.

Without thought, my hand reaches out to his own. The first graze of my fingertips against his soulmark is electric, no doubt, but the firm press is like grasping onto a live wire.

His hips thrust upward sharply, coaxing a loud moan from me as he states the words long since considered taboo by my pack. Forbidden words, ones that meant certain unhappiness and unfulfillment.

But with Atticus... it feels like coming home.

"Let it be known that thee are found," comes my ragged whisper, "and my soul awakened. The stars incline us, my love, and so we are sealed."

What occurs next is blinding. All sensation drowns away only to come back tenfold in what is the perfect mixture of pleasure and pain. I whimper at the overwhelming thrill of it all. My fingernails dig in to his soulmark, leaving ragged marks of red as they scrap downward.

Atticus's own hand moves up the column of my spine as he breathes harshly. I meet his triumphant gaze for only a second before I find myself on my back, the air knocked from my lungs.

Nimble fingers make short work of the buttons and zipper of my pants before dipping teasingly along their waistline. My reaction is rather immediate, my hips lift in eager anticipation. Our eyes lock once more as he pulls both pants and thong down over my thighs and calves. His fingers skim the length of my legs slowly until both garments are tossed aside.

His gaze devours every exposed inch of me then. Our previous union had been frenzied and rushed. Both of us too lost to our lust to appreciate the partners giving us pleasure, but at his intense regard, I succumb to the touch of vulnerability at the back of my mind.

I have never been looked at like this before.

As if the man before me can't believe his luck.

As if I'm his prized possession.

As if he loves me.

Coarse hands run along the outside of my thighs before they slide beneath my knees and spread them apart. I attempt to resist. A blush covers me from cheek to chest as Atticus stares so hungrily at the epitome of my womanhood.

However, that doesn't stop the wetness growing at my sex or the urge to snap my knees back together.

"No hiding, Winter," Atticus tells me in a low voice that vibrates across my sensitive flesh. I quiver in acknowledgment, letting out a gasp as he yanks me forward. "Say it again," he demands.

"I love you."

Atticus wastes no more time in the pursuit of his wants. His head dives down, and then his lips are on me. Like his kisses before, there is nothing gentle about his approach to my core. His lips suck and tease. His tongue lashes out without hesitation, lapping up the growing moisture between my legs until I writhe from the exquisite torture. My climax is right before me when he retreats.

A sound, the cross between a growl and a groan, crosses my lips at the loss.

Atticus guides my legs around his waist as I whimper with need. His hands hover on either side of my head as he leans over me. The wolf's hunger is mixed with the man's. It leaves me stunned momentarily, but a rocking motion from his hips brings me back to reality.

"Again," he demands.

"I love you."

His lips steal another drugging kiss from me, far more languid and thorough than the last. I melt at the sensual touch, sighing my delight as his lips work their way across my jaw and down my neck. My chest rises and falls at a shallow pace when his hand searches out my own and places it against his chest. I know without having to see how close it lays to his soulmark.

The scrap of his teeth against my throat elicits a shaking moan from deep inside me.

Without ado, I press my hand upward and cover his soulmark with my palm. Our sharp intake of breath is a testimony to the second blaze of pleasure given to us. I don't expect the rough thrust of his confined hardness against my exposed sex, but I certainly don't mind. My back, arched instantaneously from the touch of the soulmark, slams back into the ground at the continued rocking from Atticus.

He groans against my neck, nuzzling the area as pressure begins to build between us.

"And now I lay my mark for all to see. By blood, be one," Atticus says.

I bend my neck in an offering, dying a little inside as his teeth dig harshly into the tender skin. The climax I was denied only minutes before comes to its head. Lightning bolts course through my blood, the electric moment stealing my breath only to give it back in full force as I release a cry loud and uninhibited.

I grind my slick sex against his groin. The acute feeling of pain associated with being left unfilled is driving me mad. I sob when he tugs my hand away, body trembling with the currents of the soulmark's merciless pleasure and heat.

"I need—"

His lips silence me. The kiss is gentler than any other I've received from him. Around the place in my heart and soul that belongs to Atticus, something *more* ties us together. These magical words are slowly but surely tying us irrevocably together.

The moisture at my eyes is wiped away reverently. But the tender scrape of his thumbs against my cheeks only earns more for his efforts.

"I love you too," he whispers, his voice raw. "I have for years, Winter."

"I'm sorry I hurt you. I'm sorry I hurt the pack and Zoelle," I whisper back, unable to stop the tears streaming as they stem from a snowball of emotions.

Atticus shushes me, the insistent press of his lips rhythmically moving against my own until I calm. "We'll get through it together," he says at last.

My heart catches in my throat as I run my eyes over his face. Atticus's kind, yet hungry eyes stare back at me with equal intensity. It makes my pulse flutter through my veins, and my blood begins to boil again.

Mine. All mine.

"Make love to me," I plead, searching out his lips and dragging his face to mine.

He concedes. The next few moments are filled with a hasty need to rid Atticus of the remainder of his clothes. His length, hard and ready, bobs proudly at its newfound freedom. I stop my endeavor of aid to stare and reach out a shaky hand to stroke him.

Atticus hisses and stills at the action. Lust-filled eyes stare down at me. With animalistic grace, he positions himself. His tip teases my entrance, but my hold on him tightens at the movement. Atticus releases another hiss.

"Winter," he growls in warning, but my exploration will not be deterred.

His length is heavy in my grip, and my fingertips cannot reach fully around his girth. I swallow with want, my heart pounding madly in my ear as I slide my hand up and down his erection. Atticus drops his head to my shoulder, his breath coming in strained puffs. A nip of rebuke against my collarbone is all the warning I have before his fingers find their way to my center.

I buck at the gentle contact. My body, still oversensitive from the sealing and marking, trembles at the touch and kindles anew. Without preamble, two fingers slid into my waiting heat. Our appreciation is shared in mixed moans that seem to echo about the room.

When I stare up at him, I'm caught by the beauty of his body. The fire and candlelight dance across his chest and arms, along with dark shadows. I'd admire him further if not for the his fingers curling inside me and stealing my attention. They pump with excruciating patience and draw noises from me I didn't know I could make.

My grip on his silken shaft weakens as I drown in his intoxicating touch.

"Please, Atticus."

Blue eyes clash with my slate gray, and his torturous fingers retreat to my hip. I squeeze my legs around his middle, rubbing up against him in yearning.

It takes little from there to achieve our goal.

Like water bursting from a dam, Atticus thrusts into me in one fierce stroke. Already slick with desire, he slides easily inside of me. We still at the union, taking in the sensation we've denied ourselves for so long.

My hands find a home on Atticus's strong shoulders. They clench down as he begins to slowly slid in and out, building a steady rhythm that threatens to steal my breath away.

"Christ," he murmurs, the sharp line of his jaw in stark relief against the firelight. Sweat glistens on his brow as he clenches his jaw with restraint. "I forgot how tight you are."

I writhe beneath him, winding my hips in encouragement for faster movement. But Atticus draws it out. His pace remains unwavering and controlled, though his features betray his self-torture.

"Faster," I pant, hooking one arm around his back and dragging my nails down to his ass.

A hand slips to my calf, where he proceeds to raise said leg and bend it up over his shoulder. I groan and gasp at the maneuver, adjusting and wiggling to accept the deeper reach inside me.

"Oh, God…"

The whimper is all I can muster as he pulls entirely from my molten core then glides back in. Atticus curses and trembles above me. A mix of a groan and whine tears through me in encouragement, and he gradually begins to quicken the pace.

I arch and writhe in delicious agony.

Soon, our panting breaths are our only form of communication. Another fever pitch builds inside of me, daring to leave me in pieces by the time we are through.

As Atticus thrusts turn harder, it becomes difficult to tear my eyes away from his body. Beads of sweat drip down his chest to his toned abdominal muscles that are flexing and stretching. How I long to drag my lips and tongue over each scintillating, marble crevice.

It's incredible how Atticus is able to read my body. Whenever my teeth find their way into the bruised flesh of my lower lip, I earn deliciously harder thrusts. When my nails dig into his skin, he keeps up his fast pace seconds longer to prolong my pleasure.

His attention makes me feel like a goddess, and I lose myself in what he offers.

Tonight we have ventured past the point of no return. Despite our efforts, there is slim hope we will reverse the curse of the moon or soulmark. But heading into the unknown with Atticus makes the journey less terrifying. Whatever happens—be it the wrath of the Blanc or Wselfwulf pack against us—I will cherish every last experience with Atticus from this moment further.

Careening upward, I crash my lips against his. Sudden dizzying desperation courses through my already feverish nerves. Sensing the change, Atticus settles us into a new arrangement.

Seated and with his back to the fireplace, he moves me to straddle him.

"Closer is better," he says as he rights me in his lap.

I cross my ankles behind him, breathing harshly and unable to control it. As I snake my arms around his neck, he starts to thrust and grind in our new position. Our new embrace does indeed bring us closer together. Thoroughly intertwined, I relish in his breath darting across my breasts and the way his mouth reaches out to taste my salty flesh.

There is something bold and intimate about our new position. It makes my already sensitive body more responsive to his touch.

I don't know how much longer I can take it. And Atticus can tell. His hands tighten their grip on my waist as he thrusts in earnest. The ride is rough and exhilarating. His name drops from my lips in a loop.

Whimpers turn into small cries of passion as the seconds pass, Atticus whispering his encouragement crudely into my ear.

"I want your cum on my cock, Winter," he pants. "I want to feel you come undone. Do you understand?"

I nod weakly, head tilting back as my lashes flutter shut while waves of euphoria overtake me. Atticus snarls his approval. His hands move confidently around my bottom to guide my movements.

I allow my hand to stray to his soulmark. My fingers circle the dark embellishment until he is forced to grab my wrist and stop my teasing. The moment I touch the sacred mark, we fall together.

"I bind myself to you," he says, his voice husky and low as he spills himself inside of me.

My mouth opens in a silent cry. The final ties of the soulmark wrap so tightly around us I fear I'll never breathe again. When precious air finally fills my lungs and releases in a startling exclamation, I go limp against Atticus, even as the ecstasy of it all rides hard through my body.

Stars collide in my vision, but it is Atticus's warm and smiling face that enters after it. The brilliance of our union ebbs slowly and retreats in small aftershocks as my hand drifts from his soulmark. It's minutes later when Atticus is able to move us to the bed. He lays me carefully down and runs his gaze across my body.

An indescribable shiver draws a lazy path down my spine.

I can feel Atticus's pleasure. And his returning lust.

"Well," I rasp, "I'm not quite ready for bed just yet. Are you?"

THE CHALLENGE

- Chapter 22 -

The weekend comes again far faster than I would like with the days racing by like the end of the world is hurtling at us. In some ways, it is. We plan to confront my parents and garner the tonic's ingredients and its full list of effects. If they cannot provide us with the details, then we will demand to know who they purchased the tonic from and go from there. Our plan to do this leaves me immeasurably nervous as it will be me doing the confronting.

As for the issue of the curses, we will only have Luna attempt to talk to the tree if all goes well with my parents and the opportunity presents itself. Hope both fierce and strong swells in my chest as I rehash the plan once more in my head. Everyone in the pack and coven is counting on our success, but none more so than me—I have promises to keep after all.

I stare at the cream-colored batter sitting next to the stove in a pale green ceramic bowl. *Pancakes shouldn't be this hard to make.*

If my pancakes aren't cooked through enough, then they are most certainly burnt. Only two have managed to come out a pretty golden color and are suitably fluffy, though their shapes are a bit abstract.

They sit alone on a plate on the island, becoming cooler by the minute.

Atticus needs to wake up soon if he wants to enjoy them properly. Just the thought of the man brings a crooked, self-satisfied smile to my lips. I duck my head, hiding my blush from the world as I think over the week we've had.

Though riddled with a healthy amount of anxiety over what is to come, things between Atticus and me are good. Really good. I haven't felt this light in years… or loved… or sore.

My blush deepens as I recall our kitchen escapades just two nights ago.

"Atticus, if you don't stop, I'm going to get you all wet," I say, trying for something stern even as I grin like a lovesick fool.

Firm hands glide across my stomach in a tease. "The point is *to get you all wet," he purrs back.*

His hands continue to move at a hypnotic pace, drawing south as my hands still their idle work in the sink. One more warning lies on the tip of my tongue but is stifled by a tremulous noise from the back of my throat.

Restless energy swims through my veins at his intimate touch. The plate I wash slides from my hands and lands with a clatter against the stainless steel sink. I rock against the pressure at my sex. The motion is gentle and unhurried.

The cut of the counter against my stomach slowly increases its pressure. A hiss escapes me as the sculpted body behind me relentlessly presses forward. A cold draft plagues the kitchen and rides over me to leave goose bumps in its wake while new skin is exposed to its pursuits. Atticus's shirt that I borrowed this morning finds its way pushed far above my hips.

His free hand scratches a delicate path down my exposed flank and hip.

"I like you in my shirt," Atticus tells me in a voice that makes me lick my lips in anticipation. "But I like you much better in nothing at all."

Digits, long and lean, stroke my tender folds. The action makes my knees tremble, and immediately I am grateful for the sturdy body behind me. When those same fingers plunge within me, dragging out my nectar to swirl over my nub, a weak cry tumbles past my lips.

His name follows closely behind in a whimper.

With his cock digging into the small of my back, I lean further against him, leveraging myself against the sink.

"Don't tease," I beg.

Because that is what I am immediately reduced to, and have been for the past few days—begging for mercy at his studious touches and excruciating patience. Until, that is, my begging turns into desperate cries of the wanton nature.

A knee nudges my legs further apart, and then a more insistent length presses against me. Atticus's hot breath at my ear stirs my blood into a frenzy. As his second hand continues its work down south, the other crawls north between the valley of my breasts to wrap loosely around my neck.

My labored breath sounds in return, leaning into both avenues of his clutches and bending my body to do it. He lets out a strangled growl, fingers pressing just a touch more heavily against my neck.

With a shifting of hips, he enters me sharply to draw a pleased noise from both of us.

My toes curl and strain against the mosaic tile. They push me up onto their tips when he thrusts again just as forcefully. I hook an arm over my shoulder and grapple for Atticus's neck to hold on to for dear life as he proceeds to fuck me against the kitchen sink.

A chorus of moans and grunts fill the spacious room. They build just as the momentum between us does. My fever pitch arrives quickly, those lean fingers still strumming against my clitoris and the hand at my neck demanding my complete submission to his will.

There was never any doubt in this... but giving in to his power is thrilling. Intoxicating.

As the sounds of our flesh meeting in angry slaps break into the symphony of our sounds of pleasure, Atticus holds me tighter. And when I fall, he is quick to follow.

Needless to say, learning each other this past week has been enlightening. So has finding ways to tease and ride the electric surge that occurs with every brush of the soulmark.

We also—

"Shit!"

With fluttering feet, I dance back over to the griddle, quickly tossing the ruined pancakes off onto the designated trash plate. For breakfast's sake, I should stop dwelling on our sex marathon.

Drawing my mind from the soulmark is another task entirely.

The week has brought to light the dozens of regrets I have in my life—from the way I so easily bent to my parents' will, to my most recent deceptions and actions coming to a head with Zoelle. Yet, it is allowing myself to be fooled and afraid of the soulmark that I regret most.

Going through with the sealing, marking, and binding opened not only my eyes but Atticus's.

The soulmark bond softened the connection between us. Atticus confessed just the night before that it was too difficult for him to stay upset with me over my misdeeds. When I asked why, he calmly replied that he could feel the vast depths of my remorse and guilt.

As I pour the next ladles of batter out, I hear footsteps come trotting down the stairs. Atticus enters the kitchen moments later, a bright smile already on his face as he observes me cooking.

"That smells… awful."

Our faces split into identical grins, and he comes over to me. Atticus brushes my snow-white hair over my shoulder and places a kiss at the back of my neck right between the sixth and seventh vertebrae.

"The majority haven't turned out so well," I concede, but then happily turn around and point to the plate I've left on the kitchen island. "Those, however, are perfect."

He hums a happy acknowledgment with his fingers skimming just below the indentation of my lower back, right below my soulmark. I spear him with a playful glare and step out of his reach, spatula brandished before me like a weapon.

He snatches the spatula from my hand and flips the pancakes. They retain a nice golden-brown surface. This time, the happy hum comes from my throat.

"Are you ready for tomorrow?"

The question is asked so casually it takes a moment for it to sink in. My cringe is unable to be hidden. Atticus's brows pull sympathetically together, and his palm comes to rest on my cheek.

"Not really," I mutter with a sigh. "But I suppose I'll find my strength somewhere along the way."

Tomorrow we leave on our journey to Quebec, and what a long journey it will be. We'll be driving, given the fairy that we plan to travel with is somewhat of an illegal alien.

My concerns, already expressed a multitude of times to Atticus, lie in the confrontation I am meant to lead. I still find it difficult to believe that both Atticus *and* Xander support this aspect of the plan with knowing how well my parents bent me to their will in the past. Yet, after having a day or so to let the plan sink in, I came to realize my pivotal role for what it really is: a test of my loyalty to the Adolphus pack.

I won't let them down, no matter how daunting the prospect is.

"You've always had the strength, Winter," Atticus says.

I meet his bowed head halfway and our lips meet briefly. Briefly because the smell of burning butter reaches our sensitive noses at the same time. And definitely not because of the loud clearing of a throat that sounds from the other side of the kitchen. We part with strained smiles, Atticus directing his at the griddle and mine at Jax.

The sorcerer was pushed upon our hospitality by none other than Xander himself. The alpha claims he can't deal with the added stress of someone in his house pestering him. What Xander really means is that he can't deal with the added annoyance of Jax. I can't say I blame him.

Jax Stormrow is a troublemaker.

Atticus compares him to Ryatt often but fails to explain accurately the danger he also associates with the sorcerer. Perhaps it is his magic—gifted by whatever Gods he prays too—that makes Atticus wary. I know it makes me wary.

Jax is dressed in dark wash pants, a white button-down, and deep maroon vest. My eyes travel down his trim form and stop at his feet. The derby shoes are a matching maroon and polished to gleam.

"Breakfast?" Jax struts up to the island counter and snags the plate of good pancakes with a charming smile. "You shouldn't have."

His hazel eyes twinkle with mischief, and before I can snatch the plate back, he's spun around and walks to the table.

"Would one of you bring me a fork and knife, please?"

I sigh but do as Jax asks.

"Here."

He takes the silverware from me in his own time, making a perusal of me as I did him. "Trouble sleeping?" He clucks at my blush. "I can make you something for that. It will put you right out."

I glare, but it fades along with the color on my face. Jax's eyes continue to twinkle, but that mischievous gleam isn't as kind as before.

"Too soon?" he probes, digging into the pancakes.

A snarl catches in my throat. I'm only able to hold it back from years of experience. Instead, I stiffly walk back to Atticus's side. The familiar weight of his arm around my waist is an immediate comfort.

"He's definitely worse than Ryatt," I grumble, making sure I'm just loud enough to hear.

"Rude," Jax pipes up around a mouthful of pancakes.

I watch him chew, that charming smile turning to a cheeky grin. It suits him more, and his close-cut beard that looks more like fashionably trimmed scruff only adds to its captivating quality. By the dimple etching into his left cheek, he knows it.

"I rather think of myself as a prince charming," he continues, combing his fingers through ash brown, wavy locks that could use a cut. "Though, I must say, it would be beneficial to be able to speak with the witches who performed the retrocognition spell. Their notes don't paint the picture I'm looking for. It's more of a Picasso than say a Jan Vermeer."

It's the tenth time Jax has asked. Atticus heaves a sigh.

"We've been over this. The Trinity Coven won't allow you inside their homes nor to speak with their witches. You'll have to make do."

"And how go the witches attempt at waking our sleeping beauty?" he asks. Atticus and I freeze momentarily, but the sorcerer catches our tell. "Any new *developments*?"

I fidget and fuss with my hands for a few seconds before clearing my throat and answering. "The witches are confident they took down a layer of the tonic's magic. One of several, as it happens, but in doing so, they left her vulnerable and unstable, which is why they wrapped her up in their own magical sleep."

Jax pauses with a forkful of pancake halfway to his mouth, letting his sights slant our way.

"That's a new word. *Unstable*." He lets the word roll off his tongue like a fine wine. "Unstable how, exactly?"

Atticus glances my way as I bow my head a fraction. His hand seeks out mine to provide reassurance. "She… stopped breathing," I say.

Jax takes his time chewing and swallowing the triangular morsel, but then he begins to nod slowly. "And the plan for your hometown ambush? Let's rehash it again, shall we?"

Three more perfectly cooked pancakes find their home on a new plate, which Atticus offers to me. After a delicate push to my back, I walk over to the table and join Jax with my breakfast.

"It will be the three of us, plus Keenan and Luna, to take on this mission. Thanks to Winter's knowledge and experience, we can expect to catch her parents off guard in their house before they partake in the full moon run," Atticus says.

"They don't start their run until late at night," I explain before Atticus can continue.

Atticus sends me a brief smile. "Once we're inside, we'll need you to seal the place up so that no one can get in—"

"And none can get out. Duly noted and well within my capabilities," Jax cuts in.

"And from there Winter will demand the tonic's composition and composer."

Jax sets down his fork and levels a belittling frown at Atticus and then myself. "*You*," Jax says, his hazel eyes assessing me without remorse, "are going to demand from your parents the tonic's composition? What makes you think a beta, such as yourself, will be able to pull off such a feat? Isn't that the entire reason I'm here to help fix the mess that you've so kindly put us in."

Atticus lets out a growl as I flush with contempt.

"Xander is a stronger alpha than my parents," I tell him, though working my jaw from its clenched position is a task. "Being as such, there is a more than fair chance that either Atticus or I could challenge their authority."

Jax leans back in his chair, still eyeing us with apprehension before he shrugs and his expression falls. "I can work with more than a fair chance," he announces pleasantly and digs back into his pancakes.

I toss a look over my shoulder at Atticus, my eyes pleading with him to join us. He gestures to his pancakes, and I let out an exaggerated sigh.

"Right," Jax says. "So, you make your demands, but what if they refuse?"

Atticus smiles. "We aren't leaving that house without the tonic's composition or the name of the person who made it. The whole point of going is to get it, and so we will."

Jax returns the smile. "I like your conviction. It's quite rousing."

Atticus snorts but says nothing more.

"Once we have what we need, if there's time, we go to the golden birch and have Luna speak to it."

"And if your little fairy comes through with reasonable information, I'll take a crack at your wily curses," Jax finishes. I nod. "Wonderful," he says, wiping his mouth with a napkin. "And is there a plan

B, perchance? In case, let's say, your parents aren't home or there's an ambush waiting for us?"

I look to Atticus who is stacking his plate high with pancakes. He raises a brow back at me, the corner of his lip twitching. I turn my gray eyes back to Jax.

"You are our plan B. Should things go awry...."

Jax winks at me, though the sight is mildly off putting with the measure of menace behind it. "Understood. This will certainly be an exciting venture. I've pulled off many spells and potions during a full moon... but not with a pack of *lycans* in the near vicinity. But seeing as how the proper reversal of these curses relies at the very least on this famed tree and the full moon, there's no avoiding it."

My stomach turns. "I'm sure it will be fine," I say.

Atticus comes and sits next to me, his hand coming to rest on my shoulder for a comforting second.

"You should really work on your conviction," Jax tells me.

"Duly noted," I mutter and stab at my pancakes.

Jax laughs as he sinks further back into his chair with lazy confidence. *Cracks* and *pops* sound in canon as the sorcerer works his knuckles into submission. Typically, the cracking of one's knuckles doesn't come off nearly as intimidating as is intended, but the flare of green sparks that emerge above his fists do just the trick.

"I can hardly wait," he says with that damn charming smile.

+++

We've been sitting inside the large SUV for too long. Someone on the street is bound to notice our car full of people that slowly fog up the interior windows with our combined breath and body heat. Straight ahead is a large home far more contemporary than its neighbors.

My parents' home.

Several cars line the curb in front of their abode and stack the driveway.

"Are we going in or not?" Jax asks from the back seat.

Atticus spares me a look before addressing the group. "Let's recap," he says, taking charge.

"What's there to recap? We've been over the plan a dozen times. Head inside. Execute magical house arrest. Interrogate. Save the girl and break the curses. Easy," Jax says.

"And stay together at all costs. If we're separated, they won't hesitate to strike and take one of us out," I say, my voice monotonous.

A light touch at my shoulder draws my eyes to the back of the car. Luna's eyes are somber, but she offers me a small smile of support. The witches had not been pleased to release Luna into our care, not after the arrival of Jax. But the fairy had promptly informed them that she was not their property and they couldn't control her—no matter how hard they tried.

Atticus described the scene as *epic*, after picking her up.

The fairy in question is bathed in a full body glamour, but unlike the witches itching trace of magic, Jax's brings the hair at the back of my neck on end.

Gone are the vines and flowers that curl just beneath her skin, like dancing ink.

Gone are her wings from human and supernatural sight.

Gone are her pretty violet eyes.

Even her hair is altered to a platinum blonde instead of its frosty white.

In the end, it doesn't do much to mask her unearthly beauty, but it makes our journey across the country more manageable.

"We'll be right behind you," Luna tells me, her words softly spoken.

Our fingers brush against one another, and nothing more is needed to be said between us. We all know the risks of coming here. The war that will happen if we fail, because the time for negotiation passed the second my parents ordered me to spy on my new pack.

"I thought your parents liked to be alone before full moon runs. Why are there so many people here?" Keenan asks. His face is etched from stone, impassive and severe as he analyzes our predicament.

"People come, but not until much, *much*, later. They should be alone right now," I reply, facing front once more to count the cars. My stomach drops as realization hits. "They must be hosting a *Fête de la Lune*."

"A what?"

I peer back over my shoulder to Keenan. "A few times out of the year they host a *Fête de la Lune*. A feast," I explain due to his furrowed brow, "to honor the moon. The top ten ranking wolves and their plus one's get to come. Because the bottom three ranked wolves—eight, nine, and ten—fluctuate so much, the feast is a coveted affair."

"Great, there goes plan A," Atticus murmurs unhappily, just as Jax pipes up from the back as well.

"A feast? Have I dressed appropriately?"

The question draws a snort from me, but it also manages to lessen my stark demeanor. "How we're dressed is the least of my concerns," I tell Jax over my shoulder.

Jax winks. "Well then, let's get this party started."

The clamor of buckles being undone, doors opening, and the rustle of fabric fills the air. All the while, the world shifts into slow motion right before my eyes as my hands struggle with my safety belt.

Even the sharp bang of the front and passenger side doors closing can't jar me from the time lapse.

My door opens, as if by its own accord, and the biting wind rips by my face. I suck in a harsh breath, the sting of the wind instantly wetting my eyes as my lashes combat the frigid air.

"Are you okay?" Atticus's blue eyes are filled with concern and dart to my nerve-struck hands. "Here, let me."

In seconds I am free, but my release is far from that of pleasure.

"I can't do this," I whisper to him. He opens his mouth in rebuttal, but I plow on, gripping onto his forearms as if I'd drown without him. "A week isn't enough time to prepare for this. I'm not strong enough to face my parents. All my life I've learned to *survive* them, not beat them."

"Winter." My name is but a sigh across his lips, and I watch with wide eyes as he gently brushes aside my tenuous hold to cup my cheek. I lean into it, unabashedly seeking the solace in his touch. "You're not doing this alone. I know you don't think you're strong enough, but you are. Draw on the pack for strength if you feel you need it. Draw on me. We can't lose if we do this together."

My bottom lip quivers as I suck in several breaths in quick succession to try and right my nerves.

"I'm scared."

"Me too," he whispers back in assurance. Atticus leans his face in closer to mine, so our eyes are level. Blue to gray, a perfect complementary match. "But I trust in Keenan's strength, in Luna's heart, in Jax's magic, and in your will, Winter. Your will is stronger than theirs. All your life they've pushed you down to train you not to get back up again because you are strong. Because your strength is a threat to their power."

"Atticus—"

My weak reply is met with a firm shake of his head. His chestnut curls wave with the motion; the color is darker in the fading sunlight.

"No going back," he says firmly. "Only forward."

I join the small huddle in front of the car, the cold air waking my dulled senses. Atticus rounds up to my side, closing in the circle and staring at us all gravely.

"Keenan, I want you on Luna tonight. You've got the list of elements for the curses that the witches were able to discern from their spell earlier this week." Kennan nods his affirmation. "I'll be at Winter's side, and we'll take the lead with her parents. And Jax—" The sorcerer preens at the mention of his name, standing up straight with his large staff at his side. "—don't fuck this up."

Rather than deflate, Jax flashes a dangerous grin. "Ready when you are, boss."

The walk to the house is just as nerve-wracking as I expect it to be, maybe even more so. But I try my hardest to keep my nerves under wraps knowing how it may negatively affect tonight's outcome. I need to be strong, and if that means leaning on the pack and Atticus for support, I will.

After all, I have promises to keep.

The wolf, silent in my head for so long, rumbles its agreement. It knows far better than I as to how to draw upon the strength of the pack and begins to do so. As it does, the last remaining ties between myself and the Blanc pack—those between my mother and I–sever.

Only adrenaline courses through me now. Tonight someone will die by my hand… and if my parents aren't careful, it might be one of them.

The Golden Birch

- Chapter 23 -

We don't knock before entering.

Not with Jax in our group. He strides ahead of the pack, tossing his patented roughish smirk our way before jogging forward with wicked intent.

Jax pitches his body forward, the short tails of his pea coat flapping with unnatural energy, and then he is throwing his body round in a backspin. His staff arcs widely with the whirling motion. When he lands, the earth gives a subtle shake. His hand presses against the ground and his staff is thrust upward behind him.

The door slams open.

"We were going for the element of surprise," Atticus snarls, jogging to catch up to Jax, along with the rest of us.

"Surprise." Jax chuckles darkly as we sweep past him and inside. The sound of my parents and their guests in an uproar reaches our keen ears.

The house, usually kept sparkling clean and free of any sort of unnecessary decoration, is bathed in festive decor for the *Fête de la Lune*. Twinkling lights and garland wrap around the winding grand staircase off to the left. An assortment of miniature cedar pine trees are spaced out along the perimeter of the large circular foyer and alternating silver and gold ornaments.

I breathe in the scent of fresh pine and am surprised at the touch of nostalgia I feel.

It lasts less than a moment because the stabbing *click* and *clack* of stiletto heels are storming our way. The door shuts behind us with hardly a whisper of sound. A sudden feeling of nausea comes and goes with a haggard breath past my lips.

"What in heaven's name are you doing here?" my mother seethes as she enters the foyer and sees our lot. Her eyes slip to brilliant gold as she plants herself before me. "Where is your cousin? Explain yourself."

I ignore her demand, cocking my head to listen for any who might dare interlope... such as my father.

He's probably reassuring their esteemed guests there's nothing to worry about. *How wrong he is*, I muse.

"Who are these ruffians you've brought into my home?"

"Unfortunately, Lucy had to stay behind. As for these *ruffians*, they're my pack," I reply softly, at last dragging my regard back to my mother.

She looks as regal as ever, her deep purple dress cut modestly while her hair is brushed back into some updo.

"Why are you here, Winter?" she repeats, mimicking the soft accent of my voice. But where mine is laden with nonchalance, Mother's holds a menace only she can master.

"You were right," I say, enjoying the flutter of confusion that combs over her face. "Before the wedding, you told me you and Father had doubts about me. About my loyalties to the Blanc pack. You were right to have them."

Her low snarl echoes across the checkered marble floor.

"If it's any consolation, I had my doubts about you and Father too," I add and watch her falter.

Mother takes a step toward me. *Click. Clack.* "What did you just say to me?"

"Granted, mine were proven true long ago. It's only now I've decided to stop pretending like I haven't known it since the first time you left a bruise on my face. You are unfit to be parents to any child," I say, my voice barbed and boiling thick with resentment long since pushed down inside of me.

Mother tilts her chin up, her eyes flat in their regard of me. "You were always much too *sensitive*, Winter. If it weren't for your father and me, you'd be an omega. Can you imagine the humiliation—the alphas of the pack producing an omega? The pack would have eaten you alive if it wasn't for our love and dedication to keep you abreast of their treatment with our own."

Her words jar a manic laugh from deep within my chest. It lasts far longer than appropriate. A hand comes to rest near the base of my neck, and long fingers spider out until a warm palm is flush against me. Atticus's touch brings me back to reality.

"Love?" I snarl. "You wouldn't know love if it bit you in the ass, Mother."

"Is this what you came here for, Winter? To have it out with your father and me? To flaunt in my face your defection?" Her accompanying scoff carves itself into a special place in my memory. I will never forget it.

"No doubt you thought your bold plan would earn the respect of your new pack or some other such rot, but you've chosen the wrong night to seek your peace, Winter." Mother lets loose a wicked smile. "You know what we do to those who dare leave our ranks, and I can't go playing favorites anymore."

I bristle. "Your threats don't scare me anymore."

"Oh?" A well-manicured eyebrow lifts imperiously. "If you care a wit about the wolves behind you, I suggest begging for my forgiveness at your foolish and arrogant display. Perhaps, if I am satisfied with your apology, I'll allow them to leave."

My growl ignites her smile even wider, and a dangerous gleam comes to her eyes.

"On the other hand, I wonder what your alpha would do to see your pack's safe return?" She lets out a gleeful laugh that makes my stomach plummet.

"You won't hurt them," I promise darkly, my feet shifting wider apart as my hands curl into tight fits. "You've hurt enough people to last a lifetime."

And then, to the surprise of everyone, including myself, my fist finds its way to the bridge of my mother's nose.

"You dare—"

My snarl ricochets throughout the entryway. Mother's eyes, plagued now by a sheen of wetness, widen before rapidly narrowing on me.

"No more," I fire back, just as my father enters the equation. Perfect.

Adrenaline stays true to course inside my body, keeping me poised to fight. The wolf's appetite for more retribution against these sadistic wolves heightens the chemical reaction.

"What the hell is going on here?" Father demands as he comes to stand by my mother's side.

His icy blue eyes glare daggers at our small group, but that's not what steals my attention. It's the Blanc pack's top-ranked wolves treading carefully into the room behind him.

I spot June immediately. She is herded forward by Jeffrey Terreur. Her face is without color, and when our eyes meet, she pales further.

June stumbles at Jeffrey's pressure, her feet tumbling over themselves in her shock. A breathless gasp is on her lips as she surges forward, only to be caught roughly by the arm by Jeffrey. His brown eyes belay his anger, as does the curl of his upper lip into his graying mustache.

"Behave," I hear him hiss to a quivering June.

Another snarl rips from my throat. It draws the older man's eyes to me, but unlike June, I don't shrink away. My wolf rouses to the challenge and seeps into my vision. Jeffrey lasts only a few precious seconds under my scorching glare. His eyes drop, along with his sneer.

It doesn't escape my notice how quickly the man yields to my dominance—a man who is ranked highly within the pack to an outsider like me, with no place any longer among them.

And neither does the crowd.

This precious time away from my parents has at last released my wolf from its constraints. It is strong and capable... Atticus is right. They kept me down, and my wolf for fear its strength would one day surpass their own.

Today will be that day.

Atticus's hand glides down my back in a soothing motion as he slips closer to my side. I shift back into the touch.

"Tell them, Winter," he urges in my ear.

Like a steel rod, I stand tall, jutting my shoulders back and my chest forward as I face my parents. "Your plan to nullify the fairy didn't succeed," I say.

Father's lips purse together. He sends my mother a sidelong glance and places a hand on her hip as she cups her bleeding nose.

"We don't know what you're talking about."

"For the record," I continue on, despite my father's glacial words. "I didn't give Lunaria the tonic. I gave it to Zoelle."

Mother's hand drops to her mouth to cover her gasp, while my father's shock reads in his sharp inhalation. I gift them a smile they taught me years ago, one meant to convey appropriate and civilized ruthlessness. Mother collects herself shortly after her outburst, dabbing at the blood still dripping from her nose. She smacks my father in the chest, gesturing at him with one palm open until he places his handkerchief there.

"You little fool," she hisses, eyes ablaze with anger at me. "What have you done?"

"I'm doing exactly as you asked, Mother. I'm ending this war." *And I'll be damned if I fail now.*

I step forward, away from the support of Atticus's touch and into my mother's personal space. The spirit of my wolf floods through my veins, filling me with its strength. Too long has it been leashed and beaten by my parents' commands… we will no longer cower before them.

"Unless you wish war, you will produce the creator of the tonic." I sweep my eyes over the crowd behind my parents. Some seem wary of my apparent strength after the scene with Jeffrey. Others, like my aunts, look incensed. "Let me guess, the witch or sorcerer who produced the tonic isn't here?"

"You know very well we don't associate with that sort," my mother insists, sticking to her denial. As expected.

"I know many things, Mother," I condescend. "But I am not without my leniencies, even for you. My pack mates and I will accept the tonic's recipe in place of the creator to make things simpler, then be on our way to other pressing matters here."

Father chortles in response. The sound is weakly echoed by some of the other wolves in the room. Atticus's responding growl is quick to silence them all.

"This isn't a matter up for discussion," I tell them flatly. "Give me the tonic's ingredient list. Now."

My head snaps to the side with the force of my mother's slap. The sound of it resounds throughout the room. The following snarl from Atticus is *terrifying* and mingles with my own growl of anger. But it's the familiar crackle of energy at my back that makes me stop.

"You made a mistake," I tell my mother as I straighten and step to the side in front of Atticus. "Unlike your pack, which can barely summon the courage to come to your defense and deny my accusations, mine do not take kindly to harm against their betas."

Mother squares her shoulders. "Do you honestly believe this ragtag band of wolves can take on the finest of my pack?"

"For clarification purposes, I'm not a wolf," Jax pipes up affably from behind us.

I spare him a glance and the smallest hint of a grin.

Mother's nose wrinkle. "You've brought a *witch* to show off their paltry tricks?"

"Sorcerer," Jax corrects, losing all traces of geniality.

"And a fairy," I kindly inform my mother, gesturing to Luna whose glamour is beginning to fade as she stares down my mother. "You remember? The fairy you wanted me to deliver that tonic too in the hopes of bringing down the Adolphus pack's magical border."

Whispers ignite around the room. June's lips part in shock as I glance her way. Mother takes a significant step forward, her eyes fixated on Luna.

"You brought me a Christmas gift, after all, Winter," she retorts, her words clipped and succinct. "At least you've done one thing right."

She makes a move forward, practically lunging toward Luna, but I've got a hand curled around her upper arm faster than she, or I, can blink. Mother directs her snarl my way, but that's not all.

"Let me go," she orders.

The force of her will is like a battering ram. It barrels into me without remorse, along with the other wolves in the room. The pack behind her bends at my mother's anger. Some of them even drop to their knees. I stand rigid. My grip is unrelenting as a silent battle is waged between us. To cater to her now will leave us at her mercy… and as my mother has proven time and time again, she is without mercy.

"*No.*"

Strength as I've never known rides through my veins, my wolf answering the call to arms I cry for inside. I know my eyes to be a mirror of my mother's and brilliant gold. Sweat tickles at the back of my neck as I grind my teeth painfully together, pushing, pushing, *pushing* back at the tremendous force my mother extends to put me in my place—beneath her.

I know you don't think you're strong enough, but you are.

Draw on the pack for strength if you feel you need it.

Draw on me. We can't lose if we do this together

Atticus's words beat inside my head, drowning out my worries and the dosing pain that comes with pitching my will against my mother's. I repeat them to myself, over and over again until the words slip past my lips in what feels like some kind of incantation.

The world falls away from us, which leaves only one of us to drop away with the rest.

It won't be me.

Because Atticus is right again. I have a boundless source of strength at my disposal. My pack mates wouldn't hesitate to bend a knee in a generous offering of what power they have to give. Whereas my mother *takes* from her wolves and drives them to the ground.

This makes all the difference, for my mother will always take. But not I, I offer myself up to my pack bonds and call out for their might even from so great a distance.

And slowly but surely, they respond.

"No," I say once more, shoving my mother back with a triumphant growl and prowling forward into her stumbling retreat. "No more."

"Winter!" My father's brash call is cut off by Atticus's fist. My father topples into my mother, an animalistic noise tearing from his throat in a rebuke to the slight, though he does nothing to defend himself.

"No more power plays. No more of your twisted games," I breathe harshly. "You will get us the ingredients of the tonic or have someone fetch the witch or sorcerer who did it. Now."

"You will regret this," Mother promises darkly. She trembles at my order. "Margaret, go to my study and fetch the parcel from Claudette."

My mother's sister, June's mother, is quick to act on the orders. She rushes from the room and out of sight. The room waits in a tense reprieve for her to return.

As for me and mine, we stand tall.

There is power in my body unlike any I've experienced before. It brings every hair on my body to stand and makes the wolf inside me howl for more. For this triumph is not only mine but one for the entire Adolphus pack. An unspoken acknowledgment ripples through the pack bonds and brings even more strength to our pack.

Aunt Margaret returns. She passes the small parcel into my mother's waiting hands, then scampers to the back of the gathered ranks. Margaret is one of the fluctuating wolves.

Mother's chin juts up with defiance as she thrusts the parcel onto me.

"There will be consequences, Winter," she whispers, her sights slanting in the direction of June none too subtly.

"You aren't going to do a thing, Mother," I snap back, my voice thick with authority.

The wolfish gold begins to seep from my mother's eyes, kowtowing to my command—and my alpha's will. From far away, his immense power bolsters me. His desire to put this pack in its place thrums through me like a storm on the verge of mass destruction.

"There will be no retaliation. No claims of fault or slander of my pack's name," I continue on, my voice hard and unyielding. "And when we're done saving your pathetic hides, don't get any ideas of sending your lackeys after us. From this moment on, we are beyond your reach."

Father glares hot daggers at me. "Mind your rank, girl."

I let my upper lip curl back. "My rank is far above anything you could hope to achieve," I bite back savagely. "And one last thing. There will be no more shackling these wolves to your pack. For too long you've kept them confined with the promise of retribution should they dare leave. To themselves and to their loved ones.

"If any so choose to leave with us tonight… there will be no penalty. No wolf should be made to lick after the heels of an alpha whose love they'll never have. You've disgraced this pack," I say, my emotions keeping my delivery tight and cutting. Even as a mix of torrid relief from years of steeped anger threaten to spill hotly over my cheeks.

I take in a steadying breath, making sure to level them both with a flat, disappointed stare. "You've *ruined* the Blanc name."

Mother's almost unable to rip her gaze away from mine. Her lower lip trembles slightly as she keeps her head held high. My father's pale face is thoroughly flushed.

Neither of them says a word.

A faint shift in the room's power dynamics ripples over all of the wolves who are present. Instead of showing deference to my parents, with either their heads bowed or necks bent submissively in their direction, they direct it to us—to Atticus and me.

My chest rises up as I roll my shoulders back and step away from my parents. Steadfast fingers splay across my lower back over my soulmark. A dizzying warmth spreads all the way down to my toes as I place myself back at Atticus's side where I belong. And then my eyes search out the only person who matters to me amongst the Blanc pack.

"June?" I say softly.

I stretch out my hand to her, ignoring the strangled growl my father emits.

"June, please. It doesn't have to be this way. You don't have to stay here and be used."

She looks nervously at Jeffrey before tossing a scared look her mother's way. "Mom?" she whispers. Her gaze darts back and forth between the two of us.

Margaret stays silent. Her face is ashen and unreadable as the room waits for her answer. Then a new growl lets loose in the grand foyer as June is yanked roughly into Jeffrey's side.

"Don't be absurd, Margaret. The contracts have already been signed. The girl is *mine*."

Jeffrey's outburst makes the room stir uneasily. No matter how formidable his rank may be, it is unwise to speak to any girl's mother in such a way. Margaret's husband, Thomas, flanks his wife's side.

"Go with Winter, Juniper," he commands, his eyes flashing gold.

"Dad?" June shakes visibly, weakly attempting to dislodge her arm from Jeffrey's hold. Her tears come pouring out to no one's surprise. "Dad, I—"

Her words cut out with a startled cry as she is thrust back. Tripping over heels far too tall for her doe-like legs to manage, June falls to the floor. She stops mere inches from one of the miniature cedar pine trees. Her slim and slightly gangly form spread callously along the marble floor.

Several gasps tear through the room as Margaret sprints to her daughter and Thomas barrels toward Jeffrey. No one expects the little pine to begin to shake violently. It's porcelain white pot cracks down one side, then another, before it falls completely to pieces as the pine's roots reach out to June.

June lets out a shriek, attempting to scramble back. She does not succeed.

Whereas the rest of the gathering watches in fear, releasing their own sounds of terror, I turn sharply to stare at Luna. Her glamour flickers in and out of effect as she concentrates on her task. When my gaze inevitably returns to June a second later, the roots are tentatively supporting her efforts to stand.

Margaret reaches her daughter's side at long last, tugging her away from the plant's wandering roots and into her embrace.

"It's okay," she says hoarsely, pressing a kiss against Juniper's head as she stares wide-eyed at the docile pine. "Come along, Junebird. We're leaving."

Nobody, not even Jeffrey, stops them as they stride toward our small group. Thomas follows resolutely at their heels, having left Jeffrey without a mark of retaliation, in favor of joining his family.

"Anyone is welcome to join us back in Branson Falls," Atticus reiterates once they are safely in our circle. He turns his eyes to my parents, and I feel his body stiffen beside me. "Winter's terms stand, and if you wish to break them or further interfere with our pack, my alpha will take it as a declaration of war. If you wish to dispute our terms, you may take up the issue with either our sorcerer or fairy."

As Atticus delivers his last line, the foyer reverberates with the sound of breaking porcelain and the rustling of roots.

No one says a thing.

And yet, as we stride from the room clumped closely together, the sound of footsteps follows hurriedly behind us. I stiffen, prepared for an attack by either my mother or father, but the steps come from fear-struck wolves pursuing our escape. I pass them a reassuring smile, watching the tension slip slowly from their faces as they reach us.

"You can't do this!" my mother shouts at our retreating backs.

"Of course, we can," Jax calls back, unperturbed as he spins his bo staff leisurely. "Just watch."

+++

I am in shock. There is no other way to explain the rolling blankness of my mind as my feet blindly lead our growing group to the golden birch tree. It's located three blocks over, at the very end of the neighborhood near the Marster's house. June is a whirlwind of questions. She spits off too many *hows* and *whys* and *what*s for me to keep up with, but I don't have to. Atticus patiently explains what is happening and our next plan of action.

He advises everyone who wishes to follow us back to Branson Falls to leave and pack their things. When none immediately go, he warns them our orders might not stick for long once we leave the Blanc territory. Those who don't get out now might not get the chance later.

Several run away at his advice. Their phones press against their ears as they dictate the happenings of what occurred and order their families what to do and pack. Others stay to see our efforts made.

June included, and her mother.

As our ranks decrease and then swell with curious interlopers watching our progress, I lean more heavily into Atticus's side.

"You were amazing in there, Winter," he murmurs to me when June begins directing questions to her mother. Toby's name is rattled off at least four times before Margaret gives a reluctant sigh and peels away from our group with June in tow. "Winter? Are you all right?"

My answering nod is weak enough that Atticus stops our advance to turn and face me. His hands plant themselves on my shoulders and anchor me back to the earth.

"It worked," I say breathlessly. Atticus replies with a gentle smile. His eyes scan our small crowd momentarily. "It actually worked."

"Of course it did," he teases, stepping closer and pulling me into the hug I didn't know I needed. I wrap my arms tight around his middle, pressing my face against his broad chest and breathing in his familiar scent and the leather of his jacket.

My rankled nerves settle further with each drag of breath.

"Winter?" A brief pause is given for me to pull back and look into his beautiful blue eyes. "We're not done."

This time, my answering nod is stronger than before, but by no means has the full shock of events slipped away from me.

"I know," I respond, taking another step back and giving a firmer nod. "Let's go. It's just up ahead. We can send a copy of the ingredients to both Xander and Diana while Luna does her thing."

Atticus's smile warms like the dawn, though around us the world fades to dark with dusty navy hues thanks to wayward clouds. When we reach the ancient tree, its ashy branches quivering in the breezy early dusk, we stop. I turn, expecting to see only half the number of who walked out with us.

I am wrong.

There are at least two dozen wolves in total. Some are from my parents' home; the others are the curious interlopers who wandered from their homes to be part of the commotion. They all wear the same solemn face, but there is no mistaking the curiosity and hope that burns in each of their eyes.

"I want to remind everyone of what Atticus said earlier. We can't guarantee the commands we laid upon my parents will hold for long. For those of you who wish to leave this pack and join another, or even be on your own, now is the time to go," I state plainly.

None make an attempt to leave, though there is a rustle of feet and shifting of facial expressions into something less somber and more determined.

I sigh and turn to face Atticus. He guides me forward to where Jax and Luna stand before the tree. Luna's cheeks and nose are a brilliant scarlet, despite her layers upon layers of outwear. She casts worried glances between me and Jax, bringing my own worry to the forefront.

"What is it?" I ask softly.

Luna shifts uncomfortably, folding her arms around her stomach. "He wants to do things differently than we planned."

"What?" I hiss, glaring pointedly at Jax as Atticus echoes my sentiments with a low growl. "We're not changing the plan—"

"We are," Jax states, the epitome of cool and collected. "Because we don't have time to do it the way we previously planned. I can't guarantee a speedy analysis of Luna's interpretation of events along with the witches. Hell, it could end up taking days."

"How long have you known?" Atticus asks, his voice flat.

Jax shrugs, that infuriating grin sneaking up onto his lips. "Let's just say I had a sudden feeling. What would be better—far better—is allowing me to piggyback off of Luna's conversation."

"What does that mean?" Luna asks as tears threaten to spoil her vision. "He keeps saying that. Why are pigs going to be involved?"

Despite myself, I have to bite back my own grin at her naive response. But instead of Atticus or me jumping to offer an explanation, Jax steps between us to stand directly in front of Luna.

With a delicate sigh, he takes off his gloves and raps his staff against the ground twice before abandoning it in favor of giving his complete attention to Luna. The staff stands at attention without his hold.

Jax reaches out and brushes the back of his fingers against Luna's jawline, all the way up to smooth back her hair. The action knocks off her hat, and Luna's eyes widen. After a moment, her tears vanish as Jax continues to stroke her hair back. She stares at the handsome sorcerer, mesmerized.

Although I cannot see Jax's expression, I can only imagine what devastating smile he levels at Luna to raise such a blush to her cheeks.

"It means, gorgeous," Jax purrs, "that I want to be a bystander in your mind as you talk to the tree. I've already memorized what notes the witches took... but hearing what you do directly from the source would be best."

A stuttered breath tumbles past Luna's parted lips. "Will it hurt?"

"Only a pinch, gorgeous. I wouldn't do anything that would cause harm to the divine creature before me."

Oh, dear God.

"Enough flirting." Atticus places a hand on Jax's shoulder and pulls him a step away from the fairy. But Luna makes a small noise of protest, her love-struck gaze unable to be torn away from her flatterer.

"I'll do it," Luna agrees. "As long as it doesn't hurt too bad."

Jax shrugs out of Atticus' grip, moving far faster than I expected him too. He is swift to guide Luna the remaining steps to the tree's trunk, whispering reassurances in her ear.

"You needn't do anything different. I'll merely stand behind you and place my hands as they were moments before upon your crown. Does that sound all right, gorgeous?" Luna nods, her focus torn between her task and the charming sorcerer. "Have at it then."

As Luna places a hand against the rough bark, Jax does precisely as he promised. His fingers comb through Luna's hair until they reach her temples, and he allows his palms to cup her skull.

"*Omnis helos, banos.*"

His head tilts back to stare at the sky as an eerie wind begins to curl around our feet. Luna makes no sound of protest or any indication of discomfort other than a slight pursing of her lips.

The scene is an uneasy one to watch. The magic Jax pulls from the air around us makes my skin sickeningly tight. My heart beats faster as fever itches at the nape of my neck. Atticus drags me into his side, and the sensation of discomfort alleviates some.

The gathered wolves watch the happenings in a tense reprise. Our shared anticipation draws the group closer together.

"What's taking so long?" someone whispers from the back.

"We should go before someone sees and reports us," another voice says, this one closer to the front.

The whispers and doubts continue to rise. They pull at my heartstrings for the position I have put them in. Once again my good intentions have turned awry. Before I can tumble down a path of self-doubt, Luna lets loose a terrible gasp and stumbles away from the tree.

Jax is there to steady her. He tucks her against his chest but keeps his head held high as his own senses return to him. We wait with bated breath for either to say a word—to say or do anything at all.

I don't expect Jax to speak, not with the way his jaw is clenched so tightly that it makes a vein throb near his temple.

"I know what to do," he says. His words are delivered in husky notes, but I also hear their breathless quality and am filled with trepidation.

The magic recedes from the air. The act is reminiscent of some phantom touch drawing away from my skin. Though it brought about discomfort moments before, I cannot deny the odd hunger I have for its return.

I eye Jax with renewed skepticism. Whatever magic he deals with is far different from the witches. His isn't elemental... it is primal and pure energy. Addicting in its own twisted sense of pain and pleasure.

"What do we need to do?" Atticus asks as he signals Keenan forward to collect Luna. She goes into his embrace, trembling like a leaf and her breath coming in short bursts. Keenan makes a soft whine in his throat, rubbing her arms gently to calm her as he walks her farther away from the group's prying eyes.

Jax motions us forward with a jerk of his head, retrieving his staff and meeting us halfway.

"What do you know regarding the reversal of spells and hexes?" Jax asks, his hazel eyes ablaze with their intensity. I spare Atticus a glance, noting we wear the same troubled expression across our brows. "Fear not, friends. I merely wish to gage your knowledge so I may better explain what needs to occur next."

I sigh and watch my breath cloud before me. "My understanding is... limited. From what the aunts explained, certain components of the original hex must be present in the spell that reverses them. Like the full moon and tree."

Jax nods, his gaze still smoldering. "Anything else?"

"You need to know the words of the hex, and what hex belongs to which curse, the lycan or the soulmark."

"Very good," he mutters and rubs his hands together briefly. "We have two of the components necessary for both curses already—the moon and tree. Just as your witchy friends gathered."

"And you were able to learn the hexes from Luna's... conversation?" Atticus asks.

Jax's eyes darken. "Yes. I know the words to says for each curse. But there is more."

Atticus squeezes my hand so tight I feel my bones shift beneath his grasp. "What else do you need?" Atticus asks through gritted teeth as his patience thins.

"Blood," Jax replies, "given by me during the reversal of the lycan curse. Ever your servant—until my Lord Vrana deems otherwise—I shall willingly give it. Additionally, I will need a wolf spirit for the lycan curse to be performed correctly and a soulmark."

A deep chill settles over my bones as the crowd behind us begins to chatter excitedly. Something tugs at my memory as Atticus begins to ask more questions. Jax doesn't respond, and his eyes do not stray from me.

I have a feeling there is an element to our efforts we have forgotten. But I cannot fathom what....

We need a direct bloodline....

Soul sacrifices are powerful things, whether done willingly or not....

"The wolf spirit and the soulmark," I speak softly, breaking into whatever one-sided conversation Atticus is having the Jax. I lift my eyes to Jax. "They need to be sacrificed, don't they?"

Atticus looks to me sharply. "What?"

"We need a sacrifice," I repeat, unable to look away from the grim truth hiding behind hazel eyes. "Don't we? The aunts said the necklace contained three soul sacrifices. The witch's soul sacrifice to conceal the curses in the necklace, and a sacrifice for each hex. A wolf... and a soulmark. Isn't that right?"

Jax nods. The gesture is given in small measure so as to keep his eyes locked on me. "It isn't just some components that must be recreated for the spell. It is all of them, though some must be adjusted to steer the course of the reversal. The moon, the tree, and the blood remain the same. The words of the counterspells are composed of the original hex along with nullifying incantations. As for the wolf and soulmark sacrifice, they must be given willingly."

We three stand silent as the crowd behind us swells with eagerness for whatever is to come. The promise of our curses' end blinding them to what will need to be done. Sacrifices... willingly given. I swallow thickly when I note the tightness around Jax's eyes.

"What aren't you saying?"

An ear-splitting howl interjects at the tail of my question. It captures the attention of Atticus, who turns to look out into the forest stretched out ahead of us.

Jax tilts up his chin. "These sacrifices also adhere to a blood stipulation."

"What does that mean?" Atticus asks, tearing his eyes away from the forest line. He sports a callous frown, unlike any I've seen before, and his blue eyes rage with a storm. Through the bond, I feel his ire rising and force myself to retain some modicum of calm to tide the swell of his emotions.

"It means the wolf spirit sacrifice and the soulmark sacrifice must be of a certain blood... Blanc blood, to be specific," Jax explains patiently. He does not spare Atticus a glance, even as my husband's answering growl cuts through the air like lightning. Jax only has eyes for me.

A disturbing hush culls the crowd of any more commentary. Even I find myself struck mute at the revelation.

"Anything else?" I ask, the words rolling thick off my tongue.

Jax twists his head from side to side.

"Exactly how do these sacrifices work?" Atticus demands roughly, earning back the sorcerer's regard.

Jax hikes up one brow. "I thought it obvious," he remarks far too casually for the situation at hand.

Another howl pierces through the air, this one closer than the last. Unsettled murmurs break out among the wolves behind us.

"The first sacrifice will remove the wolf spirit from its human counterpart. The second will require aid in the form of a knife to remove the soulmark from the skin and offer it as sacrifice," Jax tells Atticus, his voice full of condescension. "Does that clear things up for you?"

A surge of protest rises from the crowd. Jax rolls his eyes to the heavens and looks out to them.

"Now, now, do calm down. None of you will have to sacrifice your wolf spirit or soulmark tonight." Jax returns his gaze to me. "After all, I do believe I stated the sacrifice must come from a Blanc."

"Take Malcolm!" someone shouts.

"Yes! Let's get, Malcolm."

Panic hits me full force as the wolves behind me cave to their raging emotions. The full moon only intensifies their reaction and lust for blood. My eyes shutter closed for one scintillating moment to block out the roar of the crowd and allow my wolf to come to the forefront of my mind.

My throat tightens inexplicably.

We have only just begun our lives together, I think with great sorrow as my heart is cut and torn to pieces inside my chest.

Every journey must end, sister, the wolf's voice whispers back.

A sense of peace overcomes the wolf as it acknowledges and accepts our fate. Our farewells ring in my mind against the noisy crowd as my eyes flutter open.

"No," I say aloud. My lashes are already dampened from the tears that have gathered in my sights. "No!" I say louder. Firmer.

It catches the crowd off guard as I turn to them; I know my eyes to be a brilliant gold.

"Winter…." Atticus's voice is but a shadow at my ear. The urgency in his tone leaves little to the imagination of what he wishes to say, but my decision—*our* decision—has already been made. The wolf softly snarls its agreement.

"The sacrifice must be *willing*. Who among you believes my parents to be capable of such a feat?" None answer, and I feel the shift of their anger into one of dread and sorrow. "As the last of the Blanc line, it is my *honor*"—the word cracks on my tongue—"to end the curse that has plagued our kind and our pack for so long."

"Winter, no!" Atticus shouts, yanking me back around. I place my hands on his leather-bound chest.

Tears rush down both our flushed faces. "Atticus…." My voice trails off brokenly at the pure tragedy of his expression. The lines of his face are in shadows thanks to the light of the moon, but I see every crease and line wrought with grief and anger.

"I just got you," he says.

Worn leather caves to the insistent curl of my fingers. Our bodies collide in equal urgency. Hands paw at my hips, locking on to the slim plane as if they alone can keep me from doing what I must.

"If not me, then who?" I whisper back. "I know my father, Atticus. I *know* him. He would rather damn our kind and this pack than relinquish the power he's accumulated. The same goes for my mother."

"That doesn't mean *you* have to," he growls back.

I run a hand up his chest and hook it around his neck. Chin trembling, I answer. "Yes, it does, baby." The sad whine that breaks free from his throat says otherwise. I rush on to quell whatever pleas he might make. "I'm the only Blanc left. If I don't do this, the curse will never be broken. For the rest of time, our kind will be bound to the moon's whim, and the Blanc pack will never know what it is to bring a child into this world with their soulmark."

He shakes his head, cupping my face and bringing our lips together in a desperate kiss. My small sob breaks the intimate moment and draws a rough cry from Atticus as well.

"Why?" he questions. "Why would you sacrifice yourself for them? Why sacrifice our bond? What have they ever done for you?"

I tilt my gaze to my old pack mates, watching as they bow their heads with guilt. True, they had never questioned the methods my father and mother took to raise me "appropriately." Even more so, several of the women here had challenged my rank and slandered my name… but what had I done for them? My parents' cold and cruel behavior hadn't only been directed my way, and when their sights had been set upon *them*, I'd done nothing to stop it.

"I want a clean slate," I admit and muster a small smile. "A real, *new beginning*. And none of this means I won't still be your wife, Atticus. And I might no longer be a lycan—" I suck in a harsh breath, my wolf howling a mournful song in my mind. "—but I'll still be pack."

Atticus stays silent a moment as his lips thin in his regard of me. "I could order you not to," he tells me quietly, his voice hard. I flinch back, shaking my head and letting my hurt flood the bond between us. Atticus groans and dashes away his tears with his jacket sleeve. "No, I couldn't, could I?"

"Just promise to still love me after," I ask.

His mouth slants over mine in a bruising kiss, one to which I willingly submit.

I take this time and ingrain it into my memory. The coarse stubble that peppers his jawline. The purposeful stroke of his tongue along mine. His lips and how they mold perfectly over mine. The way his hands hold me with reverence.

Someone will die by your hand, Aunt Mo's voice whispers in my head. I weak smile flickers onto my lips. *How was I to ever guess it would be my wolf spirit?*

"*Ahem*," Jax says rather loudly. "I don't mean to break up this precious moment, but time is of the essence. Winter, if you are willing to sacrifice your wolf spirit and soulmark, then come with me."

Taking a wobbly step back, I marvel at the fact that this—leaving the safety of his embrace—won't be the hardest thing I do tonight. It is these steps I take toward my fate.

A sound like drums beats inside my head and with the sound of paws racing across the earth from generations ago. My ancestors—all of our ancestors—coming to welcome my wolf home. I know this only through the rippling anticipation of my wolf.

It will proudly lay down its life for our kind. For the greater good of the pack.

There is no greater honor than this, my wolf assures me as the beating grows louder in tandem with my racing heart.

Jax leads me to the base of the tree, guiding me so my back is to the birch's trunk. I lean against it for much-needed support, my breath coming out in soft pants.

"I need to ask you once more," Jax says seriously, his voice low. "Are you willing, Winter? This spell will strip you of your wolf spirit *and* your soulmark. I cannot guarantee that either sacrifice will see you still standing at the end... The original wolf sacrifice ended in death. If you do survive, the bond you have with Atticus will be severed. I need not tell you what pain that will cause both of you."

His words shake me to my core, but still I nod.

I spy Atticus around Jax's shoulder and see his solemn nod. His lips move slowly, mouthing two words: *Together. Always.*

"Yes, I'm willing," I whisper, refusing to take my eyes from Atticus.

He slips a small knife from his pocket into my hand. "You will know when the first spell is complete. This is for the soulmark counterspell. You will need to—"

"I know what to do," I tell him, my gray eyes turning to him. The Blanc pack has been removing soulmarks for decades. But placed on my lower back as it is, the process will be precarious at best.

I bite my lip and nod once more to Jax. He responds with a curt nod of his own and walks back several feet, sweeping his staff out around him. The snow on the ground begins to melt instantly and steam rises from the ground as Jax inhales deeply. From afar, the sound of angry snarls breaks the night air.

"I require absolute concentration," Jax says, his gaze steadfast on me, but his words address the wolves behind him. "Am I understood?"

A rumble of agreement comes from the lycans at his back. Their eyes light up like brilliant golden flames as they advance to guard the tree and us.

"Hear me!" Jax bellows once the last lycan has taken their post at his six: Atticus. His eyes burn as brightly as the others as they watch me. "By all that is powerful and just—hear my blood claim!"

Jax draws the diamond-shaped head of his bo staff across his palm. Red pools in his palm and spills over his hand in copious amount. He pays the loss no mind and thrusts his palm forward and begins to chant.

"*Brious macab aos sole ave;*
Folle d'astalle ne lios.
Brious macab aos sole ave;
Folle d'astalle ne lios."

With each line I find myself simultaneously pulled forward and yanked back. The push and pull become more intense with each grating line. But it isn't just me being pulled forward; it's not me at all, I realize. It's the wolf.

"*Brious macab aos sole ave;*
Folle d'astalle ne lios.
Brious macab aos sole ave;
Folle d'astalle ne lios."

My hands claw at the tree bark, desperate to find purchase as I lurch forward then dive backward. Air rushes from my lungs at the impact, my scream of pain quenched by the loss of breath and my wolf's mournful cry of pain.

"*Brious macab aos sole ave;*
Folle d'astalle ne lios!
Tov mal sintave!"

Pain racks my body. Every vein inside me is fit to burst as something so ingrained in my bones and blood begins to seep away. My cries are but a distant chorus of the wolf's soft whine and the pounding of the ancestors' paws. Until, with a shuddering gasp, it ends.

I slump against the tree, wide-eyed and hysterical as my mind and body reel from the loss. A hand claws at the side of my head, searching desperately for what was once there—a hand that cannot possibly be my own.

"No, no, no," I hear myself muttering as I lose myself to my grief.

Foreign words tumble past me on the wind, whipping around me and standing me upright.

A delirious moan crawls up my throat. Everything hurts, and there is a piercing pain in my heart as if a stiletto knife has sailed straight through it. I look to the circle of wolves with reluctance, expecting to find sympathetic faces or ones of firm resolve. But I see none. I see no one but *her.*

She limps forward, a woman in a sullied gown with dirt and muck embedded in her wild hair. I inhale sharply, the bark cutting into my back as I pitch away from her wretched form. She is wrong.

Wrong, wrong, wrong.

Wolf instincts or not, my very soul shudders at her unholy presence.

A startled scream jostles the winter fog rising around us. *My scream,* I think with panic. Because one moment she is over there and now she is here, mere feet in front of me with her stained teeth and haggard face glowering at me. The knife falls from my hand.

"Who dares claim themselves worthy of sacrifice? Who dares attempt to reverse my claim of fault?"

Her mangled lips move, but the words do not sound from her mouth. It vibrates through the tree and slithers among the fog. My painfully human hearing can barely keep up.

"I do," I say with a quiver taking over my voice. I am unable to tear my eyes away from the hag's flat, dark stare.

"Your name."

A searing pain, much like claws, scores down my back. My jaw drops, a scream on my lips as the horrible torment begins again.

"Your name," the hag hisses again.

"Winter," I pant, my consciousness beginning to fail. "Winter Blanc."

She screams and pitches herself backward. "You," she bellows. "Your blood is tainted! You're—"

"*Veratum! Mai ovræ playus outum e capasus natas!*

Viest ne tocrum o sath vorce.

Sacrum vol colorus, alst om duay cultost, nallem!"

The hag whirls at the haunting overture. Her wild eyes careen this way and that as she begins to foam at the mouth.

"This is not to be born!" she seethes and lunges magically forward again. First there, then *here*. She is inches away from my face and breathing rot into my nostrils.

"Your hate cannot live forever." I gasp, back arching as an unseen force cuts at my lower back savagely. "I am a willing sacrifice."

Her vile breath pants across my cheek as I grope blindly at my soulmark. The area is slick with something wet and sticky—not sweat, but blood. I release a desperate cry, allowing my hand to fall away as I begin to sag against the tree.

"I am a willing sacrifice," I gasp again.

Out of the corner of my eye, I see the hag's mouth opens wide. Her stained teeth are broken and ragged, and for a tenuous moment, I'm sure she means to eat me alive. Body, mind, and spirit. What's left of them, anyway.

"Enough."

I freeze at the addition of the new voice. As does everything else, even the hag.

"Enough," the soft, feminine voice repeats.

The suffocating pain that digs its jagged edges into my body begins to recede. I slump further as the hag staggers back. She throws her head this way and that, searching out the voice and letting out a tormented sound.

And then the hag is gone, and I am alone.

My eyes slip closed in defeat as I suck in ragged breaths to fill the empty space inside me. I feel… incomplete. Lost. Abandoned. Alone… so terribly alone.

"My dear girl," the feminine voice coos from nearby, "you are not alone."

Howls rise in a symphony around me, and when I open my eyes, the most beautiful woman stands before me. Her skin is opalescent, with hair and eyes as dark as night. She wears a lilting smile, and around her stand dozens of wolves. One of them circles calmly around the ethereal woman in her Romanesque silver gown. Its coat is a brilliant white.

When the wolf meets my eyes, I am struck with recognition and fall to my knees.

My wolf. Mine.

"And now she is mine," the woman says. "Oh, my dear, sweet, Winter. I've been waiting for a heart like yours for a very long time to set my children free."

"You're…."

The Goddess of the Moon inclines her head. "Merida's hex was born of true hate. Even those of my kind cannot intervene when such offerings are interwoven into hexes such as hers. And so I waited, just as all my children did, for the willing one to step forward and set them free."

"It worked?"

My mouth is dry. My throat is raw. And though my question is coarse and unrefined, she smiles genially at me. A yip from one of the many wolves sounds behind the goddess. And then another, and another. Until the lot are barking and yipping in excitement.

"You cannot feel it because your wolf spirit is part of my pack now, but yes. Your sacrifice—both of yours—have set your brothers and sisters free."

"Atticus?"

Her smile dims, and the goddess dons a look of mild reproach. "Do you think I would allow your great sacrifice to go unrewarded? Merida's curse on the soulmark was weak but protected by her first and last of concealment. That you and your mate would willingly sacrifice my greatest gift to you for that of your kind… I cannot bear the thought of it. Be at peace, my child. Your soulmark remains."

I shudder a cry. The song of the wolves a sudden symphony—and then gone as the air around me shifts. The cold air of night is like a slap to the face.

"Winter? Winter, wake up!"

The passionate words are more than just a plea but an order. My lashes flutter valiantly to shake the filmy haze that still clouds my senses. My sight sets upon the figure cradling me in their arms.

"Atticus?" A whimper of relief sounds from my husband as he pulls me into a crushing hug. "Too much," I wheeze. "Too hard."

His hold relaxes, guiding me back as red-rimmed eyes study my weak form with grave intensity. "You weren't breathing," he says, his jaw shaking with barely suppressed emotion.

"Be at peace," I murmur, my hand smoothing over his chest to his heart. "All is well. Everything is back in its rightful place."

Atticus inhales deeply several times. "I thought I lost you," he confesses quietly, almost too softly for me to hear.

"Never."

The world around me comes back into focus as Atticus presses his face into my neck and inhales once more. I scan the crowd. They are crying with relief and hold each other close.

You cannot feel it because your wolf spirit is part of my pack now….

"It worked," I whisper, growing weaker by the minute. "The curse—"

Atticus shushes me, his teeth grazing the skin at my neck lightly in rebuke. I bend my neck submissively—old habits still etched firmly into my new human life.

"Yes," he says. "And now we're going home. We can't stay here any longer."

I pass my troubled frown to Atticus, but he only shushes me again. Love and reassurance, so sweet and full, flow through our soulmark bond. A whimper of relief slips past my sore throat as I rest my head on his shoulder. I slowly begin to succumb to the darkness treading into my vision.

"Atticus?"

He hums his response as he pulls us up and strides away from the tree and the Blanc pack—from the hardest decision either of us has ever had to make. I spy Jax already several feet ahead of us, casting curiously dark looks over his shoulder. His face is terribly pale and drawn, but when he catches my eye, the dark expression immediately melts away and he sends me a wink.

"Excellent work, Mrs. Hayes," he says.

I can barely muster a nod, my train of thought lost one moment before regaining it in the next.

"Atticus, everything is going to be different now."

As much as hope and happiness swell inside my chest at the thought of my pack running free as they were meant to be, fear follows closely after. With all lycans free of the curse that has bound us for centuries, what chaos might ensue? As the thread of my distress runs through our bond, Atticus slows.

"Everything is different now," he agrees solemnly, his crystal blue eyes locking onto mine. "But not between us, Winter."

I smile softly back, completely unaware of when I finally lose consciousness to this tiresome day. Never between us.

EPILOGUE

It wasn't the fairy's first winter in the decidedly human dimension, but it didn't lessen her utter astonishment at just how *cold* it could be here. She didn't like the cold. The only things that survived it were ghastly tall evergreens whose attitude Lunaria found particularly standoffish.

The fairy missed her home.

She missed the Hollow Wood. She missed her closest and dearest friends, Alekos and Celosia. She missed the nightly revelries and even the tedious chore of pruning the underbelly of the *rafflorondi*.

This dimension, with its unpredictable weather and people, had lost its shine to the fairy long ago—right about the time she realized the witches who gave her shelter and food had little interest in truly helping her home.

And why would they? the fairy thought. *I provide protection against their enemies, even from afar.*

The fairy was connected to their precious crystal, the one they proclaimed hailed from Dan Furth. Her nose scrunched at the thought. The witches were wrong about its name and origin, but her attempts at explanation when she first arrived had gone awry. She had never bothered to correct them again for it mattered not.

The crystal's mystical powers were what mattered, and the witches had known that at the very least. The fairy smiled. The crystal was indeed special for it had dual abilities to bolster the land where it resided and protect it.

Lunaria did not understand the specifics as to why her presence increased the crystals ability, but she assumed it came from her own ability to bolster and nurture the land.

"You know," the sorcerer piped up from the driver's seat, his hazel eyes slanting from the road ahead and to the fairy. "You're not the first mind I've gotten to peek into, but yours is by far the most... magnificent."

Lunaria blinked, and tiny rosebuds blossomed on the apples of her cheeks. "Oh?"

Jax smirked and turned his eyes back to the road. "Truly. I—" He cleared his throat. "—also saw a few glimpses of your home," he said, more subdued than his usual bright commentary. "It was beautiful."

The fairy looked to her lap for an answer and then out the window to her right. When neither offered their advice, she took to chewing her bottom lip until the appropriate response came to her.

"Thank you," she said, matching the soft inclination of his voice. "No place compares."

"Now that I believe. So what made you leave, gorgeous?"

The fairy's eyes widened considerably as she kept her sights trained out the window. "The crystal called for assistance as it was in disrepair, and I was the nearest to help. Really, it was quite by chance that I arrived and helped its passage. It could have been any *Cultivator*, really. The only problem is... I haven't been able to find a way home after seeing it through to this plane."

Lunaria peeked back to Jax whose face was caught in a look of concentration. When he noticed her regard, it slipped away to be replaced by a lazy grin and sparkling eyes that didn't quite capture the fading light of the sun. Lunaria didn't pay much mind because it was startlingly easy to find herself spellbound by the sorcerer's good looks. *Well, his good looks and sweet compliments.*

"Well, gorgeous, you're just in luck for I have the favor of multiple gods. If you like, I can take a crack at sending you back home."

"Thank you," Lunaria said bashfully, "but Winter is going to help me. But perhaps, if she cannot, I shall call on you?"

Jax nodded, and Lunaria relished in his generous offer. A rush of feelings swarmed her body—appreciation, hope, and excitement from anticipation and attraction. Her bottom lip found its way back between her teeth again, and the sorcerer let out a rumbling chuckle. Jax glanced quickly at the road before his eyes looked back to Lunaria. He reached over carefully and pried her bottom lip free with the pad of his thumb.

"You're going to eat your lip if you keep gnawing at it like that."

The action lit the fairy's face on fire, and Jax released another confident chuckle. He was well aware of his effect on the fairy and was unafraid to take advantage of it. Not to mention, he found her innocent reactions genuinely refreshing after time spent in the Dark Court, where the innocent were eaten alive—literally. Jax slanted another look in her direction and winked when she caught his gaze.

What remained of Lunaria's weak glamour shuttered away as her body became inflamed with red roses at the suggestive wink. Jax blinked, taken aback by her rather enthusiastic reaction.

It was there and then, only an hour's drive away from Branson Falls on a backcountry road, that Jax almost killed them all. Lunaria had finally torn her eyes from the charming sorcerer and taken one glance at the road before she released a shrill scream. The brakes let out an ear-splitting shriek as Jax slammed the pedal, his eyes now glued to the body laid out in the middle of the road.

The others in the van came awake with a jolt, letting out curses and prayers as the car came skidded to a stop.

"What the hell, Jax!" Atticus snarled and snatched the sorcerer by his jacket to shake some sense into him. "Are you trying to get us all killed."

Jax growled back as he tried and failed to release himself from the beta's grip. "There's a body in the road! Or did you want me to drive over it?"

Winter gasped and began to look out the window. "A body?"

"Keenan, go check it—wait, Luna!"

But the fairy was already out of the car and running to check on the male outside. The car had stopped a few feet away from the prone body. It was clear that the male was injured. The others had joined her by the time she knelt at the muscular man's side.

He must be a giant, Lunaria thought, for even prone on the ground he seemed to dwarf her.

"Oh my God," Winter whispered.

Luna reached out to the deep cut across the bridge of his nose. Perhaps she could—

"Don't touch him!" Winter shouted. Lunaria froze and peered back at her friend, filled with sudden fright.

"What's wrong?" Lunaria asked as she noted the confusion laid bare over the men's faces.

A roughened palm and fingers seized Lunaria's wrist, and the fairy shrieked in surprise. Her regard lashed back to the figure on the ground to see the man's dark eyes cracked open. Lunaria sucked in a sharp breath as her violet eyes clashed with the stranger's own abysses of black. *No*, she thought with great fear striking her body still. His grip belayed a dangerous aura, one Lunaria knew all too well.

"*Rokama*," she stammered as recognition dawned upon her.

The stranger's eyes lit with anticipation as greater consciousness found him. "*Lunaria*."

Did you enjoy Lycan Legacy?

THANK YOU FOR YOUR SUPPORT

Your reviews not only help readers choose their next book, but they also help authors get the word out about their work.

PLEASE LEAVE A REVIEW :)

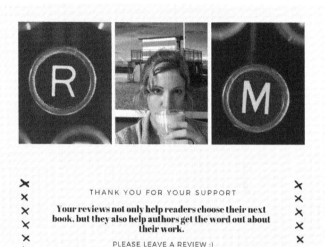

If you have a moment, please review Lycan Legacy. Help other paranormal romance readers find a new story and tell them what you enjoyed most about it!

Ready for the next installment in A Soulmark Series?

Coven (Book 1) — *Out Now*
Midnight Scoundrel (Book 2) — *Out Now*
Wardens of Starlight (Book 3) — *Out Now*
Mr. Vrana (Book 4) — *Out Now*
Lycan Legacy (Book 5) — *Out Now*
Lunaria (Book 6) —TBA 2019

Let's Connect!

Want to stay in the know on updates and bonus content?

Join Rebecca's Readers
rebeccamain.com

Like me on Facebook
https://www.facebook.com/AuthorRebeccaMain/

Follow me on Instagram
https://www.instagram.com/mrs_rebeccamain/

Follow me on Pinterest
https://www.pinterest.com/authorrebeccamain/

Acknowledgements

To my incredible husband who has been there every step of the way—thank you.

Thank you for pointing out the holes in my plot.
Thank you for encouraging my ideas.
Thank you for pushing me and constantly asking, "Have you finished your book yet?"

While a majority of the time this question made my eyes roll as you insisted on asking it in the *earliest stages of my writing* and *frequently*, it nevertheless remained a driving point to complete my work. So thanks for that too, I guess.

To my friends and family, you are wonderful and mean so much to me. Thank you for your belief in me all this time and introducing me to *your* friends and family as your "writer" friend. It's very cool and will never get old.

And an extra special thank you to Hot Tree Edits, especially Virginia, for her editorial efforts!

About the Author

Rebecca Main published her first romance novel—Coven (A Soulmark Series Book 1)—in June 2017 and hasn't put down her keyboard since! Quitting their respective jobs in May 2017, Rebecca and her husband now travel the world. Their calico cat, Dorcas, waits patiently for their return to become a "city" cat once more. Rebecca is an avid reader, travel-hacker enthusiast, and karaoke queen (after a shot or two). Her current writing passion is romance with a hearty dash of supernatural and paranormal thrown in for good measure.

Tear-inducing accomplishments include hitting #1 on the Amazon Top 100 list in Fantasy Romance and Paranormal Witches & Wizards, free climbing out of Belize's Crystal Cave, also known as the Mountain Cow Cave, and starting a publishing house—Via Graphia LLC—with her husband.

Made in the USA
Columbia, SC
11 June 2020